CULT OF SACRIFICE

CULT OF SACRIFICE

J. GREYSON FIKE

Rev. date: 11/17/2020

To order additional copies of this book, contact:
Xlibris
844-714-8691
www.Xlibris.com
Orders@Xlibris.com
819314

This novel is dedicated to my wife Bonita,
whose help and support made it possible.

CONTENTS

CHAPTER 1

BEGINNINGS I

In a gray stucco bungalow at Seventh Avenue and Madison Street, fourteen-year-old Harvey Davenport sat holding his mother's wrinkled, cool, deeply veined hand as she lay wheezing through her last hours. She slipped in and out of consciousness, uttering words he could not understand. When she moaned, he thought she was in pain and tried to comfort her.

Mrs. Brown, whom his mother called Stephanie, had brought him supper around six that evening. She lived in a shabby gray house down the block. Her greens, grits, ham hocks, and sweet potatoes were his favorites. He had little appetite, though, and ate the food only because she'd been kind enough to prepare it.

During the long hours of the night, he sat in his mother's ancient straight-backed chair, reading his latest Zane Grey novel from the library by the light of a single lamp on the small square table he'd pulled up to her bed. The maelstrom of grief and uncertainty, however, punched repeatedly through his concentration.

He was losing his best friend and teacher to what her doctor called "liver cancer" and "scleroderma." He didn't understand those terms, but the doctor added that she'd been poisoned by industrial chemicals. An hour's subsequent research at the library had clarified the doctor's words. Now he understood why people coughed when the sulfurous smells and smoke became really intense, and why his family had to drink bottled water.

He and his mother had been companions for each other since his father, Melvin, had died two years before in a rollover semitruck accident out on Route 22. He'd seen the battered ancient green cab and winced when he thought about what it must have felt like to crash through that windshield to the pavement at sixty miles an hour. He felt certain the collision had resulted from one of his father's frequent coughing fits, when he spat blood into the blue paisley handkerchief he carried in his back pocket.

What would he do when the neighbors no longer brought food? Soup, sandwiches, and scrambled eggs stretched his cooking skills to the limit.

Where would life lead him now? He had just completed his freshman year at Westfield High. He wasn't even old enough to drive—legally. He'd have to fix his bike to get around. But it needed two new tires, and there was no money for what she had called "extras." Besides, the gas, electric, and phone bills awaited payment on the kitchen table, and while his mother had arranged for him to sign checks, there was precious little in the account. Too sick to work, she'd been living off of social security disability for two years. Consequently, he had no income.

Through the night, he rehearsed the context in which his parents had become so irretrievably ill. Most of his friends in school had family members who were habitually sick. Some folks seemed convinced that being ill was part of being poor. Others believed the cause was air pollution. Still others said the water was poisoned. Old Humphrey Marshall, longtime friend and neighborhood resident, had sat with him one afternoon, recalling a story handed down from his great-grandfather.

In 1852, the mine owners of Westfield and Mayor Dylan Koch agreed the city would waive pollution restrictions and allow them to dump tailings and chemical residues in the Bottoms, a name carried over from the old days when the mine workers lived close to their work. The mine owners drove a hard bargain, but in the end, Koch's reward was to have his four boys educated at Harvard at no cost to himself. "The effects of that shady deal," Mr. Marshall said, "have lasted till this day."

When he was younger, Harvey's arms and legs had itched with sores. When he scratched them, they became infected. Then his mother would take him to the clinic for a shot to prevent blood poisoning. He'd heard the older boys say the pollution was getting worse. The families of three friends from school—Scott, Thad, and Bobby—had all moved away from Westfield. Was he himself being poisoned? Maybe this was a good time for him to leave before things got worse. But where would he go?

Sometime later, old Mrs. Brown passed silently into the room and put her hand on his mother's forehead. "She's goin', son," she whispered, shaking her head as she straightened the blankets. "Not much time left."

Long after midnight, a tumult of voices tormented him. Chemical names he struggled to pronounce—benzene, butadiene, styrene, sulfur dioxide—swam in company with memories of the people he knew who had died. His grandmother Pearl, his aunt Libby, and cousin Joe's sister and father all passed long before their time. It seemed everyone in the neighborhood fell prey to cancer, leukemia, asthma, and immune deficiencies. Though no one had said in his hearing why people got sick and died younger, the evidence seemed clear.

Once strong and beautiful, his mother had lost so much weight she now looked wasted and thin as a scarecrow. Yet she was unable to eat.

"You go ahead and have it, Harvey," she'd say when he made her a can of tomato soup and a grilled cheese sandwich, a meal she had once enjoyed. "My pain's so bad I'm not the least bit hungry." Watching her waste away broke his heart.

Sandra and Melvin Davenport had married right after college and settled in Westfield because it seemed like a nice town. Melvin managed a McDonald's franchise in the early days of fast food.

Sandra taught sixth grade in the elementary school ten blocks from their house, which was situated in an area people called the Bottoms.

All went well for the Davenport family during their first ten years. Then both parents became ill. By the time he was twelve, neither could work full-time. His mother worked a few hours a week as a secretary, and his father gave up managing fast food and became a truck driver.

They'd enjoyed living in a neighborhood that included Blacks, whites, and Hispanics, most of whom commiserated with and found solace in one another's company.

"Where we live makes a statement about race and prejudice," she'd often told him. "People who live together understand one another and get along better." Unfortunately, the people were also mostly poor and uneducated, which brought him ridicule and embarrassment when he began attending the new Westfield Consolidated High School south of the river.

Toward dawn, he awoke with a start. He listened for the rattle of her breathing, but the stillness of the room blanketed his ears. Only the ticking of the ancient kitchen clock remained. While he slept, her hand had slipped from his grasp as her life flowed away, leaving him an orphan. Now that her pain had ended, grief poured over him like scalding-hot oil. He said a little prayer from a book he'd once read.

Great creator, please care for my mother.
May your light shine on her, and her soul rest in peace.
Amen.

Then, with no one to observe, he let the tears flow with great wracking sobs. The source of his life, the one who had taught him history, math, and life, was gone. She had been the interpreter of his world, the one who had read to him stories that incited his imagination. Not always gentle, she was definitely concerned for his well-being.

"You see what I've done for you, Harvey," she'd said. "Go do that for others. Spread it around. The world's a mean, tough place. Anyone you meet needs your caring, if only you're willing to give it."

When it became light outside, he stood up, blew his nose, stretched, turned out the light on the table, and raised the window shade. Through the glass, he saw men unloading lumber from a pickup truck parked in the alley behind their house.

In a few minutes, Mrs. Brown returned. She'd brought him breakfast, but he still felt no hunger. She'd also brought a pile of sheets and a washing tub.

"You go on out, chile," she said. "There's nothin' you can do for her. She's in heaven now, feelin' no more pain. We'll take care of your momma, get her ready for the funeral."

He walked down along the river and under the Bennett Industrial Bridge to where the discharge pipes from the shops spewed their gunk into the river.

"You killed my mother!" he screamed. "I hate you! One day you'll pay!" Though no one heard his cries echoing beneath the bridge as heavy trucks rumbled overhead, those inchoate words released him from the grip of terrible anger threatening to overwhelm him.

When he returned home, the men of the neighborhood were building his mother's coffin in the backyard. He walked over to inspect.

"Need any help?" he asked at length. *Might as well do something useful*, he figured.

The men looked at him with uncertainty. Then one of them said, "Fetch me that board leanin' against the house."

That small gesture transformed him into one of the crew. Working alongside them, he realized he still had something he could call family.

At ten the next morning, the famous bell of historic Bethel AME Church called the people to Sandra Davenport's funeral. There had been no money, except a $1,500 insurance policy with the mortician, who offered only the simplest possible arrangements for such a pittance.

As the sanctuary filled with his mother's many friends, the head usher accompanied him to his designated seat in the front pew. In such an exposed position, he was constantly on display; he resolved not to let his feelings express themselves in tears.

The organist played familiar hymns, among them his favorite, "The Old Rugged Cross." White candles graced the communion table, and six bouquets of flowers filled the chancel with their distinctive fragrances. Disease had disfigured her face so cruelly that he'd asked for the casket to remain closed.

Staring at the stained glass figure of Christ on the cross, illuminated by the morning sun, he meditated on the way his mother had been sacrificed on the cross of industry's convenience. A thousand questions plagued him. Why that disease? Why had it taken her when she was so young? Why such a notable difference between people on the two sides of the river? To keep his composure, he put these troublesome thoughts aside for the moment, certain that somehow, some day, he would discover the answers.

The pastor, Amos McElwain, welcomed the mourners, then asked four of his mother's closest friends to share words about what she had meant in their lives. None of those speakers mentioned the cause of her death. That omission made him squirm in his seat. Didn't they know? Or were they afraid to say? He'd learned in school that the smoke and chemicals coming from the shops and factories were poisonous. What dismayed him was that nobody seemed ready or willing to speak about it or stop it. Maybe they'd gotten used to the smell of rotten eggs. Maybe it was easier just to ignore it and keep living one's life, as his mother had done. Maybe that was just the way life was.

These thoughts made it impossible to hold back his feelings any longer. He bent his head to hide the tears of anger. From the sound of sniffles in the pews behind, he concluded others had similar feelings.

A deacon read some lines of scripture, the Rev. McElwain gave a brief homily, and then the congregation stood to sing "Amazing Grace."

After the service, the people gathered for a brief graveside ceremony at the cemetery just a few blocks from the church. When he was offered the chance to throw the first spadeful of dirt on the lowered coffin, he stepped away from the grave. Why heap more poison on the poor woman's remains? He turned and strode angrily the six blocks to home.

That afternoon, Humphrey Marshall, the wise old mentor who had helped so many of his neighbors, came to see him.

"Too many of us are getting sick from all the poisons," said his friend. "If you stay here, exposed to these chemicals, Harvey, you won't have a chance. Let's get you that insurance money from your dad's accident, and I'll put you on a bus to go to your aunt Harriet and uncle Theo's. That'll get you out of danger, and they have the wherewithal to give you a decent education, help you reach your goal to be a photographer."

After having ruminated most of the night, Harvey was ready with his answer. The old man's advice seemed better than anything he himself could conjure. However, he had to think seriously about the risks. When he was younger, his family visited his aunt and uncle during the time they lived in a small house in downtown Binghamton, many years before Theo inherited his wealth. Even then, Theo had a violent temper and a slave owner's mentality. He'd beaten Harvey several times over his parents' protests. Furthermore, he'd be walking in on Theo and Harriet unannounced after quite a few years. Who knew what trouble that might provoke? However, if living the next seven years with his aunt and uncle afforded him a leg up on his career as a photographer, allowing him to pursue his dream, then it was a chance he'd have to take.

"Action is a sign of hope," his mother had said. It was her benediction.

Two hours of rolling along under cloudy skies through endless fields of corn and soybeans slowly transformed his grief and dark thoughts of revenge into curiosity about his surroundings. When they stopped in Des Moines for a half-hour layover, he grabbed the Brownie camera his father had given him out of his suitcase and raced for the terminal to see what he could shoot. Nearly all the photography magazines he'd read advised that a budding photographer should take pictures every day. He'd vowed to himself that he would practice this approach, and this was today's chance to keep that discipline.

First, he shot the buses lined up outside, then a bus being repaired in the shop. Then he bought a hot dog with everything and settled in the waiting room. Among his likely subjects was an old fellow laid out on a bench in the waiting area, snoring softly and covered with newspapers. One meaty hand grasped the shoulder strap of a small equipment bag. When Harvey snapped his picture, the flash awakened the man, who sat up, rubbed his eyes, and groggily introduced himself as Thurston Samuelson. "Just call me Sam," he'd said.

As it happened, Sam was a photographer bound for Chicago, and they struck up a conversation that lasted the rest of the day. Sam examined Harvey's photo album and was quite complimentary.

"You have a natural talent," Sam said. "You're doing commendable work with what most of us in the field would say is a rather crude instrument." He went on to explain how he'd gotten his start thirty years before at a small community newspaper in the northeast. "I just retired after fifteen years in my own studio in Des Moines," he said. "I'm on the way to Chicago to help another young friend of mine start his own studio and give him a chance to have the same fun I've had."

At the next rest stop, they exited the bus and found a park, where Sam let Harvey use the Nikon he kept in his equipment bag, giving him pointers on taking newsworthy photographs.

A flush of adrenaline made Harvey feel a little breathless.

Thornton Park was spacious and green with lots of amenities—swings, a sandbox, a jungle gym, some walking paths. Everything a photographer could ask for.

"What's your first experiment going to be?"

"Depth perception," Harvey replied.

They walked over to the swing set where ten wood seats hung on chains from a large, steel A-frame. A father and two children occupied three of the swings.

CULT OF SACRIFICE

"Good afternoon, sir," Sam said to the father with a gentle smile. "My name's Sam, and this is my protege, Harvey. We're experimenting with a new camera. Would you mind if we took some pictures of your handsome children on the swings?"

"Sure, we don't mind. Do we, kids?" the father yelled so the children could hear him from the lofty heights of Swingdom.

"No!" they shouted in chorus, then pumped until they were flying even higher to show off their skills.

"Okay, Harvey," Sam coached. "Let's see if you can keep those swings in focus and stop them in midair."

Harvey set the shutter speed and aperture, then cranked the telephoto until the young fellow on the swing was in the height of his arc. He then squeezed the shutter. Again and again, he experimented with different camera settings.

While Harvey took pictures, Sam talked with the father, who said his name was Steve Wright, and his children were Stephanie, nine, and Michael, seven.

"We're taking the bus to Grandma and Grandpa's house. Aren't we?" He paused for effect.

"Yay!" shouted the mighty chorus of kids above.

Later, when the bus pulled up at a Howard Johnson's restaurant for another stop, Harvey asked if he could do a portrait of Stephanie.

"Oh, yes!" She was more than ready for that, being dressed in a new white dress with red trim and black patent leather shoes.

Harvey worked hard behind the lens of Sam's Nikon, relishing the challenges Stephanie's young imagination threw at him.

"First, I want you to photograph me looking at my full bottle of Coke," she said, then giggled as she put on a happy smile. As queen of the party, Stephanie blossomed with every smile and frown— drinking the Coke, eating the burger, looking sad when it was all gone. Harvey found he had to reload the Nikon frequently.

Just after they departed at six thirty that evening, the bus driver announced there would be a three-hour layover in Chicago for engine repairs.

"That's fine with me," Sam confided to Harvey. "In three hours, we can eat dinner, get our film processed, and still have time to review our work."

Outside the terminal in Chicago, Harvey and Sam stepped out into a mild southeast breeze along State Street. Sam introduced him to the Loop with its skyscrapers and department stores. They visited Waterman's Camera store, a huge emporium of photo equipment. There were so many items he'd never seen and didn't know existed— umbrellas, studio cameras, backdrop paper, strobe lights.

"Everything you'll need for your own studio," Sam told him.

He tingled with excitement at the possibility of setting up his own studio.

"Are you hungry?" Sam inquired when they were back out on the street.

"Sure am!"

"Let's go to the Berghoff for dinner. My treat."

They walked across the street and down a block. As he held the door open, Sam said, "This is an old, traditional German restaurant. I want you to experience the *taste* of Chicago as well as the sights and sounds."

They selected a booth with black leather and walnut trim. "We call this elegant style Bavarian Alpine. A century ago, those chandeliers held wax candles."

He'd never been in such a place and had never eaten such rich, delicious food served by attentive waiters elegantly dressed in black pants and vests with white shirts.

"I have something to propose to you," Sam said after they had eaten.

"What sort of proposal?" he asked. Expectation ignited his mind. Sam had so far been full of good surprises.

"I propose we trade cameras. You take my Nikon. I take your Hawkeye. Even trade. What d'ya say?"

Stunned by Sam's suggestion, he hedged. "You mean like this afternoon—to do more experiments, right?"

"I mean permanently, young man," Sam replied with finality. "When we walk out of here, you will carry your very own Nikon, and I will have your Brownie. And remember ... that Nikon isn't even a year old."

Confusion overwhelmed him. Kindness was one thing, but why would Sam want his Brownie? The Brownie was precious—his first camera. A gift from his father. It symbolized a decision he'd made to be a photographer. Furthermore, why would a successful professional like Sam have any interest in a rank amateur like himself?

"But why such a generous offer? Once I get back on the bus, we'll never see one another again."

"True enough, my friend. Let me explain. First of all, I have many cameras. Most of them I used during my professional career. Many are now antiques. This new Nikon is the latest of nine I've owned and used."

Experimenting with this sharp, new camera during the afternoon had energized Harvey. It opened a door to becoming a real photographer. Yet something in his mind refused to accept Sam's authenticity.

"I bet you're a collector of Brownie Hawkeyes too."

"Good for you for thinking of that. But money's not the issue. Giving you my camera takes you to the next step of your journey. One of my goals is replacing myself with young professionals like you. That's worth a lot more to me than the Brownie."

Harvey was breathless, giddy with delight. Sam had taken part in their experiments, coached him on technique. Now his proposal was like the creamy, smooth ice cream that had topped his apple pie.

"I accept!" he blurted out. "Thanks for taking an interest! You're the first person who's ever been so encouraging." He swallowed hard to keep back the tears trying to leak out the sides of his eyes. One door closed, and another opened.

"You're good, kid! *Very* good. Just keep shooting. Every day, at least one roll. Think—composition, light, shadow, speed."

"I will, sir, and thank you *so much!*"

Sam hailed a cab and climbed in. "Before I go, if you get the chance, get your degree here, from the Art Institute of Chicago. It's the best. And my alma mater."

He looked Sam in the eye. "I'll do that, sir."

Before experiencing Sam's kindness, he had not understood that everyone needs a hand up at some point in life. Just as his mother had said. From that time on, Sam joined Harvey's mother as primary influences in his professional and personal life.

When Harvey eventually arrived at the Binghamton bus station, no one came to meet him. Tired and anxious as he was, necessity and the desire to make the most of this opportunity moved him to find a taxi and take it to the address Humphrey Marshall had given him. Much to his amazement, it turned out to be an elegant mansion in the suburbs.

Aunt Harriet met him at the front door, invited him inside, then bade him sit with her in their luxurious living room. He sat breathless, wide-eyed with wonder. Her answers to his many questions revealed that their financial situation had improved considerably from the last time he and his family had visited them.

"Before Theo took over his father's investment company," Harriet said, "he'd become so mean and contemptible I was ready to divorce him Then the old man died and left him the business. That gave Theo what he couldn't achieve on his own. By the time we'd been here a year, we'd discovered we needed each other."

"You needed *Theo*?" he exclaimed. "I can't imagine why."

"It was the money. He needed to look successful. I needed the lifestyle. *He* also needed *me,* because I'm his ticket to acceptability. Our marriage makes him seem legitimate to his clients. So, we stuck it out."

Hans the butler interrupted briefly with much-needed iced tea and homemade chocolate chip cookies. In those few moments, the realization hit him that even those who didn't deserve it could win at life and get rich. *How ironic!* He also learned his first lesson in patience: some life situations take years to work themselves out in positive resolutions.

Then Harriet resumed their conversation. "So, what brings you here, Harvey?"

When he related how Mr. Marshall had worked out the details with his uncle Theo, Harriet's body stiffened and her hand flew to her mouth to stifle a gasp.

"You mean I'm supposed to be your surrogate mother?" she exclaimed. "For the next six years?"

When he nodded, the color drained from her face.

She paused for a moment, recovered herself, then said, "Theo's into shock and awe these days. He's probably pretending you don't exist." Her face hardened, and her eyes went cold as she raised her chin. "He knows damned well I'm not prepared to accept that kind of responsibility, and the shit's gonna hit the fan as soon as he walks in that door."

"Do you think he'll try to use me? Maybe extract something from me?"

"You learn fast, boy," she teased. "Real fast!" Her eyes met his. "Yes, he will. I'm certain of it."

Just then, Theo burst into the living room wearing an executive's navy blue suit and red tie. He strode to the dark wood sideboard, removed a bottle of Jack Daniels and a glass, then poured himself three fingers and drank it down in one gulp.

When his hawklike eyes spotted Harriet's guest, he said, in a voice loaded with sarcasm and disrespect, "Look who's with us this afternoon, boys and girls!" He refilled his glass, then dropped into a plush wingback chair.

"Say hello to your nephew," Harriet said, with an acid tone. "You were supposed to meet him at the bus stop this afternoon!"

Theo stared with narrowed eyes. "Son of a bitch!" he pronounced slowly, his face flushed with color. "Harvey?" His eyebrows shot up. "You actually *got here*?"

Harriet briefly recapped the facts about the death of Harvey's parents and the afternoon's conversation.

Rising from his chair, Theo approached him, hands on his hips, chin thrust out, eyes ablaze with anger,.

"Stand up!" Theo ordered him.

He stood, stretching to his full height. He was a good four inches taller than his uncle.

"Now you listen to me, bud. If you're gonna live here, you'll obey *my orders*. You hear?"

"Loud and clear, sir," he replied, feeling his blood pressure rise.

"Theo!" Harriet exclaimed, raising a hand to interrupt. "There's no need to attack the boy."

Harvey stood at attention, rigid, his hands balled into fists, trying to control his anger and resentment.

Harriet stood, arms akimbo, her head raised in indignation. "What rules are you making up, Theo?"

Theo flapped his hand back and forth, spurning her insight. "First, you're gonna get a job and bring me your income! That'll be your rent. Number two, no private school for you. You're not my kid." He poured himself another whisky. His pudgy, bulbous nose was already red from drinking. "Rule three, whenever we have guests, you'll stay in your room. I will give the staff orders to that effect."

Theo's tactics hadn't changed a bit. He was dangerous, chunky, and well built. He'd clearly been working out. But fear faded as Harvey neared the boiling point.

Looking him straight in the eye and pointing a stubby index finger in his face, Theo shouted, "Give me my money from my dippy brother! And if I catch you holding out on me, I'll kill you!"

Harvey reached for his wallet and extracted four one-hundred-dollar bills Humphrey Marshall had given him and handed them over. Good thing he'd put the other five hundred in his shoe as a rainy-day fund.

"That's not enough!" Theo shouted. "Give me the rest of it."

"That's all the insurance money there was," he murmured as he looked at his shoes.

"If you're holdin' out on me, I'll kill you! Take your clothes off!"

"Theo!" Harriet roared, her voice commanding, her face a mask of disbelief. "Don't you dare strip-search him!" She inserted herself between them, eyes glaring, nose to nose. "You touch him, and I'm gone. And *that*'ll cost you millions!"

Clearly, Harvey had found an ally, though a very self-willed one.

"Uncle Theo." He began with a calm, reasoned approach. "The role of victim doesn't appeal to me. You want to rule the roost? Fine by me. It's your roost. But you will not sacrifice me or my future for the sake of your ego. Hear me, when I say"—he was near to shouting now—"don't … tread … on … me!"

Quicker than lightning, Theo backhanded him with his right hand. It stung, but he rolled with the slap and recovered with a roundhouse left to Theo's head and a solid, fast right to the solar plexus that doubled the old man over. He followed with a stiff uppercut to that bulbous red nose, which spurted a thick stream of blood.

Stepping back, winded, Theo gasped for air, then went into a fighter's crouch, his face a mask of sheer malice under the blood. He smashed Harvey's nose with his right fist; he heard it crunch and stumbled backward. Blood ran down the front of his green shirt as Theo hit him hard in the stomach. He doubled over, falling to his knees. Then Theo hammered him on the nape of his neck with both fists, forcing his broken nose to the carpet. He screamed in pain.

As Theo started to wrench him over, a swish followed by a loud crack startled him. Theo gave out an enraged cry and released his hold. Harvey rolled over, disbelieving, as Harriet stood just ten feet away. Her right hand held a bullwhip, and her left hand pointed a Glock 26 at Theo's head.

"Stop it, Theo!" she screamed with the authority of God on her side. Her electric blue eyes shot sparks of anger. She'd split Theo's suit jacket down the middle; it flopped over his midsection. The swish and crack came a second time, even closer. The business end of the bullwhip wrapped itself around Theo's right arm, just above the wrist. "Leave him alone, or I'll break your arm! Move and you're a dead man."

15

"All right, all right! I give!" Theo yelled with a look of terrible hate and fear.

Harriet yanked the whip loose, which brought another sharp cry.

Theo tried to get to his feet, but the whip cracked again, splitting the arm of his suit from shoulder to wrist. "Two more lashes, I'll cut that suit right off you."

"Ow! Christ! No!" he shouted. "You've made your point!"

"Best you go to your room, Theo, and clean up—mind and body. No booze! Your alcohol ration for this evening is hereby cancelled. You're already over the limit."

"Okay, okay," he muttered, breathing hard. He turned and left the room, muttering, "Goddamned bitch!"

Harvey laughed to himself. He'd actually hurt Theo! It felt mighty good. Soon he'd be able to bully the bully. In that spirit, he determined he would survive that place and leave in one piece. As soon as possible.

For the next two years, Harvey continued to struggle against Theo. Nothing he did or said was good enough for that newly minted robber baron. He'd learned that term in school the previous year, and it seemed to fit his uncle perfectly. Punches, slaps, and epithets prevailed whenever Aunt Harriet was out of earshot. It was a confusing time; he was a guest, staying out of their way, living by Theo's rules. But he survived.

With Theo's help and insistence, the *Daily News* gave him a job. From 8:00 a.m. to 5:00 p.m. in the summer, he gathered trash, mopped floors, and cleaned bathrooms. He ran errands for the typesetters, composers, and pressmen. This was a good place. He learned a lot, liked the people, and enjoyed the work. One of the photojournalists, Mike Seymore, occasionally let him tag along on assignments. That was a wonderful bit of fun.

Once he'd settled in and started high school, he also shouldered a paper route serving one hundred fifty customers. Each day at four o'clock, he loaded his bike with papers and pedaled the length of the city's west side. He saved his earnings and put them in the bank, minus Theo's percentage for the bicycle.

When six months passed without a paycheck from the newspaper, however, he went to Mr. Shipman, the manager.

"Where are my earnings?" he inquired. "I've never been paid for the work I did inside the plant."

Shipman explained how the paper paid Theo directly as a trustee for Harvey's money.

"Since you're asking, I take it he's not given you—"

"Nothing!" Harvey interrupted with a sneer.

"Your uncle's obviously cheating you," Shipman said with an understanding smile. "From now on, you'll pick up a weekly check right here from the cashier, and I'll raise you from three twenty-five to four dollars an hour when school's out."

"Thank you, sir," he said, elated.

"I'll notify your uncle of our new arrangement. If he blows up, let me know. I'll fix his little red wagon."

Lesson learned—know the whole contract, right up front. His mistake had been letting Theo negotiate for him.

Next, he asked Aunt Harriet's support on cutting Theo off from his paper route earnings. From then on, the old man never got a cent from Harvey's labors.

By now, he'd made three friends among the news carriers, who also needed to escape from home, for similar reasons. They often talked together about their problems One day, they found an ad in the paper for a low-rent shack in a wooded neighborhood just outside of town. That was their excuse to set up housekeeping. Another milestone accomplished. At last he was free from Theo's grip, leading his own life as he pleased.

In another year, he left the *Daily News* when Mr. Nickerson, owner of the hardware store, offered him more money as an inventory manager. To his dismay, however, he soon discovered Nickerson abused some of his customers.

One cold, wintry day, an elderly black woman came in for a snow shovel. Nickerson hurried to help her choose one.

"Special sale today, ma'am. They're regularly twelve dollars, but for you, the price is ten." But he sold the same model to his friends for six dollars.

A hill family came in to buy a toilet, regular price thirty-five dollars. They ended up purchasing it for fifty and were convinced they had gotten a bargain.

After he'd worked for Nickerson a year, he realized nothing in the store had a marked price. Nickerson's preferred customers tended to be white guys with beer bellies, looking for wheelbarrows, lawn mowers, cement, and tools. They all paid the lowest price. But when an old white lady came in for an ironing board, the price doubled.

One afternoon, he asked Nickerson, "Why do you raise the prices for certain people?"

"Because I don't like 'em," Nickerson shot back. "They deserve to pay more."

"Why is that?" Harvey pressed. "They have less to begin with."

"Don't be so weak and stupid, Davenport!" The old man spat a wad of tobacco in the wastebasket. "They're sittin' on a pile of government cash—welfare and social security. Wherever I see a pile of money, I want my share. The government's got a *lot* of *my money*, and I want it back!"

"But that's illegal and immoral," he objected. "Are you blind? Or just stupid?"

"Now look here, boy," old Nickerson growled, sticking his ugly mug in his face. "Don't be talkin' to me like that. Tell you what. As of now, you're fired!"

What a liberating moment! Harvey had long thirsted for revenge on the multitude of Theos and Nickersons who loathed and cheated minorities and the poor. His encounter with Nickerson intensified that craving—radicalized him.

Once outside the store, however, he realized having no job also meant he couldn't afford the next month's rent. He crossed to the bank to withdraw funds from his account, but the teller reported his balance was only $37.50. The previous week, it had topped five hundred dollars. So he asked to see the branch manager.

"Your uncle Theo Davenport came to the bank, saying he wanted to grow your account faster. So he withdrew five hundred dollars to invest it for you."

"And you let him take it? Just like that?" Harvey exclaimed in disbelief.

"Bear in mind, young man," the manager said, "you're still a minor. In this state, any parent or guardian can determine when, where, and how a minor in their charge handles money."

Another bit of learning. Never let the enemy know where your assets are.

"Thank you," he replied, still in shock. "I'll take the balance, then close the account. I won't be banking here anymore."

He returned to the *Daily News*, and, fortunately, Mr. Shipman seemed glad to see him.

"With Theo as your uncle and Nickerson as your boss, I knew you'd be back."

Shipman's frankness and thoughtfulness impressed him.

"You need a job, right?" said Shipman, with a smile.

"Sure do," he said. "Theo stole my bank account. I've got thirty-seven fifty, and the rent's due. I was hoping ..."

"Your timing is perfect!" Shipman crowed. "I just accepted the resignation of my pressroom manager last week, and here you come in. I know you're only ... what? Sixteen this year?"

"Yes, sir, that's right."

"Well, you've more than proven your ability to handle a job. How about I put you and our retiring pressroom manager together for two months, so you learn the job backwards and forwards?"

"U-u-unbelievable!" he stammered in shock. He could hardly believe it. "Yes, I'd like that very much. Thank you, Mr. Shipman!"

The new job meant he'd probably not return to school that fall, but he had confidence something would turn up in his favor if he worked diligently and searched methodically for whatever his next course of action might be. Time was in his favor, and he'd already begun selling photographs to the *Daily News*.

He was learning how to be on his guard, to have resources in reserve, and to be flexible. He'd happened across a good guy, but until he learned who to trust and under what circumstances, caution would be his watchword. Otherwise, he'd suffer the consequences.

CHAPTER 2

BEGINNINGS II

Half a century later, having returned to Westfield, Harvey Davenport celebrated his sixty-fourth birthday. He settled in his office chair in the studio he'd remodeled from an old barn fifteen years before. His smile broadened as his associate, Mina LoPino, sang "Happy Birthday" to him. Her warm, mellow voice filled his heart with gratitude as it echoed through the workroom. Then, dressed in black as usual, wearing a blue paisley scarf, she presented him with a diminutive chocolate muffin, on top of which a tiny candle emitted a friendly glow. He nodded, enjoying her sense of humor. Immediately, Lord Nelson, his Russian blue tomcat, jumped into his lap to taste the frosting. His year of retirement was off to a promising start.

"The lady at the French bakery removed these fresh from the oven as I passed," she cooed. "Couldn't resist bringing you one."

Mina had come to his studio one spring morning three years ago, looking for work. She was a photography major from the Art Institute of Chicago, his alma mater. Tall, graceful, with a short, black, pixie haircut, pale face, and dainty ears, Mina was an accomplished photographer already at twenty-six, having garnered many positive reviews of her work. She didn't cook, bake, or sew, claiming she knew what happened to girls who did and wanted to avoid that outcome at all costs. But she certainly knew her way around a photographic studio.

She also reminded him of his daughter, Laura. When he was thirty years old, he met and married Bernice Trombley, a Londoner, newly graduated from Oxford, and brought her to this country. They had Laura while living in New York City as he established himself in a well-known photography studio. Then, suddenly, in the winter of 1991, his wife died tragically in a car crash on an icy curve in the road, coming home from a book signing in Poughkeepsie. From that time on, he'd raised Laura by himself. She had been an intelligent, energetic, self-motivated teenager, very much like Mina.

Memory lane also revisited him with shadows of his fourteenth birthday, seemingly a lifetime ago, following the untimely deaths of his mother and father nearby in the Bottoms of Westfield. On that day, his elderly friend Humphrey Marshall had presented him with a gift that contributed immeasurably to his professional success. The money from his father's meager life insurance policy had set him on the journey to Binghamton, New York, where he'd lived with his uncle Theo and aunt Harriet until he was eighteen. The confusion and dismay that assailed him in those years returned to him now, prompting a tightening in his stomach, for once again he stood on the verge of an unknown future.

When he'd first returned to Westfield in 1996, he'd taken time to visit his mother's grave in the Bethel AME Church cemetery and explore the old neighborhood. The cemetery was well maintained, and he found his mother's gravestone easily. He spent a few minutes placing a bouquet of bright yellow daffodils on her grave, letting memories from his adolescence bubble to the surface. The house where they'd lived was still in use, though thirty years had taken their toll on its exterior. The present family's youngsters played in the dirt just as he and his pals had done. Unfortunately, they also evidenced the same sores from which he'd suffered at that age, thus evoking within him a renewed commitment to fighting industry's misdeeds.

As he stared out at the countryside, a chilly spring rain soaked fields soon ready for planting. "I love the rain," he said to Mina. "The sound of it calms my nerves and refreshes my spirit." But twinges of envy and nostalgia tightened his chest. "Those five old oaks out there along the drive mock me. They stand so straight and tall. They've provided shade for these pastures since long before this barn was built, and I will probably not outlive them."

"No reason you should," she replied. "But you can enjoy them for the years you have left."

"What I want is another season of spring!" he exclaimed with sudden intensity. "Another time of growth and discovery. I'm not *that* old. Yeah, sure, my body might be developing a few quirks, but the thought of harvest fast approaching doesn't improve my attitude one bit."

He'd heard the cliché, that in this modern era, the elderly could expect a full life in retirement. But which group of elderly? During his adult years, the best features of modernity had been steadily eroded or reserved only for those with wealth. He worried that the quality of life for people like himself seemed destined to decline in the next thirty years. Yet, if one considered the breadth of human history, hadn't that always been the fate of the common people, especially the elderly?

"You don't have to live the next thirty years all at once," she said, evincing her mischievous smile. "Just take it one day at a time. Take the good and the bad as they come. Most likely, you'll continue to make the kind of life you want."

Considering his beginnings, he'd been fortunate to lead the life he had. If he was completely honest, he'd spent the decades living moment to moment, enjoying life and work to the fullest. After graduating from the Art Institute of Chicago, he'd enjoyed an exciting and often perilous career as a photojournalist, gathering a worldwide reputation. He'd survived the jungles of Southeast Asia, endured the deserts of Arabia, and outlived the wars of Iraq and Afghanistan. He'd been lucky—far more so than many of his comrades. And luck was still with him now. He'd been able to return to Westfield toward the end of his career to satisfy a long-held yearning to cleanse his birthplace of the industrial waste that had killed his parents and so many others for more than a century.

"We'd better get back to work," Mina advised, moving into the workroom.

As usual, she was right. However worrisome they might be, retirement and his agenda with industry would have to wait a while longer. There was work to do. They were in the last stages of creating a photograph commissioned by a longtime friend and client, Tom McIntyre, the biggest oil magnate in the state. They had just two days to create a six-by-ten-foot masterpiece called a "vanitas" for McIntyre's new headquarters in the state capital. This would be a contemporary version of an art form developed in the Netherlands in the seventeenth century.

The vanitas form had long been used as a social commentary. Such a painting typically displayed a background of healthy, sunlit flowers against a foreground of decay, such as dead rabbits, rotten fruit, bugs, and worm-eaten instruments. He felt himself in league with those old Dutch painters, though few national leaders of the time had taken their message to heart. Nevertheless, McIntyre, being an optimistic fellow, wanted his vanitas to make a similar statement about the use of fossil fuels and the acceleration of global warming in his own time.

The prospect of creating this photograph made him tingle with anticipation, but his heart occasionally raced with anxiety whenever he considered the short deadline. He'd never assembled such a work of art on so tight a schedule.

He wheeled a cart loaded with fresh flowers to his worktable under the lights of his production studio. They had been handpicked by Brazilian growers just the day before. As Mina opened their shipping boxes, they gave off heady fragrances of verbenas, roses, tulips, irises, and chrysanthemums. Meanwhile, Harvey chose a graceful, deep blue vase from his storage cabinet as the vessel that would display them.

His pulse quickened and his senses came alive as he selected one lovely, shocking-pink chrysanthemum, cradled it in his hands, then placed it in the vase. He complemented this blossom with a stunning red rose on its right and a graceful purple iris on the left. The warmth of happiness spread through him like sunshine as his creation began to take shape.

A call from George Spencer momentarily interrupted his work. George was a copyright attorney and a friend for many years. Lately, he'd been leaning on Harvey to run for city council as Ward Six's representative. Service to the ward and the city would fit his skill set and allow him to help his neighbors and pursue his quarrel with industry. Though he'd been hoping for such an opportunity, the time was at hand when the ward committee would make a decision. He had to give George his answer that evening.

As soon as they'd agreed to meet at the Succulent Sirloin at seven, Harvey returned to his worktable. He had a job to do and a deadline to meet. Seated once again at the worktable, he added three more proud purple irises, balancing them with three Delft blue tulips on each side, then two additional red verbenas and three bright orange tulips. Finally, he added his monarch, a huge, dazzling crimson rose, in the center. He smiled to himself with pleasure. She was a magnificent, fierce queen.

Mina sauntered over to look at his arrangement. Her work on the vanitas involved making clay models of various symbols of social decay. "Fabulous!" she cried as she touched his arm and held it for a moment. "McIntyre will fall in love with it!"

The phone rang, and she answered. "It's your aunt Harriet," she said to him.

The hairs on the nape of his neck stiffened with aggravation. He didn't need another distraction. Still, his aunt had supported him in dealing with his violent uncle Theo during his adolescence, so he owed her a moment of his time. He was her only living family member since Theo had died of a heart attack thirty years before.

After he'd given her some advice about a problem she was having with her IRAs, he had a sudden impulse. "What do you think of my running for city council? Would I do well at that?"

"What a marvelous idea!" she said. "It's the first step of your plan, isn't it?"

"So far, yes," he replied.

"It'll keep you out of trouble, and you'll soon be mayor!" The hint of playfulness in her voice suggested she was poking fun. But now she became serious. "No, Harvey. It's not a good idea. As I've told you before, you're not cut out for that kind of craziness. You're an artist, not a civil servant. Don't dirty your hands in the muck of politics. You're better than that."

"Well, I thank you for your advice, Aunt Harriet. If you think of a better way to accomplish my objective, please let me know. Unfortunately, I've gotta run. We're working on a tight deadline today."

He leaned back in his chair, taking several moments to distance himself from her autocratic posturing. At eighty-six, she wasn't going to change, and he was in no mood to argue.

By this time, the floor around his stool was littered with green paper, cardboard boxes, bits and pieces of flowers, and scraps of clay. Lord Nelson, with his narrow face and wide-set green eyes, had a delightful time pawing at anything that caught his attention. Harvey reached down and picked the cat up, hugging him to his chest. The prospect of someday finding himself among the detritus of his own career gave him a moment of unpleasantness. He curled his shoulders forward around his lovely, big kitty, focusing on more sanguine thoughts like evenings beside the fire, reading his favorite novels.

Meanwhile, Mina had moved ahead, fashioning symbols of decay such as tiny ants, wasps, and bees out of clay, then hanging them among Harvey's flowers with microfilament invisible to the camera. She also molded and painted models of wrecked Volkswagens and Cadillacs. Her master stroke was a mash-up of a demolished Concorde and a battered old Apple II computer, which she positioned just in front of his flower arrangement.

She cocked her head to one side and looked up to him with a nervous little smile at the corners of her mouth. "Looks like we've got ourselves a mighty strong graphic here."

"Yes. And, as always, Mina, you've done excellent work!" he said.

"Thanks, Harvey. I'm happy to hear you say that," she replied in her soft voice. "But …" She bit her lip, and her expression suggested an urgent question she didn't know how to ask.

"Go ahead, Mina. Tell me what's on your mind," he said with a gentle smile.

"Well, since you're talking about retirement, have you thought any more about your succession plan for the business? I sense you're getting serious now, aren't you?"

Years before, he'd been in a similar conversation with the principals at the Handy & Hardhardt Photographic Studio in New York before going out on his own. He could easily sympathize with her position.

"I admire your sensitivity and your boldness, Mina," he said, beaming at her and giving her a thumbs-up.

"I don't want you to think I'm being too"—she shrugged her shoulders and tilted her head to one side—"forward."

"Not at all," he reassured her. "I've made up my mind, and you're the person I trust to take over. If you want it, I'm ready to sell it to you."

With a gentle, cautious smile, she peeked at him from underneath her black eyelashes. "Thank you, Harvey. I am so relieved!" She took a deep breath and let it out slowly. "I've been trying to decide what my options are for the future."

"We'll have more years here working together," he said. "You need time to build more experience and equity, and I hope you'll put up with an aging partner a while longer." He grinned at her.

"I've always enjoyed working with you," she said. "I hope you know that."

Together they maneuvered the large, rotating platform on which they'd assembled the vanitas to the center of the light table. Then Harvey sat at the lighting console to make the first round of exposures.

As he sipped his beer that evening in the bar of the Succulent Sirloin, waiting for George Spencer to arrive, the pungent odors of sweet potato fries and grilling steaks made him hungry. Pushing his glass and coaster around the table, sardonic amusement overtook him. What would happen if he refused George's offer? They'd both be shocked, wouldn't they?

When they'd been seated in a booth and had given the waiter their orders, he unrolled his napkin slowly and deliberately, then arranged his silverware next to his beer glass.

"Put my mind at rest, George. Why is the committee so eager to have *me* on council? There are other people more qualified."

"You're well known, and you've helped a lot of people in the ward. You have the residents at heart. The streets are full of potholes, streetlights need repairing, the garbage might or might not be picked up. Sewers are backing up all over town, as you well know."

He laughed and nodded his head. He knew about the troublesome sewers all right.

"What we need is a driving force, and you're the guy the committee thinks can provide it."

Harvey crossed his arms and leaned into the table, returning Spencer's stare. "So why don't *you* run for council, George? You have the training and experience. I'm a rank amateur." He didn't relish sparring with one of the city's most prominent attorneys, but he felt a compulsion to dig a little further into George's motivation.

"Because I don't want the job," George said, raising his palms faceup on either side of his shoulders. "I've got a thriving practice that keeps me busy. Besides, I'm an idea man. I prefer to take the long view and stay away from hashing out the minutiae of policy." He paused to take a sip of his water, then looked him square in the eye. "Here it is, Harvey. We need some dynamite under city hall—analysis, communication, persistence. You're the guy who can do it. The question is, will you?"

Well, who could argue with that? Certainly not a fellow on the verge of retirement with an urge to make things happen. "You make a strong case, George. Yes, I'm in. Ready to do it."

"Fair enough, my friend." George relaxed in his chair. "Glad to have you with us. Let's look forward to our meeting with the ward committee."

After dinner, Harvey drove to his downtown studio to pick up two bright white reflectors he'd need for the vanitas shoot the next day. He also wanted to check on the sewer repairs being made in his block. The city had neglected to deal with massive tree-root problems for years. Now all the families on the block were inconvenienced, perhaps for as long as a month, while new lines were laid. This was the reason he and Mina were working in the barn studio out in the country.

Since the streetlights on his block had been out for a month, the street was almost dark. Peering through the gloom, he made out the familiar six-foot trench ringed with orange mesh in front of his building.

A quick check of his downstairs commode and kitchen sink confirmed that the sewer problem still existed. Upstairs in the workroom, he poked around in the utility cabinet till he found the reflectors, each one folded and stuffed into a white acrylic case that resembled a coconut cream pie. He jammed two under his left arm, then headed for his car.

Crossing the street in the dark, he fumbled in his right pants pocket for his keys. Just as he freed the keys, his left foot hit a large, jagged pothole. He fell to the pavement as his ankle gave way with an audible snap. He emitted a sharp cry of pain as the car keys flew toward the construction hole and his reflectors careered across the pavement into the gutter beneath his van.

Gingerly, he rose to his knees and crawled to the van, wincing with eye-watering pain as he pulled himself up by the door handle. Then he spent several minutes hobbling back along the edge of the construction ditch, trying to see the glint of keys in the dark. All at once, his foot hit them, nearly knocking them into the trench. They stopped four inches from the edge.

Next, he lurched to the van's passenger side and lowered himself to the pavement on bruised knees to retrieve the reflectors. A neighbor's porch light revealed that when he'd parked the car, a fire hydrant had smashed a large dent in his lower rear quarter panel. A wave of anger washed over him a second before the ridiculousness of the way he'd phrased that situation in his mind hit him and he burst out laughing.

Back in the driver's seat, he rested a while. Then panic hit him. Who would hang the McIntyre photograph? He'd have to hire a professional installer. The city's negligence was costing *him* money now.

Yes! Of course! He *certainly by God would* run for council! And he'd dig and dig until he found out why the streetlights, the sewers, and the potholes weren't being fixed. And while he was at it, he'd find out why the council had never put a stop to the toxic waste killing machine too!

Half an hour later, back at the barn studio, in his bed with a book of short stories in hand and his aching foot propped up with an ice pack, the world looked slightly better. The fragrant aromas of the leftover flowers Mina had put into a vase and set on his walnut bookshelf soothed his mind and brought a smile of satisfaction to his lips.

Now, if only his neighbors would support him, his retirement plans might seem a little more solid.

Harvey and Mina returned to Westfield late Wednesday night, April 14, after installing the vanitas for the opening of Tom McIntyre's headquarters. Since his right foot was still unable to bear much weight, he'd had to hire Felix Vogel, a local newspaper reporter, to help with the installation. The arrangement worked for everyone because Felix was covering the event for the *Westfield Independent*, and he seemed grateful for the extra cash and a free ride.

Having returned well after midnight, he'd spent Thursday on the couch in front of a blazing fire, with his sprained ankle propped up on pillows, a cup of hot Dutch chocolate in one hand and the latest Stephen King novel in the other.

By evening, however, he was eager to join the ward leaders in their discussion of candidates for city council. The Sixth Ward comprised the heart of downtown Westfield. Average election turnout was 74 percent—highest in the city. Political awareness and participation bound these folks together like glue. He donned his office costume and limped the two blocks to Claudia Douglas's nineteenth-century brownstone. Now was the time to take the next step toward his dream.

As he climbed the stone steps to Claudia's front porch, the jonquils and crocuses in the front yard leaned forward to inhale the clean, fresh scent of spring. Instead, they were assaulted by the stench of sewage. Across the street, three yellow hard hats bobbed up and down in a muddy trench similar to the one outside his studio.

Claudia flung open the door with a welcoming smile. "Saw you coming, Harvey!" She laughed. "Gosh, it's great to see you! Come in."

This highly charged, little half-pint of a woman, with shoulder-length chestnut-brown hair graying at the temples, commanded the ward. She ushered him into her spacious living room, gave him a brief peck on the cheek, then dashed to the kitchen to extinguish her oven timer. The odor of fresh-baked bread and a taco casserole soothed his nerves. A master of culinary arts, Claudia had arranged a buffet supper.

"Check out the goodies in the dining room," she called from the kitchen. "Don't you just love this spring weather?"

He fell into a blue velvet couch, which wrapped him in a soft embrace. Jazz tunes from the sixties played softly on the stereo. He'd lived in the ward for fifteen years and had been part of the ward committee for ten. He knew these folks well and trusted them. They'd bitched and griped together many times about the pathetic lack of city services; it was a shared irritation.

Nancy Caruthers and Susan Mintz entered the living room chatting about the spring sales. Nancy was a buyer for a local department store, Susan a partner in the public relations firm of Meyers and Mintz. Both hugged Harvey enthusiastically as he stood to embrace them.

"You're looking fantastic!" cooed Nancy. She fluffed her honey-blond hair with her fingers. "Haven't seen you in ages."

"We thought we'd lost you." Susan fixed him with piercing green eyes from underneath a shock of auburn hair. "Where have you been?"

"I spent a month photographing in Central Asia," he replied. "Took two weeks on Hawaii's beaches to recover!" He laughed at the memory.

"Poor baby, you do lead a tough life, don't you!" said Nancy.

Bill Ferman and Joe Lingonberry strolled into the room chatting about GMOs. Lingonberry was an academic, with elbow patches on his herringbone jacket to prove it. Ferman, a veterinarian, headed the United Way board.

Claudia next ushered in Herb and Retha Galloway. They owned the largest men's clothing store in town. Herb's dark navy suit and bright yellow tie rendered him a walking advertisement.

Behind them, George Spencer breezed through the hall and into the living room. "How're you feeling, Harvey? How's the foot?"

"A bit nervous and a little sore in that order," replied Harvey with a shrug. "Otherwise, good. And hungry!"

"Just remember—in this ward, you're known and loved. The people will definitely support you," George assured him.

Just then, a tall man in a green sweater and khakis bustled in.

"That's Sam Beresford," Michael Douglas whispered in his ear. "In his forties, specializes in mergers and acquisitions. He also owns a ton of real estate in downtown. The short guy with him is Richard Collins, owner of WWFL-TV, Channel 5. They're both here from the chamber of commerce."

Just then, Natalie Peterson, in a blue periwinkle dress, flowed to Harvey, embracing him with a rather unmotherly hug. But he returned the hug and thanked her with a peck on the cheek.

Thankfully, the deep tones of Claudia's immense Han dynasty gong interrupted Natalie's embrace, announcing it was time to fill their plates. He loaded up on taco casserole. As always, it was delicious and the conversation lively. Twenty minutes later, when everyone was comfortably seated with their food and drinks, Claudia welcomed them.

"As you know, we're here to discuss the upcoming election for city council. This is informal, so proceed at your leisure. What are your thoughts?"

"My question," said Susan, green eyes spitting fire, "is why aren't the buses running? We need public transportation, and we used to have it."

"Same reason we're hearing that construction noise across the street," Spencer offered. "The city's falling apart financially."

"Whenever I tried to talk with Gerry Fraubeck, our previous councilman," said Harvey, shaking his head in disgust, "he blamed the city manager, and I could never get a straight answer on anything I asked him."

"But the sewer was never fixed," Claudia complained. "We had to engage a private contractor. That's who's working out there now." Her intense blue eyes sparked with anger.

"If we don't elect a reliable and accountable representative," said her husband, "it'll get worse. Our infrastructure is hopeless. We've got to do something—now."

"Whenever I go to city hall, I put on my track shoes," said Nancy Caruthers. "Running from one office to another—no one answers my questions."

"Have you heard? Manfred Quentin has declared for this ward," George Spencer interjected. "He's the chamber's candidate. Should we support him?"

That bit of news had escaped Harvey, and the fact that George raised the point set his heart to pounding.

"I can tell you without hesitation we do not want the junior manager for International Taconite as our councilman!" declared Herb Galloway. "They've dumped poison into the Staminon River for at least a century."

"Actually, friends," said Sam Beresford, "I think Manny's a fine candidate. What's your objection?"

"Quentin would weaken regulation and pamper the corporations," Galloway replied, an edge in his voice.

At last, Harvey's brain made the connection: Beresford and Collins were shills for the chamber. The warmth of embarrassment flooded his face. They were here to persuade the ward to back their candidate.

"The chamber may have registered him for our ward," Claudia steamed, "but he is *not* our candidate! We want a candidate we know we can trust."

"Why can't you trust Quentin?" Collins inquired with obvious irritation.

"Inappropriate values," said Nancy. "Plus, we just plain don't want him."

"You mean the values of business aren't appropriate?" Sam Beresford exclaimed. "Listen, little lady, without business, this city would go bankrupt—fast! Business keeps the economy humming!"

Faces around the room wore thunder clouds. The two pitchmen reminded Harvey of his uncle Theo—slick, ruthless, and dishonest, resorting to violence to get their way.

"I can tell you now, fellows," George said to the two shills, "you chamber guys may have burned us once, but you'll not do that again."

Relief spread through Harvey as he took a deep breath and relaxed. Most likely, George had been playing devil's advocate just to get past this part of the meeting.

"Wouldn't you prefer a candidate who will continue to build the city's economy?" Beresford pressed his point.

"Certainly not," said Nancy. Cold steel infused her voice. "Our values are services to the residents, money for the schools, help for people who suffer, and regulated markets that give everyone an equal chance at a good life."

"I would add honesty, transparency, and accountability," Bill Ferman offered. "Most businesses stay far away from those principles."

"Let's move on, shall we?" said Claudia Douglas. Her spread hands indicated she meant everyone in the room. "Who can do the job for us on city council?"

"Someone who will attend the meetings and put our needs first," said Natalie.

"Bring back the buses!" exclaimed Susan, her green eyes boring into Collins with a vengeance.

"A person who can give the job the time and attention it deserves," said Bill.

"Maybe someone who's retired?" offered Nancy.

"Good reputation's important too," Galloway chimed in.

"My vote goes to Harvey Davenport," said Natalie. "I think he's an ideal candidate. He's helped us before. He knows our needs."

His stomach flipped at the mention of his name. The welcome nomination had come faster than he'd anticipated. Was it for real? Would it stick?

"What do you say, Harvey?" Spencer asked, as if they'd never discussed it before. "Are you willing to take this on?"

He paused to calm his nerves. He couldn't quite believe he was this close to his goal. "Yes, I am," he said finally, with a measured cadence, steepling his hands in front of his face. "I've been thinking about retirement, and I'm looking for a way to be of help in the community. This is the perfect opportunity."

"Nah! You guys!" exclaimed Sam Beresford, shaking his head with obvious disdain. "No legal experience, no history in municipal government."

"He has no name recognition," Collins chimed in. "He's a political amateur! That's crazy!"

"Never mind them, Harvey," said Joe Lingonberry, gesturing over his shoulder at Beresford and Collins with his thumb. "The big question is, do you want to do it?"

"Yes," said Harvey with a confident nod. "We could do a lot together to improve our community."

"Amen to that!" Nancy Caruthers cheered.

"But he knows nothing of municipal government!" Collins objected.

"So, we'll teach him!" Ferman countered.

"Takes a lot of money to campaign," Beresford persisted.

"We'll work together to raise what we need," said Harvey, with unusual calm.

Without warning, Collins jumped up from his seat. "You people are incredible!" he bellowed. In his excitement, he stumbled into his tray table, sending dishes crashing to the hardwood floor. "You have no idea what you're doing, electing an incompetent amateur to a governing body!"

Beresford rescued Collins's tray table and Claudia's broken plates, put them on the coffee table in the center, then said, "If you didn't like Gerald Fraubeck, you'll get a lot worse with this guy!"

"You're trying to ram your candidate down the throats of ward residents, and I'm not having anything to do with that," complained Collins.

That's exactly what you're doing to us. Interesting how they turned the facts around to suit themselves.

"Get out!" growled Michael Douglas, anger inching up his neck, a cold glint in his eye. When Beresford and Collins didn't seem to understand, Douglas rose from his chair, pointed a finger, and roared, "I said *get out of my house!*" and moved toward Beresford, as if ready to enforce his words.

The two men left swiftly, grumbling angrily all the way out the front door.

When the fireworks had ceased, George Spencer said, with a calming voice, "Now that we've heard from Mutt and Jeff, let's resume our discussion."

Audible chuckles arose from the group as tension diminished.

"What would you do first?" Spencer asked, looking at Harvey.

"I'd examine the budget," he said. "That's the most important diagnostic tool. It'll tell us what's wrong. Then I'll report back to you. From that point, we work together on how to shake things up. It's time the residents were heard!"

"Good campaign speech!" Nancy cheered. Turning to the others, she said, "If we want accountability and transparency, we couldn't have a better candidate."

"Perfect!" said Claudia. "Did you know? In its first meeting in January, the council always deals with the budget. We'll be waiting to hear what you have to say, Harvey."

The affirmations of others around the room echoed her sentiments.

Unalloyed excitement throbbed in his veins. His confidence and readiness to serve were in high gear. Now it was up to his neighbors. If they agreed with the committee, he'd be set to drive real transformation. Nevertheless, the appearance of Beresford and Collins suggested trouble lay ahead.

CHAPTER 3

TESTING THE WATERS

A brilliant sunset illuminated the copper dome of city hall on a bitter-cold first Monday in January. Harvey twitched with nervous energy as he walked to the municipal complex, because tonight was his debut as a newly elected member of the city council.

Swinging open one of the huge white entrance doors, Harvey entered the reception hall, which was carpeted with a gaudy flower pattern on a red background. He winced at the abrupt brightness of fluorescent lights. To the left was the city council chamber, also accessed by white double doors. He pulled one open and entered.

The oval walls of the council chamber were clad in wallpaper with soft ivory-and-burgundy stripes. Theater-style seating covered in a plush, dark red velvet welcomed the public, but in the few times he'd sat in on council sessions—tales among his ward residents to the contrary—he'd seen very few citizens in those seats.

At the front, three sturdy tables hosted support staff, special guests, and reporters. Desks for council members and the mayor were positioned on a raised dais. The city's charter stated that the mayor would run the meetings but vote only to break a tie. Representatives from the First through Fourth Wards sat to the mayor's right, the remaining four to his left.

As Harvey took his seat, Mayor John Timmerling arrived in animated conversation with councilmen Mike Dwyer and Rhett Bennett, representing the Fifth and Seventh Wards respectively. The mayor, a tall, slim man in his midfifties, CEO of a local manufacturing firm, wore a sharkskin gray suit with a bright blue tie. A worried expression counterbalanced a perpetual tight-lipped smile. Dwyer, dressed in his signature navy blue suit and red tie, headed the First National Bank of Westfield, the largest bank in town. He exuded the frank confidence of a man used to controlling people and situations. Rhett Bennett's booming voice, half-bemused smile, and carefully styled mane of grayish hair bespoke his position as CEO of Superior Plastics, located in the old industrial park in the Bottoms and a major contributor to the area's pollution.

Clarence Williams entered the chamber talking animatedly with Marty Angelo, councilman from the First Ward. Williams was the black representative of the Second Ward, the Bottoms—the neighborhood of Harvey's birth. He worked as a production line foreman for Bennett at Superior Plastics. Rumor had it that Bennett had backed him for election at Dwyer's request. Angelo was the tactful, unpretentious owner of a local beverage distributorship. He, too, had been selected by the chamber for election to office.

Harvey's pulse quickened with excitement as Mayor Timmerling gaveled the meeting to order. The first item on the agenda was the city's budget. Here was his chance to perform for the residents of his ward.

Another new member of the council and personal friend was Stan Matthews of the Eighth Ward. Like Harvey, he was an independent candidate who had soundly defeated his chamber-sponsored opponent. He had previously been married to Sherry Matthews, daughter of Clarence Williams and former director of the city's Environmental Protection Department. She had been fired four years earlier for publishing a report giving the true pollution figures from the city's field engineers. Immediately thereafter, she'd been abducted and murdered, her remains having been discovered in a cement mixer used on a city construction project.

Media representatives crowded around three tables in front of the dais. Curious citizens filled the public seating area. The number of people in the gallery surprised him, especially considering the wintry weather. Their keen interest in the budget suggested the residents of his ward weren't alone in their discontent.

To begin, Mayor Timmerling invited city treasurer Pauline Trebenko to guide the council through her carefully prepared budget. Midforties, wearing a navy blue suit and white shirt, Ms. Trebenko looked to be the paragon of civil service.

"Ladies and gentlemen," she instructed, "please turn to page four, where you see a comparison of current year against the proposed budget. Note that increases for next year are limited to executive salaries plus streets and sanitation. That's for continuing repair of our crumbling sewers. Net increase for the coming year is three percent."

"Ms. Trebenko, why is there such a slight increase over the present year?" Harvey asked the question burning in his mind when she'd completed her summary. "The city is growing, and the residents in my ward are angry at the condition of their streets. Where's the growth one might expect for a vibrant city like Westfield?"

"The council's informal policy is to keep increases below five percent," the mayor interjected in a subdued tone.

"Who enacted this policy?" Third Ward council member Alice Morrison asked in a firm, peremptory voice. Just a hint of a smile complemented her yellow suit. She had retired three years previously after thirty-seven years of teaching in Westfield's public schools. Tall, slim, and elegant, she had a reputation for her fiery temper and dislike for hidden agendas.

"It's been our standard practice for the past twenty-two years," the mayor muttered with a frown. His pleasant, affable demeanor had given way to a guarded effort to control the discussion. "We don't want the budget to get out of hand."

"The practice is consistent with the prudent man rule," Mike Dwyer of the Fifth Ward interceded. "That's our standard for fulfilling our fiduciary duty. By law, we must handle the city's assets as if they were our own." Dwyer, besides being president of the bank, was also chairman of the board of directors at the chamber of commerce. He seemed a little jumpy this evening, like someone anxious not to lose control.

"Sounds like you're listening more to the chamber of commerce than to the residents of the wards," Alice commented. Her smile broadened to a grin.

Having an ally on the council calmed Harvey's nerves. It might be worthwhile getting to know Alice a little better.

"We're just being conservative about our fiscal responsibility," Rhett Bennett countered in his big, booming voice, furrowing his brow. Physically, he was the most formidable member of the council.

"But why starve the city for revenues?" Harvey rebutted. "My people deserve a better budget and better services!" The heat of simmering anger crept up the side of his face.

Polite applause from the public gallery suggested he was on the right track.

"The reason is people don't want tax increases," said Bennett, clearly agitated. "We hear it all the time."

"What we need," argued Clarence Williams, "is less government interference. That always means fewer dollars wasted on taxes and leaves more to spend on our families." He spoke with authority in his immaculate black suit, his manner smooth and composed.

Harvey promised himself he'd inquire how Williams balanced the needs of the poor residents of his ward and the preferences of financiers and corporate owners. What would his own mother have said if she'd known that an employee of a major polluting industry professed to represent her?

"Our citizens are satisfied when taxes are the same year after year," said Dwyer. "Keeping taxes low means shepherding every department's bottom line."

"But, Mr. Dwyer," Harvey argued, "don't new citizens coming into Westfield need services? Are those people just parked outside the city in tents like refugees from a war-torn country?"

"Every year the cost of services goes up," said city manager George Howard from his position at the staff table. His visage featured deep-set eyes, hooded under closely knit eyebrows. "As our costs increase, we must decrease the number and types of services." He was known as a good friend of Mike Dwyer and had once chaired the local chamber.

"What happened to the concept that taxes are just the way citizens contribute to the cost of services they receive?" Stan Matthews offered.

"Mr. Mayor!" Alice called with a buoyant air as she waved her hand. "I've brought copies of the last ten years' budgets." Rising from her chair, she placed one on each council member's desk. "In the past decade, there has been only a three percent total increase in the overall budget."

Timmerling looked at Dwyer, who shrugged.

"My research shows our population has increased thirty-two and a half percent in the same period," said Stan Matthews, taking advantage of the pause. "One would expect the city's budget to keep pace with such growth."

Warm applause issued from the gallery. People smiled at one another.

"Why have top executive salaries increased ten percent a year while other staff remain static?" Harvey queried after examining Alice's exhibit. "And why are their fewer employees on the payroll every year?

"We must pay salaries comparable to industry to keep good people heading our government," replied Howard.

"Cutting programs, and therefore staff, keeps costs down," said Dwyer. "The citizens of Westfield demand it. We're just doing their bidding."

"Which citizens would that be?" asked Stan Mathews. "Have the residents been given an opportunity to directly express their opinions for the record?"

"We always assume," said Howard with calm authority, "that citizens want more services than they're willing to pay for. They want something for nothing."

The 155 seated members of the public commenced grumbling. Obviously they weren't buying Howard's presumptions.

"Why not consider equal pay?" Alice suggested. "Ten percent annual increases across the board?"

"We'd never be reelected if we did that," Rhett Bennett asserted.

"Is reelection the goal of city council?" Harvey pressed. "Aren't we supposed to serve the citizens by providing services they're entitled to by law?"

"By any chance, is it only the business interests who say no to tax increases?" Alice asked.

The mayor blanched, as did the city manager.

Mike Dwyer's reddened face looked as if he'd explode, but there was no time for his comment. Looking at his watch, Timmerling gaveled the group to attention.

"Ladies and gentlemen, we have an order of the day scheduled at this time. We'll turn now to Mr. Norman Taylor, president of the chamber of commerce."

Norm had a reputation as a born charlatan and huckster. Tall, muscular, with jowly cheeks and a paunch, he looked like a former bouncer. He'd been a prominent advocate for business in the area for thirty years.

Standing at a microphone on the floor below the dais, wearing a blue dress shirt open at the collar and sleeves rolled, Taylor said, "Ladies and gentlemen, the Chamber Players now present for your pleasure *The Tax Man Cometh*."

Two dozen players in costume began to process around the chamber. Heads down, they chanted repeatedly in a low voice, "Taxes are killing us. Taxes are killing us."

"The players represent the city's residents," Taylor narrated. "Here comes a teacher, carrying books and charts. Over there's a nurse in uniform. Here we have a lawyer in the front now. You also see the secretary with her pad and pencil.

"Do you see those strange animals hiding out in the corners of the chamber?" Taylor continued.

Actors in wolf costumes with fedoras anchored between their ears crouched behind the public gallery. They began to slink about the chamber, each furry, dark back carrying the moniker "Tax Man" in white.

"The wolves of government are ready to grab citizens' hard-earned dollars so bureaucrats can amass great wealth," Taylor pronounced. "This is unjust. We who have so little should keep what we earn."

Without warning, two of the wolves grabbed the doctor in his white coat, knocked him on the head, then dragged him out of the chamber. Seconds later, another pair arrested the secretary, tied her hands, and hauled her out.

The remaining players continued to chant as they marched around the room, "The taxes are killing us."

"There goes the nurse!" shouted Taylor as the wolves hustled the woman in a white uniform from the room. "There goes the teacher's small savings. Ouch!"

Her books and charts crashed to the floor.

"There's the corner grocer getting it in the neck," Taylor continued.

The man's head lolled as the wolves hauled him away.

The few remaining players and the wolves disappeared. Then, from the outer hallway, the players shouted in unison, "No more taxes!"

"Thank you, ladies and gentlemen!" Taylor said as he bowed first to the council members and then to the audience.

When the presentation finished, silence descended on the public gallery. Only Timmerling, Dwyer, Bennett, and Williams applauded. When their scant applause became embarrassing, the mayor coughed, then said, "Let us continue with the budget."

"Mr. Mayor." Harvey had his hand in the air.

"Yes, please, Mr. Davenport." Timmerling seemed almost to beg.

"I move that Stan Matthews, Alice Morrison, and I be designated to work with Ms. Trebenko to create a more fitting budget for the city. We will bring our proposal to next week's meeting."

"Absolute nonsense!" Dwyer exploded. He rose from his chair and stomped back and forth on the dais. "How often must we say it? The public wants no increase in taxes!"

"Mr. Dwyer," said Timmerling, wrinkling up his face. "Please sit down. Your actions are excessive and an embarrassment."

Dwyer resumed his seat, his red face a mask of anger.

"I second Mr. Davenport's motion," said Matthews.

"Agreed, Mr. Mayor," said Alice. "I call the question."

Having no choice, Timmerling called for the vote. Five council members were in favor, three against. Unexpectedly, Doug Thompson and Marty Angelo voted with Alice, Stan, and himself.

Cheers and loud applause erupted from the gallery, giving the unmistakable impression that the citizens might well not be opposed to paying for services they received.

Nonetheless, Harvey was well aware he had just made a dais full of enemies, which might well impede his long-range purposes.

By the following day, Harvey's curiosity about the inner workings of the treasurer's office overpowered him. The council's resolution suggested he work with Ms. Trebenko on a new budget, so he decided to pay Pauline a visit. When he called, the secretary set the appointment for two o'clock.

An unidentified previous administrator had stuffed the city's financial center and several other departments into the bowels of city hall. As he traversed the overheated subterranean cavern, the smell of old dust and mold, overlaid with soap and disinfectant, assailed his nose. The dull yellow walls and mottled gray floor tiles recalled office buildings of the 1950s. Ancient green file cabinets piled high with boxes of documents waiting to be filed clogged the walkways.

Ms. Trebenko's secretary ushered him to an ancient, scarred wooden chair next to the treasurer's desk. After a few minutes, despite the insufferable heat, the treasurer breezed into her office with a smile, shook his hand, then sat in her chair leaning toward him, elbows on a green desk blotter.

"Good afternoon, Mr. Davenport. What brings you to our fourth level of hell?" she chirped. She looked about midforties in her sleeveless, flowered shift and ponytail.

"I'm a curious fellow," he said. "Since we'll be working together, I thought we should have a chat. My first observation is that you did a superb job Monday night under difficult circumstances. But I also noticed you didn't seem to enjoy yourself. May I ask why?"

"We've just met, sir." Pauline paused as she touched her lips with steepled fingers. "I sense, however, from your comments last evening, you seem something of a standout, if you'll pardon my saying so."

"How so, Ms. Trebenko?" Harvey inquired. Was she sincere or just pulling his chain?

"It's been decades since that august body has heard questions like you and Ms. Morrison and Mr. Matthews raised last night," she said. "In my book, it was the *three of you* who did outstanding work. We need more of that."

He shrugged. "I promised my neighbors I'd be accountable to them," he replied, meeting her gaze, "and I intend to keep that promise. They've charged me to bring back an explanation of why they can't have the services they're entitled to, so I dug in on the budget."

"Then you may appreciate knowing," she said, a slight smile broadening her slender face, "that Councilman Dwyer visited me last evening to say I needn't be concerned to work with the three of you on a new budget. I don't know why. I just do what I'm told. But he runs the mayor and five of the council members, as you may have observed, in addition to most of the city department heads."

He hadn't yet reached that conclusion, but it seemed appropriate. "How long have you worked here under those conditions?"

"I've been here since Dwyer was at Notre Dame," she said, chuckling. "I attribute my longevity to a pleasant demeanor, tight lips, and not raising embarrassing questions."

"I hope you don't mind my saying so, but you don't look that old," he said. "You must have come here right out of school."

"Thank you for such a nice encomium," she said, flashing a brief but dazzling smile. "Yes, I did arrive fresh out of Oberlin. I've always looked younger than I am, and I still remember the years when that led to frequent embarrassment." She shook her head at the memory. "But it's also true that Mike Dwyer is aging fast. The financial and behavioral control he exercises must be weighing him down." She paused to sign three letters placed on her desk by her secretary, then resumed her direct eye contact. "Please understand, I'm sticking my neck out here. So don't help them chop it off, okay?"

"No need to worry," he assured her with a smile. "Your secret is safe here, and I thank you for your candor." The thaw in her manner made the prospect of working with her seem most inviting.

"Yes," she concluded. "Dwyer runs the show. The business interests win on every issue; they're the boss. I just do my job. Which has become more difficult since they've assumed the reins, albeit illegally."

"Can we still work together, sub rosa if necessary?" he asked.

"Count on it," she said with a smile. "Alice has already called me to suggest we meet Thursday afternoon."

"She's way ahead of me. That leaves me with just one question. What was the budget before Dwyer and his cult took control of city council? I'd like to establish a base point from which to project an alternate budget."

"Glad to provide that," she replied with a smile. She rose from her desk, disappeared down the hall, then returned in less than a minute. "Here's a copy of that last budget, the year 1987. I can tell you that prior to 1987, the budget increased annually, approximately in sync with the city's growth in population. It wasn't always the same, but it never lagged more than a year or two. Consequently, I rely on that year as a baseline for my own projections."

"Thanks, Pauline," he said, placing the exhibit in his portfolio and standing. He held out his hand. "I look forward to seeing you again on Thursday." They shook hands, and he left her office.

If Alice had the same story about Dwyer and company, he could reasonably assume self-interested manipulation. Claiming that the citizens themselves were to blame for the loss of services to which they were entitled was a ridiculous lie.

After his encounter with the treasurer, Harvey needed corroborating evidence, someone trustworthy to tell him more about how city council handled not only the budget but other matters. He made a quick phone call to Alice Morrison to see if she'd have coffee with him on this sunny, calm Saturday. She agreed, and they met at the Beanery Cafe at three the next afternoon.

The Beanery Cafe was a little hole-in-the-wall, lodged in the storefront of the oldest commercial building in Westfield's downtown. It was a popular hangout for shoppers and residents—not glitzy enough for the tourists, too old-fashioned for the teenagers. Inside, the place was a warm cave, semidark, with clunky wood tables and handmade ceramic cups. The odors of exotic coffees and home-baked pastries made his mouth water.

"What're your thoughts on the budget?" he asked when they'd found their seats. "Your fire and directness on Monday night were impressive." He bit into his peach-and-apple Danish, savoring the flaky pastry and syrupy, smooth chunks of fruit.

"You too!" she exclaimed. "And Stan certainly helped our cause. It felt so *good* to have *friends*! It's been a lonely three years." She seemed friendlier somehow in jeans and a cardigan than she had at council in her yellow suit.

"Two questions," he said. "Does everyone take their cue from Dwyer? And is the majority intentionally constricting the city's budget?"

"Yes and yes," she replied, wrinkling her nose. "These guys work together like a cult. Their worst nightmare is to have the minorities rise up and take over. Service to the community isn't their style. They do as they please, and if trouble comes, they'll take the easy way out. If they can't actually get their hands on the pile of money the city collects, they're eager to choke off the supply to at least keep their profits growing. If you and Stan hadn't won the election, they'd still be ramming their own agenda through."

Certainly a heavy indictment but no surprise. He suspected Alice was venting, which was fine with him. No reason she shouldn't. But what she'd said did square almost precisely with his own observations and those of Pauline Trebenko.

"I talked with Ms. Trebenko yesterday. She said Dwyer told her to forget the budget resolution to work with us."

"She's sharp," Alice mused. "Does an excellent job, but she knows who's boss. She also knows that what they're doing is immoral and probably illegal."

"Why did Timmerling use the phrase 'informal policy'? Strange way to put it, I thought. Is he hiding something?"

"There is no policy! What a crock!" Alice scoffed, adding a high-pitched laugh. "Except in Dwyer's head. He directs the others, including George Howard and Timmerling. The clique is headquartered in Dwyer's bank and the chamber. Norm Taylor is second-in-command. You're a member; you probably already know that."

He nodded.

"They have three objectives—cut services, never raise taxes, and focus solely on the chamber's agenda for the city."

"How does that help anyone?" he asked.

"It doesn't. Their goal is profits. Taxes cut into profits. Money's vastly more important than the people."

He found Alice's straightforward approach appealing. Perhaps the harshness of her words resulted from years of frustration. Nevertheless, it offered him a way to quickly establish the cause of the city's problems.

"Why are there so many business types on the council?"

"The chamber registers candidates a year in advance. They go to the wards and suggest people follow their lead. Hey! If you can't trust a businessman, who can you trust, right? Know what I mean?" She let loose with another hilarious cackle.

"I heard Sam Beresford make that pitch in our ward committee meeting last April. An interesting mantra. Our leadership asked them to leave."

"The great thing is we're not alone. The voters elected you and Stan—two new people. Next year, maybe two more. Who knows, we might be gaining on 'em."

Afterward, as he walked the downtown streets back to his studio, he ruminated on their conversation. Despite Alice's confidence, he suspected loosening the grip of business on city hall would take more than three city council members and the treasurer.

For dinner that evening, he devoured a plate of his own homemade beef stew with bay leaves and basil. (It always seemed to taste better the third day.) As he ate, he recalled the time eight years before, when he'd been assigned to photograph a printing press in Ohio. No ordinary printing machine, this was a rotogravure press. The brilliant colors of lacquer-based ink flowed like water, filling millions of tiny divots carved in the surface of huge brass rollers that transferred the ink to great ribbons of paper moving through the press at incredible speed. The result was stunning color and detail in pictures and text.

Reflecting on this technology led to the recognition that his mother's death had been the result of a similar transaction between industry heads and city officials—a transfer of power instead of ink. Otherwise, without such collusion, how else could a sacrifice zone be created? So, perhaps the way to stop the poisoning and death of thousands of people like his parents would be to separate the manufacturers from the regulators.

That Thursday and Friday, Harvey worked with Alice, Stan, and Pauline to forge a remarkably different city budget, one that restored a balance in favor of the common good. By projecting systematic annual increases, they discovered revenue could be restored to appropriate levels in five years. The new budget also demanded transparency and accountability and called for public education to help residents accept the necessary changes. Tough to accomplish but effective nonetheless. The only question now was whether the council would approve it.

Walking to city hall through slushy, ice-filled streets the following Monday evening, he shivered. How nice it would be to have enough plows and men to do a thorough job cleaning up after such a snowstorm.

In the council chamber, he, Stan, and Alice provided visitors with copies of the budget. Excitement and tension filled the room as residents took their seats. People seemed eager to witness this discussion.

Adrenaline pumped in his veins too. He reminded himself to focus less on speaking and more on listening and let the new budget speak for itself.

Mayor Timmerling, in his sharkskin gray suit and purple tie, called the meeting to order, then asked the team to present the highlights of their new budget.

"On the expense side," Harvey began, "we've increased salaries five percent for employees below department heads. Executives received a one percent increase. This will help rebalance the relationship between those two groups."

"The allocation for public works doubled." Stan Matthews picked up the narrative. "Within that, Streets and Sanitation obtained the largest raise. This will show residents immediate improvement in services."

"Public transportation received a healthy increase," Alice Morrison added. "This will enable us to offer limited service so that in five years, the buses can return full-time."

"On page two, you'll see that revenues are up fifty-five percent," Harvey said. "I hasten to add, this is not how far we've dropped behind over the past twenty years. But at this rate, we can raise enough revenue over the next five years to provide better service in every department."

Enthusiastic applause arose from the gallery, but on the dais, silence greeted his comments. Dwyer's clique seemed stunned at having their tight control of the purse strings exposed to public view. If residents had enjoyed a tax holiday for two decades, they'd also suffered the consequences in sharply cut services.

In the gallery, buzz evolved into excitement. Was it possible the budget team's forthright approach had refreshed people's spirits?

Suddenly, Mike Dwyer stood, looking powerful and grave in his immaculate, tailored navy blue suit and red tie. "Totally irresponsible!" he shouted, his face a thundercloud.

"This will never fly with the voters!" Rhett Bennett rose to exclaim in his deep, booming voice, shaking his big, shaggy, graying head.

"I am a voter, and I approve!" shouted a male voice in the crowd.

The two council members sat down.

"We've got to walk before we run," Marty Angelo pleaded in his tactful voice, bushy brown eyebrows furrowed. "This plan scares me!"

"All you're doing is letting people dream," Clarence Williams scolded. "Dreaming doesn't help anybody."

During the public discussion time, many people offered positive comments. They seemed to accept that receiving better service meant paying higher rates.

At length, Mayor Timmerling called for the vote. A hush of anticipation fell over the room.

"All those in favor of the new budget, raise your hands."

Harvey, Alice, and Stan raised their hands.

"All those in favor of the treasurer's budget, raise your hands." Five hands went up.

Muttered comments, shaking heads, and faces earlier filled with excitement now showing disappointment answered the vote.

Harvey's stomach clenched as anger flooded over him. The cult may have kept their profits intact for another year, but the budget fight wasn't over. Not by a long shot. He hoped his ward residents would protest, bringing greater public pressure for responsible financial management.

With three city council meetings under his belt, it was time Harvey talked with his people. Sixth Ward leaders met again in Claudia Douglas's home the following Saturday. When the twelve committee members were seated and served coffee and cake, Claudia called them to attention with her huge gong.

George Spencer began by turning to Harvey. "So, what have you found out?"

"Three weeks into the new year, the city of Westfield has a budget," he said, smiling. "But"—he pointed his index finger in the air with a mischievous grin—"it wasn't our fault. We did everything possible to sidetrack, backtrack, and coax them to be realistic." He threw his hands in the air. "In the end, nothing worked."

He related how three council members and the treasurer had created a more appropriate spending and revenue pattern.

"Had we won, however, you'd be in shock!" he continued. "And most of the residents seemed amazed at the budget we proposed. But the city's growing so fast we had to find ways to catch up to where we should be."

"Let me get this straight," said Nancy Caruthers. "Are you saying that our streets are turning to cow paths because the chamber convinces the citizens of Westfield to hate taxes?"

"Well, that too. Actually, the leaders of the chamber have convinced *themselves* that citizens hate taxes. Then they spread the word that it's the *citizens' fault* for starting the myth in the first place." He laughed. "Dwyer and Timmerling argued there would be a popular uprising if we raised taxes. But the residents seemed open to paying more to receive more service."

"I would've been too," said Nancy.

"Industry advertisers and public relations people have whined for decades that government is bad and taxes are worse," said Susan Mintz, the marketing pro. "Corporates discredit government to serve their own needs."

Harvey nodded. "Now we know why the buses sit in the barns."

Amazing. People in his ward actually seemed eager to hear about the budget. He took pleasure in fulfilling a campaign promise and delivering immediate, firsthand information.

"We can't just let council's decision stand without making a fuss," said Natalie Peterson. "Surely there's something we can do?"

"Let's get Felix Vogel involved," said Herb Galloway. "He can write a high-powered exposé about the whole thing."

"Let's put it on cable TV too," said his wife, Retha. "People need to hear it firsthand. Lots of people listen to Felix's weekly summaries of the news."

"Let's write a letter to all the other ward leaders," said Joe Lingonberry. "They need to know how much they've lost by letting the chamber choose their candidates for council."

"I volunteer to write the letter," said Susan. "Anyone want to help?"

"You can run it by me. I'll give you my comments," said Nancy. "Write it so the chamber folks know there's a price to pay for taking over the city."

The meeting lasted another hour as the place buzzed with ideas. How fortunate that his people were willing to dig in and contribute. The work had begun. But the chamber was strong, the general public still largely apathetic. The road ahead looked like rough traveling.

CHAPTER 4

DISCOVERY I

Calming breezes on an unusually warm evening in March dispelled the effects of a frenetic, client-filled day. On the short walk to the weekly city council meeting, Harvey met a lone tabby, his only companion on the mostly deserted downtown Westfield streets. As he approached city hall, his attention was drawn to the heights of Westfield's last remaining elm tree by the harsh "Wraak! Wraak!" of two ravens feeding the next generation. Below, among the shrubs adorning the municipal building, the remains of a badger, no doubt a hit-and-run victim, received last rites from the evening air while being hoisted to the leafy dining room.

When the antique walnut grandfather's clock in the council chamber chimed seven, Mayor Timmerling rapped his gavel three times, calling the meeting to order.

Immediately following the invocation, city manager George Howard rose from his seat. "Mr. Mayor, before we launch into our agenda, we have an urgent matter that needs a council vote," he said, staring at his notes through hooded brows. "We received word this afternoon that the last piece of financing is now in place for the waste disposal plant that's been in the works for two years. We need council's approval to start construction."

Word had it that Howard's predecessor had been fired because
he had too many scruples, which interfered with the corporate
community's designs for the city.

"Proceed, George," the mayor said.

"I'm happy to announce that Harry Perkins of the Perkins Family
Foundation has made a grant of four hundred thousand dollars to
our waste disposal project. This completes the raising of the two and
a half million needed to construct the facility."

Howard summarized the project's financing, noting especially
a federal Brownfields grant for $500,000 that tied the project to a
location where its construction would involve remediation of polluted
soil.

What he did not say, however, though it was well known, was
that during public hearings the previous year, both area residents
and media representatives protested that the Bottoms was an
inappropriate location for a waste disposal facility. City staff and
several council members, however, dismissed those objections, saying
the city was locked in financially. Nothing could be done.

As Howard spoke, the left entrance at the back of the chamber
opened just enough to admit an aging African American woman
wearing a black dress with a floral pattern, carrying an old-fashioned
ladies' purse. Her immense black hat cast a shadow over her face,
preserving her identity. She sat in the back row next to the middle
aisle.

"With your approval," said Howard, "we can start tomorrow
morning. Any questions or comments before we vote?"

"Am I correct that you're planning to build the WDP in a
residential area where poor people, elderly, and racial minorities
live?" Harvey ventured.

Stunned silence spread throughout the room.

Finally, Mayor Timmerling took a deep breath and said, through
clenched teeth, "That's correct, Councilman Davenport."

"Why would you want to add another source of pollution to the
industries that are already pouring so much toxic waste into that

community? Can't we find a site farther from places where people live?"

"There is no better site!" Rhett Bennett's deep, booming voice rang with an impatient, commanding tone as he frowned. "A huge portion of our funding comes from federal Brownfields assistance. This mandates that the WDP be placed in the Industrial Park. That federal money depends on it being right where it's planned!"

"Besides, Davenport, what do you care?" Mike Dwyer added with a softer, more ironic tone. "The place is a trash heap anyway. What difference will a little more smoke make?"

The callous remark stunned him. Was this Dwyer's way of rationalizing such a lethal project? Or was his othering a call for social reinforcement, perhaps to make discriminating against a perceived enemy more acceptable?

Both Dwyer and Bennett sounded like a fellow he'd known in Binghamton, New York, when he was sixteen. He'd worked in a hardware store for a Mr. Nickerson, who had a penchant for catering to white men while mistreating minority and female customers. The old man's excuse had been that "those people" deserved to pay more because they received what he called "undeserved" government money.

He'd learned early in life that some businessmen were bullies who used underhanded ways to extract extra profit from those they disliked and had a talent for inventing reasons why their methods were perfectly acceptable business practices.

"Looks to me like the staff focused on construction costs, irrespective of the needs of the people directly affected," he answered. "Was the attraction of federal funds so compelling?"

Alice Morrison's face brightened. She sat back in her chair, looking relaxed. A tiny smile crept over her face. "George, why have you brought this up without prior public announcement that funding is complete? I think you knew the people would raise strong objection, didn't you?"

"Mr. Mayor," said Howard, a marked chill in his voice. "The public has had numerous occasions to comment. Ms. Morrison seems unaware that without the feds, the WDP would take another decade."

The corporate crowd seemed hopeful that federal money released them from the need to raise taxes or attend to the needs of residents. Was that extra little profit margin so much more important than finding a safer, more responsible site? And had they considered the cost of a public uprising that might result from their decision?

Life with his uncle Theo, the real estate tycoon, had taught him that when corporate enterprise wanted to dump waste, the easiest, cheapest way was to dump it nearby. If it happened that the homes of employees, minorities, or the poor were in the way, that was just too bad. They were waste people anyway. Half a dozen owners, lawyers, and bankers could easily secure the waivers needed to dump with impunity. Everyone who counted would agree.

His mother's ghost railed against such a cynical, uncaring attitude.

"You're being irresponsible and unaccountable, George!" Alice pressed her point, shaking her teacher's finger at him. "There's no one here from the Bottoms to object."

"We've had the requisite hearings," Dwyer countered, color rising in his cheeks. "They've had their say. All that's in the past. Anyway, it's just a few renegades who objected. The vast majority have no objection, and why should they? One of these days, we'll clean house over there and move the lot of 'em out. The WDP won't be an issue any longer."

He'd heard it said that Dwyer was the kind of person who would ditch his own mother if it meant achieving his objectives. Unfortunately, Mike could never have done that to his mother because she had dominated him unremittingly.

"No!" Harvey shouted as he stood, holding up his hand. "If this involved the white community, you know very well they'd be up in arms. You'd never get away with it!" Resuming his seat, trying to calm himself, he continued in a more dispassionate tone. "When enterprise wants its way, you dominate. When the people ask for justice, they have no option but to take to the streets. Then you arrest them and put them away. How easy it is for powerful officials to ignore the people whose needs we're supposed to serve!"

"I polled my ward," Stan Matthews interjected. "The majority of my people say the WDP should move to another location, and they're willing to raise taxes as needed to fund it. We calculated the increase would be three dollars and twenty-five cents per year per household. Government subsidy and miserliness is not the key to prosperity in our community." As a top-level management consultant for government agencies, Stan was a wizard at math and a stickler for managing according to the facts in any situation.

"Have you asked Chief Barnes how he'll deal with a rash of civil disobedience if you do start construction?" Harvey inquired. "I move we delay the WDP until a more citizen-sensitive decision can be made."

"Why can't you people get behind and help us on this instead of fighting it?" Dwyer demanded, his cheeks glowing with anger.

"I can assure you," Clarence Williams offered, "the WDP is not an issue in the Bottoms. Let's move forward, please."

Facing a strategic threat, the forces of corporate enterprise had lined up to push the matter through.

"I move we approve construction to start as soon as possible," said Rhett Bennett in his loud, booming voice.

The vote was five to three, granting permission for construction of the WDP to start immediately. A gross insult, he thought, to a fifth of Westfield's citizens.

As the mayor's gavel brought the matter to an end, the elderly woman in the back row stood up, purse in hand, and marched down the aisle. Harvey caught Alice's eye and raised an eyebrow in question. She answered by mouthing the words, "Martha Ruggles."

"Gentlemen!" the woman announced in a clear, strong voice as she came toward the dais. "Your decision is evil and unjust. Why do you poison our people? Our health is degraded. We're already under constant threat of disease and death. And now you add insult to injury. Where is your regard for us as human beings and for our rights as citizens of Westfield?"

"Madam," cautioned the mayor, "your comment is out of order—"

"I'll show you what plagues our community." Martha cut the mayor off, ignoring him. She reached into her purse, pulled out an orange sphere, and hurled it at the mayor. Bull's-eye! It exploded on his chest, soaking his suit and shirt with slime.

"This is what we live with day in and day out!" she roared.

"Guard!" shouted George Howard, backing away from the staff table. But the guard was in the far corner of the room.

"Out of order!" shouted the mayor, dabbing at the orange glop with a handkerchief.

She reached into her purse again. In seconds, Mike Dwyer had a comparable helping of brown goo on his front.

"You'd never in a million years want this in your neighborhood, would you, Mr. Fancy-Pants bank president? You who are grand wizard of the Cult of Sacrifice! But you don't mind if *we* have to live with it, do you?"

A sickening chemical odor permeated the chamber as a sticky green ball ricocheted off the edge of the staff table, scoring a direct hit on the city manager with an oily, yellowish-green liquid.

"You dared put this before the council when none of us could protest! You were wrong, George Howard! Dead wrong!"

The guard was on his way. The mayor was too shocked to say anything. His mouth opened and closed like a dying fish as he fought for words. A huge gob of sewage hit the desk in front of Clarence Williams, splattering him and Marty Angelo.

"You should know better, Clarence, than to push this plague on your own people!" Ruggles shouted.

A side-arm shot packed a wallop to Doug Thompson's chest, painting his front with a sticky mess of bright blue fluorescent jelly. As the guard grabbed Martha's left arm, her right hand let fly with a ball of greasy mud, which arced high in the air, just missing a chandelier, then descended gracefully to splatter councilman Bennett's desk, soaking his papers and his suit.

"No more sacrifice zone in the Bottoms!" Martha screamed.

The guard pushed and shoved her off balance.

Her broad, floppy hat slipped down over one side of her face. "We're not going to take it anymore! The WDP *must go!*" she yelled repeatedly.

The guard held her in a hammerlock and pushed her toward the exit. She fought with all her strength until she collapsed on the council floor just three feet from the door.

The chamber was in an uproar. People rushed to help the woman.

The mayor pounded his gavel maniacally. "This meeting will come to order!" he shouted. "Everyone. Please sit down. Calm yourselves!"

Martha's drama buoyed Harvey's spirits, despite his fear and distrust of his powerful colleagues. This was how the people of the Bottoms—and the people of Westfield—*should* sting when commercial interests sacrificed the people's well-being.

"As I see it, Mr. Mayor," he said into his microphone with a smile on his face, "you fellows got what you deserved!"

"Second that motion!" Alice called out. "Don't even have to vote on it!"

As the council members stood, Harvey gave two thumbs-up and danced a little jig behind his council desk. Alice slipped him a little smile.

Seeds in the sidewalk. Could concern for the public good rupture the concrete slab supporting the race for profit? Only time would tell.

Following the tumultuous meeting, Harvey needed to vent. His effort to derail an immoral and thoroughly wretched policy decision had failed. The train wreck of his emotions begged for a brisk walk to sort things out. As he exited the building, Alice Morrison caught up with him, Stan Matthews in tow.

"Time for coffee?" she asked.

"Sure."

Escaping city hall into a fresh northerly breeze, they walked toward the Busy Bee, hugging their coats about them. The temperature had dropped a good ten degrees. Just what they needed.

The Bee, as most people called it, was a popular family-owned diner a block south, then two east, of the municipal building. According to rumor, more city business was conducted there than in city hall.

"Those pigs!" Alice shouted into the wind, marching along in her yellow half heels with determined strides. "The sneaky bastards got their way again. Damn it! I'd like to kick every one of 'em down the street and back."

"Amazing how they stick to this lie that lets them discriminate and shun their responsibility all at one slice," Harvey added.

"Perfect combination of race and class hatred while building wealth," said Stan, smoothing his goatee as he struggled to keep up.

"I'll tell you one thing," Alice said. "This issue's not dead. There will be hell to pay, and I intend to exact the full price! Martha Ruggles, bless her heart, pulled off an amazing stunt. I hope somebody got a few pictures."

"I hope they took good care of her at the hospital," said Stan. "That guard was pretty rough on the old lady."

"She deserved a standing ovation, not a trip to the hospital," Harvey replied. "The way that guard manhandled her."

They continued in thought for a few minutes, walking off their frustration.

"I'm sorry, Harvey, I shouldn't be so emotional," Alice suddenly blurted out. "Here I am blowing off steam, and you probably think I'm a nutcase."

"Already knew it," he said with a chuckle. "I'm pretty angry myself, so don't feel bad."

"I take it that whole thing was a charade," Stan added. "I hope that isn't par for the council."

"Pretty usual. It's money, money, money with these guys! It's infuriating!" she bellowed into the rising wind. "There's nothing for the people!"

They walked another half block.

"They're a cult. They like to dominate," Alice said at length.

"Is that why they're in city government, just to promote business interests?" Harvey asked.

"It was such a blatant move," Stan said. "I bet news of it'll turn the Bottoms into wildfire."

When they arrived at nine o'clock, the Busy Bee was tired. It had buzzed all day. The place was quiet, the light subdued. Show tunes from the fifties played softly in the background. The front counter was empty, and Jerry, the owner, was cleaning out the coffee urns. An old woman in a booth shared a sandwich with her miniature poodle. Three old men chatted around a table, sipping coffee and munching doughnuts. The place would close in an hour.

Amazingly, the hostess, Darlene, greeted them with a cheery, "Good evening, Councilwoman and Councilmen," nodding to each. "Would you like a booth near the window?" She showed them to one with wood trim and seats clad in a warm red nylon. Then she set a basket of banana muffins on the table. "Let me start you off with these," she cooed. "Fresh out of the oven a few minutes ago."

Alice tried one. "Hmmm, excellent!" she pronounced.

Harvey ordered ham on rye and a bowl of homemade apple crisp. Scrambled eggs, sausage, and toast were Alice's choice. Stan settled for grilled cheese on rye with fries.

Alice turned to Stan. "So, what was your reaction?"

"Flabbergasted," came the reply, spoken around half a muffin. "Simply flummoxed beyond belief. I didn't know this kind of nonsense happened in city council."

"Harvey?"

"How can private enterprise claim to offer better service and efficiency? Those clowns tonight had no inclination for service and little talent except for follow the leader. Since January, I've seen more than enough to understand why the people in the wards suffer."

"Smoke and mirrors." Alice forced a laugh. "A ruse to disguise the fact that they want our tax dollars for themselves."

"I've seen that they love to cut the budget," Stan offered. "No more buses. Let the sewers back up!"

"The streets in my ward look like a woodpeckers' commune," Harvey added

"Have you ever seen the streetlights in the new developments on the south side?" Alice asked.

"No, I haven't," Stan replied.

"That's because there aren't any!" She laughed as she threw up her hands.

"Do you think we put even a small crack in their cement wall tonight?" Harvey asked.

"Nah! Solid as ever," Alice replied, shaking her head. "They'll never split up. Too much money at stake."

After Darlene brought their orders, the silence of chewing and thinking replaced conversation for some time.

"There was a neighbor fellow, when I was growing up in the Bottoms," Harvey said after he'd finished his sandwich. He looked around to see which of his colleagues gasped with surprise. Up to now, he'd not spoken about his past. He doubted it would be well received, but these two didn't seem to mind.

"His name was Campbell—*Mr.* Campbell to us kids. He told us a story of going to city council to demand they take action to protect people's health. But they laughed at him and ignored his ideas. This was the sixties, and by then, Westfield had long since become a company town. Industry held the schools, the churches, the hospitals firmly in their grasp. No one talked about the connection between the foul-tasting water, the sulfurous air, and increasing numbers of kids with leukemia."

"You grew up with this stuff?" Stan inquired, sounding incredulous.

"Sure. The air we breathed was laced with benzene and sulfur dioxide. At night, I could read by the light of a bright orange sky because the refineries burned off fumes and gas. The neighbors complained of respiratory problems, sinus headaches, skin allergies. But for many years, I thought that was just the way life was."

"Then what happened?" Alice asked.

"My mom died of liver cancer and scleroderma," he replied. "My father was working on an advanced case of TB when he was killed in a truck crash two years before my mom died. My grandfather died of cancer too. So did a lot of our neighbors."

"Oh, Harvey!" Alice exclaimed. "That must have been awful!"

"It was. Suddenly, I was an orphan. But it taught me a lesson—industry has to be controlled because left alone it will deal more and more death and destruction. It's the nature of the beast. I vowed to come back here one day and stop the poison!" He choked back a sob, but a tear escaped and rolled down his right cheek. He tossed his head to regain composure. "In the meantime, I learned the history of the Industrial Revolution. They've been killing people and tearing us apart for four hundred years."

"How'd you escape?" Stan asked.

"An old man—family friend, in fact, Humphrey Marshall—persuaded me I wouldn't live long enough to do anything about my vow if I didn't leave. He made sure I had the insurance money from Dad's accident, then drove me to the bus station. I went to live with my aunt Harriet and uncle Theo in the northeast. He was a big shot real estate developer."

"How old were you?" Alice wanted to know.

"Fourteen." He took a few moments to recover from his revelation before shifting the subject. "So, what led you into politics, Alice?" he asked picking up his cup of coffee. "You sounded like a real radical tonight."

"Oh, you should talk!" Alice rebutted, grinning. "After what you said?"

"Just letting you know you had company," he said, returning the grin.

"The reason I ran for council," she began, "was that four years ago, Stan's wife, Sherry, when she was head of the city's Environmental Policy Department, published a report that gave the actual field figures for various pollutants in and around Westfield. Though they tried to hush it up, the report got out, made the papers, and made a lot of the city's industrialists hopping mad. I decided to be on council to get to the bottom of who and how that report had been sequestered, and why no report since then has given the real figures."

Stan nodded in agreement. "That event changed my focus too. Sherry, my wife, headed up the Environmental Department. She was determined to buck the system Dwyer had in place. He threatened her numerous times, but finally they just put a contract out on her. Two days after Mike's last attempt to shut her up, they found her …" His face crumpled, and he couldn't speak for a few moments. "They found her in pieces in a cement mixer!" he wailed, reaching for his handkerchief and dabbing at his eyes.

Alice reached over and grasped his hand. Conversation ceased for a few minutes. Then she said, "The TV and newspaper reports were gruesome. Were you aware of that when it happened, Harvey?"

"I was away at the time, but I heard about it when I returned," he replied.

After Stan had recovered his equilibrium, Alice picked up a piece of toast. "Remember how we talked about taxes back in the sixties?" she said, adding more butter and looking toward Harvey. "Everyone paid their fair share. Nothing like that today. My mother taught us kids to care for the people around us, especially those who had less. No more of that either. How did we get from great promises to no-can-do?"

"Hey! Remember *Law 'n' Order*?" Harvey suggested. "It's still with us. That's a large part of how we got here."

"Yep, the backlash is still with us." Stan growled, shaking his head. "Both conservatives and liberals cut out progress to focus on behavior control."

"Well, they're gonna exert control till it's wrested from them," Harvey declared. "Someone's gotta do it, because these fellows on council now are a danger to the people of Westfield, not a help."

"My preferred solution," Alice said, "is to put a good, tight checkrein on the mustang of capitalism. What's yours?"

"Government has to be a buffer between commerce and the people," said Stan. "Control profit making and markets. Then we can all enjoy a decent living."

"One could wish it would happen!" Harvey echoed as they rose from the table.

"I admire your spirit," Alice replied as they walked through the restaurant. "But I want to hear more."

"I'm not really a radical at all," Harvey admitted. "Radical is a matter of perspective. Is justice radical? I think it's as old as Solomon."

As they exited the Bee, a woman dressed in a pink flowered housecoat and white tennies, her hair in curlers, ran up to Alice in a desperate hurry.

"Thank God I caught you!" the woman exclaimed.

"This is Teresa Marks, my neighbor across the street." Alice introduced the woman to Harvey and Stan.

"Someone has absolutely destroyed your rose garden! I think there were four of 'em. Masks and black outfits, carried sickles and hoes. I just happened to look out my living room window and saw them. They ripped up your prize collection of roses, Alice!" she wailed.

"God damn them to hell!" Alice burst out, her face distorted in disbelief and anger. "You see, Harvey? When you stand against them, they make sure you pay. I'll bet this is Clarence's doing. He's Dwyer's stoolie. These guys never stop until they get their way." She turned to the distraught woman. "Thank you, Teresa," she said in a hushed voice. "I appreciate your having walked all this way to tell me."

Harvey, Stan, and Teresa walked Alice back home and stayed with her until she was calm. Then Harvey quickly walked back to his studio, anxious lest the miscreants had wreaked similar havoc there.

The following Saturday was a magical spring day. The sky was soaked in ultramarine, and the clouds had been given extra bleach. Harvey and Mina decided to drive to the county zoo to relax. It would be the perfect antidote to a hectic, client-driven week. Just for fun, Harvey wore his black beret and gray herringbone sport coat. Mina donned a red scarf over her usual black top and tights.

They pushed the dolly loaded with their equipment around the paths, uphill and downhill, until they came to the bear exhibit. He favored the bears because although they seemed ungainly, they moved like the big cats. A few shots of bear antics would make graceful additions to his portfolio. He muscled the Hasselblad while Mina took the 35mm SLR, looking for action.

Mama bear and two cubs exited their stony burrow and played on a grassy knoll in the glorious, warm sunshine twenty feet from the pedestrian path. Their rich brown fur glistened in the light. The little ones experimented with biting the mother's paws and ears. She cuffed them with her paws, then gave them a few mollifying licks. The cubs mimicked her actions.

As he captured this family frolic, an unruly gang of middle schoolers descended on them, showing off with reckless, maniacal antics.

"Here come the nincompoops and halfwits running around, pushing each other," he complained to Mina. "It's a waste of time bringing these kids here. How can they learn anything? They're acting like idiots!"

"Easy, Harvey," Mina cautioned as she took a few photos of the little parasites, which made them act even crazier.

"Don't come here, kids! Please, go somewhere else," he growled at them, waving his arm to shoo them away.

A woman who appeared to be a teacher walked up to him, planting herself right in his way, ready for a confrontation. She was tall, about forty, with stringy brown hair. She wore faded jeans and a red-and-black checked shirt. Aggravation had deepened the lines in her face.

"Is this your group?" Harvey asked.

"Buzz off, buster!" she barked. "The children have a right to be here. Don't go muscling in on these kids, or I'll call the management *and* the cops. We'll see who has the right to do what!"

Three more teachers with peevish expressions crowded around, energetically agreeing with their colleague.

Time to move on. He caught Mina's eye and nodded toward the equipment. She caught his sign and moved their equipment farther down the path.

"Bunch of imbeciles!" he muttered when they were out of earshot. "They shouldn't be allowed in a place like this."

"You're othering again, Harvey," Mina countered. "You have no use for them, so you demean and dismiss them."

More harassment! Sure, she had a point, but he was in no mood to appreciate it.

Seeking relief from school tours, they headed for a little copse of birch in the back corner of the park. The light might be better on that side. Perhaps they'd spot a zebra, a white rhino, or something even more exotic.

They advanced to the meerkats. These humanlike animals, standing on their hind legs, looked like politicians or advertising executives—regal and wolfish with nothing but mischief on their minds.

This time, he grabbed the SLR and just started shooting anything, indiscriminately. He was sick and tired of all the goddamned interruptions. The meerkats picked up on his mood and imitated his movements, taking imaginary pictures of one another. For a few blissful moments, everything appeared copacetic.

"We've got company again!" Mina gasped. "You will not like this."

Sure enough, a troop of Girl Scouts settled on a grassy bank behind the meerkats, within camera range. They set their huge picnic basket on a garish red blanket and began setting out their food.

"What is it with these people?" he seethed. "You'd think they'd have sense enough to see what we're doing. We've got all this equipment and the cart, and we're shooting pictures. Why don't they have the good sense to go somewhere else for their five-course lunch?"

"Those scouts have the same rights we have," Mina mused. "But let's shoot them having a picnic with the meerkats. Don't you think the kids resemble the animals?"

Good move, Mina! She could always find a way into his mood, a place from which to deflate his self-conceit and elicit a smile. It was at once endearing and aggravating.

"What say we get some lunch?" he suggested. "Maybe we'll have better luck this afternoon."

They made their way to the zoo's cafeteria. Since it was a nice warm day with a slight breeze, they decided to enjoy their lunch on the patio in the sunshine.

They waited fifteen minutes for a waiter to take their order.

"Whaddaya wan' today?" the youngster said with the air of a hot dog vendor at a ballgame.

Mina ordered a salad and corn bread. He chose the day's special—slow-cooked southern fried chicken and dumplings. Comfort food was what he needed.

"I'll grab it!" was the careless reply.

Half an hour later, the kid delivered their food.

"Why is the service here so abysmal?" he asked.

"Busy day at the zoo," Mina replied in an almost too cheerful voice. "The place is crawling with visitors."

"Maybe we should come back in winter when we can shoot the animals in their wooly winter finery," he said. "You know"— he paused to find the words—"the zoo would be a marvelous place to come if it weren't for all these people! If they'd just stay home and watch television!"

"Horrible thought!" Mina exclaimed with a sour look. "Your othering's really on a roll today. Is there anyone you don't hate?"

"Can't think of anyone," he replied with half a smile tugging at the corners of his mouth. She knew how to get to him.

He bit into the first piece of what should have been "slow-cooked southern fried chicken." It was rubbery and unchewable, as if the chef had fried it on the exhaust manifold of a Mack truck.

"What happened with this chicken?" he cried. "It's terrible! Inedible!"

Mina's jaw dropped. She shook her head and focused on her plate.

He seized his plate, marched to the kitchen door, and barged through. A half dozen men in white hats descended on him, pushing him back past the entryway as he screamed, "Who's responsible for this abominable, wretched garbage? Where is the manager of this godforsaken dump you call a restaurant?"

Suddenly, Godzilla in a chef's uniform burst into the dining room, meat cleaver in hand. In three strides, he took Harvey by the shirt and lifted him till they were nose to nose, then spat in his face.

"You no like my chicken? Listen to me, old man, you're nothing but a little pile of shit. I make the best food in the USA, and don't you forget it! Now get your stuff and get out before I give you something to complain about, because I don't like you!"

As the chef brandished the meat cleaver, the kitchen crew rolled up their sleeves. Obviously, it wasn't the first time this team had played together. It would have been funny, except for the feeling that he was seconds away from being thrashed.

"Let's step outside and finish it across the street," the chef continued. "Me and my friends will decide if your conduct is abominable, wretched, and garbage. Whaddya say, chump? Now get out of here and don't come back! Ever!"

Harvey muttered, "I'm sure you're right, Mr. Chef, ssssir." Sibilance with relish. "Since you're the one with the meat cleaver and the muscle, I'll consider my lunch on the house."

"Get out, or the house will be on you!" were the chef's parting words as he and his henchmen stomped back into the kitchen, presumably to prepare the same schlock for the next unsuspecting customer.

He vaulted the retaining barrier to the sidewalk outside the zoo. Thank goodness Mina had possessed the foresight to move their equipment to the van while he'd exchanged unpleasantries with Godzilla. He hopped in the passenger side, and she wheeled the van through the parking lot and out of the zoo's confines. Minutes later, they were on the highway back to the safety and sanity of the studio.

"Close call," Mina commented, staring at the road with its Saturday-afternoon traffic.

"Interesting act, wasn't it?"

"*Act* nothing! You almost got your clock cleaned!"

"They're just being tough. They've done this before. God knows how many times, given the food they serve."

"You feel justified in what you did?" she asked.

"Mina, I respect your opinion, but you're pushing my limits."

"Well, you've spent the whole day pushing the limits of anyone who got in your way. You've been the perfectly miserable king of the hill all day, reducing everyone you don't like to objects."

"So what?"

"Othering's a nasty attitude. Unpleasant to be around. It makes your fellow human beings into strangers, people you have no feeling for, people you can safely ignore, or worse. That doesn't sound like the justice-seeking Harvey Davenport I know."

"Oh, nonsense. I'm just irritated, that's all." He slumped into the corner between the seatback and the doorpost.

"What about?"

"The high nuisance value of my fellow human beings."

"Other people are just like you and me. Can't you see that?"

"No, they're not."

"Why not?"

"Because every one of the rotten sons of bitches will turn on you in an instant, that's why," he said, sitting up straight as he recovered his pique.

"Where's that come from?" she asked.

"Oh … family. School. My rights were violated when I was orphaned because industry poisoned my parents. At school, it was the ins and the outs. Between you and me, the animals are much better company." He paused as they turned a corner. "And animals don't kill their own species."

"You're playing with a mental trick that lets you push people out of your way. You're sacrificing all these people for the sake of your personal pride and need for revenge."

He froze. That's what he'd thought about his parents all those years ago. They, along with thousands of others, had been sacrificed, and he'd become an orphan practically overnight just so industry could reap easy profits. Yes, she was probably right about his attitude.

"Give it a little thought," said Mina. "I respect you greatly, Harvey, and I'm both honored and happy to be working with you. But I see this othering habit of yours eating away at the heart of a fine artist and an otherwise magnificent and thoughtful human being, and it makes me sad."

Bingo. Nail on the head. Nice play, Ms. Shakespeare!

His biggest embarrassment of the day, however, was having discovered that he shared with Dwyer and friends the tendency to denigrate and disparage those they didn't like or for whom they had no use. For the rest of the drive home, his cheeks burned with the shame of it.

CHAPTER 5

DISCOVERY II

Harvey's encounters with the council majority raised serious questions about their motivations and principles and their understanding of the distinct roles of enterprise and governance. So, when he received an email from the chamber of commerce that Mike Dwyer was giving a presentation on growth and dominion, he thought he might attend and find some answers.

He arrived early and found his seat in a corner of the conference room at the back. The pale yellow conference room walls bore elegant portraits of presidents and financiers, reputedly Mike's favorites, in handsome mahogany frames. Brown and yellow runners embellished with vases of colorful spring flowers graced the attendees' tables.

Following his introduction by chamber CEO Norm Taylor, Mike rose from his chair and stepped to the podium.

"Good morning, ladies and gentlemen," he began. "First, I'd like to share with you that the private-public partnership has two components. The first is enterprise—the production of goods and services for the masses to consume. Secondly, we must consider the mass of citizens we call the public. Your enterprise should have a solid, productive relationship with both."

He paused to allow the notetakers a chance to catch up. When heads had popped back up above their laptops, Mike continued.

"When we speak of people working together, we're talking about local citizens supporting the local business climate through activities such as participating in citywide festivals or publicity events.

"Our objective here is to keep the public's attention riveted on the threat of hard economic times. Why? Because fear leads people to action. Without it, minds wander. Then, when we speak to the general public, we can relieve their worries by reminding people that business is the place of expertise—always leading in the right direction that will benefit everyone."

The scream of a fire engine's siren interrupted Dwyer momentarily. The banker's blatant encouragement of manipulation made Harvey want to scream in harmony with the fire truck. To quell his irritation, he selected a chocolate eclair to go with his second cup of coffee.

"Now, by contrast," Dwyer continued, "when we speak to individuals, we have a different message. Here we talk about striving, achieving, helping people grow themselves and their businesses so they can outperform their competitors, friends, and neighbors. Don't forget — our success depends on separating each consumer from the pack, then focusing their attention on the new and exciting products they should be buying to enhance their own personal lives."

A bit crass, perhaps, but simple nonetheless. As Harvey typed a few notes into his phone, the memory of his uncle Theo appeared in his mind. "Only the fittest deserve to survive," he had admonished his nephew. "So you must strive to be among the fittest. Those who don't survive deserve their failure." The old social Darwinist claptrap still persisted a century after its fabrication.

Dwyer shuffled his note cards, then continued. "My next point is that deep inside, we all strive to be top dog, king of the mountain, building empires that satisfy our inner desires to dominate. Each of us knows, in our heart of hearts, that success—winning, dominating—is the name of the game."

The age-old call to war, that all true men should feel good about beating the next guy in the race to grab any and all available resources. Here was the root of great inequality.

Dwyer's message seemed to be, "You want it, just take it. Grab it away from others. It'll make you feel great!" *How repulsive!*

"When the chips are down," Dwyer continued, "and the struggle against the competition is fierce, one must set priorities and eliminate all distractions. Therefore, when we fight no-holds-barred in the midst of the battle for dominion, there are—and there *must be—no rules*. We can and do use every trick in the book to come out on top. What matters is that we win. To come in second, or third, or tenth is to be found among the dead and wounded. Am I right?"

Some clapped their hands over their heads. The buzz became cheerful, and a couple of loud "You betchas" could be heard over the din.

For Harvey, it was too much. Like being at a football game. *Maybe Dwyer should have come dressed in a short skirt, waving pompoms.* The thought made him chuckle.

"When the fighting's dirty, when there's blood everywhere," Dwyer continued, "that's when we need the support of our team. This is when we need government to take off the shackles of regulation so we can strike the enemy a death blow. We need the masses of people to be focused on how right we are, how bad the enemy is, how bad the economy will become if we lose the battle!

"As we fight for our individual goals, we must also grow. In order to grow, we must fight government expenses that could, for instance, raise"—he lowered his voice to a whisper—"taxes! Let's not use our profit dollars to pay taxes. That's self-defeating."

Cheers and applause poured forth from the audience.

Coaching his audience to ignore their responsibility to the community seemed to Harvey the antithesis of what society needed to function for the benefit of all.

"To accomplish this, two things must happen," Dwyer continued. "First, entrepreneurs need to influence public policy so it benefits our interests. Second, we need the public behind us as we do this. For example, it's helpful if we have a majority of the city council on our side. So we go to the wards to get their backing for our chamber's candidates.

"That's how the system works," Dwyer concluded. "It's been working that way for two and a half centuries. When public policy leans in the direction of the entrepreneur, the entrepreneur rewards the public with a growing … fruitful … productive … economy!" He punctuated the last four words with his index finger.

When Dwyer had finished, the audience stood to applaud as he gave them a big smile and a two-thumbs-up sign. Then Norm Taylor rose to shake his hand and escort him down to the buffet lunch.

As they passed the front entrance to the conference room, Harvey waved at him just as Dwyer glanced to his left. Mike's neck reddened as he turned back to Taylor and tilted his head in Harvey's direction. He was willing to bet there'd be hell to pay for that.

Having spent most of the winter discovering how the city operated, in the second week of April, Harvey decided it was time he learned how to make industrial polluters pay for sickening and killing people. For that, he needed a good look at the landscape he would soon traverse. So he called his lawyer, Frank Pederson, and learned that a local attorney, Charles Higgins, had great depth of experience and could answer his questions.

"I've heard about you, Mr. Davenport, and applaud your recent vote against constructing the WDP in the Bottoms," Higgins said when Harvey contacted him. "How can I help you?"

"I want to sue the manufacturers who dump industrial waste in the Bottoms. Can you show me the landscape and procedures involved in doing that?"

"That's a pretty complicated subject, Mr. Davenport. Why don't you come over to the office and we'll chat?"

The next day, Harvey walked over to the Carruthers Office Plaza where Higgins had his offices on the fifteenth floor. From its black Marmara marble and glass exterior to its plush interior boasting an art collection that would be the envy of many museums, the Carruthers building exuded an atmosphere of luxury.

Higgins's lavish office was similarly appointed with floor-to-ceiling cherrywood cabinets and floors inlaid with marquetry using light and dark woods. Mirrored walls and ceiling reflected and enhanced the palatial ambience surrounding the large, oval desk and white, wingback executive office chair complemented by two upholstered white armchairs.

When they were seated at Higgins's mahogany conference table, the attorney, wearing a brown three-piece suit and dark, well-shined shoes, invited his questions.

"How can I sue Westfield's industrial polluters to make them pay for the death and destruction they've caused in the Bottoms over the last century and a half?"

"That won't be an easy task," Higgins cautioned him. "First, you could make a complaint to the Environmental Protection Agency. They can levy fines for each manufacturer who exceeds the amount limited by law. Occasionally that works, but it takes them months or years to act, even on multiple complaints. The amount of the fines is pocket change to the manufacturer.

"The second approach is to sue an individual manufacturer for specific damage caused to specific persons or families. That, too, is a long and expensive journey."

The shock of Higgins's statement made his stomach flip. This sounded complicated. It sounded impossible.

"Let's say, then, that I want to sue Superior Plastics for causing my mother's death."

"When did she die?" Higgins asked.

"Fifty years ago," he replied.

"What killed her?"

"Liver cancer and scleroderma. Industrial pollution, the docs said. My father had tuberculosis, also attributed to the heavy smoke that regularly drifted through the area."

"What period of time was involved?"

Harvey explained the circumstances.

"You have a problem. You cannot prove exactly how or whether it was pollution from Superior Plastics that caused your mother's death, or even her illness."

Another strikeout. Harvey rebelled. To him, there was a perfectly logical connection, but apparently that wasn't enough.

"All right," he conceded. "Let's say I want to sue Superior Plastics for the deaths of ten people in the Bottoms over the past five years because of the trichloroethylene they've dumped into the ground that seeped into the aquifers and turned up in the well water these people used for drinking and washing."

"Ahh," Higgins said. "Now you're getting the idea. But you're still not close to understanding the system. First of all, you need to designate and extensively interview a dozen or more families and take their statements. Then you need to create a logical progression from the manufacturer to the chemical to the individuals in your study."

"Okay, show me the steps it takes to bring a corporate polluter into court and win a case for wrongful death."

Charles rose from his chair and tugged a newsprint easel from its corner to the conference table.

"Let's take a hypothetical example," Higgins began. "Suppose you find fifteen families living within two blocks of an old well they've used for many years, which is situated, say, four blocks from the company's location."

He wrote the key words at the top of the newsprint and sketched a diagram.

"First, you must establish the symptoms the individual family members experienced. Then you need the official diagnosis for each. This must be backed by medical records and doctors' testimony. The symptoms should be nearly the same among all sufferers in the cluster."

He continued writing key words on the newsprint.

"Next, you must document the water they used, how they used it, how much and for how long each day. For example, did each member of each family take a ten-minute shower every day? You must look at skin absorption and the inhalation of vapor. Trichloroethylene gives off a vapor when heated, so people showering in contaminated water breathe the vapors as well as absorb the chemical through their skins."

This was inconceivably complicated. Days and months of work lay ahead.

"Our next step," the attorney continued, "is to show specifically what chemical contaminated the water they used. Was it TCE, or benzene, or mercury, or something else? We must also establish to what degree the water was contaminated in parts per billion."

He wrote *chemical* and *parts per billion* on the newsprint.

"We must also establish that the chemical is a proven carcinogen."

"I see where you're going, Charles. I'll bet the next step is to prove which manufacturers use the chemical that caused the diseases and deaths for these families?"

"Exactly right," said the attorney. "And you want to establish how close the manufacturer's location is to the water source these families used."

"Must we be absolutely precise in linking source, chemical, use, and disease?"

"Yes," said Higgins, nodding his head but then holding up his right hand, palm forward. "There are a few more steps, however. We must show that the manufacturer's employees were allowed to dump the chemical on the ground or put it into barrels subsequently buried in the earth, which—let's say—rotted away and spilled the chemical into the ground, for a specific period of years, in quantities large enough to have contaminated the wells these families used with enough chemical to poison and/or kill them."

"Are you next going to tell me we have to establish the path the chemicals traveled to get into the well?"

Charles nodded. "Now you're starting to think like a lawyer for the defendant. You're now in a position where a jury might—and I emphasize *might*—find a corporation guilty of damaging these individuals by their careless disposal of a known carcinogen. Or you could settle the case out of court."

"Seems like a monstrous task!" Harvey exclaimed. "Where do we start? There's twenty-five thousand people living in the Bottoms!"

"Indeed," Charles agreed. "And one thing more to remember, Harvey, is that these large corporations have vast resources to pump into fighting a lawsuit. To get their attention, you'd have to sue them for at least one year's worth of profit. They will outlast and outfight you, even though they might use incorrect or falsified data. You cannot win a political or moral victory over these guys. The game is money. Get as much as you can, by settlement or a jury's verdict. These fights take years, sometimes decades, and will occupy you and your attorneys until you're ready to drop. And that's exactly what the company wants. So start raising money, my friend. You're going to need a lot of it! Millions. Or else a very determined lawyer who is willing to bet on a positive jury award or settlement covering his expenses and fees. The probabilities of winning such a suit are quite small."

As he rode down in the walnut-paneled elevator, a flood of disappointment nearly drowned his aspirations. He'd virtually have to climb Mt. Everest to achieve his goal. He envisioned teams of lawyers trying to prove or deny the connections from factory to ground, to water, to families, to disease, and death. He imagined having to enlist experts in management, chemistry, hydrology, medicine, and other related fields. Would such a project eat up all his retirement years just to avenge his mother's death?"

The following day, Harvey received an unexpected call from Mike Dwyer.

"Could you meet me for lunch?" Dwyer said. "I'd like to discuss the waste disposal project. Norm Taylor will be there too."

"Fine," he replied. "I'll bring my attorney, Frank Pederson."

"Just a friendly exchange of views, nothing more," said Dwyer, suddenly sounding cautious. "See you at the Athletic Club at noon."

Westfield's entrepreneurs often enjoyed conducting their business affairs in solemnity and seclusion at the Athletic Club. Heavy, dark wood paneling offset by stone pillars, leaded glass windows, and floors made of Ohio blue limestone stabilized the dining room. The waiters dressed in formal attire and conducted themselves in the German manner. Harvey thought of it as the Arthritic Club.

He and Frank arrived early, greeted by the elderly and smiling Hugh Pringle, the club's gnarly, stooped doorman for more than fifty years. Within minutes, Mike Dwyer appeared in his navy blue banker's suit and red tie as Norm Taylor trailed along behind in a green sport coat over a yellow shirt, open at the neck, waving and nodding to everyone he knew.

When the group was seated and had ordered their food, Dwyer spoke first.

"I want to mend fences over the WDP," the banker began, distrustfully eyeing Pederson. "Could the three of us establish a partnership? I think we have some objectives in common."

"Why do you suggest a partnership?" Frank Pederson interjected. "Sounds to me like you're asking for accommodation. Or is it perhaps acquiescence?"

"As I see it, Frank," Dwyer replied, "Harvey's most sensible move would simply be to step aside and not take part in public protests against the WDP. That would be more in keeping with his role as a city councilman."

"Nonsense!" Leaning into the table, arms akimbo, Pederson persisted, looking straight at Dwyer. "You're just one of eight council members. Who gave you the right to prescribe anyone's behavior? I suggest you're assuming more control than you have a right to exercise."

"I would not, for one moment, consider stepping aside," Harvey interjected. "I'm committed to helping the people of Westfield get justice on the WDP and freedom from business domination."

Dwyer winced at the word domination. "How can you not see that putting the WDP in the old industrial park is the least financially oppressive option?" said Taylor, eyes wide, finger pointing in scorn. "The federal Brownfields funds keep the cost of this project manageable."

"Sorry, Norm," Harvey countered. "That's not the real issue here. The chamber is just one interest group among many. And businesses, like everyone else, should pay their fair share of taxes to support a government that serves all residents of the city—whatever the costs."

"A lot of socialist rubbish!" Dwyer muttered, baring his teeth and shaking his index finger. "Without firm guidance, city council would have us paying the world's highest taxes, just to keep the city looking prosperous. Fact is the city can't prosper unless we in the corporate sector are profitable, and there's no profit in paying taxes."

"Burgers are here, gentlemen," the waiter intervened. "Who had the shrimp salad?"

Frank Pederson put up his hand and received his choice.

"Same old clichés," said Harvey, shaking his head in disgust. "For you, *taxes* is a dirty word, right? At least, you'd like everyone to think so. But I'm not buying it." He was about to launch into one of his favorite subjects, but Pederson touched his arm, and a furrowed brow advised him to take it easy. "What's so distasteful about simply being a conscientious, caring citizen of the community?" He lifted both hands in the air, palms up. "Get real!"

"Everything north of the river is a waste pit anyway," said Taylor, shrugging his shoulders. "Why can't you just accept that fact?"

"Let's not degenerate into exaggeration," Pederson advised, holding up his hand. "We can talk civilly without suggesting that some of our citizens are trash."

"The real issue," Harvey chided, "is justice—removing the poison already there and prohibiting any more. Putting profit ahead of people is immoral."

"Way over the top!" seethed Dwyer. "No! The real issue is making the city work." He took a sip of his coffee. "Let me share a little history you may not know. In the seventies and eighties, the members of city council were at each other's throats—every meeting! People were divided into camps whose views soon hardened. Over time, the willingness to negotiate declined sharply."

"I take your point, Mr. Dwyer," said Frank Pederson. "Democracy won't work if the citizens won't negotiate and compromise for the common good. But your method breached the election rules just so you could load the council with like-minded business people. That's not democracy' it's despotism."

"Gentlemen," Harvey interrupted, his hands forming a T. "Let's get our terms straight. Democracy is governance that places a premium on *equality and diversity*, which are needed to find avenues of change to make society better. As an economic system, capitalism promotes *inequality*. That's what made the situation you describe in the seventies and eighties so unbearable."

"The marvelous engine of capitalism pushes us toward ever greater material prosperity," Dwyer countered. "Democracy only pushes us toward chaos and indecision."

"In your system, money becomes the good, the true, and the beautiful," Harvey bored in on the issue. "When that happens, we're all diminished because the people strive only for material objects they cannot have. Happiness becomes a matter of having more than one's neighbor."

"But you can't get away from the financial reality that every mode of sustenance has its price," Dwyer insisted. "Each meal has a cost, as does a tractor, or a painting, or an education."

"That's irrelevant," Harvey countered. "When industry dominates government, you lose the ability to rein in corporate striving so it doesn't destroy the humans who support it. Regulation by government is necessary for the health and well-being of both our people and our planet. Without that, commerce and industry become irrelevant and destructive."

"Look here!" Dwyer's voice increased a notch. "Winning's what life's all about, not betterment," Dwyer countered. "Some win, some lose. That's all there is to it."

"No, that's *not* all there is to life," Harvey insisted. "If the society exists only for winners, then each person craves only what he doesn't or cannot have. Where is there room to pursue the mind, or love, or creative solutions to our problems? Material possessions leave us lonely and wasted. What you saw in the seventies and eighties—and even to this day—has been the result of starving our society of anything besides gadgets."

"Winning and losing is just part of our nature," said Dwyer. "Someone must win election, others lose, perhaps to come back another day."

"Nonsense," Harvey retorted. "Our founders were capitalists who were also aristocrats and bigots. They chose majority rule so they and people like them would always be in power. Creative thinking and involvement of the people was replaced with controlling the populace and activity in the markets. But it's never been enough, and we've been sliding downhill morally for two hundred years."

"That's just sissy stuff!" Dwyer murmured. "You need to get on the right side of things, Davenport. Be a winner for a change."

"Don't forget," said Taylor, "that business has made Westfield one of the premier locations in the state. People love to come here because we have a low, stable tax rate."

Pederson shook his head and waved Taylor's words away with his hand in obvious disgust. "What's good for business is definitely *not good* for the people. Surely you can see that."

Trying hard to ignore the sour tone of the conversation, the waiter gingerly left the receipt for lunch at Dwyer's elbow.

As he lifted the bill, Dwyer leaned toward Harvey, his face a rictus of anger. "We are America's aristocracy!" he said. "And as such, we are the masters of this nation. Those of us with the money always win!" He scrawled his signature on the bill with an imperial flourish, then underlined it. "That's the way it's supposed to be. And we will do whatever it takes to keep it that way. We'll beat you and your trashy black and brown friends into the ground, Davenport, if that's what it takes!" He nodded to Taylor, and both men rose, threw their napkins on the table, and left the dining room, marching in step.

Harvey imagined swastikas appearing on the backs of their suit coats as they disappeared down the hall. But he was glad for the clarity their discussion had produced. He and Dwyer were both committed to controlling the people's governance. Their fight would be over whether business or the people themselves would be in charge. It seemed a long way from his original quest to stop pollution in the

Bottoms. But until this issue was decided, the matter of industrial pollution could never be settled in the people's favor.

Outside in the fresh air of the club's parking lot, he opened the door to his van and discovered a white card on the driver's seat. Printed on the card, in large type, was a message that chilled his blood.

"It's so easy to get to you! Watch your step!"

I'll ride that bull to the finish line. He'll have to kill me to get me off his back.

Not twenty-four hours later, Harvey received an invitation to lunch from Doug Thompson's office. Since Doug had voted with the majority on the WDP issue, he was curious as to why the attorney wanted to talk with him. They met at noon in the Busy Bee.

"My reason for inviting you here," Doug said, "was to tell you a story. I thought you might like to know a little history. My story isn't well known or remembered today. Too many generations have passed. But it is relevant."

"I'm all ears and ready to hear," said Harvey.

"As you may already know, from the city's beginning in 1847, entrenched industrial powers were king of the hill in Westfield until after the Civil War. The monied owners of the mines, logging operations, and railroad car manufacturing took turns filling public offices. Often they served gratis or for small stipends. Running their business operations and running city government were considered pretty much the same.

"By the time that first generation of US millionaires had passed, things had changed. The city was larger, more diverse by 1880, as industry expanded and many more types of industry made up our local economy. Additionally, a wider range of well-educated professionals served the area, including a large percentage of women. There was a general quest for a new moral order in the minds of many citizens."

"Sounds a lot like the sixties," Harvey said. "We thought that time was when the women were becoming active."

"On, no," Thompson replied. "In the year 1880, Melinda Travers, Cynthia Marmalese, and Virginia Stout banded together as community-minded activists advocating for a more moral, nurturing, and service-oriented city government. One of their efforts involved pressuring the mayor, Michael Seccomb, and the city council to enact a public ordinance prohibiting the dumping of industrial waste in the river or within a mile of the city's boundaries. Since the city council still comprised mostly middle and upper managers in local industry, many had misgivings about such an ordinance. But the ladies were so organized that the wives of city council members brought their own pressure to bear and the measure passed on a unanimous vote."

"Hurray for them!" Harvey cheered. "But I bet their husbands were furious!"

"Indeed they were, according to the newspapers of the time. Then one day the chemical manufacturer Trublood Bennett came to town to establish his manufacturing firm, then called Superior Products, as a supplier to local and statewide industry."

"Was this Rhett Bennett's great-grandfather by any chance?" inquired Harvey.

"The very same," replied Thompson. "When he'd built his plant and filled the first orders, Mr. Bennett came to Mayor Seccomb and made a request. Keep in mind, Michael Seccomb was not a captain of industry, as previous mayors had been. He was a well-educated politician and economist with a history of reforming city bureaucracies. The ladies found his results and his personality much to their liking.

"Then one day, young Bennett came to Mayor Seccomb and said he needed a variance in the dumping ordinance. He further explained that Superior Products was a burgeoning industry and would soon provide many jobs for the locals as well as a contribution for the city's new library.

"'Well sir,' said the mayor, 'I cannot do that, and you're very improper to ask for such a favor.'

"'How so?' Bennett asked.

"'It wouldn't be right. If we give you a variance, others will want one too. A lot of people could be damaged or killed. Besides, the ladies would be up in arms!'

"'But I know something else,' said Seccomb. 'You've been seeing Virginia Stout on the side, and reliable sources tell me you're getting quite cozy with her. How'd you like it if I had a conversation with her husband? Or perhaps with Melinda, your wife? How about that journalist fellow, Ed Freeman at the newspaper?'

"Seccomb, of course, acknowledged that would not be good.

"'All right, give me the variance, and I'll keep my mouth shut.'

"That clinched the deal. Then Mayor Seccomb went to city council with this request, and since the entire council comprised the local good ole boys from industry, they approved the variance, laughing behind their hands.

"That very night, Superior Products started draining chemical effluent into the Staminon River, and the next day, they dug a large hole outside the back of their plant—right on First Street—and buried four tons of sulfuric acid that had been used to clean steel parts in their machines. A year later, the newspaper reported multiple cases of acid poisoning resulting in the deaths of fifteen people in the Bottoms."

Harvey realized at once how this story fit with the way Dwyer advocated for dominion of business over governance. Clearly, sacrifice zones were the product of collusion—and often coercion—between business managers and government officials.

It also made him mad.

CHAPTER 6

FINDING ALLIES I

On a warm, muggy day in early May, Harvey drummed his fingers excitedly on the steering wheel of his van as he drove to the senior center in the Bottoms to talk with Martha Ruggles.

Her performance at city council meeting, when she'd tossed balls of sludge and goo, had aroused his curiosity. Clearly she was a fearless and outspoken advocate for her neighbors in the area where he'd once lived half a century ago. He hoped she would share her views about relationships between the races and the effects of industrial pollution.

Distrustful of the aging building's elevators, he climbed five flights of stairs in the gray, dimly lit, unventilated stairwell to get to her sixth-floor apartment. He recoiled at the smell of mold, urine, and disinfectant. How in the world did these old folks manage to climb such horrible stairs?

Waiting at her door, Ms. Ruggles offered him a cup of cold water with a wide smile on her deeply furrowed visage. She looked respectably stylish in brown slacks and a white blouse, An eye-catching red ribbon in her hair hinted at a sense of humor and balanced the patch over the wound on her cheek where the guard had slugged her. Inside her apartment, a smoke-laden breeze wafted through her windows.

"Welcome, Harvey," she said in a gentle, somewhat raspy voice as she stepped back from the doorway. "Come over here and look at the beautiful view out my picture window."

He walked with her, letting her grasp his arm.

"Isn't it marvelous? Too bad the factories spew all that smoke in the air. It's such a hot day, I gotta have the windows open."

The view was indeed spectacular. The panorama of the Bottoms lay spread out before them. She remarked on the community's highlights, including the old industrial park, the elementary school, the larger churches, the main streets. The Bottoms had changed measurably from what he remembered, so this bird's-eye view helped reorient him.

"That's the high school over to the right behind the elementary school. My memory's not what it used to be, but I think I remember you from when I was in high school. Did your family live on Madison at Seventh Street?"

"Yes, on the corner about two blocks from the Bethel AME Church." Not only her memory but the coincidence of their ages amazed him. He was meeting a former neighbor for the first time.

"I thought so. And I'd guess you're just about retirement age. Is that right?"

"Sixty-four this year."

"Well, I'm seventy-one, and now I do remember you, Harvey. The year I graduated from high school, you were in fourth grade. I remember you as a tall, skinny white guy walking home from school each day, loaded down with books, usually by yourself. I lived just two blocks north of you on DuBois. I always wondered what it was you were studying so hard with all those books."

"My focus was always on photography," he said. "I read everything I could get my hands on in those days."

She turned back into the living room. "Now come on over here. Let's sit in my comfy chairs from Goodwill." With a sly wink, she motioned him to her two burgundy velvet wingback chairs, which matched her sofa. When he was comfortably seated in one, she plopped down in the other, breathing heavily.

"You like cookies?" she asked, gesturing to the plate of cookies on the coffee table. "Just baked 'em this morning. Please, have your fill. 'Cause if you don't, I'm afraid I will." Her eyes twinkled above a self-deprecating smile.

He nodded, reaching for one. "They smell heavenly and taste divine." He munched his way through one, then reached for another.

"As you know," Martha said, "Westfield's charter dates to 1847. The mines were here on the north side of the river, and the miners lived nearby. The owners and bosses built homes on the bluff south of the river, away from the pollution and noise.

"Machine shops came with the railroads in the midnineteenth century, then the cement plant in the twenties. Clothing factories and asphalt plants arrived during World War II."

Heavy dark blue draperies softened the bright light from the window. She had covered the sisal carpet with several aged hooked rugs.

"My grandmother made those rugs." She pointed to them as if reading his mind, then took a sip of tea before continuing her story. "From the time I was a little girl, I heard politicians and business leaders stand at one podium or another, spouting the myth that America is the land of equality of opportunity." She puffed out her chest and raised her voice, imitating a pompous orator. "Anyone can get ahead if he only works hard and plays by the rules. It's the American way! Only the fittest will survive." Relaxing after her mimicry, Martha arrived at her point. "It sounded so fine, so simple, so desirable. Even today it's enticing, isn't it, Harvey?"

He nodded, afraid that if he didn't, she'd skewer him to the wall with those perceptive brown eyes.

"And that message really is very simple." She said the words slowly, thoughtfully. "So simple anyone would be tempted to believe it. In fact, Americans still hold the myth of survival of the fittest in one hand while concealing in the other the methods by which they arm themselves with the weapons of white supremacy." Her eyes challenged him.

She'd revealed a crust of acrimony baked in the fires of life's hard experience around that passionate, perceptive heart.

"But y'know what I've found?" She continued holding his gaze. "It's simply untrue—neither America nor the city of Westfield have ever really been interested in equality." She sat up straight once more for her imitation of a politician, this time lowering her voice and pretending to strut with her upper body and shoulders. "Though they sure do like to talk a lot about opportunity, don't they?"

Harvey laughed and nodded, encouraging her to go on.

"The first clue," she lectured, pointing her index finger at him, "that all this pompous chatter about equality is BS comes when they say, 'Play by the rules.' Because whitey makes those rules so some succeed while others are forced to fail." She reached for her tea and gave him a wicked smile over the top of her Power-to-the-People mug. The flames of resistance danced in her deep brown eyes, which crinkled at the corners when she smiled. "Because some people are worth more than others."

He drew a deep breath. "Ms. Ruggles, as I'm sure you know, a few wealthy business leaders of Westfield have controlled city government for at least two decades. This clearly hasn't helped people living in the Bottoms, has it?"

"This is true." Martha nodded, waiting.

"Why haven't you and others banded together to expose such practices and work against them?"

The silence mushroomed, exposing the ticking of the kitchen clock. Martha glared at him. Was it antipathy or embarrassment?

After several moments, she drew a breath and said in a quiet, steady voice, "Because the minority businessmen support the chamber of commerce. Their only sources of capital are the local banks. When the people of the Bottoms protest city decisions that hurt us, the money spigot gets turned off." She paused, as if in thought. "There goes the bread on many tables."

When he was growing up, life seemed simpler. White industry managers did as they pleased to a docile, uncomplaining populace of worker bees. The minorities who could work labored at menial jobs—factory hands, truck drivers, secretaries, even a few schoolteachers, like his mother. In fifty years the two groups had apparently become much more enmeshed with and invested in one another. Martha's comment seemed to reveal the complexity of such interdependence.

"Why are you interested?" she asked, with the hint of a smile twitching at the corners of her mouth.

"My parents were killed by the pollution here in the Bottoms in 1962, and today people are still getting sick and dying from it. That pollution was enabled by collusion between industry heads and government officials going back at least a century. What's everyone been doing for the last fifty years? Why aren't people out in the streets protesting the pollution, the lack of good wages, the disrespect, the injustice?" he burst out.

"Excellent questions," Martha said, nodding slowly. "The answer is simply that some folks are worth more than others. They consider us waste people, so it's all right to starve us, sometimes even burn our houses down, to keep us in line." She took a sip of tea, then almost whispered, "Of course that doesn't mean that whatever whitey puts on the table satisfies our hunger. But whenever we reveal our dissatisfaction, there's always a price to pay. And it's always an ambush."

She shifted position in her chair to place her tea cup on the coffee table.

"Disease comes on slow. You can take a pill to stop coughing and ease the pain. You can put death off another day—until it catches up with you, but by then it's too late. What keeps the people of the Bottoms in line is the ambush we know will come. So stick around, Harvey. You'll see what I mean. They want to punish you as much as you want to punish them. Watch out where and how you take your revenge, because they have infinitely more power, more muscle, and more money."

Early on the second Friday in May, as Harvey, Mina, and Lord Nelson organized a dozen robots for a client's product shot, he received a call from a fellow named Paul Johnson, head of a social service agency in the Bottoms called Renewal House. Johnson called to thank him for his vote against the WDP and to suggest they get together for lunch to chat about mutual objectives.

They agreed to meet at a little place on Sixth Street in the Bottoms called Mama Lulu's Grits and Hocks. When he asked if he might bring Mina, Alice, and Stan, Johnson agreed.

"We need all the help we can find," Paul had said.

Three hours later, they walked along Sixth Street in bright sunshine to Mama Lulu's. Inside the front window of the ancient storefront, a middle-aged man lounged on a grime-encrusted crocodile-green sofa, reading a newspaper as he held a cigarette in his right hand. His feet were propped up on an ancient thrift store coffee table piled high with vintage magazines. Two red-and-white-striped wingback chairs faced each other, sitting on an ancient, warped hardwood floor. Each chair hugged an aging gentleman in black clerical garb, frowning in concentration over the checkerboard between them.

As they entered, tantalizing smells of barbecue sauce and pies fresh from the oven teased their noses. Chubby Checker played on the jukebox. Visible in the kitchen, through the opening behind the counter, a woman in a white apron stirred a pot on the stove. Warm feelings washed over him as he remembered how his father had brought him here for lunch when they needed to talk man-to-man. To his amazement, not much had changed since then.

Along the wall opposite the serving counter, from the lounge area to the rear exit, ran booths upholstered in ancient black Naugahyde, featuring wood tables. Tables with old-fashioned ice-cream chairs occupied the open space in between. Halfway to the back sat a tall, muscular but handsome man in blue jeans and a brown dress shirt with the sleeves rolled. Paul Johnson rose from his white Formica-topped table and hurried to greet them with large, gleaming brown eyes and a wide smile. A full head of close-cropped, black, curly hair crowned his high, smooth forehead as he ushered them to the service counter where they could place their orders.

"Friday, big choice," Mama Lulu advised with a broad, inviting smile as she stood behind the counter. She was a large seventy-ish woman, dressed in black, wearing a white apron. "Ham 'n' scalloped. Barbecue chicken. Smothered chicken. Ham 'n' grits. Fried catfish with peanuts. Take your pick."

When they'd placed their orders, Mama Lulu escorted them to a cave-like back room smelling of old hardwood, dust, and cigarette smoke, which had been reserved for their meeting. They sat on ancient ice-cream chairs from the fifties—the kind with strands of twisted steel for legs—positioned around two square black tables resting on scarred, round chrome bases. The walls were dark green and featured placards from shows of the sixties and seventies.

"What do you think, Harvey?" Paul asked. "You seem pretty much at home here. I bet you've been in joints like this before."

"Used to come here as a kid," he replied in a voice thickened by memories. "My father brought me here for the first time when I was ten. The place hasn't lost a bit of its charm."

"I don't believe it!" Paul exclaimed, looking shocked.

"My mother died young from liver cancer and scleroderma," he said with a flat tone. "Docs said it was toxic waste. Now I'm interested in breaking up the bittersweet marriage of business and government that made this place a sacrifice zone."

"Well, then, I'm glad we're havin' this meeting," Paul affirmed. "I think we can help each other."

Harvey smiled happily to himself in gratitude. This was a good place, and Paul seemed like a solid, trustworthy fellow.

"So, what's Renewal House all about?" he inquired.

"Ten years ago, when I became director," Paul began, "teaching, counseling, and organizing for action were still very much needed. I adopted Alinsky's methods, and things progressed well for a while. Then one day, we had a surprise. The Economic Development folks broke ground for the Belle Riviere industrial park without a word. One morning, bulldozers showed up and leveled forty homes. In a month, we saw footings for ten new businesses."

"Sounds like a threat," Stan Matthews said in a quiet, concerned voice that matched his traditional gray sport coat and goatee. "What did you do?"

"We had to change our mission. Why promote health if more pollution stared us in the face? Why improve housing when extensive remediation might mean the demolition of thousands of homes?"

"And I suppose you refused to give up?" Alice suggested with a wry smile.

"You're reading the tea leaves correctly, my friend," Paul acknowledged with a mischievous grin.

"Must have been a drastic change for you," Stan speculated.

"Community development became priority one," Paul continued. "We began to train people to help each other become economically mobile. We're building self-esteem and initiative within our families. We're getting people ready to move out, because their health and survival depend on it. Tough going. Our people crave stability, but the prospect of death and disease is a powerful motivator."

"Are the people still passive?" Harvey wanted to know. Under the table, his foot began to bounce as anxiety preyed at the edges of consciousness. "Or are they taking an active part in removing themselves?" Martha Ruggles's answer to a similar question had left him dissatisfied.

"A bit of both," Paul affirmed. "When the chamber put Clarence Williams up for election, ordinary people at first just accepted him, even though he was enmeshed with Superior Plastics. Made life easier, or so they thought."

"Sounds like colonialism." Mina wrinkled up her nose.

Paul nodded. "Gradually, they figured out industry's strategy was to make life so completely hellish they'd all move out. And that galvanized everyone's attitudes."

His spirits brightened as Harvey realized there was still much he could do. He guessed the accomplishment of Paul's objective was still a generation away.

Just then, Mama Lulu called out, "Come and get it!" They went to the counter and picked up their trays.

Back at their tables, silence prevailed as they ate like hungry lions. Harvey lost himself in his heavenly potatoes and ham. "Best I've ever had," he mumbled with a mouthful. "Oughta come over here more often."

"Best place in the Bottoms," Stan murmured around his chewing.

"Now that you've settled into city hall," Paul said, looking at Harvey, "what do you want to accomplish?"

"My larger goal is justice," he replied. "Find the corporate root of injustice, shine a big, bright light on it, and cut it out."

"Sounds like you want revenge, not justice," Paul responded as he stuck another toothpick in his mouth. "And I can tell you right now, that'll take a very long time. Too many forces working, too complicated. We have to remember—revenge is a personal quest, not something that gets other people charged up."

"What I see is a city run by the profit motive," Harvey replied with a shrug. "That does the people injustice in so many ways. When I see industry poisoning and killing people, I'm out to bust 'em, make them pay, give 'em what they deserve."

"Can't say I disagree with you," Paul conceded. "But at Renewal House, we have a little different approach. We try to build solidarity among the people and accountability within industry."

"Oh! Sounds so slow and tedious!" Harvey protested, shaking his head.

"My point," Paul persisted, "is that we can transform the bully by denying him satisfaction. And by collectively shining the light of public scrutiny on his intent."

"That I can support," he replied. "But why haven't you been successful? I see the corporate bullies haven't stopped polluting. To my mind, solidarity just makes people feel good, but it does nothing to the bullies. They care only about money."

Paul looked down at his plate and dropped into silence. "You win," he said at length, looking abashed. "We haven't been as effective as I'd hoped."

"My analogy for business," Harvey offered, "is cancer. Greed for growth has eaten away the tissue of our human values, like cancer eats away our bodies and toxic waste destroys our planet. Owners want industry to grow, consumers demand cheap products. That leaves labor, minorities, and the poor suffering in the middle."

"Hold on, Harvey!" Paul cautioned. "Not all businesses are bad."

"Oh, yes they are!" he interrupted, letting an angry twinge seep into his voice.

Paul persisted. "Lots of good people own and operate businesses and serve the community well. You can't throw all those good folks in with a few rotten apples."

"Yes, you can!" he insisted, then snorted angrily. "Look at it this way—somebody once said humans have evolved to gossip, preen, manipulate, and ostracize." He flashed a cherubic smile. "Second, the nature of business is self-interest, so when infected with outsized ambition, it transforms into a fast-growing cancer."

"Are you saying the cancer of enterprise eats up our society the way cancer destroys a body?" asked Mina.

"Yes!" he exclaimed. "It destroys our values and corrupts society. But three treatments can cure cancer—the surgical knife, radiation, and chemotherapy. I liken those three cures to tight regulation, stiff fines, and taxation."

The silence of reflection descended as they finished their lunches. When they'd emptied their plates, Mama Lulu and her crew removed them.

"Would you folks like dessert today?" Mama Lulu asked.

After they'd ordered, Alice was ready with a challenge.

"Let's get a plan together, fellows," she said. "You guys have rattled on long enough! We all know what we want to accomplish. How are we going to do it?"

"First thing I want to do is direct action," Paul proclaimed, taking her lead. "There's a community meeting coming up soon about the WDP. We have to decide what we'll do now that city council is determined to start construction."

"Hold on a minute," Stan Matthews interrupted. "I think we should get Charles Higgins to introduce us into the nationwide antitoxins movement first. There's a ton of resources we'll need. That will help us with direct action too."

"Yes, like attending training sessions for air monitoring," said Mina. "The people themselves need to be involved. This would be a good way to do it."

Just then, Mama Lulu and her servers brought their desserts. The room was silent again except for chewing noises as they indulged in these delicious treats.

"Okay," Paul said when he'd washed down the last bite of his cherry pie with coffee. "Let's also have Charles show us how to file civil complaints against these polluters so we can put them on notice that we're coming after them."

"I had a conversation with Charles back in April," Harvey said. "He named the steps of filing a civil action and going to trial. A very complicated set of steps, I must say. He also advised me that suing a polluting company for personal damages is quite expensive and can take years to accomplish."

"Can't we sue them for violating laws against pollution?" Mina queried. "Wouldn't that be simpler?"

"No, that's EPA's territory," he replied. "We could talk to the governor about appointing an emergency city manager, however. I've heard he's an advocate of the separation of commerce and state."

"We'll need solid data to persuade the governor," Alice suggested. "We could measure levels of toxins in the water and soil and do other kinds of research among our residents."

"Sure," said Mina. "We could have volunteers walking through the Bottoms surveying residents door-to-door about their health in recent years."

"That makes me think of phone surveys," said Stan. "Let's sample families all across Westfield about cancers and other diseases."

"I'd be happy to do some in-depth interviews with the residents," said Mina. "I can also provide photos. They communicate faster than prose."

"Higgins thinks we need to sit down and write a compelling case stating that our residents are being sickened by emissions," said

Harvey. "We can take that statement to the state assembly as well as to the governor."

"We can also take it to the EPA and show them what they're missing," said Alice.

"I'd like to see Harvey, Alice, and Stan introduce legislation in city council to protect public health more aggressively," said Paul. "Part of that could be an ordinance prohibiting any kind of pollution and fining violators substantially."

"If we have a public demonstration," Mina offered, "let's have a group of people wearing bright yellow T-shirts that have WCEQ on the front—that would signify Westfield Citizens for Environmental Quality."

"I've been thinking we need to convert Doug Thompson and Marty Angelo to our way of thinking," Stan ventured. "They do sometimes vote with us."

"Let's also work with the ward committees," said Alice. "Help them select their own candidates for office instead of accepting the chamber-selected candidates."

"Looks like we've got a plan!" Paul announced, beaming as he pushed back his chair and rose. "Sorry, folks, but I've gotta run. Staff meeting, you know? They're probably wondering where I am." Then he hastened to the counter to pay the lunch bill.

As the others preceded him to the front door, Harvey did a little one-legged twirl and kicked his heels with excitement. Mina's questioning look made him laugh. Did she think he was crazy? Well, maybe he was. But he certainly enjoyed the ideas and support he'd found in this group.

Out on the street, as they said their farewells, a '68 Dodge Charger and a late-model Ford pickup pulled up on the sidewalk, blocking them from moving.

"What's up, James?" Paul said to the driver of the Charger, showing irritation. "Is this business?"

"Sure is, Mistah Paul," James replied. "Y'all come with us. Some of you can ride with me; the rest get in Sid's pickup."

"No can do, fellows," Paul said with an outstretched hand and the voice of command. "I have four guests here. I need to get them safely on their way back over the bridge."

"No, sir, not okay," James countered. "We're to take you to Mr. Williams right now. Get in my car or the truck, please. No trouble, or things'll get nasty." He pulled an automatic pistol from his hip pocket to enforce his words.

Ordinarily, Harvey would have insisted that the threat of a drawn firearm was a matter for the police. But he'd been around the city long enough to know that even if he did report the incident, there would be no follow-up because Chief Barnes was not going to step up to Clarence Williams or any of his thugs.

When they arrived at Clarence Williams's office, the councilman kept them waiting twenty minutes while James stood guard.

Back in the day, when Harvey was a teenager, such seizures were not uncommon. But for an elected member of the city council to accost citizens on the street was unthinkable. Who did Councilman Williams think he was?

"Well, James, what have we here?" Clarence said affably when he finally appeared.

"As you requested, sir," said James, saluting in military style.

"Mr. Davenport, Ms. Morrison, Mr. Matthews, so glad to see you this afternoon," Williams oozed. "Usually I listen to your mellifluous words of wisdom in city council meetings."

Harvey remained perfectly still, waiting to see what Williams would do.

"You folks down here stirring up trouble, I hear," Williams said with a sneer.

"That is none of your business," Johnson said. "But aren't your grandchildren being sickened by the industrial sludge and heavy smoke? I'm surprised you tolerate that."

"You boys stay outta here!" Williams shouted. "You've no business nosing around my ward!" He looked toward Alice. "You all stay on *your side* of the river, understand?"

"We were forced here at gunpoint," Paul said. "You know you're breaking the law, don't you?"

"Let 'em go, James," Williams said, raising his chin as if in defiance.

"Yes, sir, Mr. Williams," said James, opening the office door.

"Let this be fair warning. You stay out of the Bottoms, or things'll get quite a little livelier for all of you."

"Lovely as usual, Mr. Williams," said Paul Johnson.

The ambush we know is coming keeps us in line. Was that what Martha Ruggles meant? That connected to the destruction of Alice's roses. Perhaps this thought was premature, but he worried about providing security for volunteers as they canvassed the neighborhoods.

CHAPTER 7

FINDING ALLIES II

As his first step of carrying out the plan they'd devised, Harvey chose to freshen his acquaintance with the people of the Bottoms by attending a community workday scheduled for the following Saturday. The purpose of this event was to engage the friends and neighbors of Paula and Isaiah Jones in painting their entire two-story home, inside and out, in one day.

This was part of Renewal House's program of community development, a way to strengthen the spirit of amicability and mutual reliance among the people and overcome the isolation and fragmentation of the community.

People turned out in such droves that Harvey and Mina had to park several blocks away from the Jones's home.

"What a beautiful neighborhood!" Mina exclaimed as she took a few pictures.

As they walked along, they admired newly planted trees on the parkways and carefully tended lawns. Beautiful day lilies, hyacinths, and hollyhocks graced several front porches.

Paul had earlier explained that buying and refurbishing their house had been a struggle for the Joneses. When the Westfield National Bank refused them a mortgage, they turned to friends and their local credit union. They also rented out the upstairs to a young couple starting their own family. Soon after they'd moved in, an industrial accident caused by poor safety standards in the workplace disabled Isaiah. Thankfully, he was now back to work.

Meanwhile, Paula had had several bouts with breast cancer, plus migraine headaches and lesions on her spine. The doctors said these ailments resulted from chemicals in the water and soil. Since her condition limited her ability to work, the cost of medications depleted their savings. So, to make ends meet, Paula worked as a secretary for the elementary school a few days a week. In sum, the house painting project brought welcome relief.

Laughter and friendly greetings met them as they entered the Jones's backyard. People seemed to have a fun time. The men erected ladders and organized supplies while the women gathered in the side yard to discuss feeding sixty hungry workers two meals. The smell of fresh-ground coffee enticed the volunteers to sample breakfast goodies set on tables in the side yard—fresh fruit, homemade biscuits, muffins, pies, cakes, and cookies.

Harvey signed up for the prep and trim crew upstairs, and Mina joined the downstairs paint and roller crew. At 9:00 a.m., Paul Johnson, in jeans and a black T-shirt, gathered everyone.

"We're making history in the Bottoms today," he told them. "Helping a neighbor, helping a whole community—it's all part of our struggle for freedom." After a word of thanks from Paula and Isaiah, everyone began work.

Sixteen-year-old Peter Jacobs and Rachel Jackson, who looked twenty but was probably only seventeen, were Harvey's crew mates in prepping the master bedroom. Pete wore a bright red painter's cap over faded blue bib overalls. Rachel had come in jeans and a flowered shirt topped by an old striped railroad cap she said had been a present from her grandfather.

"What made you come here today?" Harvey asked Pete when they'd settled into their tasks.

"Probably same reason you did," Pete replied with a broad smile. "I want to help. The Joneses are longtime friends of my family. They've done a lot for me and my sister. Now it's payback time."

"Same here," Rachel chimed in. "Paula was my teacher in third grade. Best I ever had. We used to have long talks about things I didn't understand."

"What's it like living in the Bottoms these days?" he asked.

"Not much of a life," Rachel replied, wrinkling up her nose.

"Pretty much like slavery," the young man added, scrunching up his face.

"Any way to change that?"

"I like what Paul Johnson says, 'When we work together, we get more done.' He's helping us change these streets one house at a time," said Pete.

The two of them launched into a discussion of ways to change a neighborhood. Their teenage debate impressed him. They talked about cooperative finances, debt, and the recent history of the Bottoms.

An hour later, as they washed down the walls of the second bedroom, Rachel stopped working and looked at Harvey.

"Ever since I was little, I've wanted to learn everything possible. It's become my passion. I don't know why."

"Good passion to have," Harvey said, trying to reassure her.

"The thing is it's hard to learn here."

"What do you mean?" he prompted.

"We have these old raggedy textbooks at school. A lot of what they say isn't true, and I don't know what to believe. The elementary school has a library, and I've read the history, geography, and science sections. But I still have lots of questions."

"Have you tried the public library?"

"My mom works and can't take me, and now there's no bus service."

"What will you do with your knowledge?" he asked.

"Be a doctor. I want to work here in the Bottoms. I want to help people have a better life."

"Can you go to Westfield High School?"

She looked down, shook her head. "Can't get there. Besides, I've heard the white kids make fun of us. I couldn't learn much in a place like that."

The look on Rachel's face melted his heart.

"The white kids make fun of our skin," said Peter. "It's all blotchy." He pulled up the sleeves of his shirt to show numerous sores and scabs. "You see these? A lot of kids around here have 'em, and they get infected. There's poison in the ground. When you're little, you play in the dirt. When you're older, you play ball in the vacant lots. Grown-ups work in their yards or gardens."

"We get colds easily too," Rachel added. "A lot of kids have asthma."

Pete chuckled. "You know … last spring I spent more time going to funerals than I did in school. People are dying so young now. It's cancer or TB or heart attacks."

"There's a good side though," Rachel said. "Sometimes, after a large release of chemicals, they'll send a man around offering fifty dollars to anyone who'll sign a letter saying they have no complaint against the company."

Before he could respond, the lunch bell—an antique school bell mounted on a table in the backyard—interrupted them.

At lunch, Harvey spotted the attorney Charles Higgins and went to sit next to him at one of the long tables set up in the side yard.

"Come on, join us!" Higgins exclaimed. "Plenty of room here." He had a smooth, mellow voice, kindly frank eyes, and a dimple on his chin. He wore a light blue shirt with sleeves rolled to the elbows as he introduced his wife, Sara, and their two teenage children, Hassan and Sybil. Sara looked very professional in a black chemise accented by an amber pin and red scarf.

Just then, Mina came along with a fully loaded plate. When Harvey introduced her to the Higginses, she sat opposite Hassan and Sybil. Within minutes, the three had bonded, and Harvey spotted a camera around Hassan's neck.

"Taking a few pictures?" he asked the young man.

"Good place to get candid shots, sir," Hassan replied. "I've already got a half dozen real sweet ones."

"Keep at it," he said. "You'll soon be a magazine photographer."

Through reading an article in the *Westfield Independent*, he learned that Charles and Sara were well-educated, wealthy business people. Reaching middle age, unable to have children of their own, they'd adopted Hassan and Sybil as infants. Their decision had created substantial controversy.

"I'm interested to learn why you decided to live in the Bottoms," he said.

"We were bluebloods," Sara replied with a laugh. "Brought up in wealth, taught to seek and appreciate it. We had the breaks we needed to be successful as a lawyer and an entrepreneur—a good education, fabulously supportive parents, and friends."

"We live here in the Bottoms," said Charles, "because we want to make a statement that people here are the same as people everywhere. We haven't changed our professional lives. I work in the Carruthers Plaza Building as always. Sara's businesses are growing."

"But our personal lives changed drastically," said Sara. "The water here is unfit to drink; it has so much chemical waste in it. We've had to refurbish our house with absolutely airtight windows to keep out the pollution. The streets are falling apart, and we have vacant lots and old, dilapidated houses everywhere. We live amid poverty, yet we're reasonably well off."

"Things are starting to change though," said Charles. "More people are fixing up and caring for their homes. We're learning to help each other."

Following their conversation, after they'd finished eating, Harvey walked away with a lighter step. Here were pioneers whose experience and judgment were tested and who might be willing to assist his work in Westfield.

After that, he spent the afternoon with camera in hand, shooting pictures as the volunteers continued their work. Like a dog sniffing its way through field and forest, he shot whatever took his fancy. Over the next two hours, he shot the equipment, the colors, the food, the people.

One of his more intriguing shots was of seventy-year-old daredevil, Herb Martin, perched high atop a twenty-foot ladder. With a gallon of paint in one hand and a loaded brush in the other, he stretched far out to his left to paint wood siding.

"Hello, Mr. Davenport," a voice surprised him from behind.

When he turned, he saw a young man in brown chinos and a navy T-shirt holding an ancient Brownie camera.

"My name's Derek Robinson," the young fellow said. "Paul Johnson said you're a photographer. Do you mind if I hang around and pick up some pointers?"

"Always glad for a little company," he replied.

For the next two hours, he discovered Derek had a penchant for shooting anything having to do with pollution. The young man had the same model of Brownie Hawkeye he'd had as a youngster when he'd had his adventure by bus with Sam from Chicago. By the end of the afternoon, they'd become fast friends.

Around six thirty, Harvey joined the Joneses and a few friends in their newly painted living room for supper and relaxation. Walking through the immaculate living and dining rooms, he was mightily impressed with the community's efforts. Isaiah and Paula had big smiles on their faces. A project that had taken years was finally completed, the result of tremendous hard work and sacrifice.

"It surpasses my fondest expectations," said Isaiah.

"It's our very own castle!" Paula declared. "How great to have such a friendly, warm safety net around our family. Never thought it could feel so good."

Harvey had to agree.

"Any of you night owls interested in a hand of poker?" Isaiah asked.

Within seconds, he had four takers—Lonnie, Bobby, Justin, and Clem.

Isaiah rose and walked to a corner of the dining room where he'd stashed a fold-up poker table behind a handsome wooden hutch.

Then he motioned for Lonnie and Justin to lend a hand with the chairs. Finally, just for peace of mind, Isaiah closed the side windows in the living room, which had been opened to ventilate the paint fumes. The six players took their seats, cut a deck of cards, and began the game.

How pleasant it was to spend a peaceful evening relaxing with new friends after a day of hard work. Reflecting on the day's conversations renewed his confidence in his ability to accomplish what he'd set out to do.

By nine o'clock, Bobby Nelson was in hock, tired and disgusted. "I'm goin' home, you guys. This just isn't my night."

"Stay with us, man!" Isaiah coaxed him. "We won't be so hard on you. Your luck will change. You wait and see."

Justin Morris said nothing. On the edge of his seat, he drummed his fingers on the table and bounced around on his chair. His corner of the table had the most chips.

"What'd you put in these cards, Isaiah?" Harvey asked. "Must have been some pretty powerful mojo. You sure this deck is regulation?"

"Right as rain," Isaiah replied.

"Speaking of rain," said Lonnie, "was that thunder I just heard?"

"Some kind of boom," said Justin. "It's coming faster now. Can you hear?"

"Also louder and more distinct," said Harvey. Both sides of the house reverberated like drums but with no lightning.

"What're you guys doin' in there!" Paula yelled from the kitchen. "Can't you just be quiet and play like nice fellows?"

"Something's hitting both sides of the house!" Isaiah exclaimed.

Rising quickly from his seat, Harvey moved to the dining room window. Gingerly, he parted the drapes just enough to see through the late-evening dusk. Yellow splotches covering the window made it difficult to see. A figure dressed in camouflage, wearing a black antifog mask, was shooting projectiles loaded with paint that burst when they hit the house.

"The house is being paintballed!" he cried. He dreaded having to confront something like that at this hour.

Isaiah and Bobby headed for the front door. Flinging it open, they encountered a fellow aiming an automatic rifle at the front porch. Isaiah hit the deck to the right. Bobby started to run to the left across the porch, but a half dozen projectiles nailed him. He stumbled and fell.

Leaning out the front door, Harvey froze in terror for three heartbeats. Then the firing stopped. Three attackers jumped the front fence and fled to a waiting vehicle, slipped inside, and slammed the doors. In the gloom, what looked like a pickup truck began to move, but he heard no noise other than a jet engine overhead. He bolted forward across the porch, slipped and slid down the soppy front stairs, then ran down the sidewalk trying to get a better look at the truck—maybe the license plate. *Dear God, let me get something on these idiots!*

As the truck gained speed, one of the paintballers fired a gunshot, bringing him facedown on the sidewalk. The pain in his right leg radiated throughout his body. The shattering of glass told him a second shot had hit the house's picture window. Somewhere in the distance, a voice talked to 911.

His face felt like it had been in a fight with a sanding machine. Hands tried to help him stand, but the pain was excruciating, so they sat him upright on the sidewalk.

"Where're you hurt, man?" Bobby murmured, still trying to catch his breath.

"Hit me in the right leg," he gasped.

"Help's on the way!" cried Isaiah, wiping his hands on his pants. "We hope."

"What the hell happened?" Harvey croaked when he'd been helped to sit up on the sidewalk.

"Those guys unloaded a river of paint on Isaiah's house!" Bobby shouted.

"Didn't they know how to use a paintbrush?" Harvey asked, feeling a rush of delirium creeping in behind the brave front of his smile.

"Should I call the police?" Lonnie asked.

"Hang onto that for a bit," cautioned Isaiah. "Let's talk first. I'll be there, soon as we get Harvey into an ambulance. Call Mina and let her know he's wounded. Call Paul Johnson too."

When Johnson arrived, he took one look and scratched his head. "Let's think carefully before we call the police, my friends. The wrong move could make us more trouble. Looks to me like someone at city hall was in on this."

Heads nodded.

"Let's call our friend Charles Higgins. He'll tell us who's our best bet in the police department."

As he lay in the ambulance on the way to Westfield Memorial, Harvey ruminated on the attack. Was it retribution for having a community workday, or was it punishment for his having participated? Either way, he concluded, the price of revenge was ramping up. Nevertheless, he now had a strategy and some allies. It was time to get to work.

By the following Tuesday, Harvey had devoured newspaper articles on scientific evidence linking diseases like cancers and leukemia to industrial waste. His research, plus Charles Higgins's summary of the steps for filing legal claims, had alerted him to the need for accurate, current data, which piqued his interest in monitoring devices.

As a result, he accompanied Alice Morrison, Sara Higgins, and Stan Matthews to a statewide training session on monitoring air quality in an urban setting. On their way out of town, they picked up Isaiah Jones and Melissa Gravely, pastor of the Westfield United Methodist Church.

Forty-three volunteers from communities across the state attended the training sessions, which were held in the ballroom of a downtown hotel in the capital. The state's Department of Environmental Quality sponsored the event.

Their room featured a carpet with a multicolored roseate pattern. They sat on traditional hard, stackable conference chairs. Their windows overlooked the state legislative building with its portentous classical Greek columns.

Trainers included engineers who explained the technical details and experienced community organizers who coached them on recruiting and motivating local project workers.

At break times, they enjoyed sharing experiences and common problems. Surprisingly, they learned that the movement against industrial pollution had gained strength in numbers and in greater social recognition in the early decades of the twenty-first century. The prospect of broader social support energized them.

By the end of the morning session, their heads swam with technical details. Monitoring air quality was more difficult than they'd imagined. The monitoring equipment required precise adjustments for the many types of gases and particles they would measure. Sensors had to be cleaned frequently, attached securely, and located in areas where pollution would reach them. They learned how to fasten the devices to light poles, porch posts, fences, and other improbable locations. Sampling air quality was not a simple task.

"Not sure I'm ready for this," Isaiah complained as they ate lunch together in the hotel dining room.

"We're in over our heads!" Sara exclaimed. "We need a technical advisor."

"All we need is a little practice," Stan replied with a mollifying voice. He had been one of the fortunate few able to examine a sensor thoroughly. "I played around with it for a while and learned how the adjustments work. It's really pretty simple."

"I think we've got a real fundraising job ahead," Melissa announced. "They call them low-cost but these things aren't cheap, and we might need as many as a dozen of them."

"Where should we place them?" Sara asked.

Everyone had suggestions.

The coaches for the afternoon session were a different sort than the engineers. Their focus was people—their hopes and fears and their urgent need to obtain relief from the toxins surrounding them.

They suggested making a list of reliable people who might keep odor logs that matched pollution incidents with how people felt during and after each waste emission. The coaches also gave instruction on how to approach people, easing their fears and motivating them to participate.

The trainers then gave the group time to start those lists of prospects. During this period, the Westfield group identified twelve people south of the river and another dozen prospects on the north side.

On the trip back to Westfield, they talked excitedly about discovering for the first time the measurable amounts of toxins in the air around them. Rumors of a connection between pollution and sickness were one thing. Facts from data collected were more substantive, harder to ignore.

Back in his studio, Harvey ordered nine sensors from the manufacturer. Melissa had been right; the devices cost a thousand dollars each. Sooner or later, they'd have to do some fundraising. In the meantime, however, the ability to take this leap ahead in his plan made it worthwhile for him to pay for this initial investment himself.

When the devices arrived a few days later, Harvey reconvened his team in the new community center of the Bethel AME Church. Once again, excitement filled the air as Isaiah and Melissa spent the first hour opening the boxes and assembling the sensors on one of the conference center's brown collapsible tables. Harvey had brought tools for assembling the devices. Then Sara instructed them in how to install them, handing out sheets of instructions for attaching and recalibrating them. For each sensor, there was a USB device to plug into a computer for receiving data. That meant each location had to have a computer associated with it. In a matter of minutes, they'd almost become experts.

Meanwhile, Harvey and Mina made a list of the places and people, both north and south of the river, who would help with installation. They established five locations in the Bottoms, four to the south.

After an hour, Rev. Ben Booker, in black shirt and clerical collar, stuck his head in the door to introduce himself as Bethel's pastor and welcome them. He became so fascinated with the sensors that he took one and put it up in the church's bell tower. This was an ideal location to catch anything industry might throw at them.

Felix Vogel, photojournalist for the *Independent*, arrived just in time with a laptop in his backpack. They set it up in the conference room to test Ben's newly placed sensor. When everything worked to their satisfaction, a cheer arose as they celebrated progress.

In response to phone calls, Paul Johnson and Stan Matthews arrived to help with installation. Paul took a sensor for mounting on Renewal House, and Stan agreed to install one atop his brother's furniture store. Rev. Nate Kline from the Assembly of God Church picked up one for his building. Even Martha Ruggles claimed a sensor for the senior center, where she knew the building supervisor would help her. Melissa and Sara instructed each of the installers until they were proficient in all aspects of caring for the devices.

"I'll get some folks to help me with this," Martha said with a furrowed brow. "There's a lot of detail here, and my memory's not what it used to be."

Once again, before they left the community center, Melissa Gravenly brought up the issue of fundraising. "We've got to get ourselves together on this," she cautioned. "Harvey's been generous, but he can't foot the whole bill by himself. Our church board has pledged ten thousand dollars. Nate and Ben, would you ask your people to help?"

"Gotcha covered on that," Ben answered. "We'll do five thousand."

"I'll ask my congregation," said Nate, with obvious hesitation. "I'm sure they'll do something. My folks aren't that wealthy, but my guess is we could raise twenty-five hundred."

Another cheer arose from the group.

Two days later, when the eighteen pollution sensors had been installed, Harvey and Sara Higgins started another new project, to recruit fifty individuals in the Bottoms to keep what the experts called an "odor log." Sara selected five volunteers from among her friends and relatives. She started with Rachel Jefferson, then added Amy Cunningham and Rev. Melissa Gravenly. Betsy Rawlings and Paula Jones also volunteered. Thus she had three adults and three teenagers as volunteers.

She met with them in the Bethel Church Community Center parlor. Harvey brought needed materials. Mina handed out bright yellow T-shirts that had WCEQ on the front for Westfield Citizens for Environmental Quality.

After some instruction and a question and answer session, it was time to practice on real prospects. An adult went with each teenager to supervise. Upon exiting the church, Sara and Amy went to Monroe Street, Paula and Betsy worked up and down Madison Boulevard, while Melissa and Rachel took Catalpa Avenue. Since Harvey's gunshot wound was healing well, he tagged along to observe and keep a lookout for Clarence's bunch.

When the teams had each completed three interviews, they regrouped back at the community center for a question and answer session. Remarkably, everyone seemed to feel at ease with interviewing. Two of the teams had snagged new odor log volunteers on the first try. Next, the pairs split up, putting six volunteers to work canvassing the neighborhood.

As he stood on the corner of Monroe and Catalpa Streets observing traffic, however, Harvey noticed a red '68 Dodge Charger with two men, massive chrome, and loud exhaust manifolds cruising through the area several times. He could hear shouts down the block on Monroe Street, so when Sara and Amy returned, he asked if they'd heard anything from the Dodge.

"They said the rudest things!" Sara exclaimed. "But we just ignored them. Thank goodness they didn't stop. But if they had, I was ready." She patted the pocket of her skirt meaningfully.

He didn't ask what she meant—didn't want to know. But Sara was a savvy gal who knew how to fend off danger. Still, the incident suggested that his fellow Councilman Clarence was still observing their work. What that might lead to, he could only guess.

It had been a rewarding week. He'd made some new friends, received beneficial advice, and set out workable strategies, which he'd begun pursuing. What he needed now was more help with the mountain of work that faced him.

When workers off-loaded heavy equipment at the waste disposal construction site in the first week of May, popular sentiment held that the speeding freight train of enterprise was once again on track to overpower the people of the Bottoms.

He fervently hoped that this Saturday's community gathering, six weeks later, would agree to a mass mobilization to focus public attention on the disease, suffering, and death that were bound to happen when that facility was operating.

Arriving early on this balmy mid-June evening, Harvey recognized the man with the clerical collar setting up chairs at the back of the sanctuary as Pastor Benjamin Booker.

"Need help?" he asked.

"Oh, you are a saint, Mr. Davenport!" exclaimed the pastor. "Thank you!"

As they worked, Booker recounted Bethel's history and philosophy. He described the church founder, Jeremiah Hartshorne, as a free black man, educated in Boston, who came to the Midwest in the 1850s by means of a network of people seeking a strong spiritual leader with a powerful message of freedom.

"He was a dynamic speaker," said Booker. "He told people to be free and help each other on their journey. He also had a passion for hymns that encouraged thoughts of freedom."

"Sounds like he had to be smuggled in," Harvey commented with a dour expression.

"As a matter of fact," said Booker, nodding his head, "he *was* brought here under cover of darkness. He wasn't the kind of person whites tolerated easily, and throughout his ministry, he was in and out of trouble with the establishment."

Booker went on to describe Hartshorne's view that there were three types of faith. Anesthetic faith removed people from an intolerably painful existence. Imitative faith gave people the illusion they could be like whites, with the trappings of high society. Revolutionary faith helped people cope with life by inventing creative ways to be free.

"Our people at Bethel, of course, espouse the third type," Ben concluded with a smile as he bowed his head.

"What does that mean for the people?" Harvey asked.

"It's like working in a diamond mine for most of your life, then finding out you're the owner of the mine," Ben replied, opening his arms wide. "We generate new ideas for being free and living as equals. We challenge our people to innovate in every aspect of life."

In the sanctuary, Harvey found a peaceful haven of grace and mystery. At the front, behind the communion table with its fresh flowers, hung a huge, rough, hand-hewn cross wrapped with shackles from the days of slavery. Four windows festooned each side of the sanctuary. The brilliant colors of hand-painted stained glass depicted inspiring biblical scenes, while the lower panels revealed elements of contemporary life.

"Those windows were handmade by our members," said Booker. "Free artisans contributed their work." He then turned and pointed to the multiple rows of framed photographs mounted on the rear wall. "Those pictures show the leaders and events of the church's history."

Rev. Booker ushered him out onto the front sidewalk, then turned around, looked up, and pointed to the steeple. "That's the original bell," he said. "Hartshorne named it *Eleftherias*. It means the bell of freedom. This church has burned to the ground twice, and each time the people rebuilt it themselves, always careful to replace that sacred instrument in the belfry."

Booker impressed Harvey as an erudite, well-spoken preacher, with a humble demeanor, who used common words. Had he been religious, Harvey might well have joined a church led by such a man.

By seven o'clock, the sanctuary was full to bursting with neighborhood folks ready to participate in the discussion. Rev. Booker appeared from a door at the front of the sanctuary, stepped to the middle of the dais, and called the meeting to order.

"Many weeks ago, my friends, the city council voted to construct a waste disposal facility in the old industrial park. That means another century of increased pollution of our air, water, and soil. Construction started early last month. Paul Johnson and I immediately requested interviews with the mayor and the city manager. But they said we'd had two chances to give our input; now they're moving ahead. This meeting is your opportunity to tell us what you want to do in response."

A young man in the center of the crowd stood, waving his hand.

"Go ahead, Justin Morris," Booker said.

"A year ago, sir, I attended both public sessions. Lots of us spoke against the project. Are they just deliberately ignoring us?"

"We're no more than waste people to them!" a woman called out from the middle of the crowd.

"We have three city council members with us tonight," said Booker. "Alice Morrison, Stan Matthews, and Harvey Davenport. Let's hear what they have to say."

When they'd made their way to the front, Alice was first to speak. She looked quite fashionable in her yellow suit and red shoes.

"For two years, I witnessed the WDP being planned for the Bottoms. It wasn't an accident. We're up against business people who dislike taxes and a tradition of poisoning this neighborhood with industrial waste."

"I was shocked!" Harvey admitted. "The project was not on our agenda that evening. The city manager slipped it in just as the meeting started, saying it was a last-minute gift that had clinched the deal. I spoke against the request, so did Alice and Stan."

"In the end, they outvoted us," said Stan, frowning through his mustache and goatee. "We're ready to join you in a public protest if that's what you decide to do."

Booker recognized a tall man in his eighties. "Yes, Clem Sanders, what's on your mind?"

"I say the only way to get this thing out is to blow 'er up!"

"We need to make a big stink about this!" said a short man in a green shirt near the front. "Need to get the media involved. Get ourselves on TV."

Midway to the back, Isaiah Jones, whose house Harvey had helped paint, said, "I agree we should blow the damned thing up, burn it down. Tell city hall we won't stand for being dumped on anymore."

"These white folks are always so arrogant," said an older man in a railroad cap and bib overalls. "Gets on my nerves. Are we too afraid to come up against 'em?"

"We're not afraid, Sammy," said a voice in the third row. "We 'bide by what the Bible says, 'Vengeance is mine, saith the Lord.'"

The crowd seemed full of anger yet incapable of making a decision. He began to suspect focusing on collective action might be too much for such a large group. Consequently, doubts about Paul's appetite for involving the people crept into his mind, dampening his hopes for success.

With a flutter of activity at the back, someone helped an old lady to her feet. Martha Ruggles shuffled down the aisle and turned at the front. He'd have known that ancient, deeply furrowed visage anywhere.

"We're like the people of Israel," she said in her preacher's voice. "We begged and pleaded with Pharaoh, but ole Pharaoh said no. People in power are stealin' away our rights and our lives. They think black folk aren't worth a damn!"

"Remember, brothers and sisters," a voice in the middle of the sanctuary interrupted her. "We let them do it to us. We been too patient. Now we're hurtin' bad. We gotta stop being patient."

"But some whites," Ms. Ruggles continued, "are with us tonight." She gestured to the three city council members. "We are not alone. We are not helpless!"

Clapping hands and cheers greeted her. Many shouted, "Hallelujah!" or "Preach it!"

"Now is the time to take the first steps to free ourselves of pollution, disease, and death. Time to say *no* to Pharaoh and the WDP!" Martha ended with a shout.

Paul Johnson, shifting a toothpick from one side of his mouth to the other, rose to stand beside Martha, and the people became quiet.

"I take it by your response to Martha's words that you think we should make a nonviolent, public demonstration against the WDP," he concluded with a broad smile.

The room exploded in affirmation, shouting, "Yes! Yes!"

When the elation had run its course, Rev. Booker led the people in electing a leader of the demonstration and a planning committee.

While that work went on, there was a commotion in the back of the room. Clarence Williams entered the sanctuary, and Harvey caught Alice's attention and raised an eyebrow. No doubt Dwyer would soon hear of tonight's decision.

Just then, Rev. Booker stood to recognize Rev. Melissa Gravenly, pastor of First United Methodist Church, and Rev. Nate Kline, pastor of the Assemblies of God. "Come forward, my fellow pastors," Booker called to them. "Let us hear your words of encouragement."

Melissa Gravenly stood tall in brown slacks and blue shirt with a clerical collar underneath her shoulder-length black hair. She had a reputation for encouraging her congregation to support minorities and the poor. Nate Kline was shorter, rotund but not fat, with a full beard. He and his congregation were more moved by relationships than politics, so Nate had made an effort to bring them closer to their sister churches in the Bottoms.

"Nate and I are here," said Rev. Gravenly, standing in the side aisle, "to let you know you have a ton of support behind you south of the river. We're ready to work with you to remove the WDP."

For a moment, there was unexpected silence. Did she mean what she'd just said? Then suddenly, everyone came alive with applause.

"We join with you in solidarity to bring your desires and your efforts to full fruit," said Rev. Kline.

Once again, the people rose in celebration. When calm was restored, Rev. Booker announced the four steering committee members to strong applause. "Furthermore," he announced, "you have overwhelmingly elected Martha Ruggles as our leader and spokesperson!"

After several moments of enthusiastic cheering and clapping, Booker said, "Ms. Ruggles, please bring the meeting to a close."

Martha rose, tears streaming down her ancient face, wrinkled by years of struggle for her people's freedom. "My brothers, my sisters, thank you for your trust and affirmation. Let us sing 'We Shall Overcome.'"

Ben led the congregation in four verses of the famed anthem of the civil rights movement, then pronounced the benediction.

Once again, the courageous little white church with its ancient bell had birthed a freedom revolution. Of course, there would be no revolution if the media failed to do its job of publicizing and commenting on their demonstration, or if those who held power refused to budge. The lack of a surefire way to force change for the people's benefit nettled him. But they'd know in a week whether it was revolution or dissolution.

CHAPTER 8

PUBLIC ACTION I

At seven thirty on a cloudless Thursday morning toward the end of June, Mike Dwyer sat at his desk on the sixth floor of Westfield National Bank. From the corner windows of his presidential suite, all of Westfield lay before him. Pedestrians and cars moving along the streets looked like miniature figures in a silent movie. Without the noise of humanity, life seemed so much more tractable, even pleasant.

He had just risen to swipe a forefinger across the top of the frame around Picasso's *Women of Algiers* when Dana Schecter, his secretary, breezed in, delivered papers to his in-box, and scampered out leaving a slight but distinct trace of a scent he didn't recognize. Something new perhaps? One never knew with Dana.

A phone call from his city clerk advised him that the parade permit for Saturday's demonstration had been picked up by Renewal House staff. He immediately dialed Stan Davies, one of his most reliable runners.

"Could you arrange a little incident for us at Saturday's event?"

"Glad to oblige," Davies replied. "What degree of impact did you have in mind?"

"Swanson's getting the nod from Barnes, but he's scared. Put enough sting in it to make him want to clear the streets."

"Sure, we'll give him a kick in the pants," Davies replied.

"If you use Kravitz, tell him if he has a shot at Davenport, now's a good time to do it."

"Gotcha covered."

"Thanks," he said and hung up.

Half an hour later, he walked to city hall to attend Police Chief Ronald Barnes's briefing of his executive officers. Barnes was one of the few blacks who had grown up in Westfield and had economic mobility, thanks to his grandmother, who sent him to college and the police academy. Just one of the ten thousand scholarship loans the bank had made over the years.

He and the chief had planned this event in exhaustive detail. Barnes had chosen his top officers with great care because discretion prevented incidents—the one thing Mike hated with a passion. The police presence would be widely scattered along the demonstration route, but the heaviest concentration of men, weapons, tear gas, and tanks would be at the construction site. How the officers received their instructions held great importance for him.

"Keep a lid on things," Barnes cautioned his team. "No rash decisions. Before you give orders, have a backup plan. And a backup for that too, if possible. I'll expect detailed reports when this is over."

"Yes, sir," the team affirmed, many nodding their heads.

"Please." Barnes paused for emphasis with his right index finger in the air as he made eye contact with each officer. "Take it easy on the people. They have a right to redress their grievances. Here's a chance to prove yourselves under stress."

"We'll do our best, sir," Captain Brent Swanson said on behalf of his colleagues.

"Thank you, Brent. And I want to be certain you, sir, understand that this is not a military operation. It is a civilian police action. It calls for flexibility and a firm hand, *not* bravado and recklessness. Understand?"

"I understand, sir," Swanson replied. "No rough stuff."

Despite the chief's thorough instruction, on the slight chance an incident might occur, Mike had suggested Barnes order up all the department's heavy, military-style equipment for transport to the construction site. He wanted to provide the officers with absolute control. After all, the feds had paid for it as a reward for an upsurge of drug busts. Why not use it?

When he was satisfied with the arrangements, he returned to his office to review mortgage loan applications.

Harvey woke up early the next Saturday morning as the Mongolian chimes rang on his second-floor balcony. The west wind was up, and the day was forecast to be warm. As the sky turned from purple to yellow-orange, he showered and dressed, then walked to the Busy Bee.

As a local decision maker, his role in the demonstration against the WDP would be to advocate for justice for all the people of Westfield. If that put him in the crosshairs of those eager to use city policy for their own purposes, so be it.

At nine thirty, in high spirits, having enjoyed a hearty breakfast and animated conversation with Alice, Stan, Felix, and Mina at the Busy Bee, he joined a growing stream of expectant people headed toward city hall.

Haze and smoke from the factories lay over the Bottoms, just beneath the morning breeze. He'd read one of Felix Vogel's articles in the *Independent* the previous week, saying that the people living there had more respiratory diseases and cancers than those living south of the river. Not exactly news, but he was grateful for the well-timed publicity.

Seeing two of the block captains from his ward, Herb and Mary Cornell, he hurried to catch up with them and chat a bit. Upon spotting Isaiah and Paula Jones debarking from the Renewal House bus, he introduced them to the Cornells, hoping they'd chat about the previous month's paintball disaster.

Seeing the vast numbers of people coming in for the demonstration calmed his stomach and gave him more hope for success. To his surprise, Doug Thompson, councilman from the Fourth Ward, caught up and walked with him for a while.

"What's up?" Harvey asked. "It's great that you're here, but I didn't expect to see you."

"Ever since Martha Ruggles's outburst in council meeting, I've lamented my vote," said Doug. "She's right, and I want to help."

"Great news!" exclaimed Harvey. "Thanks for letting us know. We need your voice."

By eleven, a crowd had gathered on the lawn in front of city hall, overflowing onto Bridge Street. Demonstrators queueing for the march also filled the side streets. A forest of picket signs paraded in the air—"WDP is not for me," "Out of the Bottoms, WDP!"

As microphones were set up and tested, Paul Johnson sidled up to him. "Can you speak a few words at the press conference? Let the media hear about your motivation for the march."

"Glad to do it," Harvey replied.

Martha Ruggles opened the affair with a short homily reminding her audience that this public protest was "only one step on a long and difficult journey to freedom." She then introduced Alice, who wore a yellow sleeveless top and navy blue pants. "It's time Westfield stepped into the twenty-first century respecting the rights of all citizens," she told the crowd. "Let's put the WDP in a place where no one is harmed."

Enthusiastic applause and cheers issued from her audience.

Stan stepped to the mic, then wiped a hand down across his mustache and stroked his goatee. "I believe the people of the Bottoms should be free to live as they see fit, without pollution from industry or the city."

Harvey now stepped to the microphone. "As many of you know, corporate leaders are planning a future for the Bottoms that doesn't include minorities or the poor and elderly. They want to redevelop the area and turn it into profit. For them, the WDP won't be a nuisance. But for all the rest of us, we'll continue to suffer the effects of pollution for many decades. That's why we're marching this morning."

"Too much profit, not enough sense!" someone shouted.

"People before profit!" another voice called out.

The march began, then, with Johnson, Ruggles, and Booker plus a half dozen ministers from both white and black churches walking behind a huge, multicolored banner that proclaimed, "Remove the WDP!"

Next came Harvey, Alice, Stan Matthews, and Doug Thompson representing city council. Mayor Timmerling was noticeably absent. Behind them marched a contingent of thirty young people wearing bright yellow T-shirts with Westfield Citizens for Environmental Quality printed in black on front and back.

Banner and marchers moved to the center of Bridge Street, then turned north, proceeding toward the Arthur T. Macawber Memorial Bridge. Many carried picket signs with slogans such as "Nobody Asked Us," "Unfair to Blacks and Browns," "City Hall Unfair to People of Color."

Once across the Macawber Bridge, the marchers advanced to the Belle Riviere Industrial Park. The line extended a mile back into downtown.

Inside the industrial park, a counterdemonstration of some forty or fifty people snaked around the park, strung out like ants through the jobbers, crafters, and manufacturing firms. The Belle Riviere marquee announced this was a promotion backing the WDP headed by Norm Taylor of the chamber of commerce. Police officers kept the two groups apart with cones and barricades. Several top brass from the police department met the Renewal House staff to inform them of the situation.

Paul Johnson spoke to the marchers through a bullhorn. "Please, everyone, avoid the counterdemonstrators and follow the marked lanes until we've crossed the street to the elementary school."

Wizened patriarch Clem Sanders then borrowed the bullhorn to advise the crowd. "This is an insult to our community," he shouted. "Just like ten years ago, when this industrial park was built. Are we going to let that happen again with the WDP? Or are we determined to stop it?"

Clem received hearty and appreciative applause as the demonstrators moved west toward the construction site.

As the demonstrators advanced beyond the elementary school, Robert Kravitz exited an old, bleached-out gray Chevy Malibu driven by Stan Davies at the back of the federal housing project.

He'd made himself up as a haggard-looking, weather-beaten old man with dark skin, dressed in a dirty gray, raggedy sport coat and faded blue jeans. Ancient tennis shoes and a washed-out baseball cap from which sprouted tufts of disorderly white hair completed the ensemble. In one hand, he carried a cloth grocery bag loaded with unwashed laundry packed around a fiberglass case. He hadn't shaved in a week, and he smelled. Just another homeless bum trudging along the streets of the Bottoms looking for a handout.

He entered the shabbiest building by the side door, then climbed five flights of stairs. No one had lived on the sixth floor for years. He walked down the hall, turned left, and stopped at the third door on the right, apartment 613, then let himself into the vacant apartment.

As arranged, the living room window was open about ten inches—no blinds, no screen. He had an unimpeded view of the construction site's main gate.

He removed the smelly laundry and piled it next to a wall. Then he extracted a collapsible tripod, which he set up six feet behind the window. Next he removed the case containing his disassembled rifle. With unerring precision, he assembled the gun, opened the chamber, slipped in a single cartridge. Finally, he affixed the rifle clamp to the tripod, then slid the gun into place with an affirmative click. Looking through the telescopic sight, he focused on the guard standing by the gate.

Perfect. He relaxed on the stained, gray-carpeted floor with a paperback novel to await action.

As the front ranks of the march rounded the corner of First Street, Harvey discovered Swanson had transported his officers to the site hours earlier. They stood every ten feet up and down First Street, Faurot Avenue, and Douglass Street as the demonstrators streamed first to the main gate, then encircled the five-acre construction site, remaining on the sidewalk at all times, shouting epithets about the WDP.

With face masks lifted and body shields in front of them, the police seemed nervous. Many fingered their batons and checked weapons and radio equipment.

People in the housing project across First Street resented the police for their frequent intrusions in search of drugs. A few residents hurled insults out their windows. Someone threw a pop bottle into a street corner cluster of officers, spraying glass shards that injured one man. Volunteers soon cleaned up the mess with brooms and a shovel. Paramedics tended the officer.

Mattie and Mollie Watson, elderly unmarried sisters living across from the main gate, had opened their home as a media center and a place for tired protesters to rest and relax.

As he marched, a worm of fear crawled in his gut. The extent of police armament seemed vastly heavier than necessary. What made all this armament so dreadful and frightening was its purpose—to beat down a nonviolent attempt to bring relief to a suffering people. Why should the police fear the very people they were sworn to protect and defend?

He walked a block to confer with Johnson and Booker.

"What'll we do if Swanson uses all this hardware?" he asked.

"Same thing we learned in school as kids," said Johnson with a smile, throwing his hands up and crossing them over his head. "Duck and cover."

Three horse vans turned from River Road onto First Avenue. "Here come the Mounties," Ben Booker said with a note of worry in his voice.

The fifteen mounted officers rode huge chestnut Thoroughbreds and carried pistols, chains, and whips. Shotguns were nestled in scabbards hung from saddles.

Johnson directed the marchers to gather for an assembly at the media tent in front of the main construction gate. As Johnson called the crowd to order, most of those parading around the construction site sat down on the sidewalk for a much-needed rest. A small contingent remained circling, brandishing signs and singing sixties freedom songs.

When Paul introduced Martha Ruggles, the crowd welcomed her with warm and extended applause and cheers. She was a queen in a voluminous multicolored African caftan.

"My friends," Martha began, "today we take the first steps to free ourselves from a new component of the sacrifice zone we call the Bottoms."

The excited crowd cheered and applauded.

"This whole neighborhood should never have been made into a sacrifice zone in the first place. It was a handout to business and industry, contrary to the laws of that day."

Several in the crowd called out, "Preach it!" and "Tell it like it is, sister!"

"Therefore," she continued, "we are protesting yet another source of pollution happening in our community—the Westfield Waste Disposal Project."

People pumped their picket signs and fists up and down.

"We're also protesting the failure of the city to place the WDP where it will be less invasive."

Hands up, she waited for the crowd to calm itself.

"We come here today to tell city hall and the corporations that *we don't want the WDP here and will not stand for it to be put here.*"

The crowd cheered wildly, and everyone stood.

Robert Kravitz aimed his rifle and confirmed Harvey Davenport was in the crosshairs. When the crowd erupted in response to the old black woman's last challenge, he took a deep, smooth breath, held it, then pulled the trigger. The rifle jumped a bit, but only a muted thud escaped the silencer.

He didn't have to look back; he knew he'd hit his target. He always did.

As Harvey stopped to confer with Paul Johnson, something stung his left shoulder, and a policeman to his left collapsed to the pavement.

He brushed his shoulder with his right hand, thinking he might have been stung by a bee. But his hand came away with blood running across his palm.

Within seconds, paramedics arrived to treat Harvey's wounded shoulder. Then they loaded him onto a gurney and headed for an ambulance that had backed up First Street almost to the media tent.

After several minutes, other EMTs wheeled the fallen patrolman to another nearby ambulance. The officer's shoulder had bled through his shirt, but he seemed to be conscious.

Meanwhile, the demonstration line reformed, and once more protesters marched around the construction site.

In less than half a minute, Kravitz broke down the rifle and tripod and slipped them into their case. Then he stowed the case in the bag's bottom and piled the dirty laundry on top.

Bag in hand, he crept to the door and opened it. Hearing nothing, he closed it from the outside, listening for the click of the lock. He turned left and went back the way he'd come, doddering like an old man on his way to the Laundromat for a lazy afternoon of suds and comics.

He walked through the alley to the street, then slid into the waiting Chevy Malibu. With a slow, deliberate motion, Stan Davies rolled the Chevy down the block, turned east on Monroe Street, and headed toward the Macawber Bridge. Neither man knew that Harvey Davenport was still very much alive.

Sitting up on his gurney outside the ambulance, Harvey had a good view of the street as the med techs cut away his shirt and swabbed his arm. When he looked up, Swanson stood in the middle of the street, facing south, talking on his communication device.

"Attention, all officers," barked the police loudspeaker atop the command post. "An officer has been shot and wounded. Everyone not wearing a police or emergency uniform must vacate the area immediately. Officers Miller and Hammond, report to my location now."

Face shields flipped down; body armor went up, batons at the ready. After a moment's consultation with Swanson, Miller and Hammond lined up officers on both sides of First Street along the six blocks from Monroe to Wilkerson. A water cannon moved up First Street spraying everything in its path. Walkers marching east from Faurot Avenue and Douglass Street came to First Street to confront chaos without knowing there had been a shooting. People were upended, blown over, soaked with powerful streams of water.

Swanson beckoned his cavalry as he spoke into his shortwave. "Mounted officers, clear Faurot, Douglass, and Wilkerson. Now!"

The horsemen rode five abreast in three columns up First Street following the water cannon. The first column peeled off at Douglas, then the second column tackled Faurot. The third column rode past the media tent up to Wilkerson. The officers charged into clusters of protesters, beating those who could not escape quickly enough, riding over those who fell or objected, trampling them with their horses' hooves. They gave the people no quarter. In minutes, the battered and broken bodies of screaming, crying people who had simply exercised their right to protest littered the streets.

Meanwhile, ambulance crews tended the wounded on First Street while paddy wagons stood by to transport those arrested in the scuffle that ensued. The water cannon mowed down more demonstrators coming along Wilkerson from the senior center. The people had been pushed into chaos by officers who controlled them with an iron hand.

Just as the paramedics discharged Harvey, Chief Barnes's black-and-white sped up First Street to Swanson's location with its lights flashing. Barnes leaped from the car, then ordered Swanson into the rear seat. "All officers, return to the command post for further instructions!" he shouted over the PA system.

Mike Dwyer received a call from Stan Davies a few minutes after noon.

"Success!" Davies said. "Kravitz stirred things up all right."

"What about Davenport?"

131

"Don't know yet. Nothing on police radio about a civilian death. I think an officer was wounded."

"Where'd you leave Kravitz?"

"Chevy to the junkyard, no ID, Kravitz on a bus out of town."

"Good man!" he affirmed.

"Always do my best," Davies said as Dwyer hung up.

Dammit! Couldn't Kravitz find Davenport, or had his aim been off? Either way, he'd still have to put up with the councilman's obfuscation.

Meanwhile, Harvey, whose wound had not been serious enough to require hospitalization, walked around behind the projects and into the Watson sisters' apartment by the back door to keep abreast of happenings on the street.

After a morning taking hundreds of photos of the demonstration, Felix in his camo and Mina in her black tights and top also sought refuge in the Watson sisters' apartment.

"Martha Ruggles just called," said Mattie Watson. "They're ransacking the senior center now. She got home and found her place torn apart. I guess the police thought someone hid out over there."

"Those white officers won't be gentle with the seniors," said Mollie.

"No one can keep track of 'em over there," said Felix. "No one supervising. Lots of winks and pats on the back from fellow officers."

The phone rang again. Mattie answered it. When she hung up, she said, "That was Mary Greensboro. She said the cops've got everybody on the upper four floors outside standing in the mud along Wilkerson."

"I've gotta go get this!" Felix exclaimed, picking up his camera bag, heading for the back door.

"I'll go with you," said Mina, jumping up to follow him. "Someone's got to look after you!"

As the two left the building, Harvey wanted to scream. The protest had barely begun before the police made a mess of it. The media would shout about the shooting and bury the demonstration.

The public would never notice the real issues, let alone absorb their meaning.

Late that afternoon, Harvey met with Mina, Felix, Stan, and Charles Higgins in Alice's apartment to watch the five o'clock news.

Alice had prepared a light buffet of shrimp canapés, sliced meats with mozzarella and cheddar, steamed veggies with olives, and cheesy biscuits.

"Strawberry shortcake for dessert," she said. "With ice cream."

As they ate in the living room, waiting for the news, conversation turned to the day's events.

"People certainly came out in force, didn't they?" said Stan Matthews. "We must have had a thousand marchers."

"What was that counterdemonstration all about?" asked Mina.

"Just the cult's need for recognition," said Charles, looking quite fashionable in his tan summer suit and brown shoes.

"The police were long on violence," Harvey commented. "I thought it destroyed much of the PR value."

"They certainly were primed for action," Higgins reflected. "I thought the shooter either played into their hands or was hired. It seemed fabricated to show off police power."

"The church people certainly showed up in great numbers," said Alice. "There's growing unrest in those congregations. People are paying attention."

She rose from her seat, then wheeled three television sets from the dining room into the living room. "Channels 5, 7, and 9, for your viewing pleasure," she said.

Stan and Felix chose Channel 5, Harvey and Mina chose Channel 7, while Alice and Charles took Channel 9. They moved their TV sets and chairs to three different corners of the room to watch. When the broadcasts finished, they discussed what they'd seen.

"Not much substance," Harvey ventured. "Looked to me like the media pretty much ignored the whole thing."

"Nine didn't report the event at all," said Alice. "I wonder now if the public will ever know about the WDP."

"Five said the police responded to a shooting that happened during a demonstration in the minority section of Westfield," said Stan. "Nothing about the demonstration."

"Seven had some good cuts of your speeches," Mina said.

"I had hoped the protest would make the public sympathetic to our cause," said Harvey. "But I doubt that happened."

"In today's world," said Higgins, waving his hand in dismissal, "protest demonstrations get little attention. Nobody cares. Everybody protests something."

For the rest of the evening, Martha's word "ambush" tormented his mind. *What keeps the people of the Bottoms in line*, she had said, *is the ambush we know will come.* But surely there must be some way to reach the hearts and minds of the public and move them to oppose such practices. If, that is, the public could be said to have a heart.

Two days after the public demonstration, at the regular city council meeting, the public gallery was filled to capacity. The atmosphere was electric.

As Mayor Timmerling gaveled the meeting to order, Harvey's hand was in the air.

"Mr. Mayor, I move we take the WDP out of the Bottoms and relocate it where no one will be sickened by its emissions. How can we ignore a fifth of our population who demand this?"

"I second that motion," Alice agreed. "We need to turn this immoral fiasco into a moral policy decision."

"We have a motion on the floor," said the mayor. "We will now receive comments from council. Councilman Dwyer, I see your hand."

"We have three choices," Dwyer summarized, his face a mask of indifference, his tone dismissive. "Not build it, move it, or stay with the plan. The first is ruled out by our urgent need for it. The second is negated by its cost. So, staying with the plan is our only option."

And just how did we get there, Mike? Wasn't it through following your lead?

Alice texted him. "Good ole Mike. Seems so inchoate, so bland. But so absolutely culpable! I can't stand it!"

Harvey nodded back with a thin smile. He'd begun to sense that publicly unmasking the pomp and pretense behind the WDP wouldn't be enough.

Many in the gallery shook their heads in obvious disbelief at Dwyer's persistence in sticking to his script.

If Dwyer were captain of a sinking cruise ship, he'd probably sell his passengers life vests for a hundred dollars each before they jumped into the sea!

"Thank you, Mr. Dwyer," said the mayor. "I now recognize our special guest, Mr. Norman Taylor of the chamber of commerce."

"Every day we delay construction," said Taylor, "is another day the city dumps are open and the housing developments planned for those areas are delayed. The city urgently needs new housing because our population is growing and people need homes. We need to move ahead, immediately. The developers are running out of patience."

City manager George Howard stood. "We have only the money presently allocated. We need to be in compliance with federal rules, and we know our residents won't stand for a tax increase. Very simply, our hands are tied."

The classic excuse for immoral decisions!

"Ms. Morrison, your views, please."

"The WDP is injurious to the people of the Bottoms. What we've done is unjust and inhumane." Her hands shook. She was clearly having difficulty holding back. "The council's decision to go ahead with construction was *ill considered* and *morally wrong!*"

Her statement brought comments of agreement from the onlookers.

"We must decide to pay the true costs of having this facility, and having it in a place where no one will be harmed! We *should not* force the burden of more pollution on these neighborhoods!"

"Thank you, Ms. Morrison. Mr. Angelo, please."

"I want the WDP as much as the next fellow," Marty added. "But we cannot make people sicker. That's not the way to govern."

"Mr. Thompson."

"We've come this far," Thompson remonstrated. "We need to build it and go on. We've waited ten years for this facility. Let's just carry the ball across the goal line and get the job done."

Doug's consent to go with the cult on this issue contradicted what he'd told Harvey at the beginning of the demonstration. He had to wonder which side the attorney really supported and what had caused him to change his view.

"Councilman Williams. Your thoughts, please."

"Won't be that much extra pollution," Clarence began. "Most of our people understand this is just the way things have to be. We're an adaptable community. Inconvenience and smell don't bother us. Long as we're makin' progress."

"Councilman Davenport, you're next."

Without warning, a streak of sheer stubbornness gripped him. Caution? To hell with it. The cult could do what it wanted. There probably would be more punishment. But why be afraid now? He'd met the demons and knew their tactics.

"For at least a century and a half," he said, "we've thoughtlessly, heedlessly dumped huge amounts of industrial waste into a place where twenty thousand of our citizens reside. That's not governance; it's usury at its worst. It was a monstrous, immoral series of acts against residents we're sworn to serve and protect."

Though the spectators applauded, he was shaking, and his stomach had tied itself in knots.

"The reason we're in tight financial circumstances," he continued, "is that this council has starved the city of revenue for twenty years. In the name of higher profits and increased economic growth, you've sacrificed the whole city. Deliberately. Against our laws. Contrary to the principles of good municipal governance."

Heads nodded, people murmured. Comments were audible here and there.

"What's good for business is *definitely not* good for the people!" He stabbed the air with his index finger. "The corporations are no longer responsible citizens; they're working *against* the community!"

The people in the public gallery stood and cheered as they applauded. Alice was on her feet, raising her arms in the air, much to the dismay of the cult members, whose faces were glum. Their eyes inspected the wastebaskets under their desks.

"Thank you, Mr. Davenport," the mayor acknowledged. His face had gone white. His lips were pulled into a rictus of disapproval, his eyebrows met at the middle in a frown. "Microphone one, your comment please."

"We don't need no more pollution, Mr. Mayor. Please take the WDP away."

"Microphone number two."

"My name is Martha Ruggles."

"Thank you, Mrs. Ruggles. I hope you haven't brought more vials of that smelly stuff with you tonight?"

"No, sir, I haven't," Martha affirmed with a Cheshire grin. "White folk been doing this to us for three hundred years, and it's time you stopped. In the twenty-first century, we've developed the technology to rid ourselves of industry's reckless ways, but you're using it to bring us sickness and death instead. It's time you stopped that too!"

Applause greeted her remarks.

"Number three," barked the mayor.

"Most people I've talked to are realistic about paying for the services we need. You're just fooling yourselves when you say people will rebel if you raise taxes. The people are willing, but you corporate guys're makin' a lot of money from holdin' us back."

"It's time to put this matter to a vote," the mayor called out, pounding his gavel. "All who favor relocating the waste disposal project, please signify by raising your hand."

Harvey, Alice, Marty Angelo, and Stan Matthews put their hands in the air.

"Those opposed, likewise."

Dwyer, Harris, Thompson, and Williams raised their hands.

"I see we have a tie," the mayor intoned with a dour expression. "According to our charter and bylaws, a mayor may vote to break a tie. As mayor of this city, I do not favor stopping construction on the WDP and locating it elsewhere. Given our circumstances, it is, in my estimation, exactly where it belongs. I hereby cast my vote as no. Therefore, the motion to relocate is defeated. We move now to our next item of business."

People murmured and muttered as they rose to leave. Alice's face bore a look of total disgust.

His own gut churned, and his pulse beat wildly in his ears. That's what came of majority rule. The minority was by default left out in the cold. Justice? A relic of the past. No more than a sack of empty words. It burned him up. Notwithstanding, the situation now required a more forceful response. He was not yet sure what that would be. In the meantime, there were other tasks that needed his attention.

CHAPTER 9

INDIVIDUAL ACTION

Building a solid case against industry required Harvey and his team to demonstrate the general state of people's health in the Bottoms as compared to an average population. Consequently, at ten o'clock on a balmy Saturday morning at the end of June, Harvey and Paul Johnson assembled a crew of volunteers at Renewal House to canvass local residents asking about their health problems.

Four high school students volunteered for this day's interviews. Tyler Smith was a tall, skinny fellow with an Afro, Samuel Washington was short and squat with dreadlocks, Hassan Higgins came dressed in a brown suit and well-shined shoes, and Derek Robinson carried his Brownie Hawkeye and wore bib overalls over a red T-shirt. Councilman Stan Matthews and Rev. Nate Kline helped out as adult supervisors.

Harvey enjoyed working with these young people. They learned fast, worked hard, and competed fiercely with one another. They reminded him of his daughter, Laura's, teenagers.

"The assignment's fairly simple," he told them when they were seated around the tables in the Renewal House conference room, eating homemade Toll House cookies. "Before you knock on someone's door, check the address against your pink sheet," he said as Paul Johnson handed out the four sheets each interviewer would use. "These are the people already working on odor logs, so we don't want to bother them with this survey."

He next gave a few pointers on introducing themselves and their purpose before launching into the health questions. "Be sure to wear your yellow WCEQ T-shirts."

"What kinds of questions?" Derek Robinson asked.

"You might start by asking if anyone in the household has cancer or liver or heart ailments. Next would be cold and flu."

"How will we know if their illnesses have anything to do with pollution?" Sam Washington asked.

"Well, you don't. Neither do most people. But you're asking them because you want to know their experience and their opinions about their health."

"I'm with you," Sam replied.

"Next, you should ask what kinds of pollution they see most often around their house and what kind of toxic waste is present on their property."

"What if they don't know?" Tyler asked.

"Ask them if the soil around their home has greasy brown material in it with a disagreeable odor. If they've got it, they'll know. And when you've finished the interview, be sure to say thank you."

When everyone seemed ready, Harvey and Paul led them out of Renewal House, and each pair peeled off for their assigned streets. For the initial round of interviews, an adult accompanied each teenager.

During their first hour of canvassing, all went well, except for Sam Washington, who ran into a domestic quarrel at his third house.

"Good thing Rev. Nate was with me," he said, slightly shaken, when they regrouped for debriefing on the street corner. "I learned a lot just from listening to how he handled it."

Over the next eight hours, the canvassing went well, and everyone completed their assignments as instructed. By the end of the day, though they were tired, spirits were high, and they'd generated a gold mine of health information.

They were heading back to Renewal House when a dozen motorcycles flooded the area, making a huge racket with their mufflers. They rounded up the eight volunteers and held them in a circle in the middle of Catalpa street.

"What's the meaning of this?" Paul shouted. "You know you're not to bother my people on any assignment they have from Renewal House."

"Sorry, Mistah Paul," said the fellow whose name was Steve. "Mr. Clarence Williams asks that you be his guest in his office right now."

"We're going nowhere, except back to base," insisted Johnson, turning and walking away toward his office.

"Beggin' your pardon, Mistah Paul," Steve called out, reaching in his back pocket and once again producing his pistol. Around the corner sped a transport van, and the gang members lined up the volunteers and shoved them in. Johnson and Harvey resisted, but the threat of gunfire dampened their spirit.

When they arrived at Clarence's place, the councilman gave them the usual "stay out of my territory" speech.

"Listen, you two-bit bag of wind," Harvey warned. "Let me and my people alone. We're going to be working down here for several months, and if you don't cease and desist, I'll summon the state police to set things straight. Then we'll see whose territory you command."

At that, Clarence backed off. "Let 'em go, fellas," he said, looking at his shoes. "Just wait till the next time, Whitey. We'll get you, one way'r another. I got my orders."

"From whom?" Johnson queried.

But Councilman Williams did not reply.

At the high sign from Paul Johnson, the volunteers walked away toward Renewal House. No one looked back. Harvey commented on Clarence's slip about "orders."

"He does nothing without Dwyer's prior approval," Paul muttered.

For the next three days, they were out on the streets canvassing the neighborhoods with no interference. They recruited another dozen volunteers, then set up a system that allowed them to cover the whole of the Bottoms by the time school started in the fall. Excitement built as they realized the powerful story their data revealed.

The next Tuesday, at five in the morning, Harvey picked up Charles Higgins and headed his van down I-97 into rolling hills a hundred miles south of Westfield. They were on the way to meet with Governor Hugh Fairmont at his fishing cottage.

Harvey appreciated Charles's willingness to arrange this meeting. Action at the state level now could have a powerful impact. As an African American historian and lawyer, Charles had long experience in state and municipal government. Frequent opportunities to work with Fairmont over the years had built their friendship.

After an hour's driving, Harvey turned off the interstate onto a narrow country road. Earthy, pungent smells of forest and pastureland poured through the van's windows, relaxing them both. When he stopped to allow a family of deer to cross the road, he shared a silent greeting with a demur wild turkey perched in an ancient gnarled oak beside the road. It fluffed the war stripes of its feather overcoat and winked at him with its comically decorated eye.

The governor's cottage, a simple two-story A-frame built of natural pine and white oak, overlooked the juncture of Cross and King Lakes. A solid expanse of glass facing westward gave a majestic view of lakes and forest. On the beachfront, two large gray fiberglass rowboats invited leisurely fishing.

The governor's pilot set down the Cessna 400 on King Lake precisely at 7:00 a.m. When the aircraft had taxied up the inlet, Hugh Fairmont, tall, athletic looking, with graying hair, stepped down onto a pontoon, then hopped to the beach, relaxed and smiling in a gray tweed sport jacket and black slacks.

"I've heard a lot about you, Harvey," the governor said when Charles introduced them. "You've been shaking things up at city hall."

"My neighbors elected me to do just that," Harvey replied. "My job is to find out why we can't get reliable city services and then try to fix it."

"Charles tells me you've discovered the effects of corporate dominance. We're having the same trouble at the state level. I'm interested to hear of your experience."

Learning that the state's highest executive understood at least one of his two problems, his earlier tension drained away, and hope for the success soared.

When they'd changed into their fishing clothes and installed themselves and their gear in one of the rowboats, they headed out through a canopy of lush green willow trees to the lakes. Charles generously offered to row. Security agents trailed at a discreet distance in their individual motorized rubber rafts.

As Charles maneuvered their boat under a huge, gnarly old oak tree, Fairmont had his fly line ready. With a smooth, practiced motion, the governor whipped his fly line twice in a graceful arc, letting its hand-tied red and black deer-hair bug settle just beneath an overhanging branch. As he slowly brought his line back toward the boat, he opened the conversation.

"Tell me more about what you're facing," the governor said, raising his eyebrows in invitation.

"A few more aggressive business types have organized what I call a cult of sacrifice," Harvey began.

Startled, the governor held up his hand. "All right, now what is this cult thing?" he asked.

"A sacrifice zone is a repository for industrial pollution and toxic waste bordering, and frequently encroaching on, a residential area occupied by minorities and the poor."

"Yes, unfortunately we have several in this state," said the governor. "Does that affect the rest of Westfield?"

"I discovered that the city's budget has changed little in twenty years. Population is increasing, but so are costs. City services are decreasing because this little cabal of conservatives don't want to spend any money."

"Why is that?" Fairmont inquired.

"They say if we raise taxes, the people will rebel. But I'm convinced their real motive is that taxes eat into their already robust profits. They're starving the city and our residents to bolster their own wealth."

"I like your directness, Harvey. Very refreshing! But come back to why you use the term cult. Seems like a strange word in this context."

"Because it's a group of individuals who share an interest in the principles of creating and maintaining sacrifice zones for their own benefit."

"Who are we talking about?"

"Corporate managers, the banks, the advertisers, trade associations. They provide social cover that encourages the public to support their practices."

"I get it," Fairmont said. "The support troops play on the tendency of people to harbor attitudes of superiority and racial prejudice. Charles tells me the city wants to put a waste disposal plant in the Bottoms. Given the context you've described, that doesn't sound like good policy to me."

"The people in the Bottoms agree with you," he replied. "They're angry and have initiated a public protest demonstration to publicize what's going on."

"As you know, Charles," said the governor, with thunder showing on his face. "This is a politically sensitive issue for me. Business is what runs the state's economy. Without appropriate supports, business would go downhill fast. Consequently, I'm a firm believer in government providing support for innovation and commerce."

"Yes, sir, I am aware of that," said Charles.

The realization that the governor was more enamored with business than he'd anticipated hit hard. Was it possible the discussion could turn sour?

"As you also know," Fairmont continued, "I'm due to leave next Monday for two weeks in China. Norm Taylor's going with me. We hope to return with encouraging news for the state's manufacturers."

"Yes, sir. I take your point," said Charles. "But you'll also admit there's a difference between general public support for a healthy business climate and having the corporate and finance heads running city and state government to suit themselves."

"Point taken," said Fairmont with a sigh of resignation. "Nothing's simple or clear-cut in the modern world. Everything's connected to everything else, isn't it?" He paused for a moment to recast his line. "Anything else I should know about?"

"One thing," said Harvey, "is that the pollution is spreading to all of Westfield. I've received reports that show the whole city is becoming a sacrifice zone."

"That's a new development," said Fairmont, raising his eyebrows.

"It brings another thorny issue. Not only do we need to raise taxes to get the city back on track, we also anticipate a huge expenditure to remediate the whole area. The sacrifice zone is starting to affect even the captains of industry."

"If I may say so, Hugh," Charles said, "I think you ought to take a close look at this. The timing may be right for action."

"I'm thinking along the same lines," the governor replied. "One of the things I want to ask you fellows this afternoon is what you think about appointing an emergency city manager for Westfield."

"Yes," Charles affirmed, "an emergency city manager would remove power from both the city manager and the city council until the city's finances were substantially improved. It would keep the city out of bankruptcy. No doubt it would also loosen the cult's grip on city finances."

With that, Fairmont reeled in his fishing line, then disassembled and put rod and reel in their case. They stowed their gear, then rowed back to the cottage for a further conference over lunch.

At noon, Bob Wernheim, the governor's legislative assistant, arrived in a shiny black limousine. He wore a navy blue suit and pale blue shirt. Charles had said Bob's main strength was accomplishing difficult tasks in ways that promoted the governor's agenda. He had many friends and few enemies and was exceptionally creative in avoiding political fights.

Shortly thereafter, they heard Thaddeus Newman's Cessna touch down on Cross Lake. As it taxied up the inlet, Newman, wearing a dark maroon jacket and brown slacks, and obviously in a hurry, escaped the passenger compartment and stood on a pontoon while the plane taxied to the beach.

Charles had said Thad was a large bundle of African American energy, who had made his way from Harlem to a Harvard PhD. His specialty was emergency city managers. He was in great demand as municipalities nationwide struggled with increasing costs and diminishing revenue.

When they'd filled their plates from the sumptuous buffet lunch prepared by steward Hans Grabel, featuring fresh caught trout, they gathered at the conference table.

"I invited you here to discuss the city of Westfield in relative privacy," Hugh Fairmont began. "Charles, would you give us a summary of our morning's discussion?"

When Charles had completed his assignment, Newman spoke first. "What would an ECM achieve in this situation?"

"Shine a public spotlight on important issues like control of municipal government, lack of service to citizens, and 20 percent of citizens being poisoned by industrial waste," said Wernheim.

"Do you fellows know about the cult of sacrifice?" inquired the governor.

"We all do," Wernheim said. "The problem isn't recognizing what they're doing; it's breaking them up."

"Also, Westfield's growing," said Newman. "One of the few cities in our state. Municipalities shouldn't be forced to scratch for pennies. An ECM could adjust finances before they deteriorate into bankruptcy."

"What about the political fallout?" suggested Fairmont.

"Some people might be skeptical," said Wernheim. "They seem to tolerate an ECM in a black community, but in a predominantly white city? I doubt it will be popular."

"Let's not run from that," said Newman. "We have to help people understand they'll reap huge, direct benefits denied them for two decades."

"Many people don't see business as a problem," said the governor. "An ECM might put me on the hot seat."

"We don't need to say anything about business interests," said Newman. "The ECM is there to turn the city around financially.

Ostensibly, the ECM sees nothing other than money in and money out."

"But it's tough to control that issue," said Wernheim. "The media will be all over that argument. They'll want to know who's at fault."

The fast ups and downs of the conversation whipsawed Harvey's emotions. Clearly, all three officials and Charles could argue both sides of any issue instantaneously. He was glad he hadn't stuffed himself at lunch.

"The city needs to raise taxes," said Newman. "That might be unpopular!"

"What's your greatest hope for Westfield?" Charles asked. "Why would a governor put any city through a wringer like an ECM?"

"My greatest hope for Westfield," said the governor, "is a new respect for honesty, integrity, and the rule of law. An ECM could lend increased accountability and transparency. In the end, I think the citizens will be a lot happier."

"Our campaign and PR specialists can handle that," said Wernheim. "We just need to say it's time to take care of the people."

"I agree. Depends on how we talk about it," said Newman.

"Making Westfield Safe for Citizen Participation sounds like a good slogan," said Charles, pushing.

"Gentlemen, thank you for a frank conversation." The governor rose from his chair. "I see people have arrived for the afternoon's meetings. I've got some other cities I'm concerned about too. I'll follow up with each of you after the holiday."

Was the turkey's wink a jinx or a promise? Though the discussion had ended on an encouraging note, the governor had not committed. Harvey couldn't know whether he'd won or lost until the governor's state-of-the-state message.

Harvey arrived home late that Tuesday night from his fishing expedition with the governor. Tired and a bit wobbly on his feet, he fumbled for his keys, then opened the door to his studio. As he entered, his eye caught something amiss. The set he'd been working on looked as if it had been blown apart. Chaos greeted him as he flipped on the light.

"Christ on a cracker!" he exclaimed under his breath. "What a mess!" Two of his three equipment cabinets lay on the floor, doors open, empty. Intruders had smashed large rolls of background paper. The auto parts he'd been shooting littered the floor. Three tripods he'd used to shoot those accessories were lying on the floor and missing their cameras. In the offices, equipment had been knocked to the floor, desks had been ransacked, and three client displays lay in ruins on the floor of Mina's office.

Checking the alarm system, he discovered nothing amiss. Whoever did this was a professional. He called Mina to tell her what had happened.

"Did you call the police?" Mina asked. "I'll be there quick as I can."

"Don't know what good the police will do," he said. "Barnes is in cahoots with them."

"Sounds like some of Clarence's gang guys," Mina replied. "But call the police anyway. Think of the insurance."

She was unflappable. *Leave it to Mina to think coolly under pressure.*

Twenty minutes later, when they had just set one of the cabinets upright, Mina's head suddenly swiveled toward Harvey.

"Where's Lord Nelson?" she asked in a strangled whisper. "Something's happened. I can feel it!" She searched frantically for the cat. Minutes later, a blood-chilling wail cut through the silence. "Harvey, come quick! I need your help!"

He rushed to the back porch, where she was in tears, cradling Lord Nelson in her arms. The intruders had tied him to the clothesline stretched across the porch. He took the frightened cat in his arms up to his bedroom, trying to calm him in a safe place.

When he returned to the studio, Mina had discovered a note smeared in blood on one of the cabinets.

"Get out of the Bottoms or you'll get worse!" it said.

"Looks like someone's upset," said Mina with her usual understatement and a crooked smile.

"Sounds like Clarence's idiots," he replied, shaking uncontrollably. "Anyone who would torture an innocent animal must be psychotic."

He had trouble dealing with this. It was late, he was tired, and yes, he had gotten the message. It made him angry. And scared. Not just for himself but for Mina and Felix too. And Alice Morrison. Was his resistance to the cult endangering the very people he cared about?

"Let's quit," he suggested. "Leave everything for now. We'll clean up in the morning."

"You're sure you'll be all right?" Mina inquired cautiously.

"I need rest before I can deal with this," he said. "See you tomorrow. I'll nurse the cat back to health." He went upstairs to his apartment, thinking hard about taking revenge against the people responsible, but soon after his head hit the pillow, he was asleep, Lord Nelson warming his feet and purring like a Mack truck on a hill.

The next morning, Wednesday, the Fourth of July, Harvey found Mina already in the studio in black jeans and T-shirt, starting to clean up the damage even though it was a holiday and she was entitled to be off.

"I called Paul Johnson and told him what happened," she said. "He wasn't surprised but thought that the studio was turned into a mini sacrifice zone to ward off intruders who might want to help the people. So how does that make you feel about working over there?"

What a knack she had for nailing an issue.

"I'll get over it," he said, hoping he sounded more confident than he felt.

Around midday, Johnson showed up. The three pulled chairs around a display table, drinking coffee and wolfing down pastries and fruit.

"So, how are you feeling, Harvey?" Paul asked, a sympathetic smile on his face. "I imagine this hit you pretty hard."

"It did. I certainly got the message," Harvey said. The knot in his stomach returned with the memory.

"And what are your thoughts this morning?"

"Well … I'm scared. I think it'll get worse. Nothing can stop them. They have all the power and no scruples. My nicely arranged world of photography has been trashed, and I'm pissed!"

"As I expected," said Paul. "You had a nasty shock. Mina told me about Lord Nelson too. How's he doing?"

As if on cue, the cat leaped into Paul's lap, standing on his back legs, pawing gently at his face.

"How are you feeling about the WDP and your role with the people? Has this scared you off?" As always, Paul never minced words, but his mien was pastoral.

"I'm still with the program," Harvey replied as forthrightly as he could manage. Doubt made his stomach quiver, but bullies disabled opponents to keep them in line, and he wouldn't—indeed he couldn't—let that happen. "I want to teach 'em a lesson," he hissed, looking at Paul directly. "I want to make 'em hurt!" he exploded, pounding his fist on the table as tears escaped his eyes and Lord Nelson ran for cover.

"I want you to know," said Paul, "the community is behind you 100 percent. They've set a guard on your studio for the next thirty days. All volunteers. Isaiah Jones is in charge."

"Thank you!" he said, bowing his head in thanksgiving, a lump in his throat. "And thanks to Isaiah. It's unbelievable that people are so caring."

There it was, community. Plain, simple. Gathering when trouble comes. But would they gather to make the deep changes necessary to improve their lives? That was still to be tested.

CHAPTER 10

MIXED RESULTS

To Harvey's great surprise, just three days after he and Charles had talked with Hugh Fairmont, he received a call from Alice.

"The governor's due to give his state-of-the state address tonight. Why don't you join us to watch it? Can I tempt you with some of my Texas barbecue?"

"Sounds heavenly!" he replied.

By five o'clock, he and Mina, Felix, Stan, and Paul had gathered at Alice's place. When they'd filled their plates with tangy barbecue, brown rice, spinach salad, and homemade bread from the buffet, they sat on comfortable white leather chairs in the living room. Afterward, they watched Hugh Fairmont's address. Felix had hinted there might be a surprise.

As the mariner's clock on her mantlepiece struck eight, Alice turned on Channel 5. While the announcer introduced the governor's speech, the camera zoomed slowly in on Hugh Fairmont as he stood at the rostrum before a packed audience. The governor was handsome, tall, and smiling as he bantered with his colleagues.

After being introduced by the Speaker of the House, Fairmont said, "Good evening, ladies and gentlemen. We've made great strides forward this past year."

He described efforts to improve living conditions and shared his plans for rehabilitating roads and bridges. Then he delved into the steps he'd taken to rejuvenate the economy. He also cited wins in public education and health care and described efforts at prison reform and bringing prison management back under public control.

"My friends," he said at last, "I want to talk with you confidentially about the role of government in today's society. This is an issue that has been uppermost in my mind throughout my political career."

The audience was hushed, expectant.

"Government's purpose is to serve all the citizens of our state. We must perpetuate the rule of law, dispense fair and reasonable justice to everyone, and administer reliable support services. No one should be above the law, and no one should suffer injustice from it. Neither should anyone vilify taxes—the source of revenue that provides citizen services—just to make himself rich."

The audience applauded politely, perhaps wondering where this was leading.

"We work daily to discover opportunities for business while maintaining systems of regulation and taxation that protect and serve everyone. This is always a delicate balancing act, but it must be done. And it always involves open discussion and compromise."

Was the governor opening a case of political dynamite? People in the galleries fidgeted. A slight buzz oozed from the crowd.

At that point, the feed from the state legislature was interrupted, and the screen went black, then fuzzy with snow.

"What the hell!" Felix exploded. "Something happened to the network feed!"

"Millions won't see the rest of it!" Paul fumed.

Alice grabbed the remote, punching in cable Channel 7. "Leave it to Marvin Feldkamp to have an independent line into the legislature," she remarked. Seconds later, the governor was back on the screen.

"For many years, Americans have had a love-hate relationship with taxes. A few hate to pay them, so they've made it a dirty word. But it is through taxes that the needs of our people are met. Democracy is a two-way street; we give and we get. Nobody gets their way completely all the time. But I'm convinced it's a lot better than the alternatives."

At that, the chamber erupted with appreciative applause over an undercurrent of boos.

"In a liberal democracy, we cannot denigrate taxes any more than we would shirk our responsibility to our families or our employers. Taxes are each person's fair share of the cost of providing the services we all need."

For this, the governor received more eager applause.

"And today, the demand for services, as well as their cost, is rising. There are those, however, who would put increased personal profit over their responsibility to the rest of us. They seem to feel taxes should be forced lower despite the public's growing need."

There was applause from the liberals, stony silence from the conservatives.

"This creates another issue we must face. The corporations are spending huge amounts of money to bend government to their will."

The House of Representatives was suddenly silent. Channel 7's cameras picked out concerned and doubtful looks.

"One example of this is privatization, in which private firms attempt to deliver public services and make huge profits. But this, as you all know by this time, has resulted in disaster.

"An even more insidious problem, however, results from the overreaching self-interest we see in the commercial sector. And I want to share with you a most troubling new development."

Once again, the assembly became quiet.

"I speak now of the city of Westfield. An elected member of the city council has recently been shot and his business plundered by people who wish him to keep silent on a matter of city business."

Faint muttering was audible.

"Reliable sources say local business and large corporate interests have dominated Westfield for two decades. This is abominable!" he cried as he pounded the rostrum with his right fist.

Polite applause followed his comment.

"Elections have been rigged. Some corporations seek to avoid paying their fair share of taxes. City services have declined while the city's population has increased 25 percent. Yet the city council has not raised taxes in over twenty years, largely at the insistence of corporate operators."

The House was once again silent, as if waiting for a "but." Camera close-ups of selected legislators' faces suggested surprise, disbelief, and anger.

"My friends, the city of Westfield is very near bankruptcy, and strong evidence suggests multiple failures of governance. I believe we need a careful and thorough investigation of the facts. I am therefore authorizing an investigation into the financial situation of the city of Westfield. And to carry out that initiative, I have appointed Mr. Gerald MacFarlane, whom many of you know."

Vigorous applause issued from both sides of the aisle. Apparently, MacFarlane's reputation was strong in both political camps.

"As an independent investigator, Mr. MacFarlane has great depth of training and experience in municipal government. I believe he will perform a just and fair analysis of the situation. He will report to me at a joint session of the combined legislature."

There was also wild cheering in Alice's apartment.

"That's what we came to hear!" Harvey shouted.

Alice uncorked a bottle of champagne, and they toasted the governor. Fairmont had made the right decision. But two questions remained: who cut the broadcast cable, and would the governor support the decision of people in the Bottoms to abolish the WDP?

At ten o'clock on the following Wednesday morning, Harvey struggled with the contents of a large box of prefabricated sections that were supposed to fit together into a South Sea Island backdrop for a travel poster. Blessed relief came in the form of a phone call from his aunt Harriet.

"Let's take Laura out to lunch to celebrate her thirty-third birthday," she'd said.

Well that suited him fine. It would relieve his tension and give his brain a chance to play with the poster puzzle to discern its secrets.

After a pleasant half hour's drive, he arrived a little earlier than planned at Helena's Country Kitchen on the outskirts of Cherokee Heights. That was where his daughter, Laura, lived with her husband, Tony, and their children, Peter and Jacqueline.

He took a corner table where he could see the parking lot. The dining area was an open, airy place surrounded on two sides by windows that overlooked fertile farmland with fields of corn and soybeans. Large potted shrubs and flowers complemented the white marble tabletops and Pollock chairs covered in buttery yellow leather.

He didn't have long to wait. Laura shared his penchant for arriving early for most appointments. She'd recently acquired her own interior decorating firm and seemed to be doing well. He was proud of her, and she looked very professional in a summery cotton dress printed in a colorful flower pattern, complemented by her shoulder-length brunette bob and a single strand of pearls.

Lithe and tall, Laura still had that fresh, heart-shaped face and glowing, full-lipped smile of the teenager he'd raised from the time she was twelve. Though he'd pushed her off to the College of Wooster when she was twenty, he was happy to have her back where he could keep an eye on her. In the restaurant, her brown eyes sparkled when she hugged him.

"Happy birthday, sweetheart!" he said with his most generous smile.

"Thank you, Sir Gallant," she replied with a flourish as she sat.

In a brief glance out the window, he spotted his aunt Harriet exiting her car in the parking lot. She seemed to have considerable difficulty. As she turned around, a cast on her left leg peaked out from under her dark blue skirt. She hobbled with a cane slowly to the restaurant door.

He rushed out to help her through the double doors and over to their table. She was breathing hard and running a bit late.

"Oh, I'm so glad this worked out for your birthday, Laura!" she exclaimed as she reached their table. "I hope it's a happy one."

"Indeed it is," Laura replied.

As Harvey seated her at the table, Harriet jingled with dozens of bracelets on her arms. Her wavy white hair reached halfway down her back, but despite an occasional wince of pain, her sharp blue eyes sparkled as usual. At eighty, she was still the good-looking, tough, and resolute woman he'd known in his adolescence at uncle Theo's mansion in Binghamton. Though it hadn't been funny at the time, he laughed to himself now as he remembered her pointing a gun at Theo, threatening to kill him if he didn't stop beating his nephew.

When they'd ordered, Harriet said, "Well, Harvey, what have you been up to?"

"I've been gathering allies," he replied. He explained his having met Paul Johnson, Alice Morrison, and Stan Matthews in connection with his city council responsibilities. "We've put together a plan for dealing with a few of Westfield's problems, and I think we'll succeed."

"What is it you're trying to do?" Full of eagerness, Laura leaned forward in rapt attention.

"First, I want to work on stopping industry from polluting the area with their chemicals. I'm finding out that in order to succeed, we'll need to separate industry from city government. The regulators aren't doing their job because the business owners control them."

"Well, Harvey, I told you not to dirty your hands, and you went right ahead and did it, didn't you?" Harriet frowned as she remonstrated with him.

"I had no choice," he countered. "I'm doing it for my mother, and I'm going to get the guys who poisoned her."

"Oh, let it alone," she groaned. "The poor woman's been dead fifty years. Why do you care?"

"Because she was good to me, and she died in my arms."

"I just wish you'd find something else to do in retirement besides politics," she said. "It's useless and beneath your origins."

He let it drop. She was pulling a Theo on him—forcing an issue with prejudice rather than logic. Irritating, but he could tolerate her even though she was unable to appreciate his drive to help people.

"You guys are tearing me up," Laura said, arms crossed with obvious irritation. "I don't want you to fight. Sure, you have different opinions about things, but let it go. Every human being is his own person." She wrinkled her brow, grasped a lock of her hair, and twisted it around a finger. "Dad, I just hope you'll spend more time with your grandkids. I want them to get to know you and grow up like you."

"Thank you, dearest daughter," he said. "I understand your feeling, and I'll try to get down here and spend more time with them."

"So, now I'm curious," Laura said. "Have you learned anything since being on city council?"

"One thing is that I can expect a reprisal from the opposition any time I make a move to help the city's residents."

"I saw on TV you had a break-in." Harriet changed the subject. "What are you doing that makes people want to do that?" She wagged a finger at him, quivering in discernible indignation. "I'm just fearful for your safety, Harvey."

"Yes, that upset me," he replied. "That was right after I met with the governor."

"What's this with the governor?" Harriet queried with a frown.

"Took him fishing and had a chat." He explained how the governor seemed disposed to help with the problems in Westfield.

"I sure am glad you're getting some help." His aunt breathed in relief, bowing her head.

"What do you think will happen?" Laura wanted to know.

"An investigation, most likely, and possibly an emergency city manager," he replied. He told them a few of the benefits of each strategy.

"Didn't you have a big demonstration a week or so ago?" Harriet asked.

"Very big, yes. Results were less than satisfactory though. The media had very little to say about it."

"Newspaper said you got shot," Laura commented.

"Yeah, two times this spring. Once in the leg after a community workday in the Bottoms, and the other at the WDP demonstration. Just grazed me though. Nothing to worry about."

"Heavens, Father!" Laura exclaimed, frowning in irritation. "Sounds dangerous! Are the business people picking on you just for doing good for people?"

"Afraid so, kitten," he said.

"Well, do you think the WDP demonstration made any difference?" Harriet wanted to know.

"No, it did not," he said with finality. "The city council refused to reconsider the location of the project, so as of now, it's going forward."

"I could have told you that," said Harriet, shaking her head in disgust. "Are you still hell-bent on getting revenge against the polluters?"

"That's my top priority."

"Have you learned nothing in all this time?" she inquired with a sardonic note in her voice.

"Yes. I've learned how to involve other people and how to know when and whom to trust."

"Sometimes I worry about you, Harvey," Harriet said.

"I thank you for your concern, Aunt, but I'll be all right. This isn't the first scrape I've been in." He paused to finish his coffee. "That reminds me, Harriet and Laura. Can either of you lend a hand with some canvassing in the white areas of Westfield?"

"Well, I don't know," Harriet said. "There's this thing with my leg. And speaking of that, I have a request. I need you to get me to the doctor's to get this cast off. Could you do that next Tuesday?"

"Sure. Glad to do it. Let me check my schedule. If there's a problem, I'll call you." Worry set in like a hungry cat. This was another diversion he didn't need. "What about you, Laura?"

"I'm interested," she replied in a flat voice. "But there's something I have to tell both of you. My doctor says I have melanoma."

"Oh no!" said Harvey and Harriet together.

"It's not the end of the world," Laura reassured them. "But I am worried about it. There are lots of unknowns."

The worry worm stirred again in his gut. The danger was he'd get pulled off track by family matters. Not that he didn't care about his only two living relatives, but singleness of purpose was a high priority.

"I can work with you," said Laura. "Once I understand more about this melanoma thing. Maybe a couple afternoons a week for a while?"

"That would be a good start. Bring the boys with you. We'll teach them how to approach people. It'll be fun!"

As he helped Harriet into her car, she turned to him and gave him the thumbs-up sign. "You're doing okay, Harvey. I'm with you. Just worried about you, that's all."

Laura gave him an understanding hug, then grasped his arm and sighed with a thoughtful expression. "Just don't let anything else serious happen to you, Dad. We need you with us for at least thirty more years. Okay?"

"I have to do things the way I perceive is best," he said. "I'm committed to helping people, and I'll do that till I succeed." A mark of the stubbornness typical of his family, perhaps, but that contrariness and persistence was what kept him alive.

Nevertheless, he was already having some second thoughts about the effectiveness of revenge. Paul had put it in his head that revenge and justice might not be the same thing. Could his personal vendetta actually get in the way of bringing justice to the people? He'd have to think more about that.

Every morning, as he enjoyed his coffee and day-old sweet roll, Rhett Bennett, CEO of Superior Plastics, watched the Dick Richards *Current Events Roundup* show on Channel 7. He liked to keep up on the latest happenings, but he only half listened to the show. Local events weren't that entertaining. He often used the time to check his email.

Rhett stubbed out his cigarette in the closest ashtray. As usual, it was full to overflowing, but he'd get around to that later. Then he opened a new pack and lit a fresh one. He enjoyed the taste of coffee with the smell of cigarette smoke. It reminded him of his dad's office at the coal mining company where he'd played as a child. Even now, he wore the same outfit he had then—old jeans and a faded blue work shirt. "Informal day" was every day as far as he was concerned.

Some people might have said his office was a mess. But Rhett didn't care. It was his, and he was comfortable in it. What use were file cabinets when everything he needed was right on the desk? And those eight dead geranium sticks in flower pots lined up along his filth-encrusted windows? They'd been old friends for years. He wouldn't have parted with them if his life depended on it.

This morning, however, Dick Richards's second guest arrested his attention. Gerald MacFarlane, the investigator appointed by Governor Fairmont to look into Westfield's problems, summarized his newly issued pollution report, revealing for all to see that Superior Plastics headed the list of top ten polluters in the city.

He nearly toppled over in his swivel chair, so suddenly did he struggle to sit upright. He pounded the desk in disbelief when MacFarlane called the Bottoms a "sacrifice zone." He kicked in the side of his wastebasket when the man said business had taken over city government to make polluting easier. But when the idiot further said the public should take priority over the needs of aggressive business types, he picked up his brass baseball, personally signed by Juan Marechal himself, and pitched it at his six-foot aquarium, which shattered and gave his filthy carpet its first bath in ten years.

"What ... the ... bloody ... hell?" he screamed at the top of his voice. He'd been blindsided! Why had nobody told him this report would skewer his firm and others? Why had MacFarlane gone on television to tell the public about it? Now everyone knew what he'd worked so hard to keep under wraps for more than three decades. And that bit about the health of Westfield citizens was the limit! If the investigator carried that out, his whole operation could be publicly exposed and legally prosecuted for having caused thousands of deaths over the last half century. He turned to the stock market website. Sure enough, his stock had already fallen sixty points.

"Who let that investigator get away with this?" he raged at the goldfish as they gasped for water. "Wasn't anyone at city hall minding the store?" There had been a long history of cooperation between his firm and the city administration. Why throw all that away in fifteen minutes of unsupervised tomfoolery?

"Get me Mike Dwyer on the phone!" he shouted at his secretary, Melva Dunning.

"Mike!" Bennett shouted when the banker picked up the phone. "What the hell's going on?"

"Can you be more specific, Rhett? I don't know what you mean," Dwyer replied.

"I'm watchin' the *Current Events Roundup* on Channel 5 this morning. And I hear this investigator from city hall talkin' about a pollution report that mentions *my company* as one that violates pollution standards! I wanna know what's going on and what you're gonna do about it! Have you seen MacFarlane's report?"

"Just a minute," Mike said. "Let me check my in-box. I haven't seen anything about a pollution report." In a few minutes, he was back on the line. "Yes, Rhett, I have the press release here. Looks like it came in just a few minutes ago."

"Looks like things have changed over there," Rhett ranted. "What the hell's going on with that guy? Can't somebody shut him up?"

"I take it you're surprised by this?" Dwyer queried in a careful, calm voice.

"Hell, yes, I'm surprised! Why would you ask a question like that?" Rhett let his anger explode into the phone.

"And may I ask why you're calling me about it?"

"Like I said, Mike," he insisted, "I want to know what you're going to do about MacFarlane's report! Somebody has to shut him up before he does any more damage! My stock's fallen 10 percent just since the show."

"*Get a grip and get real!*" Dwyer cautioned. "I can see why you're upset. But here's the thing—and I want you to listen very closely. Neither you nor I nor George Howard are in a position to do anything about this right now. This is the governor's appointee you're talking about."

"So what the hell does that matter? You can take him out, can't you?"

"You're not hearing me, Rhett! But you must listen to what I say. It would be better if you just sucked it up and shut the hell up about it for a while. Wait out the chief investigator. One of these days, he'll go away, and we'll take steps then. Otherwise, you and all the rest of us could be brought crashing down if MacFarlane looks too close."

"Aw, hell!" Rhett exclaimed. "That's the wimpiest answer I've heard from you in a long time, Mike!"

"Okay, Rhett, let me put it to you this way. If you don't shut up about this, I'll pull that ten-million-dollar loan you just took out. You think your stock price is down now? Just wait till that happens. Are you getting my message?"

When Rhett slammed down his phone receiver, it broke the phone's case in a hundred pieces. Dwyer had him by the short hairs; there was nothing he could do. He fumed about the office, then decided he had to take a long walk to dispel his anger. So he stormed out of the office, ran down the two flights of stairs, got in his Ferrari, and zoomed off to the country club. Someday he'd get that son of a bitch Dwyer and put him away for good.

On Monday evening, July 16, Harvey arrived at city hall early for council meeting. He was to distribute fresh copies of the proposal he and Alice and Stan Matthews were bringing to council. Their agenda item called for a community health survey. They had distributed copies of the measure at the previous meeting and were expecting to vote on it this evening.

Before the meeting, he'd eaten very little. His stomach churned with a combination of excitement and anxiety—excitement about the proposal, anxiety about whether Marty and Doug would vote for it. As he laid out copies of the proposal, he reflected on the chat he and Alice had had with them the previous week.

After the last council meeting in June, the one bright spot had been that Marty Angelo had voted in favor of reconsidering the WDP's location. Even though the mayor had broken the tie by voting against, the change in Marty's loyalty to Dwyer's cohort suggested a fracture in their ranks.

Since the May strategy session at Mama Lulu's, he'd been looking for such a moment to convert both Marty and Doug Thompson to their perspective. So the first Monday in July had seemed like a good opportunity to talk with both men about the health protection measure. Such a measure was desperately needed. It called for a survey of the history of illness and death throughout Westfield. The results would become part of their case to state and federal agencies about the effects of pollution.

Consequently, he'd arranged with Alice that the two of them would invite Marty and Doug for a conversation at the Busy Bee after the July 9 council meeting.

That chat had gone well. Marty admitted he'd had second thoughts about several recent agenda items.

"Staying with Dwyer's crowd makes me increasingly uncomfortable," he'd said to Harvey. "Your proposal makes a lot of sense."

Doug Thompson was more reserved. "I've got clients and connections on both sides of many issues," he'd said. "I voted with Dwyer's bunch because the chamber recruited me and I owed it to them. But their use of violence is repugnant. Besides, your proposal will produce much-needed information."

As Mayor Timmerling in his sharkskin gray suit now gaveled the meeting to order, the health protection measure was at the top of the agenda.

"Mr. Davenport, will you summarize the proposal for us and guide us through it?"

Harvey nodded and rose from his chair. "On page one, please note that the purpose of this measure is to gather data on health and environmental factors. On page two, we will use this data as we approach state and federal agencies for help with our pollution problem. Then the table of contents will guide you through the specific components.

"Essentially, the proposal calls for four types of information. First, a citywide health survey showing a fifty-year pattern of disease and death by ward. Second, accurate and transparent reporting of the real data on industrial emissions from the city's field surveys. Third, a review of current levels of pollution versus city policy and a recommendation for stringent restrictions on one hundred chemicals known to cause disease and death in humans."

"That completes my summary, Mr. Mayor."

"Thank you, Mr. Davenport. Questions from members of the council?"

"This is silly!" chided Mike Dwyer with a dour face as he picked lint from the lapel of his navy blue suit. "We don't need this. It would be a waste of time and money. Besides, we can't afford it."

"This will upset a lot of our friends in industry," Rhett Bennett commented in his booming voice. "You recall how Sherry Matthews was killed a couple years ago when she inadvertently published the real pollution figures?"

"We've checked with the administrators of Westfield General," said Alice Morrison. "They need the survey to plan for the future. They're also prepared to help with the costs."

"Does this request come from any recognized group?" Bennett wanted to know. "Or is it just your personal concern, Mr. Davenport?"

"The people at Renewal House suggested we sponsor this health survey," he replied. "They're concerned that the health of people in the Bottoms is a great deal poorer than for the general population. They believe this is the result of the pollution they've lived with for more than a century."

"This whole thing smacks of racism," Clarence Williams declared, looking at his desk blotter. "Why do you want to know the death and disease rate for our people? Do you think they're inferior? Would that justify your discrimination against our people?"

"It's not the survey that would discriminate," Stan Matthews offered as he stroked his goatee with his right hand. "It's the polluters who've poured waste into the Bottoms. That's where the discrimination is happening."

"From a legal point of view, a health survey would be a prudent measure," Doug Thompson advised. "It would protect us against lawsuits. We haven't been reporting accurate levels of pollution."

"I think it's a good idea," Marty Angelo said in his kind, tactful voice. "Many other cities and states do health surveys every ten years. But we never have. It's time to do it."

"Thank you all for your input," said the mayor.

"Call the question," shouted Alice. "It's time we voted."

"The question has been called. I must now ask for your votes. All those in favor, raise your right hand."

Five hands were in the air.

"All opposed, please give the same sign."

Three hands went up.

"The measure is approved. "We'll move on to our next item."

After the meeting, Harvey, Alice, and Stan gathered around Marty and Doug, thanking them for their support. It had been a victory—though just one small step on the long road to remediation. Nevertheless, it was a significant move toward the future. His next task was to discover what the people of the Bottoms would do about city council's refusal to move the WDP.

CHAPTER 11

PUBLIC ACTION II

City council's refusal to remove the WDP from the Bottoms had pushed Harvey to seek more robust ways to halt construction. In support of that aim, Paul Johnson and the staff of Renewal House had called another community meeting for seven o'clock that Tuesday evening to discuss their next move.

He arrived at Bethel Church early. Massive plantings of orange and yellow day lilies, dahlias, and cosmos at the church entrance welcomed people with bobbing heads in the warm, early-evening breeze. Sadly, odors of asphalt and chemical waste overpowered their fragrances.

The streets were quiet. People entered the church in silence. Solemn faces and hushed voices bore witness to the weight of the evening's decision. He worried there might not be enough emotional dynamite among community members to escalate their protest. The violence of police action at the previous demonstration coupled with council's refusal to move had demonstrated the difficulty the community faced.

As he once again walked through the sanctuary, perusing the photo gallery of the church's history, he drew strength from Jeremiah Hartshorne's courage in times of trouble. The charisma in the founder's mesmerizing eyes strengthened his own vision for the people's well-being. What would Hartshorne have done when the police panicked and violently forced his public protest to an abrupt end?

By seven o'clock, people filled the church. The side and center aisles were filled with people standing. Following Rev. Booker's invocation, Paul Johnson said to them, "This is your chance, friends, to tell us what you're feeling and what you think we should do next."

In the ensuing discussion, three camps emerged. The local preachers advocated prayer and meditation.

"Brothers and sisters," Rev. Jemma Bailey intoned, "we must pray about this troubling circumstance. We need the Lord's guidance. We're holding a prayer vigil tonight. God will give us a sign as to what we must do."

Others suggested further peaceful protest.

"We should keep demonstrating until they take the thing away," Janet Clark suggested. "A round-the-clock vigil, till we get respect."

Mary Biddle's hand shot up. "We should interrupt the city council meeting with a protest."

A third group advocated more direct action.

Isaiah Bell objected. "The time for talking is done. They're ignoring us. Time to take some serious action!" He shook his head in disgust.

"It's time we took our destiny in our own hands," eighty-year-old Clem Sanders admonished the group. Piercing eyes capped by bushy white eyebrows and a mantel of white hair gave his ancient, worry-lined face the command of authority. "We need to blow the thing up! If we don't want it, we should remove it from our midst. It's past time we rejected whitey's garbage."

Interesting how troubled times moved generations to switch perspectives. One might have expected the oldsters to be more conservative while the youngsters hugged militancy. Such was not the case this night.

Still standing, Clem Sanders said, "Every change in history has brought sacrifice and death. We can't expect real change without somebody gettin' killed."

That brought the sanctuary alive with buzz. Was direct action worth the price they'd have to pay?

Now Paul Johnson stood with a word of advice. "Don't forget that nonviolent action has always worked best for our people. Respect for the law is important when we insist on our rights. Let's be smart about what we do."

Half the room responded with enthusiastic applause, while others seemed less enthusiastic.

"Good idea!" Methodist pastor Melissa Gravenly interjected from the back of the room. "That would attract national attention, and our congregation is ready to join you in that kind of protest. Several other white churches are eager to help as well."

Then, at the back of the sanctuary, the irrepressible Martha Ruggles rose to speak. "I absolutely agree. It's time we engaged in civil disobedience. Time to shut down the construction. But we must do so nonviolently. That's the way we have the greatest credibility with the whites. I'd like to hear what Harvey Davenport has to say."

Up to now, he'd been happy simply listening. But the two horses of impatience to act and the desire for justice were now galloping in opposite directions, tearing him apart. What could he say?

Rising to speak, slowing his mind, taking his time, he said, "Look! Do you see how the light of the setting sun on these beautiful stained glass windows is projecting a pattern of Jesus's crucifixion over the people tonight?" The intricate patterns and glorious color of the images illumined those sitting in the middle of the sanctuary.

Gazing at its effect, some nodded in recognition.

"Looking at this magnificent and powerful symbol, I have to ask myself, 'Is Jesus being crucified all over again?' Or we could ask it another way. Are the people of the Bottoms being crucified right here, right now?"

There were murmurs and nods of assent. Others shook their heads.

"I'm tired of seeing a fifth of Westfield's population bearing the scourge of industrial waste just because they happen to be poor or black or brown."

Dead silence settled over the people.

"I believe the founder of this church, Jeremiah Hartshorne, would urge us to take bold, clear action. We've been violated. And the violators have now wrested from our grasp the means to repair the damage and put things right. As I see it, such violence must be met with unyielding resistance!" With the last two words, he pointed his index finger high in the air.

Murmurs came again from the people. Heads shook. Some nodded. Paul Johnson looked startled. Martha Ruggles frowned, shaking her head.

"Either blowing it up or stopping construction will destroy the symbol of our powerlessness," he concluded. "But we must choose one or the other."

His comments received a few "Amens" and scattered applause. The discussion continued for another hour in a similar vein.

When the comments and ideas had reached a point of saturation, Paul Johnson called for a vote. He enumerated the alternatives— continue the peaceful public protest, engage in a work stoppage, or demolish the construction site. Then the doors were locked. Eyes closed. Hands in the air. No peeking.

When at length the hands were counted for and against each alternative, Johnson reported the results.

"Ladies and gentlemen, a clear majority has voted in favor of a nonviolent work stoppage."

The room erupted in pandemonium. How radical! How frightening. How impossible!

A week after the community meeting at Bethel Church, all was in readiness for the work stoppage at the WDP construction site. After a tense leaders' orientation session earlier that morning, Harvey needed a stretch. Preparing even the most committed volunteers to risk life and limb to help their fellows had been an arduous, draining task.

To unwind and gain a fresh perspective, he climbed the one hundred stairs to the grassy knoll called Langley Memorial Park, which overlooked the construction site from the northwest. The hot, muggy air lingering after showers the night before made breathing difficult as he huffed and puffed his way to the top. By the time he arrived, sweat drenched his navy blue polo shirt.

When he reached the top, he collapsed on a shaded cement bench under a large oak tree to slow the pounding of his heart. After a few minutes, he extracted a thermos of coffee from his backpack and sipped the fragrant liquid, surveying the vast construction scene before him.

Trenches filled with massive footers outlined the growing structure of the waste disposal plant. Down at the far end, two blocks away, steel struts had been erected to support the facility's massive roof. Huge backhoes and bulldozers emitted a constant roar as they gouged out foundations for the buildings and smokestacks. Columns of black diesel exhaust drifted toward the public housing units.

The size and complexity of this growing behemoth flooded his mind with doubt. Did the people of the Bottoms really have the commitment and the prodigious strength it would take to shut this project down?

Martha Ruggles tapped him on the shoulder, then wrapped him in a welcome, reassuring hug.

"Watcha doin' up here, Mistah Harvey? Trying to keep cool?" She wheezed, and her face glistened with sweat after the arduous climb. She sat on the bench beside him.

"Just trying to figure out whether we really can stop this monster," he replied. "It's such an enormous project!" Her costume, reminiscent of the sixties, consisted of faded bib overalls and a brown cotton short-sleeved shirt. How many times had she prepared to give her life to bring freedom to her people?

"Biggest thing in Westfield," she said with a wilted expression. "Whew! I gotta rest a bit. I'm worn out." Then she turned to him with a big, broad smile that creased her face from side to side. "But we'll get it done. One way or another."

While Martha rested, he checked his email and discovered a note from his friend, the oil tycoon Tom McIntyre.

"If you haven't seen this, you should know what's out there to bite you."

The text of the forwarded email included the following words.

"People are protesting in the Bottoms today. They're trying to stop construction of the waste disposal plant. These troublemakers are bent on breaking the law approved by city council. They're a threat to our way of life. The leaders are convicted felons. If these interlopers are not stopped, they'll deprive us of our liberty and freedom. Oppose anarchy! Do whatever you can to stop the demonstrators!"

Dread chilled his blood. He'd seen how social media could stampede people into senseless and destructive behavior. If the wrong people followed these instructions, their peaceable work stoppage could be ruined by violence.

He showed Martha the email. "What do you think of this?"

"Dangerous," she said with a frown after she'd read the post. "Who did it?"

"You mean who'll take it seriously?" Alice Morrison suddenly chimed in from behind them, breathing hard after her own climb. Yellow jeans and WCEP T-shirt made her hard to miss.

"Oh, I do hope and pray our work here today is nonviolent!" Martha fretted.

"If our work stoppage doesn't force the cult to renege," Alice said, "we'll need outside intervention."

"Well, I sure hope the governor will come through for us," Harvey replied. He barked a laugh, remembering the triumphant expression on Hugh Fairmont's face as he reeled in a twenty-inch trout under a gnarly old oak.

Moments later, they descended the steps back to Wilkerson Avenue.

Walking south on First Street, eager to sample the mood, he greeted bystanders and picketers alike. The pavement was dry, but the gutters carried a murky soup of greasy mud that caked unsuspecting shoes. People had to shout over the roar of heavy equipment to make themselves heard as a light breeze from the northwest served up a generous helping of smoke and dust.

Heading south toward Douglas Street, a circle of early-bird demonstrators picketed the main entrance to the construction zone, singing songs and shouting slogans.

Two blocks farther south, a multitude of green, yellow, and blue buses disgorged crowds of local churchgoers from south of the river. True to her word, Melissa Gravenly showed up with hundreds of white faces showing enthusiastic support for the demonstration.

"Hey, Harvey! We brought a big crowd!" Melissa cheered, thrusting her right fist in the air. She wore a gray farmer's shirt, faded blue jeans, and high-top tennies. "They're rarin' to go!"

A hand touched his shoulder. Ben Booker of Bethel AME Church gave him a hug and a wide grin. "Hello, partner!" he said. "Do we have enough people to guarantee success?" He laughed.

"Have you seen the social media post?" Melissa asked. "I think it's dangerous."

Ben nodded. "Evil starin' us in the face," he said.

Harvey agreed, but Melissa's open acknowledgment of that danger released a flood of anxiety within him. From the last demonstration, he'd learned that using masses of people to redress grievances didn't always produce the expected results. Camaraderie and solidarity were at best unreliable, the opportunity for success as ephemeral as the passing clouds.

By one o'clock, however, he had decided there was no other way than to play through to the end. He joined demonstrators marching at Gate 2, just across Wilkerson Boulevard from the open public dump. This gate admitted only purchased materials and equipment. Circling the dump, an improved road laughingly called Stinky Avenue allowed drivers to position their rigs for easy access. This left Wilkerson open for the big dirt haulers to pass through on their way west to Gate 3.

When a dusty blue flatbed truck carrying rebar lined up to enter the gate, the gatekeeper opened the gate so the truck could cross Wilkerson into the site. In a few minutes, the next truck arrived with a load of steel girders. Now, protesters swarmed around the truck, four of them stood against the front bumper, and three others climbed up on the load, strapping themselves to the steel.

When the gatekeeper motioned for the driver to wait, concern about the possible effects of the social media post prompted him to approach the driver and introduce himself.

"What's going on?" inquired the young driver. The fellow wore a faded blue work shirt and a Cubs baseball hat.

Harvey explained the demonstration and told him that volunteers were ready to keep trucks from delivering their loads. In the process, he learned the driver's name was Danny.

"Why are they doing that?" Danny asked.

"To make the public aware of the pollution the WDP will cause when it's up and running. Do you have children?"

"Sure. Three of 'em," Danny replied with a shy smile. "Five, six, and eight."

"Would you want to see them poisoned by the water they splash around in or the dirt that clings to their skin?"

"No, I wouldn't," said Danny, frowning.

"Same for these people. They've had a century and a half of poison, and they're fed up with it."

The gatekeeper opened the gate. Two volunteers lay with apparent calm in front of each of Danny's massive front wheels.

"What are you going to do, Danny?" Harvey asked, backing away from the cab.

"Don't know," Danny replied, shaking his head as sweat poured down his face. "I know what my job is, but I can't run over people."

While Danny made up his mind, another truck carrying a brand-new articulated hauler taxied in behind his. Six demonstrators ran to lie in front of its wheels.

Just then a company foreman wearing a white hardhat appeared at the gate. He was a large man with a broad face, thick neck, and booming voice, wearing bib overalls and heavy yellow boots.

"Who's in charge here?" he demanded.

Harvey walked across Wilkerson to the gate. "What do you need?" A double cocktail of anger and fear convulsed his stomach.

"You people should not be here!" the foreman declared.

"We have to do it," Harvey replied. "It's the only way to get this project stopped."

"Tough shit, fella!" the foreman blasted back. "None of my business. Now get your people the hell outta here." He shouted the command as if to a disobedient child.

"Not your business?" Harvey gave a scornful laugh. "You're wallowing in toxic waste!" He pointed at the foreman. "Your clothes and boots, even your face, are covered with soil containing heavy metals and PCBs. I hope you give yourself a complete wash when you get home."

"You cain't scare me!" the foreman scoffed. "What the hell business is it of yours?"

Just then a tall young African American fellow wearing a red hardhat with a union insignia joined the group.

"I'm Thad Marshall, union steward on this job. What's up?"

The foreman summarized his predicament.

"Simple solution," said Marshall. "Since it's a Friday, the drivers can elect to take the rest of the day off, and we'll close Gate 2 to further traffic." He glanced at his watch. "Only another hour till quittin' time anyway."

"I ain't runnin' over no human beings!" Danny fumed. Then he pivoted toward his truck and marched back across the street. "Hey, Mark!" he called to the driver behind his rig. "Back up so I can turn around, and we'll skedaddle."

The other driver nodded and waved in confirmation. Then the two proceeded west on Wilkerson toward the highway.

The unexpected release of tension caused Harvey to feel weak in the knees. They'd had a victory; the gate was closed. With great anticipation, the demonstrators marched half a mile farther west to Gate 3 to take on the dirt haulers.

At this stage of construction, massive earth-moving machines scooped great heaps of contaminated soil, then deposited it on huge conveyor belts that loaded it into haulers for transport to a dump site. The deafening roar of heavy equipment, the stench of exhaust, and the overpowering odor of the soil made for an overwhelming, nauseating experience. But if they could keep the empty trucks outside, the huge conveyor belts would soon have nowhere to deposit the soil rising from the pits.

When they reached the gate, half a dozen people proceeded to where the next two trucks stood in line. The first truck was a fearsome, bright red Kenworth with dual rear exhaust stacks and double 150-gallon fuel tanks. A chrome visor and a twelve-inch reflective bumper added to its intimidating affectation. The second truck was a sleek-looking, shiny black International Lodestar with a gaudy mouthful of chrome in the shape of futuristic bat wings.

He approached the driver of the Kenworth and learned his name was Coot Dodson.

"I sure as hell *do* know what's happenin' here," Dodson railed.

"What do you think?" he pressed. "Are you with us?"

"Hell, no!" Dodson shouted. "Bunch o' lawbreakers tryin' to stop construction!"

"Where'd you hear that?" he asked.

"Read the posting on social media this morning. Said we should stop the demonstration to save our freedom and democracy," Coot replied.

An adrenaline spike forced him to catch his breath. This was it, just as he had feared.

"Are you going to run these people over when it's your turn for the gate?" he asked.

"If they're still in front of my truck, no doubt about it," Coot replied. "I will run 'em the fuck over! Gotta keep construction movin'." He picked up his walkie and thumbed it to call the driver in the truck behind him. "Hey, Pete, gatekeeper says they got room for two."

"Roger that," Pete replied. "I'm gettin' nervous with all these people standin' around."

"Me, too. But don't let it bother ya, Pete. We're on a mission. A mission for God. We're gonna teach these assholes a lesson, right?"

"Roger that, too," Pete affirmed.

Turning back to Harvey, Dodson continued his rant. "You know what a shutdown means for us?"

"No paycheck?" Harvey ventured.

"You got that right," the driver shot back, adjusting his red ball cap. "We're doin' this for ourselves *and* for liberty and freedom." He looked at the gatekeeper and saluted. "Sorry, bud, I just got the nod. Gotta roll."

Harvey hastily backed away from the cab.

Dodson stuck his head out the window to yell at the demonstrators. "Don't mar that engine cowling and chrome!" he shouted. "And try not to get blood on everything!" His loud cackle of laughter was drowned out as the engine revved, as if to scare the demonstrators with a taste of what he had in store.

The threat galvanized Harvey's fear, and his heart pounded in his chest.

Just then, Rev. Nate Kline stood with the demonstrators in front of the big hauler's cab. "We're fightin' this fight so the next generation can live and breathe free!" he shouted.

"Amen!" came the response.

From a position near Harvey, Ben Booker's rich baritone voice rang out as he began to sing. "When Israel was in Egypt Land—"

"Let my people go," the people responded in harmony.

"Oppressed so hard they could not stand," Booker intoned with a dramatic touch as he walked back toward Pete's truck.

"Let my people go," came the response.

Together they sang the chorus. "Go down, Moses! Way down in Egypt land. Tell ole Pharaoh, to let my people go!"

Leaning out of his window, Dodson lambasted the singers one final time. "Get outta here, you chickenshit motherfuckers! I'm not waitin' aroun' for anybody dumb enough t'stand in the way o' this truck. You're breakin' the law! You want anarchy? I'll give you anarchy, goddamnit!"

Dodson revved his engine again.

Two volunteers placed their arms against the truck's front cowling, their heads barely reaching above the bright steel engine.

"Let … my … people … go!" the crowd roared and clapped.

One young fellow beat an angry tattoo on Dodson's engine hood right down to the last second as Coot shifted into second gear, pressed the accelerator and slipped the clutch. In one liquid motion, ten tons of steel and rubber gave a convulsive shudder, then rumbled ahead, gathering speed.

The demonstrators fell as wheat before a threshing machine. In a last-ditch effort to stay upright, one of them grabbed the hood ornament. It broke off in his hand, and he, too, was mashed to the pavement. Two agonizing screams came from beneath the Kenworth and three more from under the Lodestar. Both trailers bounced from shoulder to shoulder, scattering bodies for twenty yards.

Ignoring the gate, and perhaps realizing what he'd just done, Dodson kept moving west on Wilkerson. The second truck was on his tail, along with two city squad cars.

The first visible casualty was Nate Kline, crushed under the Kenworth's right front wheel as he sang.

Melissa Gravenly ran to him wailing, sobbing. Harvey was right behind her. She picked up the minister's smashed, bleeding head and cradled it in her arms as she sat on the roadway.

"Oh! My beautiful, beautiful man!" she wailed without ceasing.

Harvey gasped with rage and disbelief. But there was nothing he could do for Nate now. He looked around to see where he was needed. Another man had been crushed and mangled underneath the drive wheels of Dodson's cab. Numb with terror, Harvey helped the paramedics carry his body to the ambulance.

Martha Ruggles tended the lifeless body of a woman who'd been caught by the left front wheel of the Lodestar. He bent to help her, tears streaming down his face, until the paramedics came.

Four others suffered crushed arms or legs. Red and yellow flowers lay scattered on the road. An orange baseball hat lay in the ditch twenty yards away. In shock, he walked to retrieve it, along with a cell phone. Shards of glass and bits of plastic were the sole remnants of someone's horn-rimmed glasses. For a few moments, he just stood in the middle of the roadway, shocked at how the media post had accomplished its intended purpose. Was he in the right universe?

Terror and grief gripped marchers and onlookers alike. The police cleared away the waiting tandem haulers and tried in vain to restore order and calm. Many of the marchers headed for their cars or to the buses that had brought them. A few oldsters fled to the senior center.

Flooded with grief, Harvey worked with the paramedics to care for the wounded. As the last one was wheeled to an ambulance, he stood, unbelieving, as a sudden coldness numbed him at the core.

Far across the work site, down at First Street, a mass of figures in black, wearing masks, many carrying weapons, ran along Monroe Street, crossed First, then bolted through Gate 6, which hung off its hinges at a crazy angle. They ran northwest, spreading over the construction site, converging on the mobile offices that served as the contractor's headquarters.

"Those aren't demonstrators!" Alice shouted with alarm as she rushed to join him. "They're gang kids!"

"They're not our people," Paul Johnson said, also out of breath. His voice shook with fear. "They're the drug gangs! They're opposed to nonviolence, and they're apparently out to rid the place of the WDP their own way."

Feelings of futility and powerlessness washed over Harvey. Multiple horrific explosions shook the air as the gangbangers insanely tossed grenades and firebombs into construction equipment and the cabs of many soil haulers. The drivers plodded through the muddy tracks, trying in desperation to escape the Armageddon.

This was a wild card, a disaster from a totally unexpected source. All the efforts of community residents, all the planning, all the hopes for a peaceful outcome to the WDP wrestling match were now lost, down the drain.

But perhaps there was a tie to the cult, thin as it might be. Clarence Williams was a strong influence among the gangs. Though he had voted to keep the WDP in the Bottoms, could he have put the gangs up to this? Harvey shook his head in disbelief. Surely the man would have had better sense.

"Did they read the social media post?" Alice asked.

"We believe so," Johnson replied, wiping his face and forehead with a handkerchief. His brown jeans and shirt were drenched. "Our people are trying to discover where this originated."

A splinter group of hooligans reached the construction company's trailers and ducked underneath. Seconds later those structures exploded and burned, even as the last employees scurried for safety.

"They're closing the gates!" Alice shouted.

"No one will escape now," Johnson said in obvious dejection.

They watched as Captain Swanson directed his officers into battle formation, weapons drawn, batons and shields at the ready. Several phalanxes moved forward in a pincer formation to grab, beat, and arrest anyone they could. The incident became a desperate, savage battle between the gangs and the police.

"They're bringing in the water cannons!" Harvey exclaimed, pointing toward Monroe Street. Two cannons headed north through Gate 6 toward the battle. Gang members by the dozen fell under the disabling jets of water. Many were upended or bowled over. Others tried running around the perimeter fence, looking for an opening, but were soon corralled and beaten senseless.

"I'm going to Langley Park for a better view," Harvey said. "Looks like the governor's entourage turning from Washington Street!"

"Yep! Here they come now," said Johnson. "Charles Higgins will likely accompany the governor."

The police halted the governor's motorcade, presumably to advise them of the circumstances.

"I'll alert them to come to the park," Paul said. "That's a safer place to talk." He took off, running toward the place where motorcycles surrounded Fairmont's limousine.

Harvey and Alice ran to the base of Langley Park and scrambled up the steps.

Reaching the top, Harvey collapsed on a bench. Sweat drenched his shirt, and he struggled to catch his breath. A slight dizziness and weakness in his legs assailed him, not so much from the climb but from the disheartening thought that violence might indeed be the only remedy for Westfield's predicament. His insides felt as if they were filled with ground glass.

He needed to view the chaos from afar to master his feelings of futility and powerlessness. In just a few minutes, social media meddling and gang violence had transformed the community's hope for a peaceful protest into disaster. He bent forward, burying his face in his hands as he caught a sorrowful vision of the entire nation suddenly shifting from oligarchy to destruction by the mob.

At length, he looked up at Alice, who sat to his right. He pounded a fist into the palm of his other hand. "I want retribution, dammit! I want to string up whoever posted that letter, whoever prompted these idiots to storm the site." The cult on steroids was how he imagined it.

"Do you think our peaceful protest would have achieved any lasting result?" Alice asked. Anger and disbelief clouded her periwinkle eyes. Her thin lips were closed in a gesture of what could only be frustration.

In essence, he'd made the same argument to Paul Johnson when they'd first discussed strategy. He wanted to pull together a demolition team to simply blow the WDP to smithereens. But he'd given in to Martha Ruggles's recollections of nonviolent success in the sixties. That obviously had been a mistake. Part of the new universe, he guessed. Don't negotiate, forget compromise, just blow 'em the fuck up!

Martha Ruggles's point during their interview had been on the mark—whoever held the money and the threat of death was boss. A nonviolent approach worked only when everyone held similar moral principles. And that time belonged to the ancient past.

"What's the governor doing here?" he asked.

"I'm glad he's here. Glad he got to see this fiasco," Alice replied without answering his question.

Accompanied by Paul, Gerald MacFarlane, and Charles Higgins, Governor Hugh Fairmont, in navy blue suit pants and dampened white shirt with sleeves rolled to the elbows, stepped onto the grassy knoll.

The governor recognized Harvey and shook his hand. "Can you fill us in on what's happened?"

Harvey gave a brief account of the day's events, summarized the tragedy at Gate 3, then the gangs' destruction of the site.

"One of the worst events I've witnessed in my life!" Hugh Fairmont exclaimed.

As he spoke, a series of thunderous explosions rocked the grassy knoll. At the far south end of the construction, sections of two bulldozers and a huge conveyor belt flew a hundred feet in the air. Then six steel roof support towers toppled.

"I guess they're not through yet," the governor commented, shaking his head.

At that moment, Mayor John Timmerling walked over from the steps. "Governor!" Timmerling burst out with a disparaging tone, nostrils flaring. "The decision of the Westfield city council—"

"My question is," the governor cut the mayor short. "*Why* did you do it?"

"Financial necessity!" Timmerling barked, his eyes bulging. "What else? It was the only way we could receive federal Brownfields funding." He waved a dismissive hand in the air.

"That's a crock, Timmerling!" Harvey sneered. "You've decided to make the minorities and the poor sacrifice so you rich business types and financiers can make more money." He pointed his index finger at the mayor with blistering disdain. "That's an old familiar Westfield pattern, isn't it? Dump the waste where the people with the least power live. Then they won't raise a fuss! Ha-ha. Very funny!"

"Gentlemen! Gentlemen! Enough! Please!" said the governor, hands outstretched, palms down. "Let's keep a civil tongue." Fairmont held his position staring at each of them until there was silence. Then he continued. "We will discover the facts, and you'll each have a chance to make your views known."

The governor now turned to Gerald MacFarlane and Charles Higgins. "From what you've reported so far, and from what I hear today, it seems we need an emergency city manager. Would your findings support that conclusion?"

"Finally!" Alice cried out in relief, clapping her hands overhead. Her eyes rolled heavenward as a smile spread across her face.

The governor gave her a startled, cautionary glance.

MacFarlane gave a subtle nod.

Charles Higgins gave a thumbs-up.

At last, Harvey had what he needed. An ECM would block the cult members and protect city staff.

Fairmont turned to Higgins. "I see the media reps are still on the scene. Can you put together a quick press conference in twenty minutes?"

"Sure thing, Hugh," said Higgins, taking out his cell phone.

At four o'clock, the governor's retinue assembled with the media under the white tent, and Hugh Fairmont, once again in a navy blue suit and striped tie, stepped to the podium.

"As governor of this fair state, I want our people to survive and thrive. We can build a healthy, vibrant state if we work for greater equality between the haves and the have-nots. Justice must prevail in the smallest hamlets and villages as well as in our cities. Municipal staff and elected officials must make prudent decisions that benefit the public good, not special interests.

"In recent years, Westfield has suffered from destructive influences. The city is growing, but its budget has remained static for twenty years. One by one, city services have suffered drastic cuts or disappeared.

"Last month, as you know, I initiated an independent investigation into the financial condition of the city of Westfield. Mr. Gerald MacFarlane, a career investigator with our state police force, is here with me today." He nodded toward MacFarlane, who raised his hand. "Westfield should be throbbing with life. But it has symptoms of decay and destruction, not the least of which was a decision by city council to place a waste disposal facility adjacent to a residential neighborhood that already had a history of industrial pollution. It's time for a correction.

"In light of these facts, I am now appointing an emergency city manager for the city of Westfield."

The media reps erupted in audible gasps and muttered exclamations of surprise. Was this a sign that Westfield was on its last legs?

"I am asking Mr. Timothy Benson to carry out this assignment. He is a long-time city manager and an expert with thirty-five years of excellence in city government. As emergency city manager, Mr. Benson's job will be to restore the governance of the city of Westfield to a healthy, fiscally sound, and morally enriched condition, able to meet the needs of every citizen. That's all I have for you today. Are there any questions?"

"Has the WDP project been suspended?" asked a representative of Channel 5.

The governor looked at Tim Benson, who nodded. "Mr. Benson confirms that the project has been halted as of this moment."

Just then, his limousine rounded the corner. Fairmont thanked the media. Then he and his associates climbed in and disappeared down First Street.

Contrary to his earlier expectations, the day had opened a crucial door to achieving the first of his goals. How odd that what had seemed an impossible task was now easier thanks to a businessman and politician who cared about the common good. What had begun as a question, then turned to despair, had now resolved into a success. Thank goodness the governor had appointed an ECM. Fairmont had proved he could be trusted to empower people rather than extract more from them.

That placed a heavy burden on Harvey's own shoulders, however. He had to ensure that Benson devised a way for Westfield citizens to reclaim their government and transform their city. It would not, he supposed, be a smooth and easy process.

CHAPTER 12

NEW STRATEGIES

The following Monday morning, as Mike Dwyer drove to the bank for a team meeting at ten, he pounded the steering wheel of his BMW as his mind replayed the previous week's events. The show resembled a disaster newsreel more than an adventure film.

First, the governor's decision to investigate Westfield's finances had the potential to administer a seismic shock to the public-private partnership he'd taken two decades to establish.

Then the latest pollution report, issued under the all-too-circumspect eye of Gerald MacFarlane, had stirred a hornets' nest of anger among his business partners. Rhett Bennett's explosion, plus another half dozen calls from angry CEO's strained his nerves to the breaking point.

What disturbed him most, however, was that he hadn't taken into account the possibility that Clarence Williams, unpredictable rascal that he was, would incite the gangs to destroy the waste disposal project. He should have seen it coming, but he hadn't. He'd focused on perfecting his social media post. Had his mother been alive, he would have received harsh and well deserved punishment for such a strategic error.

As a result, since his team faced a more troublesome set of circumstances, they needed a more potent strategy to deal with it.

They could not allow Davenport and friends to dictate public policy. The team had to maintain dominion because business success was far more critical to a well-run society than anything else.

As he reviewed the morning's mail and several loan applications, his three troublemakers arrived. Clarence Williams wore a navy blue suit. Norm Taylor's outfit reminded him of a clown. And Rhett Bennett wore a sycophantic smile over his bright red tie.

"Welcome, gentlemen!" he called.

They waved back and proceeded eagerly into the conference room, presumably in pursuit of breakfast goodies.

Precisely at 10:00 a.m., he rose from his desk, gathered his notes, and sat at the head of the conference table. A minute later, Dana opened the door and ushered in Marty Angelo and Doug Thompson. They acknowledged his nod as he noted their late arrival on his attendance clipboard.

"Gentlemen," he said, as if he considered them peers. "As you know, we've suffered some losses. What's on your mind and what should we do?" Allowing them to comment first let them know he required participation.

"We received hundreds of irate calls after that pollution report," said Norm Taylor. "How could you let that happen, George?"

"It was careless," Thompson confirmed. His hard, deep-set eyes shot well-deserved blame down his aristocratic nose. "Didn't you review it beforehand?"

"It was a busy time," Howard replied, shrugging his shoulders. He leaned back and picked up a pencil. "MacFarlane's presence has sent uncertainty into every corner of the administration."

"We should run as tight a ship at city hall as we do in our businesses," Mayor Timmerling lectured. "You're sitting on a powder keg, George. So handle it!"

What made these guys so angrifying was their penchant for wasting time arguing and competing. With the fervent hope that once they'd got it out of their systems they'd be able to concentrate on their problems, he banged his gavel on the table, leaving several dents to commemorate the occasion.

"What are we doing about that investigator?" Clarence inquired. "He'll soon be coming to each of us. What are we supposed to say?"

"The MacFarlane investigation is pro forma," attorney Doug Thompson lectured in a flat voice, deep-set eyes peering from under heavy, dark brows. "They won't find anything more than majority votes for a prudent fiscal policy. Plus a very well-controlled budget." He emitted a snickery laugh. "There's no city in this state as tight as Westfield."

"You may be right about MacFarlane," said Timmerling, looking quite informal in a day-old beard and blue dress shirt with the sleeves rolled to the elbows. "But the one who will make life tough for business is Benson."

"Nah, what can Benson do?" Rhett Bennett responded with obvious loathing.

"He can take over the council's work, that's what!" Timmerling shot back with obvious heat. "He can also run the city with an iron hand."

Mike had set a meeting with Benson for the following Monday morning. He hoped Benson appreciated the public-private partnership. But he knew how to handle Tim. They'd worked together on city projects before. Piece of cake. Except if it wasn't.

"Okay, friends, we need to change our strategy," Mike interjected. "What would you say to ridding ourselves of the people interfering with our efforts, chief among them Harvey Davenport?"

"Amen!" Timmerling affirmed. "And that Morrison woman too! God, she's a nuisance!"

"And Paul Johnson," Rhett Bennett affirmed.

"Give Johnson to Clarence," said Doug Thompson with a broad, toothy smile. "That's his turf."

Mike turned to Williams. "Can you handle that? Remove Johnson and keep it quiet." None of the team was comfortable in the Bottoms, except Clarence. It was a creepy place where one's back was never safe.

"Gotcha covered," Williams agreed.

"Who's got Morrison?" Mike asked.

"I'll talk to her," said Marty Angelo. "She's not as dangerous as the others. Her term's soon finished. Let me see if she'll agree to back off."

"Good," said Mike. "But, again, don't involve the rest of us, all right?"

"Understood," said Angelo with a nod of his head.

"Moving on," Mike said. "To keep the WDP in the Bottoms, we need to get with Benson early on Monday morning. Who's going with me?"

"I'll go," said Bennett.

"Count me in," said Williams.

"Thanks," Mike said with a thin-lipped smile. "We also need to restore order in the Environment Department of the city. George, can you handle that?"

"I don't know. I think it'll look like I'm cleaning house as revenge for Macfarlane's revelation," the city manager replied with a shrug, head tilted, hands palms up.

"Not if you don't clean house," he quipped with a smile. "Don't get carried away. Just reset some procedures and standards, then enforce them. Don't trust. Verify. In person. Every time."

"Yes, Mother," came the taunting reply.

"Getting to Benson is the best idea I've heard," said Thompson.

"Agreed," said Marty. "I don't like the rough stuff. What do you say, Mr. Mayor?"

"What alternatives do we have, gents?" said Timmerling. "We can't let them bully us around or kick us out. We've worked too hard, too long."

"Let's get to the legislature," boomed Bennett. "Most of those people are business types. We should ask them to pass legislation that makes it illegal to investigate municipal governments without the Senate's approval."

"Excellent idea!" Mike praised him. "Why don't you talk to the city attorney about drafting the legislation? He's also got people who can give us a leg up in the State House."

Just then, muffled commands and the rumble of dollies in the outer office interrupted the meeting. A shrill scream from Dana followed the sharp rasp of metal on metal.

"No! No! You can't come in here! This is a secure area!"

The conference room door burst open.

"Help! Mike, I need you! Get these guys outta here! Please!"

"Excuse me, gentlemen." Mike rose from his chair. "Let me see what the hell's going on!" Halfway to the conference room door, he turned to face them. "We're done here, fellows. Looks like we've got our strategy."

He turned and hurried to the outer office and headed for Dana's desk at a run. He slid, then fell on his back in a loathsome, putrid mess of black goo, just as the elevator doors closed on whoever had played this prank.

"What the *hell happened*? My God, this stuff smells like asphalt!" he yelled. Scrambling to his feet, he noticed Clarence Williams making a beeline for the stairs, a knowing smirk on his face as he ducked his head between his short shoulders. The goop had a greasy, sticky consistency, and big clumps stuck to his suit and shoes. *Shades of Martha Ruggles!*

"I'm trying to get security, but no one's answering." Dana shouted, phone in hand.

Mike clumped through the sludge and across his expensive red wool carpet to his desk, reached for his phone, and dialed his branch manager. "Tom! Security alert! Get everyone out of the bank. Shut off the elevators, now! We can't reach security. They may have been compromised … Right! … Bad guys are coming down in the elevator now."

As Marty and Doug ducked into the hall to take the stairs, Mike heard laughter echoing in the stairwell.

Rhett Bennett spotted a note scrawled in black magic marker on a piece of cardboard placed on Mike's desk. He read the message out loud.

"Your office is now a Sacrifice Zone! Hope you like it!"

Back at his desk, Mike dialed Robert Kravitz. "As we discussed. Get Davenport after city council meeting. Make it quick, and let me know when you've finished." He was about to hang up when he had another thought. "Bring me his left hand—just to make sure. I want to see the evidence."

Shaking like a leaf in a windstorm with heart pounding and sweat beading up on his forehead, running down his face, he went to the shower room to wash off the goo and don his third suit of the day. Relaxing under the warm water, he realized the intruders were all young. Probably gang members. Not even he was immune to their pranks, and Clarence Williams was their patron saint. Another complication to an already tense situation.

That same evening, Harvey arrived at Mama Lulu's just after eight o'clock. The hot, muggy night followed an intense and stressful city council meeting. He peered through the neon-lit windows of the restaurant. The place was packed! No wonder he'd had to park two blocks away. He was here to talk strategy with Paul Johnson, but the soothing jazz and loose crowd promised relief from the pressures of arguing over Westfield's future.

He'd come here to advise Paul that their top priority now had to be removing cult members from city government. As he saw it, only a city council with moral backbone and free of industrial influence could enact the strong policy measures necessary to stop pollution and clean up the Bottoms.

Since entrepreneurial meddling had produced nothing like financially sound governance in the past twenty years, perhaps Benson would be amenable to ousting Dwyer's people during the financial emergency.

As he tugged open the door soft jazz, subdued lighting and lively conversation enveloped him. Several people lounged on the old grime-encrusted, crocodile-green couches in the front window. In a corner to the left, two couples made out on an old graying sectional. On the right, chess and checker enthusiasts surrounded two sets of players. The place smelled of stale cigar smoke and ancient oak flooring worn gray with a hundred years of dust and dirt.

He sighed and lingered for a moment, soaking up the atmosphere. Precious, the house watch-cat, brushed against him, twining her tail around his legs. He paused a moment to scratch her ears as he archived this moment in his brain.

Paul waved at him from a table at the back of the room. The mess of papers spread around him suggested he'd been there several hours. A pile of gnawed rib bones on a paper plate threatened to collapse on the floor. The sharp fumes of Mama Lulu's tangy barbecue sauce reminded him he hadn't eaten all day.

Paul rose, and they shook hands.

"This is becoming my favorite place," he said.

"Glad you like it," Paul replied as he tugged an empty table over and scooped his papers onto it.

When they were seated, a waitress brought frosty glasses of iced tea, and he ordered a pulled pork sandwich and greens, plus a slice of chocolate layer cake with its marvelous cream cheese filling. His hands welcomed the cold moisture on the glass of tea, and a long swig of the delicious brew relaxed him.

"So, how'd it go with city council?" Paul asked, shifting the toothpick in his mouth from one side to the other.

Before he could reply, their waitress set two large plates before him. One held a monstrous pork sandwich, the other boasted a mountain of chocolate cake with ice cream. She then brought an enormous bowl of greens. He took a big bite of his pork sandwich and let the oily sauce run down his chin.

"You would have appreciated the disgusted look on Timmerling's face as Benson called the meeting to order," he said when he'd swallowed his first bite. "Looked like the guy who lost his best friend and his diamond ring."

"What'd Benson say?"

"A change of rules." He bit into his sandwich again. "The ECM has all the power," he said around the food in his mouth. "We won't meet every week—only on the ECM's order. We can't make policy or affect the city's financial condition without the ECM's approval."

He stopped to chew and swallow another bite. "You should've seen the uproar! Dwyer had a fit, Bennett was up in arms. The mayor stewed but said nothing."

As he spoke, the emotions of those moments revisited him. When his stomach gave an anxious flip, he laid his sandwich on its plate and wiped his hands on his paper napkin as it fell to shreds. He picked up another to wipe his chin.

"Will Benson help us?"

"Hard to say. The whole meeting left me churning with impatience." He rubbed the back of his neck as his headache of earlier threatened to return. "Rhett Bennett complained that Benson would bring the city to fiscal ruin, but Benson said that's been its condition for two decades. Alice laughed out loud!" He shook his head in disbelief. "Look at the situation. With Benson as the ECM, the council can't meddle in either the discovery process or the remediation of the Bottoms."

"Good for us," Paul affirmed. "We can involve Benson in remediation. We'll need sign-offs from city officials to get state and federal help."

"Since he's a friend of Hugh Fairmont, and the governor despises anyone dumping toxic waste in minority neighborhoods, we shouldn't have much trouble."

"Your overall conclusion?"

"Benson's relatively safe for us. Alice, Stan, and I will meet with him tomorrow morning about the effects of twenty years of business domination."

"Remediation will raise the financial juggernaut he faces by several millions," Paul countered. "We'll need the business crowd at some point."

"Sure. We just can't let them run things. That's where we run into problems."

"I can see the meeting had its difficulties."

"Thank goodness it was short!" He heaved a sigh and shook his head. "So now, what should we do?" Eagerness to hear Paul's plans kept him on the edge of his chair, a hand resting on one knee as it pumped rhythmically up and down.

"Glad you asked," Paul responded with a Cheshire smile. His eyes glowed as he rubbed his hands together. "I want to clean up the Bottoms," Paul confided.

"I agree," Harvey replied, reaching for his fork. With infinite precision, he carved a generous bite-sized portion of cake. The taste of chocolate and cold cream cheese filling soothed his tense nerves. "But I want to clean up city government because that's the only way we can create the policy foundation we need to clean up the Bottoms." He chewed his cake and swallowed it. Then, with a frown, he said, "You and I seem to be moving"—he sipped his iced tea, searching for the right words—"in different directions. You're working on remediation of toxic waste, I'm working on remediation of city management. Both take time and effort."

"What do you want to do? Should we split up?"

"No. Let's combine issues. Consider that the whole of Westfield has a double concern."

"Whites help blacks on remediation of waste, blacks help whites on removing business bullies from government?"

"It has potential." He took another bite of cake and chewed.

"We have a group here dedicated to informing our people on taxes."

"Good news," he mumbled through a mouthful.

"We've also got another group working on fed and state funding for remediation."

"Looks like it's coming together," Harvey concluded. "You handle toxic waste here and let your tax group expand into a citywide campaign. Then enlist the nonprofits in educating the public. I'll concentrate on ousting the cult and starting a tax campaign in white neighborhoods, which will join your efforts."

"If we succeed," Paul affirmed, "Westfield will be a much-improved city within five years."

"Meeting adjourned," Harvey said. He smiled as they shook hands. Months of hard work awaited them, and there was no telling what Dwyer and his crowd would throw their way.

CHAPTER 13

THE UNFORESEEN

Outside Mama Lulu's on the sidewalk, the steamy black night sucked his breath away. Reluctant to abandon the jubilant spirit of the restaurant, he strode with feigned bravery toward his van. One lonely streetlight and a rising full moon illuminated the street, casting ghostly shadows. Gradually, his pace slowed and his heartbeat quickened as fear pestered his mind about his vulnerability.

When he'd gone another half dozen steps, the sound of boots on concrete forced a glance over his shoulder. Two silhouettes emerged from the gloom, speeding toward him. An open lot where a fire had demolished an abandoned storefront offered a dismal refuge, but a glance farther north confirmed his van remained parked less than a block away. He quickened his pace.

Without warning, a large, brawny figure sprang from the vacant lot, plowed into him, and drove an angry fist into his face. "Mike Dwyer says hello, scumbag!"

He rolled with the punch, but his knees buckled, throwing him into the arms of his pursuers, who dragged him into the rubble, crushing him against a brick facade. The smell of soot and mold on the fire-blackened brick made him gag. When they turned him around, the iridescent red eyes of rats gleamed before they fled to safety. Moonlight revealed the men wore masks. One of his attackers spit a gob of tobacco juice that smacked him on the cheek and slid down his face before dribbling off his chin.

When the attacker on his right eased his grip, Harvey grabbed his face mask by the top and yanked it off, throwing it across the lot while ducking a punch by his confederate. Both men wore black costumes reminiscent of the gangs who had wrecked the WDP construction site.

Again, they threw him up against the wall hard enough to smash his bleeding nose, pinned him to the wall, and held him.

"Ready, boss," said the man without a mask, turning his head to the left.

The thugs' leader, wearing a black short-sleeved shirt, stepped in front of him. Moonlight revealed an oily smile that oozed cruelty. Multiple tattoos decorated his thick, solid arms.

"Say a fast prayer, Davenport, you son of a bitch, 'cause they'll soon hafta scrape your sorry corpse off the ground."

Lightning fast, the boss punched him in the face so hard it turned him around. Dancing backward, the man reached in his pocket to extract a set of brass knuckles.

"This'll teach you to stick your nose in other people's business!"

A punch to the gut doubled Harvey over. His knees buckled, forcing him down so that his head hit bricks and his face smacked into a puddle of muddy water. A piece of old newspaper showed a surfer enjoying the ocean. "For the time of your life!" screamed the headline. When he wiped his face, his hand came away covered in blood. He rolled over as dark enveloped him.

He regained awareness when the two accomplices grabbed his arms, forcing him up against the wall once more, exposing his chest and abdomen. After another one of the leader's powerful punches, he gasped, trying to catch his breath. His head blazed with pain. He tried to scream, but nothing came out. His hands, arms, and legs shook, and he collapsed again onto the bricks and cement blocks. He nearly lost consciousness when his head hit the iron rods of a sewer drain, but the sharp stench of ammonia roused him. In the distance, someone gasped, then retched. He realized with a shock it was himself he heard, losing his pulled pork and chocolate cake into the sewer.

"You were warned to stay out of the way," the leader growled. "Now I'll make sure you're out for good."

The boss kicked him in the lower back, then in the head. He came to the other side and kicked him repeatedly in the ribs and stomach.

Cold froze him at the core of his being. He went rigid, and his gut tightened in readiness. He might not survive this beating. This was like experiences he'd had in Iraq, embedded with the troops as a photojournalist. When he tried to crawl away, the ruffians yanked him by the shoulders and dragged him back to the brick wall.

As if in a dream, a rush of adrenaline kick-started his energy. Survival patterns from his wartime training filled his mind. He stood, reached out, snatched a head in each hand and mashed them together with all the strength he could muster. Twice. Three times. The goons fell, howling and clutching their heads.

Next, he head-butted the leader, tackling and throwing the man backward on the jagged bricks. He rolled to his left, rising into a crouch, grabbed a large brick, and repeatedly pounded the leader's head with it.

The man rolled away, sprang up in a crouch, and delivered a blow to Harvey's solar plexus that cut his breath in two. But he rolled to the opposite side and once more stood to face his attacker.

"Now it's your turn, maggot!" he sneered through clenched jaws. He drove his right fist into the leader's gut, then followed with a left to his face.

The attacker rocked backward, tripped on a piece of cement block, and fell. Rolling over, the boss pulled a Beretta 380 from his back pocket and pointed it at him.

"Not so fast, fuckhead!" the man said, breathing heavily.

But in the second it took the fellow to release the safety, Harvey was on him. He grabbed the attacker's arm and hammered it hard against a jagged edge of cement block until the gun fell through the sewer grate with a delayed splash.

Despite his injuries, inflicting some damage on his attackers felt good, but there was little time for self-congratulation.

The goons once again fastened upon his arms and pulled him away. They dragged him, stumbling, to a huge section of cement culvert halfway across the vacant lot and threw him onto it, spread-eagle. Before he could pull himself up, they tied a grimy piece of rope around his neck and fastened the loose ends to two cement blocks. He caught the sickening smell of ripe garbage and dirty diapers from an open plastic bag of refuse beside the drain pipe.

Staggering, the leader yanked a knife from his tool belt. "Hold up his left arm!" he ordered his men.

Harvey tried to scream, but in the grip of terror, he made no sound. Then the unmistakable roar of motorcycle mufflers seemed to galvanize his attackers.

"Here comes trouble!" one mugger yelled as he dropped Harvey's wrist and ran.

Within seconds, four young black men rammed into the vacant lot as the two thugs fled. They got no farther than the ally, however, before his four rescuing angels pounded them into unconsciousness.

The leader pushed Harvey's arm back down on the culvert and began sawing his left hand at the wrist, forcing him to emit a wild, incoherent scream as the knife cut through gristle and bone. He nearly blacked from the fierce, grinding pain. Before the leader could get a better hold and start cutting again, an immense, fearsome black man in a frenzy of rage rounded the corner from the street.

"No ya don't, ya little shit!" the huge man bellowed. "Get off that man!"

"Who says so?" growled the boss, turning to his left just in time to take a powerful fist in the face.

As Harvey lay on the half-pipe, the sound of the boss man's nose breaking briefly cheered him. He booted the leader in the backside, sending him sprawling back toward the newcomer, who lifted the boss like a puppet and threw him hard against the brick wall, where he collapsed in a heap on the rubble.

Meanwhile, Harvey rolled off the culvert and crumpled up inside it, cradling his useless left hand as he watched his deliverer work.

Still gripping his knife, the boss struggled to rise. Slipping on the loose rubble but regaining his balance, he rushed the intruder.

The rescuer deftly sidestepped the attack, then grasped the hand holding the knife, pushed the man to the wall, pounding his hand mercilessly against the brick until the bloody fist let go. The knife fell away with a clatter, lost in the shadows of crumbled masonry.

Then the massive rescuer gave his younger opponent a vicious beating with his fists, battering his face and pounding his abdomen until the leader sank to the ground. Repeated kicks to the groin, back, and head soon yielded an unconscious, bloody pulp.

Meanwhile, Harvey had crawled back out to the sidewalk. He pulled himself upright against a vacant storefront, then allowed himself to lapse into semiconsciousness. His left arm dripped blood on his clothing and the sidewalk, but he no longer cared.

Not even breathing hard, his avenging angel found him. "How's the world feeling, Mistah Davenport? Sorry I took s'long gettin' here. I'm Billie Marshall, but some call me Killer."

The name sounded somewhat familiar.

"Let me see that hand," Billie said. "Good God! Looks like he tried to saw it off! You're a bleedin' mess!" He extracted a large blue bandana from his back pocket and rolled it into a tourniquet, tying it tight around his left forearm. "That should hold ya till we get where we're goin'."

"Where're we goin', big guy?" he asked in a hoarse whisper, sensing he was in friendly hands.

"Hospital."

He couldn't imagine the consequences of losing his hand. The gruesome thought pushed his mind into oblivion.

When he awoke sometime later, he was lying on a gurney in a hospital corridor. An enormous sign indicated the surgical operating room was posted to his left near the ceiling.

"What happened?" he asked the man seated beside him.

"Bit o' conflict, I guess," said Billie. "Looked like the fellow was about to make a war trophy out of your left hand."

"Did you bring me here?"

"Yep. You just about fit in the back of my pickup. Hope the ride wasn't too bumpy!" He grinned and gave him a wink, then peered at him for closer inspection. "You've got a shiner or two."

"Just part of my Halloween costume," came his fuzzy reply. "Will I live? Or is this heaven?"

"Not heaven, for sure! Looks like you still got the troubles o' the world."

Then the light dawned. "You're Killer Marshall, aren't you?"

"Some call me that. And a lot of other names."

"My uncle Theo used to beat the tar out of me almost every day when I was growing up," he said with a weak voice. "A universal trait of the big bosses, I guess. Life's a game to them, a boxing match, where the object is to beat the opposition to mush."

A nurse stopped at his gurney. "They're ready for you in OR, sir. We'll take you on a brief ride."

"You feelin' some pain yet?" Williams asked.

"Not so much."

"You will. Wait till those ribs start squealin'. Then you'll know what real pain is! My advice, though you didn't ask, is breathe while you still can. It'll hurt like hell in a couple of hours. That guy was out to kill you. You know that?"

"I got the message. When did you come along?"

"Nick o' time, looks like."

"Glad you did, Killer. Thank you!"

"Just call me plain ole Billie. I like that better."

"Deal," said Harvey as the orderlies rolled him away.

"See you in a day or two," Billie called after him. "God willin' and that asshole don't come back to getcha."

In desperation, he imagined the look on Dwyer's face at the next city council meeting.

Dense fog shrouded the hollows near the Staminon River Tuesday morning as Mike Dwyer pushed his BMW at breakneck speed along the undulating curves to the newly renovated Staminon Valley Sports and Recreation Club.

The golf course now featured smoother greens and majestic varieties of maple, oak, and Douglas fir. The new marble marquee was a symbol of power, a delight to the eyes. Inside, the clubhouse was a palace. The barroom featured a panoramic view of the course through large windows on three sides. In every aspect, the club displayed the wealth of Westfield to great advantage. This had been a prominent and profitable investment for Westfield National Bank.

It was also the perfect place to celebrate with his team the demise of one Harvey Davenport, a decided nuisance from the first day he'd set foot in the council chamber. Hoping to motivate his men to greater enthusiasm and harder work for the cause, he'd prepared a few remarks for their break at the ninth hole. These guys were sheep—they had to be told what to do, when to do it, and how. They were so eager to be king of the hill and make a lot of money. Yet they hesitated to lend a hand and had difficulty working as a team. Whatever happened to initiative and drive? Since boyhood, he'd schooled himself to do whatever it took to achieve his aims.

The air was clear, the humidity low. A perfect day if one enjoyed being outdoors in the country, which Mike did not. He preferred the cool dryness of his office at the bank. Others might enjoy the great outdoors, but he endured it as a necessary price for keeping Westfield's economic future under his thumb. Ideally, the afternoon high would remain around eighty degrees.

His guests for a 7:00 a.m. tee time piled their golf bags into the backs of three golf carts covered with green-and-white canvas.

"I'll drive, if you don't mind," Mike said to his passenger, Mayor Timmerling. The four guys in the other two carts chipped in five bucks each to pay for a driver. What a waste. Why pay for a service one could provide oneself?

"Which of you ladies will turn this par-three hole into a triple bogey?" John Timmerling interrupted Mike's thoughts. His deep-set, narrow eyes squinted with caution. The mayor certainly didn't look like a golfer in his blue short-sleeve dress shirt and brown slacks. His scores tended to be high, and he usually became irritable by the tenth hole.

"Like *you* did last week, John?" quipped George Howard with a wink.

The one-upmanship had begun already. He rolled his eyes and shook his head. They were so busy competing against one another they couldn't pull together. Like a bunch of seventh-grade miscreants.

"Will you be laughing all the way to the bank today, Mike?" Norm Taylor giggled with a smirk when Mike teed up for the second hole.

Yeah, and you look like a clown in that white shirt with your big, fat red cheeks! He wrinkled his brow and kept the opinion to himself.

Mike chalked his hands and addressed the ball, fingering the leather grip of his club. He had a clear shot. He checked his stance, cocked his arms, then swung the club in a perfect arc and followed through. Just like the instructional videos he'd watched late at night in his condo. The ball flew straight toward the flag as he grinned with satisfaction. A short, easy putt, and he had a birdie. Not bad for a guy who hated golf.

On the third hole, city attorney Jon Comerford was first up. He was a quiet, reserved fellow, youngest of the group but mentally very sharp. No one fooled with Jon. He kept a keen eye on his public image and would retaliate when embarrassed. He seemed never to forget a slight, waiting as long as it took for the right moment to squeeze the balls of anyone who crossed him.

In another hour and a half, they finished the ninth hole at the top of a gently sloping meadow overlooking the river. They relaxed and watched the pleasure craft floating along for a few minutes. Then it was time for business. He readjusted his sweater with the Harvard colors over his blue T-shirt.

"Let's talk about where we go from here, gentlemen," he said, motioning for them to gather round. He inhaled deeply and projected a dazzling smile. "We're about to achieve our vision of a new city where business will grow unimpeded and investors will view Westfield as a profitable place to entrust their money."

"We came here to celebrate, didn't we?" Norm Taylor interjected. Diving into his golf bag, he extracted a flask of Jim Beam and six plastic tumblers, which he passed around, then splashed a little bourbon into each. "Here's to Davenport's demise!" he shouted.

"A toast to Davenport's being where he can't throw a monkey wrench into our plans," George Howard echoed.

"Hear, hear!" cried Taylor.

"Don't forget," Mike cautioned them. "Morrison's term is up this year. That makes two wards we can have."

"We could come out with a whole city council tuned into the business agenda," crowed Mayor Timmerling.

"The point I want to make," Mike continued, crossing his arms and shaking his head, "is that we have the advantage, and we have additional enemies to punish."

"We also need to focus on the voters," said George Howard. "They need to see we're on the right track."

"Hear, hear!" echoed Norm Taylor, raising his hand in toast and taking another swig of whiskey.

"What say we return to our game, gentlemen?" Mike advised. "Time's a-wastin'." He stepped up to the tee and addressed the ball with an 8 iron. He produced a smooth shot straight down the fairway. Unfortunately, his ball stopped a good twenty feet short of the pin. "My lucky day," he muttered. "I can just feel it!" He bent over the ball, mumbling incantations to his putter. After a few practice swings, he tapped the ball with just enough force to go the distance. It rolled over a rough spot, then remained on course until it hit a tuft of new grass and slid to the side. Five feet from the cup, it corrected. "Must have been a nightcrawler," he growled.

One or two of the fellows grimaced at the close call. Norm Taylor encouraged the ball. Rhett Bennett lifted the flag, and the ball rolled in as if it was glad to be home, ready for a cold beer.

Everyone cheered.

"Here today, gone tomorrow!" Mike cringed in self-reproach at his use of an obvious cliché. It made him sound like the rubes with whom he did business.

"Here's to Mike's unbelievable putting ability!" Norm called out as he assured himself everyone still had enough whiskey.

"Hear, hear!" the cheer rose among them.

After another forty minutes, as they approached the sixteenth hole, Mike's cell phone rang.

"You guys go ahead," he encouraged them. Dana was on the line.

"I just received a call from a Dr. Dwight Thurber," his secretary said. "He asked that you call him right away."

"Yes. I'll call him now. Thank you!"

Thurber had been a university classmate and a good friend who'd come to Westfield at Mike's suggestion. The right fellow to handle delicate matters—quiet, discreet, game for any assignment. His specialty of dermatology was a good cover, and he could keep unusual hours for double his fees.

Dwyer dialed the doctor as he walked toward the privacy of a copse of maple trees.

"I've got a fellow here named Kravitz and two of his associates," said Thurber. "They're all in bad shape. Kravitz asked me to call you."

He gasped, then clutched his throat—he couldn't breathe. How could this be? Davenport wasn't *that* strong. He was tall, but he'd be easy pickings for a guy as strong as Kravitz. Lightheadedness overtook him.

"Is Kravitz able to talk?"

"Yes, but he's thoroughly bandaged. Both arms in casts. I'll hold the phone for him."

"Mike!" Kravitz squeaked. "Good to hear your voice!"

"What happened?" Tension froze him even as his anger neared the boiling point.

"An enormous, *angry* son of a bitch interrupted our work last night," Kravitz complained. "These four guys roared in on motorcycles and beat up my men. Far as I know, the big guy appeared out of nowhere."

"How much does Davenport know?" He steadied himself against a maple tree to keep his world from spinning.

"Nothing. I swear it."

"What happened to him?" The tightness in his chest increased as he imagined the consequences if Davenport lived.

"Not sure. I think the big guy took him away."

"Okay, thanks. Stay cool. We'll sort it all out." *And I'll teach you to disobey my orders, you son of a bitch.*

In seconds, Thurber came back on the wire. "Yes, Mike."

"Can you euthanize them and make it look good?"

"Of course, Mr. Dwyer. That's why I'm here."

"Thanks, Dwight. Keep me informed."

Shaking with anger, he returned to find his team headed to the clubhouse. The slobs had finished the course while he was on the phone, then left the golf carts cluttering up the last hole for the staff to round up.

He reached into his golf bag, pulled out a 3 iron, and walked to an old oak tree behind the clubhouse, which he struck hard enough to wrap the club around the trunk.

Leaving the club where it was, he snatched his bag from the abandoned cart and charged off the golf course to his BMW. He lowered the top, tossed his clubs in the back seat, and blew down the country club drive, tires squealing on every curve. On Route 6 back to town, he accelerated far beyond the speed limit and screamed so loud his vocal cords felt as if they'd been shredded.

Gaining a measure of control at last, he shuddered as dread and guilt fought him for control. His work helping the business community enjoy dominion could fall to nothing in a matter of days. Might as well pour it all right down Westfield's backed-up sewer system! He could well end up in Stateville prison, a fate he considered worse than death. Everything rested on Dwight Procter's keeping his trap shut.

He slammed the BMW into its parking space in the underground lot next to the bank, then entered his building by the back door. He walked up the six floors to his office, allowing the exercise to siphon off some of the fierce anger and hatred he harbored for himself and the incompetent stooges he called his team.

Why had he ever thought that dominion was worth the price of ordering another human being's death? Yet it hadn't been *thought*, had it? It had been an instant of uncompromising rage that a pissant like Harvey Davenport had dared to wrest control of Westfield's future from his own grasp and deliver it to the mass of nincompoops who called themselves citizens. The impulse of a moment, nurtured through years of struggle to please a demanding mother whose approval he'd never received, seemed about to chain him in the lowest level of hell.

Seconds later, the bank's fire alarm sounded. The loud, insistent clanging produced an instant headache. Then the air-conditioning vents began blowing black smoke.

"I'm going down, Dana. Follow me, soon as you can. Just leave everything and go. You're more important than the stuff in the office." Shaking uncontrollably, he gripped the banister to keep from pitching forward as he pelted down the stairs as fast as his wobbly legs could carry him. Bursting through the fire exit, he found the fire chief next to the pumper in conversation with its driver and the crew's captain. There was no engine noise. The hose from the pumper into the bank's basement windows was flat.

"I'm Mike Dwyer, president of the bank. Can you tell me what's happening?" Perhaps it was a false alarm.

"Fire's in the basement," said the chief. "Looks like it's the storage rooms. Comin' up through the floors."

Impatience gave way to hope. "Are you putting water on the fire now?"

"Pumper isn't working. All we have is the pressure from the fire hydrant. That's okay for the basement but not if the fire gets to the upper stories."

"What's wrong with the pumper?"

"Same thing as always—no maintenance. The engine's out, so the water pumps aren't working. We've got no power. I'm calling in units four and six. They'll be here in a few minutes."

"Why no maintenance?" What the hell did these guys do with all their time off in between fires?

"You should know, Mr. Dwyer," said the chief, staring at him with obvious dislike. "No budget for maintenance on our equipment. Same all over the city. We take chances every time there's a fire. We borrow from here and there wherever we can. You guys on city council make the budget. Maybe you can tell me a cheap way I can crank out a couple hundred pounds of pressure to put a steady stream of water up to your office when it goes up in flames!" The chief turned his back and continued giving instructions to his men.

Flames licked out through the shattered windows of the basement. Then there was a loud crash, with the sound of breaking glass. *Oh my god, not the chandelier!*

He rushed to a position where he could see the entrance and look through the glass doors. What he saw horrified him. The impressive chandelier he'd had specially made for the lobby had fallen in a shower of glass, its base protruding from a two-foot cavity in the terrazzo floor. As he gaped at the flames gobbling tile and wood alike, the No. 4 pumper and the No. 6 hook-and-ladder arrived. Perhaps already too late.

Two firemen approached him.

"Gotta move you, Mr. Dwyer. Chief's orders. Let us do our jobs. There's nothing you can do to help."

He shrugged off their grasp with a snarl but moved across the street to the front of the French café. As he gazed at the action, ladders extended skyward, and the crew carried hoses through the smashed windows of the second floor. Just then, Dana appeared from the side of the bank. He waved, then whistled and called. Finally she saw him and hurried to where he stood.

"Unbelievable!" he moaned. Bank employees scampered down the exterior fire escape. "My God!" he croaked. His heart pounded in his ears, and dizziness overtook him. He staggered to the far side of Main Street and hugged a light pole for support. A spear of pain jabbed him under his left arm and over to the opposite side. He gasped, then became nauseous as his legs buckled.

Dana helped him rest on the sidewalk across from the bank his parents had established the previous century.

When she had called 911, she placed her purse under his head to make him more comfortable.

Just before he blacked out on that sun-warmed cement sidewalk, the thought came to him that everything he'd believed and worked so hard to achieve was going up in smoke. Had they lived, his parents would have been disgusted with him. Had anyone asked him, he'd have said he didn't want to live to find out what happened next.

With Harvey incommunicado in the ICU at the hospital that Tuesday morning, Mina LoPino savored handling the client work herself. She looked forward to owning the firm one day, but in the meantime, there was a ton of work to do.

This morning's task was to photograph a robot fine-tuning a guitar for *Popular AI* magazine. The robot wasn't in the mood to cooperate and kept setting the guitar aside on its stand and running like a maniac around the studio, playing hide-and-seek with Lord Nelson. Just as she screamed within herself that artificial intelligence was surely an oxymoron, Alice Morrison called.

"I just got word." Alice's voice resonated with excitement. "Tim Benson's giving a statement to the press at noon. Some big decision he's made. Let's go together. I know you'll want to tell Harvey all about it. Can you make it?"

She didn't need another interruption in an already crowded morning. If she went with Alice, she'd be working late that evening. But she'd planned on visiting Harvey later in the afternoon, and if she didn't hear what Benson had to say, how could she tell him all the news? Also, this was Alice. She liked Alice. Though a generation apart, they had a great deal in common and shared frequent confidences. Besides, Alice was tight with the boss, and who knew when that might be handy?

"All right, I'll be there," she agreed. "What time?"

"Noon, on the lawn at city hall."

She'd completed the robot shot by eleven thirty, time enough to enjoy the summer day as she walked to city hall. By noon, a hundred people had gathered at the municipal complex, sheltering from the heat in the shade of two ancient oak trees near the Civil War cannons with their pock-marked barrels and rusting wheels.

"Word is Benson's scuttling the WDP," Alice said in a conspiratorial voice. She looked attractive in a yellow blouse over a dark navy skirt.

"Too bad George Howard couldn't have done it two months ago." Mina chuckled.

"Would have saved everyone a lot of grief, wouldn't it?" Alice echoed.

As the city hall tower clock finished chiming twelve, the emergency city manager stepped to the microphone.

"Thank you all for coming today," he said. "I've invited you here because my staff has confirmed a clear injustice has been done as regards the city's waste disposal project.

"Our investigation has revealed that officials of the local chamber of commerce influenced city staff to put financial issues ahead of human health and safety. This was an inappropriate strategy, unbecoming a municipal government.

"We have also found substantial evidence of a tradition wherein manufacturing company managers have been allowed to use the Bottoms as their own private dumping ground."

A contingent led by Paul Johnson applauded vigorously for several seconds. Such candid phrases from city officials were unusual.

"In consequence, I have suspended construction of the WDP and issued an order for its demolition and further remediation of the toxic waste on that property. We will move ahead on that facility only when we have found a more appropriate site. We'll do everything possible to ensure that no one comes to harm as a result of that construction. That's my statement, and I'll be happy to answer questions from the media for a few minutes."

Hearing a responsible leader interested in improving the lives of the people gave Mina hope for Westfield.

Just then, Stan Matthews joined them. "Norm Taylor just advised the media that the chamber of commerce will have its own press briefing at twelve thirty," he said in a low voice.

"Oh, let's walk it!" Alice exclaimed. "It's only three blocks." They left at once.

"Who wants to hear Norm Taylor?" Mina asked along the way, tilting her head to one side. "Will he refute Benson's statement?"

"That's the point," Alice replied. "We should hear what he has to say so we know what they're up to."

Within five minutes, they'd arrived at the chamber's offices. The two-story complex sat on the corner of Grant Street and Homan Avenue. Its outstanding feature was a fifty-foot clock tower attached to a loathsome series of faux pediments built over the entrances to half a dozen storefront businesses.

When they arrived, Taylor had already begun. He wore chinos and a white dress shirt open at the neck, sleeves rolled to the elbows. Mud on his shoes, a dark smudge on his trousers, and a rip in his shirt made her wonder if he'd just come from the golf course.

"If an injustice has been done," he shouted, "I say it's Benson's trashing the business community that supports this city and its people," he wailed. "The retail and industrial economy of Westfield is the main attraction of our entire region!"

A strange way to say it. He wobbled a bit as if he'd been drinking.

A small cloud of bees momentarily interrupted Taylor, no doubt attracted to his aftershave lotion, detectable from where she stood ten feet away. Alice, too, looked ready to sting.

"Delaying construction on the WDP means your garbage will stink longer, and your taxes'll blow through the roof!" Taylor complained. "My friends, do you realize that without federal funding, the cost of the WDP will double? That's ten million the city'll have to pay, besides the three and a half million we'll leverage in bonds. In five years, every business, every family, will pay 35 percent more in taxes. Is that what you want? I don't think so. A federal Brownfield grant is the only thing we can afford. That's why it was slated for the Bottoms."

Several people left the area with downcast eyes as if in embarrassment at such a charade. Mina's stomach roiled too, as the warmth of anger crept up her neck. Unthinkable, but what if the public and the media believed him? Her nerves throbbed with impatience. Someone should take the mic away from the creep and tell the truth.

As Taylor paused to acknowledge the crowd's sparse applause with a smile, she stole to the platform and lifted the microphone from its stand. Taylor was quick to catch on, however. He grabbed her wrist first, then tried for the mic. The whiskey on his breath made her want to vomit, but she wrestled the instrument from his grasp and turned toward the audience.

"Ladies and gentlemen, I don't know about you, but I've had enough of this nonsense! Let's hear from a person who can tell the truth about the WDP." She beckoned to Alice, then introduced her and handed over the microphone.

"What Norm just said is a scare tactic," Alice began with the voice of calm reason. "The chamber is conjuring their favorite boogeyman—taxes. They're hoping fear will help you forget your civic duty. One of the key points Norm has taken great care to avoid is that the city prorates taxes on capital expenses for a minimum of thirty years. So whatever the WDP costs, your taxes will rise only 1 percent."

Warm applause greeted her statement. Positive comments surfaced here and there among the listeners. Alice's words warmed Mina's heart. She clapped her hands high above her head.

"The average family in Westfield," said Alice, "pays only three hundred fifteen dollars each year in city taxes. The average business pays half that much. Is three dollars a year worth having a brand-new, state-of-the-art waste disposal facility? You bet it is!"

By this time, more people had gathered, and some in the crowd cheered. They seemed to like what they heard.

"While we're at it, how about another three dollars a month to get our mass transit system back in operation? Wouldn't it be great to take the bus to work and not have to pay for gas? Thirty-six bucks a year! That's all it will cost to get the buses running again."

Several people shouted, "Go for it, Alice!" and "Tell it like it is!"

As Alice spoke, Taylor had crept to the platform. Now he reached up and tried to grab the microphone from her hand.

The brazenness of his action sent a shot of adrenaline through Mina's body. *How dare the lying bastard interrupt!*

She stepped between Alice and Taylor, fastened her hand around Taylor's wrist, then pivoted against him, turning in the opposite direction, stretching his wrist backward as far as she could. She kicked him hard in the shins twice before he released the mic. Then, while he was overbalanced, she booted him to the ground.

Standing straight, shoulders back, she pumped her fist in triumph. The crowd cheered as she mounted the platform.

"Let me show you how our leaders of enterprise *really* operate," she began. "Four men tried to kill my boss, city council member Harvey Davenport, last night."

Her lower lip trembled as enthusiasm gave way to tragedy. "They beat him so bad he's in intensive care at the hospital." She paused to stifle a few tears, then wailed, "He damned near died!"

Her audience buzzed with speculation as she recovered her composure.

"What Norm called our booming economy thrives on making people sick by using the Bottoms to dump their waste. So nice of them to do that, wasn't it? Sacrifice land they don't own? Sacrifice the lives of twenty-thousand people in the bargain? For some hundred and fifty years!"

A growing number of black hands clapped, and black faces cheered her words.

"So I'm asking myself, how could they do that? And then I found out it's because people like Norm have dominated city government for decades. Now I don't know about you, but I was brought up to believe government's job is to protect the people, not sicken and kill them. Harvey Davenport and this wonderful lady here beside me,

Alice Morrison, have worked hard to change that so-called private-public partnership so our government can do its job."

"Tell it!" and "Amen" came from the sidewalk with more cheers. But the chamber members far to her left shook their heads in anger and dismay.

With a huge smile, placing a hand over her heart in a silent "Thank you," tear tracks glistening down her cheeks, Mina replaced the microphone.

As if bidden, a large, dappled black-and-brown tabby came onstage and wrapped itself around the woman's legs. This caused them to laugh at the simplicity and appropriateness of the gesture.

Walking back to the studio, the realization dawned on her that the incident had affirmed her as a strong, competent woman who knew her mind and wasn't afraid to speak out if it concerned people's well-being. She hastened her steps with the thought that, surrounded by supportive loved ones, she'd conquer the world if it improved people's lives.

CHAPTER 14

RECOVERY

As the el-train descended into the heart of the city, the whole metropolis sweltered under a blanket of late-afternoon haze. When the train slowed, Harvey rose from his seat. The first stop was State and Main.

Arriving at ground level after descending the stairs, he explored the shop windows. He'd come downtown because he needed something, but damned if he could remember what it was. He scratched his head. Perhaps he'd recognize it as he browsed among the shops—a haberdashery, a laundry, a tobacco store.

Intrigued by the flashing blue letters of its neon sign, he entered a shop called Ancient Assemblies of America. The sound of tinkling bells and smells of oil paint, musty cloth, and dust greeted him. Raspy vintage records from the twenties played in the background.

The appliance section boasted a two-burner, green enamel, woodburning kitchen stove that looked as if it had been made before McKinley was president. He ran a hand over the stovetop, roughened by hard use. A card in front proclaimed, "Best in the West." *Wanna bet? Probably an exaggerated come-on.*

Next to the stove, he found a battered wooden icebox with one door hanging loose. Its warped varnish had cracked and peeled. Its card boasted, "Frigidaire Keeps Food Longer." Farther along, the ad card on a noisy pink window air-conditioner from the fifties offered "Greater Komfort with Kelvinator."

Two aisles over, he spotted an old, gray, forties-model Chevy with a sign, "Shop the Stores Today in Your Chevrolet." Around another corner, he found a bomber engine, a submarine, and a tank from World War II. The sign in front of that display read, "We Sell Good Things for Life."

The entire store was nothing but a museum of advertising. These products had generated substantial wealth for a few individuals but had done little to build a mutually supportive society.

Four men in dark suits and fedoras approached him. The little hairs on the back of his neck rose. *Thought police from the ad agencies here to enforce brand loyalty and stop rebellious thoughts.* No doubt they knew he was no fan of hucksterism. As he moved through the store, they followed.

Sensing danger, he bolted through the store's front door and tore west on Van Buren. His attackers followed less than half a block behind. He approached a haberdasher pushing a cart of men's suits. He yanked the rear end of the cart into the front end of a parked car and scampered around the right side, blocking his pursuers.

As he ran faster, intense pain erupted in his side, but his pursuers were relentless. When pedestrian traffic blocked the sidewalk, Harvey took to the street, dodging cars in two-way traffic. The horns of angry drivers made a dizzying cacophony of noise.

At the next intersection, he made a right turn into an alley, where he dashed through the garbage bins and dumpsters, searching frantically for a hiding place. The smell of rotting garbage and human waste nauseated him. He sidestepped greasy-looking puddles filled with dirt and sawdust. At the sound of his pounding shoes, rats scattered from underneath rusting dumpsters.

Then he saw his chance. An old fire escape loomed outside an enormous, soot blackened brick building. He jumped and grabbed the bottom stair with both hands. As he swung forward, his weight brought the lift down. He climbed up to the first landing and leaned hard on the weight that pulled the stairs up after him. Once certain the killers couldn't follow, he took a short breather. The pain in his side throbbed, slowing him down. Yet in a moment, he continued to climb higher.

Though he'd temporarily stymied his pursuers, he huffed and puffed his way up until he reached the rooftop and scampered over the ledge, safe at last! He lay down to catch his breath and let the pain subside. But it would take the ad police only minutes to come up through the building's elevator.

He found the entrance to the building's interior stairwell, then scampered down the stained, dirty staircase over broken treads and puddles of cigarette butts to the twelfth floor. Crusted, peeling paint and rippled wallpaper covered the corridors on this floor. The odors of urine, tobacco smoke, and printer's ink were strong. A fat, balding man with a paunch underneath his dirty white T-shirt and navy slacks stopped him.

"What th' hell ya doin' here?" the man yelled in a gruff voice.

"Just on my way down," said Harvey, breathing hard, trying to seem nonchalant, as if he'd worked there all his life.

"What? You got trouble?"

"Guys chasing me!" he admitted.

"Yeah I saw that. My brother-in-law and his pals. Saw you come up the side o' the buildin' too. That's dangerous, you know? Illegal as hell too." The man went on down the stairs, shaking his head and muttering to himself in obvious disgust.

A quick look around revealed an open door. He peeked in. An empty, old office. Nobody around. Since the door was open, he entered, shutting it after him, just in case old Paunchy returned.

The only furniture in the place was a desk, a chair, and a metal filing cabinet. The oak floors were cleaned and waxed. Only the window sashes revealed the age of the building. Harvey estimated 1930s construction. Desk drawers and the cabinet were empty. He sat down to let his heart slow while he thought about what to do. Perhaps he should escape now while he could. But when he tried the door, it was locked. At least for the moment, he could do nothing but wait to see what developed. He rubbed the back of his neck and shook his head in frustration.

An hour later, the door opened, and a young man stepped inside. The fellow had a crew cut and wore faded jeans, a floppy blue shirt, and black sneakers.

"Good morning, Mr. Davenport," said the man.

"Who are you?" Harvey asked with an intentional edge of hostility in his voice. "How'd you know my name?"

"I'm your safekeeper," the fellow answered.

"Safekeeper!" Harvey exclaimed. "There're no safes in here. What the hell's that supposed to mean?"

"Just making sure you're safe and sound and that you have all the comforts of home."

"Why am I trapped in here? That's not comfort."

"Because you haven't opened the door."

"I can't open the door!" Harvey complained with exasperation, gesturing at the entrance.

"Not that one, the other one! Didn't you find it?"

"There is no other door."

"Sure there is. It's the escape door. You know, in case of fire or emergency."

"Where is it?"

"Just to your left." Crew Cut indicated the long, vacant wall below the high-up window.

"I see nothing but the wall."

"See that spider on the wall?"

"What? That little bug?"

"Yes. That's a doorknob."

"No! I don't believe it! It's just a spot on the wall."

"Push it," Crew Cut insisted. "Push it with your finger."

He put his finger on what proved to be a painted black dot and pushed. The wall panels slid back, and he found himself on the edge of a six-foot opening, looking down two hundred feet. The pedestrians carrying their bagels and coffee cups looked like ants.

"Holy shit!" he exclaimed, stepping backward into the room. "Is that the door I'm supposed to go through to get outta here?" He was incredulous.

"Right as rain, brother! Help yourself. Look out for the first step though. It's a lulu!"

"Yeah, I can see that. I can't go out there. I'd fall to my death."

"That's what they all say. Sure you can. It's the only way you can leave this place."

"Can't you take me out the way you came in?"

"Nope. Can't do that. Against regulations." Crew Cut paused a few seconds. "It's not as far down as it looks."

"How do you know? Have you ever stepped out there?"

"Sure, and lots of other people have too."

"And they survived?"

"Far as I know. I'm still here."

Harvey walked back over to the abyss and took another look.

"You'll never know till you try it. Besides. What do you want most? You want to stay here in this room forever? Or do you want to get out there in the world and achieve good things?"

That hit a nerve and refocused his mind. "Yeah, that's what I want to do. Make a difference."

"All right then. You've only got one choice."

He turned and gazed out the door into the sunlit morning, out to the city limits and through the morning mist to the suburbs. He had goals he needed to accomplish. To hell with this playing cat and mouse with Mr. Crew Cut. He took three steps.

The third took him into thin air. He put out his arms to keep his balance as he … floated down, smoothly, gently. Hands held him by his feet, his legs and arms, supporting his back and shoulders. People he'd never seen and didn't know. Within seconds, his rescuers had deposited him in a department store. He was naked. The people brought him underwear and socks, a clean white shirt, a suit, and shoes.

"Put these on, brother," said a man in a French chemise and baggy pants. "You'll be a lot more presentable."

"Where are the guys who wanted to kill me?" Harvey inquired, just as a safety precaution.

"Don't know what you mean. Nobody wants to kill you. We're here to get you started on your way. You've got a lot to accomplish, and we're here to help you dig right in."

A woman's voice near him said, "Looks like you're having a little trouble breathing, Mr. Davenport. I'll place an oxygen tube under your nose. Maybe that'll relieve your breathing problem."

"O-'aaye," Harvey mumbled through his bandages. The room he found himself in was dark except for the lights of several monitors. The freshly oxygenated airflow brought relief, but he couldn't identify where he was. Cold sweat tickled as it slid down his face.

He tried to move his left arm, but it weighed a ton, throbbing with fierce pain in his wrist. When he used his right arm to place a hand where his face should have been, all he felt was gauze and tape, except over his eyes, ears, and the end of his nose. Maybe those guys had really shot him after all. He tried to feel his heartbeat, but he couldn't find it.

"You feelin' any pain?" she asked.

"Intense, yes," he said. "Where am I?"

"In the ICU at the hospital. Doctor said it's only temporary until you're stabilized. I guess you took a few hard knocks to your head." She moved around the room like a ghost.

Still on earth. "What happened to me?"

"I don't know, sir. I wasn't given that information."

"When do I get out?"

"Doctor will tell you. He'll be in after a while. I'll give you another shot of morphine to ease your pain."

"'Hank you," he mumbled, then drifted off again as the morphine took effect.

"Here's your new home," said the male orderly who wheeled Harvey down from the ICU. "Room 604. Just like the doc ordered. Anything else I can getcha?"

"What day is it?'"

"Wednesday, twenty-fourth of July."

How time flies when you're havin' fun!

"How about a nurse?"

"Nurse Phyllis will be along in a few minutes. She's tending another patient just now."

He found himself in an unfamiliar body, full of pain, wrapped in gauze and tape like a sack of smelly garbage. Excruciating pain in his wrist and ribs brought to mind Billie Marshall's words. *They'll start howlin' in a few hours.* Nurse Phyllis gave him a sedative, but it only took the edge off; the deep aches persisted with a vengeance. He spent the day curled up on his hospital bed, wandering through a terrain of frightening nightmares.

Just after three that afternoon, Billie Marshall stuck his head in the door. "How's it hangin', Harvey?"

He woke with a start, unable at first to remember where he was. With effort, he focused on his visitor. He recognized Marshall's faded jeans over Vietnam-era combat boots, a camo shirt, and an old Dodgers baseball cap.

"Could be better. But glad I'm still here," he said as he became more aware.

"You do look a li'l different in that getup. You goin' Halloween partyin' tonight?"

"What? You need a date?" he mumbled. "Good to see you, Billie!" He reached out his right arm and shook Marshall's hand. His rescuer had rough, calloused hands but a firm, almost protective grip. "What've you been doin' since we last met?"

"Just stickin' my nose in wherever it doesn't belong. How's that wrist?"

"Can't tell yet. I can feel it's still there. Painful as hell!"

"What's your doc say?"

"Says I'm lucky to be alive. A leg, an arm, four ribs each side, bashed-in face, and severed wrist. Easy peasy." He chuckled

"I got news for ya," Marshall said. "You're lucky. Those guys were out to kill you."

"I thought for a while they'd succeeded," he replied.

"But the real news is that Dwyer's dead. Yesterday afternoon, while you were in the ICU, he had a heart attack as his bank burned to the ground."

"Couldn't have happened to a nicer guy!" Harvey replied. But he didn't feel as cynical as he sounded.

In previous times, he might have said Dwyer's death was richly deserved. He was less certain now. Heart attacks happened to all kinds of people, at all ages. Was he sorry? Perhaps. At least he'd learned what to expect from the man—violence of the worst sort. But the struggle to control city government wasn't likely to end so easily, and the question of Mike's successor wormed its way into his consciousness.

"Got a question for ya," Marshall broke into his thought. "How come you just walked into that ambush? I thought you was smarter than that."

"I should have been," he admitted. "I came out of Mama Lulu's all pumped up."

"You're too trusting, man! Gotta keep those peepers open all the time. You're up against a powerful set of well-armed hombres. You might want to take things a little easier from now on."

"I appreciate the sentiment, Billie," he said. "But I'm mad as a hornet, and I'm gonna sting 'em good and get 'em the hell out of there once and for all."

"What? Out of city council?" Marshall exclaimed. "Chancy proposition, friend, if you don't mind my sayin' so."

"I've dealt with worse. Fire fights in Iraq were the worst."

"But look, Harv. In Iraq, they prepared you for it, right? You had weapons and equipment, and you didn't go out alone. Everybody with eyes in the back of their heads. But you might not be so lucky next time jus' walkin' down the street by your lonesome, whistlin' in the dark. Know what I mean?"

Let it go, Billie. You've made your point.

"I'm still committed, Billie. I won't renege on that. They don't belong there, and they're doing a lot of damage to people. What I need is more muscle working with me."

"Piece of advice?" offered Marshall. "Change your tactics. Just a little." He held up thumb and forefinger close together. "Get more people involved. Don't take it all on yourself. Hey! I know where you're comin' from. You and me, we're alike in some ways." He rose to leave and patted his knee. "Look, Harv, I know I'm sort of a rough character. But I'm not just a bouncer in anybody's bar, if you catch my drift. I've owned three businesses in this town, and I know who's who and what's what for gettin' things done around here. You need a more subtle approach. Hope ya don't mind my sayin' so."

"Before you go," Harvey interjected, "there's something I want to ask you."

"Sure, shoot!"

"When I was fourteen and just after my parents died, there was a fellow—a friend of our family—who gave me good advice and helped me claim the insurance money from my father's death, then set me on the road to my aunt and uncle in Binghamton to live. His name was Humphrey Marshall. Would he be any relation of yours?"

"I don't believe it!" Billie exclaimed, clapping his hands. "That was my old man! You knew ole Humphrey?"

"He was just as helpful then as you are now, Billie. I swear you're a chip off the old block. Your old man helped anyone in the area who needed it and always seemed to know what was going on."

They shook hands again. "Glad to have you as a member of my family," Billie said. "And now I must get outta here."

Harvey shook his head, sorry to see the man leave.

"Take it easy, and I'll see ya when you spring outta this joint."

He'd been thinking about a new direction even before Marshall mentioned a change of tactics. That dream had scared him. He didn't know where it would have ended if the nurse hadn't awakened him, only that changing his ways would take a big jump and that there would be people with him when he decided to do it.

By evening, all he could do was lie flat on his back. How could a fellow get so tired just lying around all day reflecting on the state of things? As soon as the nurses completed evening rounds, he rolled over. Yet sleep evaded him. With Dwyer dead, who would take up the reins with the cult?

Harvey lay on his hospital bed that Thursday morning amid visions of hiking in grassy hills accompanied by the sleep-inducing beeps of his monitors.

"Good morning. How's the loose cannon of city council?" Paul Johnson stuck his head in the door. The man's pointed irony and euphoric baritone voice pulled Harvey's mind to attention.

Johnson looked handsome in his gray herringbone sport coat and blue dress shirt. But as he came nearer, his jaw dropped, and his head pulled back. "Jeez, Harvey! Worse than I thought! What's weird is I didn't even know there was a contract out on you."

"Baloney!" he muttered through his bandages. "You know everything that goes on over there." A thousand ears on the streets of the Bottoms debauched their daily catch of rumors into Johnson's mental creel every day. His information tank was chock-full. Only trouble was he'd clamped the lid on supertight.

"Little bird told me." Paul gave him a mischievous wink before walking over to the large picture window. He gazed out across the awakening city in silence, then said, "Hey! You've got a great view! Mind if I move in?"

"Help yourself. The food's great too!" Harvey replied with a wry smile through his bandages.

Paul turned around, took a seat on the gray upholstered window bench, looked at Harvey, and said, "So, what are the damages?"

"Help me sit up." He struggled. "I've got the bed cranked up all the way, but my ribs are killing me."

Paul rose from his seat and strode to Harvey's gurney.

"Four on each side. They've got me pretty well sedated, but ..."

Paul put his right hand behind his back and leveraged him up, then jammed two loose pillows in to keep him sitting upright.

"Ahhhrg!" Harvey exhaled a quiet scream. "God, that hurt!"

"Better now?"

"Gettin' there. Thanks!" He reached for his water cup and took a sip. "He tried to saw off my left hand! Can you believe it? That hand wouldn't be there if it wasn't for Billie Marshall."

"Will this set you back on your taxes project?" Paul asked.

"Not a chance!" he replied with a grin. He needed ole Grandma Johnson to know he had no intention of slowing down. He'd work right through, from a wheelchair if necessary.

"Yoo-hoo! Anybody home?" came a soprano voice from the hall. Then Alice's face appeared at his door. "I love the smell of floor wax, antiseptic, and cafeteria food!" she crowed as she waltzed into the room in navy slacks and a blouse printed with small blue flowers. Then she stopped dead. "Oh my God, Harvey! I had no idea!" She shook her head with an unbelieving grimace.

"Guy tried to kill me, but I wouldn't fit into the coffin he'd bought. Just kept fighting till Killer Marshall showed up. He was almost too late."

Just then, Mina's head appeared around the doorjamb. She was wearing her typical black tunic and skinny jeans.

"Oh, Harvey!" Mina exclaimed under her breath, putting her hand to her mouth as she rushed to his bedside. "Don't talk like that!"

"Where does Dwyer get the nerve to pull something like this right out in the open?" Alice said.

"Is that who did this to you, Harvey?" Mina asked. "How do you know?"

"He may have ordered it, but I don't know who beat me."

"Speaking of Dwyer," Paul interjected. "Have you heard? He had a heart attack Tuesday afternoon during a fire at the bank. The way I heard it was he and his gang were celebrating your demise on the golf course when he got the call saying you were still alive. I guess it was a pretty bad day for ole Mike."

"He deserved it!" Alice exclaimed, clapping her hands.

Harvey raised his right hand in the air with two fingers extended in a V-sign. What else was there to say?

"So, what'll we do now?" Alice said, rubbing her hands up and down her navy slacks. "I'm ready to get to work."

That was Alice. Good strategist, always ready to swing into action. She'd been an eager supporter from the beginning and had held up well in both demonstrations. It made him glad she was on the team.

"We've got to keep working to get 'em out and stop the pollution," he said. "We can't let this little business set us back. I'll get over it, and we'll keep on going."

"Maybe it's time to let things die down a bit," Alice offered with a slow smile that built into a self-evident apology.

Allowing things to die down wasn't what he wanted to hear at that moment. "We've got to keep the pressure on," he replied. "But I won't be able to do much for a while. Doc says rehab will take at least a month."

"Well, I'm ready to work," said Alice, rubbing her hands together. "Just tell me what I should be doing."

"We need to broaden our approach," Paul advised. "The cult is swamping us right now with violence. But if we increase our numbers, that strategy won't work much longer."

Early on, he'd admired Paul. Part of it was Paul's ability to generate ideas and his open and frank way of expressing them. But Johnson's recent reliance on community and solidarity had not impressed him. It wasn't effective, and it contradicted his own belief that large groups of people couldn't make sound decisions. Maybe he'd be more effective working on the tax issue and let Paul take on remediation, like the original strategy they'd devised at Mama Lulu's.

"We've got two issues," Harvey answered. "Getting business interests out and cleaning up the Bottoms. We need to do both. And both will need broad community support. I agree we need to broaden the work, but I'm not interested in more public demonstrations. They haven't worked for us. Neither the media nor the citizens are doing their jobs."

"Well," Mina interjected, "there are three able bodies here, plus Stan and three pastors and two heads of nonprofits with us last weekend. We can all get busy and work on those two issues."

"We need a strategy so we know what we're doing," said Alice, moving to the edge of her chair and leaning forward.

"Look at it in terms of groups," said Paul. "We've got black churches and white. Then we have professional associations, like the docs and insurance folks. We've got the unions and the nonprofits. They all have well-connected staff and board people."

"But the chamber will stop those board members in their tracks," said Harvey. "Anyway, most of them are business owners."

"Oh, you're too pessimistic!" said Paul with a laugh.

Not pessimistic, just practical. Johnson's imperious tone grated on his nerves. Why this penchant for a new direction? What the man didn't seem to understand was that they needed to get more action applied to the heart of both problems—get 'em out and stop the pollution. Committees and groups, no matter how committed, couldn't do a damn thing on either of those.

"Let's work on the wards for this year's elections and start filing claims against each of the industries who are polluting the Bottoms," Harvey said, letting irritation creep into his voice. "We need a list of ward leaders, a list of polluters, and we need to involve Charles Higgins in filing specific claims."

"All right, I can get the list of polluters," said Paul.

"I can contact the leaders of those wards who elected Dwyer, Bennett, Angelo, and Thompson," said Alice.

"I can ask Martha Ruggles to get with the committee in the Bottoms," said Paul.

"I'll call Higgins and see how our case is coming along," said Mina.

"Leave the chamber for me, okay?" Harvey said. "I'm on two committees there, and I think I know just the guys to get involved. They're a different breed from Dwyer and Taylor, more community minded."

"You should hope!" said Alice as she barked a laugh.

Just then, Nurse Phyllis walked in. "Time's up, people. Time for Mr. Davenport's medication and a nap. Gotta get him healthy, you know. Tomorrow's another day. Come back then, and you can entertain him some more." She flashed them a sarcastic little grin.

In the long hours of the afternoon and evening, he mulled over the advice he'd received. *Take it easier. Don't do it all yourself. Let things cool off. Approach the city's leaders. Get them involved.* That was not what he wanted to hear.

But thinking back over his work of the last several months, nothing he'd done had come close to dislodging the business bullies, and only the governor's intervention had moved the WDP out of the Bottoms. There had to be another way to get 'em out and clean the place up.

As sleep overtook him that night, his head busied itself analyzing and questioning. If his dream had spoken the truth, his next step might have to be a leap of faith. But would that step into nothingness be fueled by faith in the people to choose their own destiny or by the exasperation and rancor that comes of being powerless? Neither seemed a satisfactory springboard.

That Friday, the orderly brought Harvey a lunch of watery soup and Jell-O through a straw. Neither appealed, and soon after the orderly removed his lunch tray, George Spencer showed up in a dark blue short-sleeve shirt and chinos.

"Well, how's the most famous city council member in the state?" Spencer said. "The papers say you got pretty well thrashed."

They shook hands.

"Glad you came by. I'm passing good. What's on your mind?"

"I need to ask," George said with a wince, "are you still able to represent the ward?"

"Of course!" He barked a laugh. "Not gonna let a little thing like this stop me doing my job."

"Sweet music to my ears, Harv!"

They paused in silence for several minutes. George shifted his weight from one foot to another and looked briefly out the window.

Harvey put a hand to the back of his neck and rubbed it through the tape and gauze. "I've a feeling there's something else you came to talk about. What is it?"

"Two concerns, Harv," Spencer began. "First, about your involvement with the WDP. Second, your statements about getting the business interests out of local government."

"Well, you know why I've pursued those tasks. What concerns you?" The usually straightforward George Spencer was turning wishy-washy.

"It's not just me. A few of the warders have mentioned it too. They're thinking business isn't so bad after all."

"Sure, blame it on the ward people. How many exactly? One? Two? They aren't here to defend themselves. You make it sound like they're up in arms."

George mumbled something under his breath that sounded like it might have been, "Son of a bitch!"

"Who said business is bad?" Harvey countered.

"All summer, you've been preaching about removing them from city government because they have no one's interests at heart but their own."

"That's 100 percent documentable. I did *not* say they were bad people."

"Point taken," Spencer said, bowing his head. He moved to the window bench and sat down, crossing his legs. "But people hear what they want to hear. Some say too much focus on the Bottoms. Others say lower your profile, work behind the scenes."

Dirty trick, putting his own thoughts into the mouths of his neighbors!

"Maybe they don't like minorities."

"They want to see you use different tactics."

"Why would they want me to do that?" He swung his legs—one of them in a cast—from under the covers and over the side of the bed, sitting up, arms akimbo across his chest. "Using our friends as cover for your own misgivings?"

First Alice, then Paul, now George. Why this desire to shift tactics in the middle of a fight? Were his allies trying to help or running for cover?

The problem with Paul and George was that their notion of justice would always be riddled with compromises.

"So, where do you stand?" Harvey prompted. "Do you still want to help me get the cult out of city government? You were hot on that during our session after you found out what was wrong with the budget."

"Yes and no," George said, screwing up his mouth, running his hand through his graying hair. "Yes, I agree government belongs to the city's residents and should serve their needs. But I'm a practical sort of guy, Harv. When I get heat from my business friends—and I do have a few." He paused to look Harvey in the eye with an ironic twist to his mouth. "I tend to go along to get along." He paused, as if for effect. "You should try it some time."

"That's what most Westfield people have done for a hundred and fifty years, my friend," he lectured, emphasizing his words with the finger of his right hand, "and now they're suffering for it. How're we going put a stop to that? You tell me."

How easily people buried inconvenient history in their minds. Where was that anger his neighbors had expressed at election time? Where was their passion to fight now that they'd discovered they and their neighbors had made themselves richer by starving the city of resources and choking off services they themselves needed? The irony was too delicious.

Spencer stood, put his hands on his hips, then lifted them to his head. "From the get-go, I knew you'd restore our services. I just didn't think it would turn into such a damned crusade against my friends and clients."

"Neither did I, until we found out what some of these friends of yours were doing. Surprise, surprise! But there it is."

"I didn't think you'd get yourself in this kind of mess!" George gestured toward Harvey's bandages.

"Hey! I didn't beat myself up, George! And you *were* with me. So were our neighbors. Sounds like you're all leaving the dance floor now you see what the bullies will do when stymied." He took a sip from his water cup. "I just went where the facts led, and it's not an attractive picture. And now you want to turn tail and run?" He sneered in ridicule. "Chickenshit! You like having your streetlights out, your garbage overflowing, your sewers backed up? What methods do you think I should change to get those results?"

"You could have used some judgment when you found out. Why blast it around in a public crusade?"

"I came to you and the warders as soon as I found out about the budget suppression. They were up in arms fast! They suggested several avenues of attack, one of which was making the whole thing public. You remember that, don't you? I thought they had excellent judgment, and they started working right away."

"Look, Harv, I don't regret supporting you, but can't we just tone things down a bit? That's all I'm asking."

"You look! If you want the people to run their government, you've got to remove the guys running it into the ground now. The only way to do that is to blast 'em out. You've got three choices. You can use public embarrassment, term limits, or provoke them to get themselves in trouble so the public can see their nasty deeds. Each of those cannons takes a while to explode. All I've done is load 'em up and light the fuses."

"But these guys are all duly elected to office, Harvey. You can't just rip 'em up like weeds in a garden."

"Well, yes, you can, George. That's what must be done. We can show they've been irresponsible holders of public office, and the people can take action on that—if they will. They can recall them. They can replace them. They can raise a hue and cry in public."

"So, you're putting it back on us now?"

"Right where it's belonged since the very beginning. Or haven't you read your history?" His right hand cut a large swath through the air. "Because for years, the people in the wards—people like you, George—have let the chamber choose their candidates for them.

They didn't go to city council meetings, didn't read the budgets, didn't keep track of what was going on. Didn't object to wrongful decisions. That's why we have to blast. And it's the people's cannon that must be fired to get the buggers out. It's a two-way responsibility. Special interests must be disciplined, and the people must use the birch rod. Why's it so hard for you to understand that?"

Now Spencer's head came up, and he stuck his chin out. "But that doesn't make me a bad person."

"Of course not, just morally reprehensible!" He smiled a crooked, ironic smile. "But your streets are still full of potholes."

Spencer was back where he'd started a year ago, wanting the services but not wanting to do what it took to bring them back

"I see where you're going, Harv," Spencer said with a slow smile. "And I know it has to happen. The people must be willing to pay for the services they want, right?"

"First step, yes. Next is the ballot box. They have to put up worthy, moral candidates and then get out and vote. After that, they have to keep close watch on city hall and what goes on there. These are the responsibilities for the citizens of a democracy. You're the attorney here, and you know that even better than I do."

"But you'll never make that happen." George shook his head and threw his hands in the air. "First, the corporations have all the resources. They're richer than God. And if you make them pariahs, rein 'em in tight, they'll just go somewhere else. They won't change. They don't have to. Why not get them together with people from other institutions? Let 'em discuss the roles of business and government out in the open. It's a good path to compromise."

Just then, Nurse Phyllis strode into the room. "All right, you two. Time for Harvey's vitals and a nap." So saying, she pulled the blinds down and cut the lights to half power.

They shook hands.

"Thanks for the chat, George. I enjoyed it."

But he hadn't. He was sweating underneath his bandages, and his heart pounded in frustration that George Spencer—an intelligent, well-educated, thoughtful friend—could be such a dunderhead about moral responsibility.

One bit of illumination, though, was this idea of having people talk together. Who among the business people had the sensitivity and discernment to engage in conversation with citizens who needed city services and accountability? There were half a dozen fellows on chamber committees who seemed to have such ideas and a better sense of morality. Maybe he could persuade them to get involved and make it happen.

CHAPTER 15

INTERREGNUM

On Saturday, August 24, four weeks after he'd been released from Westfield General Hospital, Harvey had his driver transport him in his van to the Bethel AME Church's Community Center's gymnasium to attend a photographic exhibit mounted by the students of his photography club. This had come about through an invitation issued from Paul Johnson and Pastor Ben Booker. The two had cooked up a project to keep Harvey occupied during his recovery from the massive wounds he'd suffered in the fight outside Mama Lulu's. It was the perfect gig he needed as mental and physical rehabilitation since he derived huge satisfaction in sharing his skills and experiences, teaching these young minds the art of photography.

As he walked from the parking lot to the community center's foyer, he remembered with genuine affection the first sessions of the photography club. These young people from Renewal House and Bethel Church displayed great enthusiasm and marvelous ingenuity and creativity as they carried out his assignments week after week. Though they were driven by an irrepressible desire to mount an exhibit before they were ready, he helped them restrain their drive for instant success by insisting they first perfect their skills. After a month of meetings and assignments, the students had reached the point of readiness, and this evening's exhibition would show the results.

From the time he'd crossed the Macawber Bridge, he encountered many large, colorful signs. He'd seen the copious television ads and media coverage. The publicity and sponsorship teams had done a magnificent job.

Judging from the number of buses parked outside the church, attendance would be in the hundreds. Church people, nonprofit staff, a busload of teachers from Westfield High. Even his Sixth Ward committee showed up.

In the community center's foyer, George Douglas and Pete Jacobs sat at a table, handing out exhibit brochures. George wore dark slacks and a maroon polo shirt, while Pete had donned gray slacks, a collared tan dress shirt, and penny loafers. They looked so respectable he might not have recognized them. They weren't just kids anymore.

Across from their table, the church ladies had laid out homemade refreshments. The tangy aroma of fresh-baked pastry filled the foyer. Lemon cake, mincemeat bars, chocolate swirl cheesecake, pecan buns, chocolate layer cake, and cherry and strawberry-rhubarb pie reminded him of a giant horn of plenty—enough to feed several hundred people.

On the other side of the lobby, past the exhibit entrance, people sat at tables and chairs for conversation and munching on those delectable desserts. Jeremy LeFevre chatted with his mother, whom Harvey remembered from one of Jeremy's photographs. She beamed with pride at her son, and Jeremy looked quite genteel in black jeans and a dark green dress shirt.

Harvey entered the exhibit room through the double-wide foyer doors to the gymnasium. The room looked elegant, draped with large swags of rich-looking black fabric. Inside, a sign announced the purpose of the Bethel Photo Club—"to train members in excellent photographic techniques." Another placard announced that the exhibit had been conceived "to show the best photos of club members since the club's inception." In between those signs sat Sybil Higgins, welcoming visitors and inviting them to sign the guest register. She was hard to miss in black leggings under a coral-red skater dress.

Lowering the blackout screens over the windows had transformed the arena into a darkened theater. The exhibit area contained nine freestanding panels draped in lustrous black fabric. The arrangement of these panels encouraged movement throughout the show. Each one of the nine displays used a full panel. The artist's name and theme appeared in bold letters at the top, while underneath ran an introduction and a didactic interpretation of the photos.

All photos were black-and-white, mounted on white matte board in black wood frames with thin, steel edges. Small quartz lights mounted atop the panels lit each photograph. This presentation lent a three-dimensional quality to the works.

In the center, two upholstered benches called "poofs" allowed the guests to rest or sit while contemplating the works of art. The artists stood by their works, ready for conversation and questions from visitors.

Leaning heavily on his crutch, Harvey hobbled through the exhibit, surrounded by what he estimated were some thirty people. Many stopped to talk with club members.

Hassan Higgins chatted amicably with Rev. Melissa Gravenly.

"How did you learn to do this kind of work?" Melissa asked.

"I found this old Brownie camera in a pawn shop a couple years ago," Hassan replied. "So I bought it for five dollars. I was so surprised how the pictures turned out, I asked my folks for a newer model. Sure enough, one Christmas they put one under the tree!"

"What got you into photography?" Alice Morrison asked Jeremy LeFevre.

"A couple of videos showed me how to get started," Jeremy explained. "Looked like a neat way to tell stories. That's my real thing, you know, telling stories about families."

A sense of accomplishment washed over Harvey. Doing things *with* instead of *for* them had helped him learn how to gauge who to trust and when. He stood a little straighter, bracing himself with his crutch, his shoulders back. These youngsters had real talent. All they needed was a chance to show it.

Having spent the better part of an hour in the exhibit, he had to rest. His energy was flagging as he shuffled back to the refreshment tables and selected a piece of lemon meringue pie and a fork before joining Paul Johnson and Charles Higgins at their table to enjoy the conversation and find out what they thought of the exhibit.

By eight thirty that evening, with additional patrons still arriving, Harvey hovered around the exhibit, taking a last bit of pleasure in its success. It had been a long afternoon and he was tired.

Without warning, as he gazed at Jeremy's photos of family members, he spotted someone dressed all in black sidling through the space between two of the exhibit panels. Whoever it was advanced with haste to Derek Robinson's exhibit. Then the hiss of a spray can sent a chill down his backbone. The intruder scrawled a message in white across Derek's exhibition, proclaiming, "Snoops Will Die!"

Just then, a group of five women came chattering into the exhibition and rushed past him. Seeing the intruder, they stopped cold. Several screamed.

"Oh my God!"

"It's the gangs!" Jeremy shouted.

"They're destroying the pictures!" Melissa yelled.

Then all five bolted in confusion back into the entrance hall.

In no time at all, the intruder ducked out through the panels again. When Harvey found his voice, he called for his biggest, toughest members.

"Jeremy. George, Derek!" *Oh, why couldn't they have been with him?* "Come quick!"

It took them several seconds to arrive. When they did, he could only stand mute with disbelief, pointing at the damage.

In seconds, his voice returned but in a way that almost felt involuntary. "He's going out the back door! Can you catch him?"

All three chased after whoever it was but soon returned empty-handed.

"Who was it?" he queried.

"Sonny Farnsworth," Derek muttered. "He's a Cobra."

"They call him Slippery Sonny," said George Douglas.

"He went out the door and down the alley," Jeremy added. "Way ahead of us."

The intruder had attacked the photo that showed Superior Plastics' pipes discharging toxic waste into the Staminon River.

When Derek realized how much damage the intruder had done to his photos, all he could say was, "Oh my God!" over and over. Then he sat down hard on one of the poofs, breathless. "I don't understand it!" He shook his head. "I just don't understand why!"

Harvey used his cell phone to shoot several pictures of the damage, then called the police. But several fellows in the club wanted to go out after the intruder.

"Okay, let's think about this," he cautioned. If he'd said no, right off the bat they'd want to go after those guys just to prove their manliness. But in this situation, they could get themselves killed or wounded. "Running after them now wouldn't be the wisest move. Why not let the police handle it?"

"Oh, the police won't do anything," Jeremy advised in a confidential tone. "They're powerless over here. This is a matter for people in the Bottoms."

"Why not just tell people everything's all right?" said Harvey. Responding to their nodding heads, he headed toward the foyer with the fellows stretching out ahead of him as he hobbled along on his crutch.

In the reception room, Mr. Clemens had just burst in from the parking lot. "They hit the United Way bus!" he cried. "They knifed two tires!"

Chaos ensued. Some people ran inside the exhibit for safety. Others streamed out to climb into their buses or cars to return home. In fifteen minutes, the crowd had disappeared.

He tapped Jeremy on the shoulder. "Looks like they wrecked the exhibit."

"Probably what they intended to do," Jeremy replied. "But one way or the other, I'm damned sure they'll pay for it."

"Just be careful," he cautioned the young man. "We don't want to lose a talented photographer like you just because you got pissed off at a nasty prank. You're more important than that."

He returned to where Paul and Charles still sat at the foyer tables. Johnson was on the phone with Billie Marshall. He put the cell phone on speaker so they could hear.

"From what I'm told," said Billie Marshall, "Rhett Bennett got wind of the fact that his discharge pipes made it into your exhibition. Then he freaked out. I guess he put the Cobras up to it. Kind of a shame, I know. But it's better than if one of his guards had caught the kid. They probably would have killed him."

Thanks to a nasty trick by three gang members paid by an industrial polluter, white folks who had come out in support of young black artists might now go home proclaiming the Bottoms an unsafe place. Just because the guy had a gripe against kids exposing his illegal pollution, why punish the kids? Why not just stop polluting? Sometimes money and people surely made a strange combination.

CHAPTER 16

AGGRAVATION

Following the photo exhibit, at the end of an interminable day, Harvey's wounds ached and he craved rest. But he needed to retrieve an enlarger and two strobe heads for a shoot the next day, so he had his chauffer drive him to the barn studio before returning home. If he didn't make the extra effort now, he'd regret it in the morning.

During the ride out from town, his thoughts focused on the destruction of Derek's photographs. The lad was lucky to be alive, and given Rhett Bennett's reputation for violence, the punishment of defacing his work was mild.

His ruminations came to an abrupt end, however, when they turned off the county road onto the track leading to the old farm. Three bright yellow lights he didn't recognize illuminated the night. Growing anxious, he inched forward in his seat. As they drove closer, those beacons became three separate fires. The place was burning down.

"Oh shit!" he exclaimed under his breath. What he dreaded most had finally happened.

As they inched up the driveway, the old farmhouse collapsed in flames as a burning cross defaced the front lawn. Looking left, he discovered fire spreading upward from the southeast corner of the barn. In a few minutes, he could lose the whole studio. He immediately dialed 911 on his cell. Township firefighters arrived within minutes and quickly extinguished the flames. Still, it was a nightmare come true.

A sudden coldness seeped into the core of his being. So many times, he'd questioned whether dividing studio space between two locations was prudent, especially considering his fight with the cult. As he chatted with the township fire chief, Don Rosen confirmed as much. The burning cross, however, was a unique puzzle.

"Could be a message, or it could be a ruse," said Rosen.

"Seems odd to me. I've never had anything to do with the Klan."

"Maybe whoever it was just wanted you to think it was the Klan. Probably a distraction to cover the perp's escape."

Rosen arranged for a roundup of known Klan members that evening. He also deployed an investigative team to search for clues first thing in the morning.

"Do you have any idea who might have wanted to harm you or deliver a message?" Rosen asked.

"This may connect to my work on the Westfield city council," Harvey said.

"I've been following what you're doing," Rosen said. "But I didn't think things had gone so far that somebody would try burning your place down."

"They're into punishment," Harvey replied. "They've attacked me or my people several times as we've worked in the Bottoms. You see these bandages and me hobbling around with a crutch? Just a month ago, they attacked me in the Bottoms."

"Protecting their turf, I imagine," Rosen commented.

"Will your department investigate what's happened?"

"We'll look into it thoroughly," the fire chief said. "I'll let you know what we discover, and we'll give it to the state police. That should give you reliable results."

Rosen's reassuring words unraveled the knot in his stomach.

During the drive back to town, he began to think more rationally. There was another side to the story. While his fears were daunting, he wasn't alone. Renewal House people had gathered around him after the break-in. They'd provided a round-the-clock guard in town, sympathized with him, even provided counseling. This had been a startling revelation.

Perhaps calling on a strong, supportive community was a fresh way of fighting back. Additional support was welcome, but would it be an effective deterrent? Could it overpower the cult's penchant for punishment? Regardless, the community's presence and caring eased his mind.

The next day, a bright, chilly September Sunday, Harvey knelt in the sandy loam of his garden soon after daybreak, wearing bib overalls, rubber gloves, and muddy work boots. With great care, he picked through the bed of frost-wilted dahlias looking for exceptional specimens to create a breathtaking fall photo collage.

Summer's bright pink petals had succumbed to the predawn frost just an hour ago. So far, he'd selected one flower whose stem had turned iridescent greenish-blue, another whose stamens still held their yellow color, and a third whose top-tier leaves were still green.

A vibration from his cell phone interrupted him with a call from Alice Morrison.

"Glad I caught you early," she said. "There's something you'll want to see on Channel 7 tonight."

"You know I never watch television," he replied with a friendly laugh.

She ignored his comment. "Clarence Williams is appearing on the *My People* show with Josh Bailey. It's a community forum featuring people and ideas from the Bottoms. Would you like to come over and watch? We could have dinner and see the show."

"Sure, I'll be there. Sounds serious. What time?" he asked. "Should we invite anyone else from council?"

"How about Stan and Doug?" Alice asked. "My gosh! We're a majority now!" she exclaimed. "For a while at least."

"Hard to believe, isn't it? If we include Marty Angelo, maybe he'll feel like joining us," he said. "I'll call him."

"Splendid idea. See you at five thirty."

That evening, having finished a fabulous roast beef dinner complemented by lemon chiffon pie, they gathered in Alice's living room. Lounging in one of her white leather easy chairs, Harvey rubbed his hands together in anticipation. "Now let's hear what Clarence has to say."

"If he gives a balanced analysis and comes out in favor of the impending dialogue, I'd be satisfied," Doug Thompson said.

"Oh, I'm sure he'll support dialogue," said Marty Angelo. "He knows a good thing."

"I see him discrediting dialogue," said Stan Matthews. "In our last council meeting, he complained it's just another white game imposed on the Bottoms."

"Several weeks ago, he pledged to support Renewal House programs," Harvey informed them. "But Clarence says whatever's necessary to get what he wants."

As the last commercial faded, they turned their attention to the show.

"Welcome to *My People*," said the television announcer, "a public affairs feature of Channel 7 designed for citizens from the Bottoms in Westfield to share their opinions on current issues facing them."

The camera zoomed in on the host, Josh Bailey, who introduced Clarence.

The camera pulled back to reveal Williams.

"Good evening, Clarence Williams, and welcome to our show!"

Host and guest sat in matching blue wingback chairs on opposite sides of a background displaying an aerial photograph of the city of Westfield featuring the Bottoms prominently in the foreground.

Clarence appeared luminous in a gray sharkskin suit, royal blue dress shirt, and a purple paisley tie. His swept back white mane, flinty eyes, and prominent nose exuded authority well beyond reality.

For the first minutes, the two discussed Clarence's background and lack of education. They covered his election to city council and his association with the Westfield Chamber of Commerce before delving into the issues.

"You've been an active supporter of the business community, Clarence. What's business done for people in the Bottoms?"

Intense stage lights revealed beads of sweat on Clarence's forehead. "Business has transformed our people. The Belle Riviere Industrial Park has brought us hundreds of jobs in less than a decade."

The bewitching politician, suave and handsome with the flashing white teeth, spoke in a relaxed, earthy manner, using flawless English. Yet he displayed little sense of logic and fit well within the whatever-I-say-is-the-truth school of public discourse.

"Doesn't it seem odd that an all-white council put that industrial park in the middle of the black community?"

"I came to council during that time. I can assure you it was not an all-white council. We in the black community had plenty of input on its location. We're glad it's there."

His use of the term "black community" may have played to Clarence's advantage. But the Bottoms was home to many whites and Hispanics as well.

"It seems somebody wrote him a neat little script," Doug Thompson interrupted the show with a wink and a wrinkle of his aristocratic nose.

"I've never known Clarence to stick to a script," said Harvey. "My guess is he's betting the cult will maintain control."

"He's only got one more year on council before he's term-limited out," Marty Angelo added. "Why does he want to stay with them?"

"Loyalty to Dwyer," Harvey asserted. "That's how he got elected."

"Shh!" Alice cautioned.

"Some say the toxic waste emitted by those businesses contribute to increased disease and untimely deaths, Mr. Williams. What do you say?"

"Bunch of old wives' tales!" Clarence responded with a dismissive wave of his hand. "Foolish nonsense. Our local businessmen and financiers have helped Westfield grow stronger, hold down taxes, and provide services with ever-greater efficiency."

"Some people are angry about losing city services. Shouldn't we raise taxes so people can have the services they need?"

"No, Josh, we've all benefitted from having a tight hand on the levers of governance." Williams paused to wipe his freckled brown forehead with a white handkerchief. "Fact is our people need jobs so they can consume more. If you raise taxes, they won't be able to spend as much in the marketplace."

"Would you agree with many who say the Bottoms is a big sacrifice zone for industry to dump its waste?"

"Absolutely untrue. There is very little pollution anywhere in Westfield."

That brought a laugh from the living room viewers.

"Rhett Bennett should promote him for that!" Harvey declared. "Disinformation at its best."

"C'mon, let him talk, guys!" Alice admonished them with visible irritation.

"An article in the *Westfield Independent* reported a recent survey showing pollution has spread into the white community. Is Westfield proper becoming a sacrifice zone too?"

"That was a long time ago, and they fired the city employee who published that false report," Williams said. "She was a radical reformer. Left town. Haven't seen her since."

"Rumor has it she was your daughter, Clarence. Is that true?"

He choked and took a moment to cough. "The private-public partnership of industry and government has given Westfield the economic strength it enjoys today. Business people obey the laws. They're very conscientious, and that's the reason this dialogue thing is a waste of time."

Was that a tear or beads of sweat running down Clarence's cheek?

"The *Westfield Independent* also carried a story about the need for remediation in the Bottoms and several areas in Westfield south of the river."

"Yeah, they say ten billion dollars," Clarence jeered and pointed a finger. "But I say that's a needless expense to fix a problem that doesn't exist. Let those who want to leave the area go right ahead and *move out*!" He almost shouted the words.

"What would you recommend the people of the Bottoms do to improve their future?"

"First, they should stay home, mind their own business. Forget the dialogue. It's useless. Second, we should get behind our business leaders and apply the simple but true maxims of our faith—love one another and do unto others as they do to you."

Harvey burst into peals of laughter. "Guess he didn't quite follow the script that time!"

"But you know," said Stan, "people will believe him. The audience may not have heard the slip. If it makes him seem more human, that'll bring a big positive response."

As Josh Bailey moved on to the next guest, Alice flicked off the television.

Just then, his cell phone rang.

"Mr. Davenport," said the voice on the other end, "this is Steve Hastings of the state police. The family of Derek Robinson asked me to call you. Is he a member of your photography group?"

"Yes, that's right," he answered, wrinkling his brow.

"Derek and a friend of his, Hassan Higgins, are missing. At present, we have no leads, but I understand the boys went out photographing Thursday afternoon. Do you have any idea where they might be or who might have kidnapped them?"

He hung his head, then took a deep breath to calm himself. "Only a hunch, Steve." His voice wobbled, and he mopped tears from his cheeks with a handkerchief. "Derek and Hassan are eager to tell the story of pollution in their neighborhood. They've been photographing toxic waste. Recently, I witnessed an employee of the Superior Plastics Company threaten to kill anyone snooping around their outlet pipes or their smokestacks. It might be a place to start."

"Anything else you can tell me?"

"Nothing right now." He stifled a sob. "But I'll be in touch if I think of anything."

When he'd completed the call, he sagged in his chair, wiping his eyes. He informed the others, then took his leave. With a leaden heart, he climbed into his van and was driven home.

When he arrived back at his studio, a similar message from Paul Johnson awaited him on his answering machine.

"Someone kidnapped Derek Robinson and Hassan Higgins in front of the high school this afternoon. Rumor has it they'd been down at the river photographing industrial spillage."

Calls to the Robinsons and Higginses allowed him to commiserate with both sets of parents. When he'd accomplished that, he sat in his chair and ruminated on all the many ways these two young men had helped him. Both had budding gifts of courage and altruism, which the world sorely needed. What would he do if anything ugly happened to them?

Two months after his beating, Harvey shambled into Westfield General Hospital. The pain and swelling in his right side, which had started well before his beating, had intensified, while his other wounds were healing well. At first, he'd chalked it up to stress and put off seeing Dr. Warren, his PCP, because in the back of his mind, he was afraid of what the symptoms might mean.

Two weeks ago, at his first visit with Dr. Spencer Crownover, the hospital's surgical oncologist, he learned his symptoms meant liver cancer. The doctor also suggested industrial chemicals might have been responsible. A week later, he'd undergone a PET scan, and today he would hear the results.

He took an elevator to the Charles and Sara Higgins Cancer Center on the fourth floor. As he walked down the corridor, smells of floor wax, disinfectant, and stale coffee greeted him. The walls were pastel green on one side, creamy yellow on the other. Massive windows allowed people to enjoy the courtyard below, where trees and shrubs bore the first yellow and red leaves of fall. Walking down the corridor, he passed doctors frowning in concentration, amputees in wheelchairs, families with their children, patients in slippers and sweatshirts over hospital gowns. He turned a corner and entered Dr. Crownover's suite.

As soon as he gave the receptionist his name, a med tech ushered him to a consultation room with the usual mantra. "The doctor will be with you in a moment."

Was he scared? Beyond belief. After all, he'd lived through his mother's cancer, had witnessed her pain, watched her die as the cancer ravaged her body. Thoughts about his future pulled him toward optimism, then plunged him into despair. Many people could live longer, happier lives if he could just live long enough to stop the pollution in the Bottoms.

"The PET scan shows you have a malignant mass of squamous cells about the size of a quarter in your liver," Crownover said. "Good thing we caught it early. You're a stage 1B. The mass hasn't grown into the blood vessels yet."

There it was, confirmation of his worst imaginings. A sudden chill descended upon him. This wasn't the news he'd wanted.

"I'd say you're lucky," the doc continued. "At this stage, we can treat the tumor with a high percentage of success. I recommend ablation or radiation first. If that doesn't work, there are other options."

Unfamiliar terms, new procedures. His stomach lurched. How ironic that the disease of liver cancer might take him in the midst of his fight against cancer-causing pollution. Did everyone with a sudden turn of fate feel the same sense of helplessness?

"What about the soil and water samples?" he asked.

"The lab found trichloroethylene—TCE to the layman—in all your soil samples but with lesser concentrations, plus vinyl chloride, in your water. Today we now know that both cause liver cancer, so stay out of the garden and switch to city water, okay?"

Under these new circumstances, he'd need to focus efforts on enlarging the group of friends with whom he worked.

"To start," Crownover continued, "we'll meet with the oncology radiologist next week to see what she has to say. Then we'll meet with the ablation specialist. I'm pretty sure he'll want to go ahead as soon as possible."

The cacophony of voices in his mind made it hard to focus on the doc's words. How could this be happening to him? Was he destined to be just one more victim of industry's negligence? What about the people whose lives were in jeopardy—the entire city of Westfield?

Would he be just one more of the hundreds who perished because a mayor and an industry owner had made a deal in 1847 to allow the manufacturer to dump waste where it didn't belong?

"If neither the ablation nor the radiation dissolve this tumor, we must try surgery ..."

The word *surgery* seized his attention with a jolt. He stared unbelievingly at the doctor.

"As long as you're in the early stages, we believe we'll get the entire mass without severe problems."

He clutched the arms of his chair to keep his hands from shaking. It was all he could do to stifle a scream. *Severe problems! What severe problems?*

"What are my chances?" he asked through clenched teeth.

"For the 44 percent of people diagnosed at this early stage, the five-year survival rate is 31 percent. If the cancer has spread to surrounding tissues or organs, the rate drops to 11 percent. We'll know more after the operation."

Not exactly encouraging odds. His heart beat a tattoo in his temples as the walls of the consultation room closed in on him. He had to find a way out to a place where he could think. In a fog of uncertainty and grief, he rose from his chair, thanked the doctor, then made his escape.

He bolted to his van, changed to his running shoes, then—coat blowing open, heedless of the rising wind and falling temperature— he tore across the street to the Staminon River park. Cars screeched to a halt and horns blared as he zigzagged to the riverine trail, shot through the trailhead, and sped down the path. Ten miles would never be enough to assuage his torment. Could he run fast enough, live long enough, or work hard enough to stop the pollution and transform the sacrifice zone that was his birthplace into an area safe for human habitation?

CHAPTER 17

DESPAIR

By late afternoon, the freezing north wind howling around him echoed the turbulence in Harvey's mind. The fire, Clarence's TV bomb, the kidnapping of Derek and Hassan, and now the cancer all overwhelmed his coping abilities and cast a shroud over his possibilities for success.

Still, when at last he arrived home—lightheaded, dead tired, and longing for a simple, dreamless rest—he found sleep eluded him. Experience told him this was stress, and one sure way to relieve it was to delve into some intricate problem and put the world behind him. So, he donned jeans, a red plaid shirt, and slippers, then immersed himself in his dahlia vanitas.

In his studio, he retrieved his wilted flowers from the fridge and arranged them for the photo's centerpiece. Unfortunately, the flowers were too short for the vase he'd selected. Why hadn't he measured them? The mistake aggravated his frayed nerves.

As he searched for a shorter vessel, grief at the boys' disappearance came flooding back. Were his two most promising club members dead? Were they captive in some desolate, grubby hole-in-the-wall? The thought intensified his headache. His conscience screamed that he was responsible. He had encouraged them in their desire to photograph industrial poison. Furthermore, all the members of the photo club were vulnerable now. His chest tightened, and beads of sweat broke out on his forehead. He finished his flower arrangement with two wilted tulips and a trio of faded pink roses despite the tears streaming down his face. Finally, he bent to the work surface, cradling his head in his arms as deep, shuddering sobs convulsed his body.

When the intense feelings eased, he moved the flower arrangement to the center of the table and shot a few trial exposures.

Then, as he gathered the remaining elements of the vanitas, the memory of Clarence's speech returned. The man's disrespect for the people, his globalization claptrap, and denials of Westfield's contamination plagued Harvey's mind till his chest tightened with anger. *People who believe that nonsense could cripple the city for another generation.*

He withdrew to his desk and lamented the wretched impossibility of his situation with a day-old cup of coffee and a stale pastry. When his mind began pirouetting in useless circles, he went back to work.

His next step was to cut a sheet of glass to cover the photograph. From his glass-storage bin, he selected a piece a bit larger than the three-by-four-foot he needed. This necessitated his cutting it to size by hand.

As he lifted it from the bin, his hands shook, and his eyeglasses slid down his nose on a few remaining tears. The glass slipped in his hands, struck the table, and shattered. One piece slit his thumb, and another sliced his palm, leaving trickles of blood. The third dug itself into his thigh just above the knee. He hissed with the pain. Bleeding freely, he crabbed sideways to the first aid cabinet for something to staunch the blood and bandage his cuts.

When he'd finished playing paramedic, he chose another piece of glass and shaped it with his usual dexterity. As he worked, the resemblance between working with this vanitas and governing the city hit him in the gut. Every action he'd taken had ended in grief. Maybe running for council hadn't been such a smart idea. He'd already paid a heavy price for trying to separate business and government, and that goal remained unfulfilled. Why should he bother with Westfield Dialogues? Would it make a difference? Who cared anyway?

By the time the first rays of sun peeked in the east window, he'd finished the vanitas and mounted it on one wall of the studio. Then he stood back to have a look. Staring at the photo, he frowned and cocked his head. The centers of several flowers had an odd look. He moved closer. No illusion, those were water spots on the print. Three blossoms were out of focus as well. *What a waste!* Mistakes he should have caught. Heat flushed through his body.

Muscles tense, he strode to the tool cabinet, grasped the handle of a sixteen-pound sledgehammer, and marched back to the wall. Hefting the hammer wide and high over his head, he smacked the vanitas, which exploded in an angry cloud of glass shards. He bludgeoned the fallen frame to pieces, then pounded the glass to bits, wrecking the floor tile. He tore the photograph to shreds, scattering them around the studio. Finally, he heaved the sledgehammer toward the far corner of the studio, where it smashed another hole in the wall.

He stood for a moment, breathing hard, dizzy, shaking with exhaustion and terror at what he'd done, then collapsed on the floor. Hands and leg bleeding again, he folded himself up and sobbed, face to the floor. He had no use for life. For a few moments, peaceful oblivion seemed infinitely attractive. In a few minutes, a fitful sleep embraced him.

At ten o'clock that morning, having fallen prey to a rush of serendipity, Mina LoPino decided to walk from her condo to Harvey's studio in the driving rain and wind, bundled up like an Eskimo. She paused in the foyer to remove her red boots and hang up her yellow slicker, then let herself into the first floor office with her key.

"Good morning, Harvey!" she called out to him. "I'm here to work on the Clarkson project."

Harvey was a habitual early riser. Hearing no answer and seeing that he'd parked the van in its usual spot at the curb, she concluded something must be wrong.

Opening the third-floor studio door, she discovered him on the floor, snoring like a chainsaw, hands and leg oozing blood through ineptly applied bandages.

"What the hell, Harvey!" she exclaimed, a chill coursing down her spine.

Glass chips, shards of wood, and shreds of photographic paper littered the floor. Spilled cans of stain and varnish with stiff and drying brushes cluttered the light table.

She knelt, grasped his shoulder, and shook him. "Harvey! Are you okay?"

"Mmnphn," he replied.

"Wake up! Talk to me. Why are you sleeping on the floor?" she demanded.

"I was enjoying a nightmare. Leave me alone," he mumbled. He raised his face off the floor, brushing away the glass chips with a bandaged hand.

"What's going on?" She helped him sit up. "Looks like a herd of elephants ran through here! Have you been drinking?"

"No. You know I never touch the stuff!" he growled. "I created my fall vanitas last night, but things didn't work out so well."

"Sure looks that way. Are you in pain?"

He shook his head. "Nothing more than I'd expect from a battle with plate glass. I did an excellent job with the first aid, don't you think?" He held up his hands.

His first aid looked like the work of chimpanzees.

"You had a nice time with the hammer stuck in the wall with bloody handprints on it?" Packages of Band-Aids and bits of adhesive tape lay near a puddle of Mercurochrome staining the Formica tabletop.

"I don't remember." He hung his head in obvious embarrassment. "Go away and leave me alone. I'm not feeling well."

"I shouldn't wonder! You had a temper tantrum?"

"No. Despair," he mumbled.

"Why?"

"Because I can't handle what's coming at me," he growled.

She couldn't blame him, really. He'd been through a lot. But sympathy wasn't what he needed at that moment. "Nonsense!" she said, with as much authority as she could muster. "Let's get you down to the living room where we can talk." She caught hold of an arm to steady him, then pulled him to his feet.

When he passed the mirror in his office, he stopped, then backed up and peered at his reflection.

"I'm a mess!" he exclaimed.

"Yes, you are. You want to clean up a bit? Take a shower? Go ahead. I'll wait for you downstairs."

By the time she'd made fresh coffee, he'd fallen into the living room couch, dressed in a blue shirt and khakis but still looking forlorn. She handed him a mug of coffee.

He gazed out the front window with a faraway look in his eyes. After several minutes, tears streamed down his cheeks.

"It's not just one thing," he said, voice quaking. "It's the whole lot. The beating, the fire, Clarence's dumb speech, the boys' disappearance. And now the doc says I have liver cancer."

She gasped at this troublesome news.

"It's just *too damned much!*" He blew his nose on his handkerchief. "I'm giving up and going to the mountains."

"Giving up what?"

"City council. I'm quitting, going away for a good long while."

They sat in silence for several minutes. She'd reached the limit of her skills. What he said made sense, and she'd expected something like this earlier. But she wasn't the one who could help him. She patted his hand, rose from the couch, and climbed the stairs to clean up the mess.

As she swept up the glass and sponged off the blood, the idea came to her that she might call Harvey's aunt Harriet. The elderly woman had visited several times, and they'd developed a quiet rapport. She found the number and dialed it, then explained the situation when Harriet answered.

"Oh, this *is serious!*" Harriet said. "I'll throw a few essentials in my valise and be there in an hour."

"A million thanks, Harriet!" she said, much relieved.

After a rainy drive, Harriet arrived around twelve thirty in faded blue jeans and an orange blouse that showed off her still slender if eighty-year-old body to best advantage.

Mina greeted her with a hug and a kiss on the cheek. "He's in there," she said, indicating Harvey's bedroom.

He was pitching clothes slapdash into a suitcase atop a thick green damask bedspread. Blinds and drapes were closed. Two small lamps provided only a timid yellow light.

"What in the world are you doing?" she asked as she put her hand to her mouth in dismay.

"Going away," he grumbled, not meeting her eyes. "Far away as I can."

She opened the black drapes, then the blinds. "Where?"

"Carpathian Mountains," he replied. "Back to the freedom fighters."

"Why would you do that?"

"Because I'm finished here." He sat on the edge of the bed, looking up at her with tear-streaked cheeks. "They've gotten the best of me. I need to reconnect with militants who are tough enough to conquer whatever comes at them."

She sat on a corner of the bed, folding her hands in her lap. This was a different Harvey than she'd known. In normal times, he was the fellow who'd be onto the next adventure, never looking back.

"Why do you think you're finished here?"

"Not finished," he said with a sigh. "I'm quitting. Nothing accomplished."

"And the reason?"

"Too much violence. I signed up for retirement, not a war."

"Are you talking about the business people?"

"Yes, of course!" he almost shouted. "They have no scruples!" The intensity in his voice increased. "They're too goddamned determined, too strong, too entrenched! They've got more power and wealth than God! I'll never wrest their hand from government."

Well, finally! More than two words. Maybe we're making progress. "Violence?" she queried. "Tell me what's happened."

"You know most of it. It's the break-in, the fire, being beaten half to death. They kidnapped two kids from my photo club who may be dead. And now my oncologist says I've got liver cancer, might be due to toxic waste. Just like Mother!"

"Oh, no!" She gasped, then took a deep breath and let it out slowly to gain perspective. "Okay, so what about your own personal growth? When we talked in July, you said you were learning to trust, that you had found friends to support your efforts."

"Huge mistake, Harriet. We're all helpless as newborn kittens in the face of evil."

She rose from the bed. "We'll see about that. Come, have a bit of lunch. Try to be civil while we ingest a little nourishment."

In the kitchen, there was little of use in Harvey's refrigerator. Suspecting as much, however, she'd come prepared with rye bread and salami sandwiches, scones, and fruit in her carryall.

When they'd eaten and resumed their seats in the living room, she said, "Look, Harvey, you're not a quitter. You're an inventive fellow who always comes up with a fresh angle, a new plan. Remember when you were a teenager, your old shack in the woods after lightning hit it? Remember when Theo stole your bank account?"

"Nah! That was kid stuff. I'm older now, less resilient. Besides, I have to fight an entire system of manipulation and misdirection. A thousand Theos empowered by money, drunk with prestige."

"But you have friends working with you. You may be a lightning rod, but that's no reason to run away."

"Ahh! But the opposition's turned up the voltage!" he said with evident opprobrium.

"No reason to quit! You've never knuckled under to the power of money. Look how you took care of Theo the first night in Binghamton. You were only fifteen when you knocked him down, made him respect you."

"I thought you were pretty spectacular with that bullwhip too!" He laughed.

She chuckled. "That's my point. So get a grip, Harvey! You need the bullwhip of perspective, because how you see the world determines how you deal with it. You want to succeed? Okay, how do you define success? It's all in your mind."

"No, these have all been actual events. What's in my mind right now is the tally sheet. And it says that the price I'm paying for being a decent person is too damned high. Plus, I probably haven't enough time left to be effective against the corporate polluters anyhow."

"Ridiculous!" She laughed again. "I'm not buying it. How do you think I lived with Theo for all those years without killing him?"

"I've always wondered."

"Perspective. I relied on my hope that one day I'd have my chance to leave and walk away with the money."

"Hope and booze?" He chuckled.

"Don't be smart! Yes, I had a little help. But the point stands. Theo was the goose with the golden egg. I knew he'd fly away; that was his nature. So I set myself up to be the custodian of the egg. After thirty years, I won. You can do it too."

"And you have my heartiest congratulations, dear aunt. But I have nothing even close to thirty years left."

She nodded in appreciation. "When adverse circumstances challenge, you can either see problems or you can see solutions. The cult is digging its own grave. And certainly that takes time. So gather people around you who have the time to get the job done."

"I'm up against a triple conundrum—retirement, human nature, and disease."

"So, adjust your perspective. Those are anchors, not problems."

Amazed and bewildered, he looked down at his bandaged hands lying limply in his lap and nodded. She was asking him to stare dismemberment and death in the face.

"Don't take it all on yourself. You've set the example. Now put the struggle in *their* hands. Besides, in the end, the struggle isn't yours. It belongs to the people of Westfield. Whether or not they succeed is not yours to judge."

"But I want to make sure everything happens as I envision it."

"Oh, yes!" she said, speaking softly, shaking her head. "Hubris is where you and Theo were so much alike. Maybe that's why you detested each other. But you're in a different ball game than he was. You're working for the success of the city's inhabitants. Never forget that. It's what makes you stand out in people's minds. You're a wonderful and talented person looking out for the common good."

"That's asking a hell of a lot!"

"You're the one elected to office." She gave him a smile to smooth the sharp edges of her retort. "Step up and give 'em your best. Compromise and negotiation are part of life. Dialogue, remember? Life is messy and vicious. You can't have it all your own way. Some days things go right, other days not. Everything comes down to compromise and negotiation."

"Sounds like winning is a figment of one's imagination."

"Most times it is." She sipped her coffee. "Remember, you aren't the one who will achieve your goal. Only the people themselves can do that. But you and your colleagues can set them up for success."

"Are you saying that simply by deciding to put my effort into helping the people of Westfield, I've already won?"

"Absolutely. Your actions haven't been off track, just your perception of their results. You're too much in a hurry. And now this cancer thing has you spooked."

He stood up, took a step toward her, grasped her hands in both of his, and kissed her on the cheek. "Thank you, Aunt Harriet. I think I may recover."

Would her homespun philosophy stick? She might never know. But there was always hope.

CHAPTER 18

A NEW WAY FORWARD I

Optimism and confidence buoyed Harvey's hopes for the future within days of receiving Harriet's advice. The only dismal spot on the horizon was the disappearance of Derek and Hassan. No further word had come to him. Frequent calls to the Robinsons, the Higginses, and the state police provided little reassurance. Remorse gripped his mind over their disappearance.

By nine that Wednesday morning, he and Mina waited for Paul Johnson at Westfield General Hospital, where they were to meet with Charles Higgins. Paul had said the attorney was working with researchers at State University on an alternative model for community advancement. Harvey hoped the session would offer fresh ways of removing the cult from city council. He'd also invited Alice, Stan, and Felix. All were capable of generating creative ideas.

They met at the hospital because Charles was a member of its board, and his office had made the arrangements. The commodious fifth-floor conference room overlooked Lake Lejeune, one of downtown Westfield's most popular attractions. When they walked in, the hospital staff had already decorated the large conference table with two vases of fresh flowers and platters of fruit and pastries. Beverages occupied two tea carts on the side.

When everyone was seated and Paul had introduced their guest, Harvey turned to Higgins, his face tight with anticipation, and gave a brief background of the situation with the business owners and the polluters, plus his own hopes for this meeting.

"Have you considered the possibility that groups other than industrialists and bankers might want to dominate city policy?" Charles asked.

"No, I doubt that's a concern. Nobody's tried it recently," Harvey replied.

"Have you thought that the city's residents could inoculate their government against domination by *any* faction?"

Harvey looked up and took a deep breath. "What we need, Charles, is to reestablish citizen involvement and oversight."

"Then it might be wise to create a system in which all the players, even the 'bad guys,' have input on devising creative solutions. You can do it *with them* instead of against them."

"Can such a system specify clear responsibilities and accountability?"

Charles nodded. "Yes, that's a critical component."

"Can your system suppress greed without dictatorial authority?" Stan Matthews asked.

"We can't build mutual accountability in a city as divided and racialized as we are now," Paul said with a slow shake of his head.

"Would you like to see clear, enforceable sanctions against misbehavior?" Charles asked with a hopeful smile.

"Yes!" Harvey affirmed. "But all the players have to agree, right? My guess is the corporate people will never buy it." He shook his head.

He'd never encountered anyone who didn't try to escape accountability. It was a trap, an obstruction to satisfying self-interest.

"Can you show average Westfield citizens they can demand accountability?" Mina asked.

"We do need rules," said Alice. "But, as Harvey says, the players would have to agree."

"Actually, they don't," Charles responded, sitting up straighter in his chair. "At least not at the outset. They only commit to whatever rules are agreed on for *each specific project*. Later on, they'll allow themselves to be held accountable because they trust the other players."

"Not all of our people are ready for that," said Paul, folding his arms against his chest.

"Same's true for the people in my neighborhood," said Stan.

"If the new policy meets their needs, they'll see the advantages, and everyone benefits. Confidence won't be there right away, but over time, the process will prove itself."

"Are you saying," Stan interjected, "that policy made by this process won't isolate or reject minorities holding opposing views? No more majority rule?"

"Have you ever seen common purpose grow within a group of people?" Charles asked.

"Community meetings at Bethel Church have developed considerable common commitment," Paul said.

"Would you say shared experiences could help people work together on a community-wide project?" Charles asked.

"Yes!" they answered at once.

"When human beings work together, they attach mutual emotional feelings for one another," Charles summarized.

"Is that why we feel a sense of solidarity at a community meeting?" Stan inquired.

"Exactly," Charles confirmed. "In those moments, we share the values that make us want to do whatever it is—win the game, shovel the dirt, make the garden, fill the potholes."

"That's just what we need," said Harvey. "But it will be a long, hard slog."

During the next few minutes, Charles coached them in the differences between debate and dialogue, the two ways humans tend to talk about their concerns. Debate, he said, was making statements, arguing, and competing, whereas dialogue involved asking questions and sharing experiences. Harvey liked this direction because it involved boring in on the roots of people's concerns to see what past experiences motivated them. Somewhere in his past, he'd learned that experience shapes a person's values, which in turn drives their behavior. So if one could uncover and possibly reinterpret a person's prior experience, one might be able to change the person's behavior.

"When we get behind the mask, the bluster, the defenses and discover the root causes for each person's viewpoint," Charles said, "the sum of experiences had by all players in the group becomes a frame of reference for further discussion and eventually the recognition of shared values."

"And this is how we develop fresh perspectives on the issues?" Alice inquired. "Looks to me like it's all about trust and building feelings of mutual support."

"Sure," said Harvey. "Fresh perspectives give us new ways to look at a familiar subjects. Like taxes, for instance." He grinned. "Just what we need, and the policy we make together in dialogue comes out of our common knowledge base, so it's more likely to satisfy each person's needs."

"Now you've got it," Charles affirmed with an encouraging grin. He then shared with the group the process of getting a dialogue started in Westfield using the governor's office and the university to set up a Citizens' Dialogue Council and then working on down to establishing dialogue groups in the neighborhoods throughout the city over two or three months.

"It's an exciting idea!" Harvey exclaimed, slapping his leg with his right hand. "If the people believe and participate, I bet we could develop a governance strategy lasting generations!"

"Inclusiveness and effectiveness are the two biggies in my book," said Paul, leaning forward in rapt attention.

Here was an answer Harvey hadn't envisioned—policy made through compromise and negotiation for the common good. He hadn't considered that those business bullies were also members of the community, with legitimate needs and values based on their experiences. It would be more effective than winner-take-all. So he had to conclude that life wasn't a conflict—like sports or parlor games or wars—but a series of negotiations. Life was working together to find mutually beneficial solutions to common problems.

Now all he had to do was get this immense ball rolling and see what the people of Westfield would do with it.

By five thirty Monday evening, the intense rain had let up a bit. Two days of steady downpour had residents who lived along the river calling to complain about flooding. Forecasters insisted the river was far from cresting, but who knew? The increasing frequency of bright jags of lightning presaged another drenching storm.

Nevertheless, Harvey prepared his notes for the city council meeting called by Tim Benson for seven that evening. Then, wearing his black nylon slicker and zippered rubber boots, he tromped through wide, muddy puddles to the Busy Bee for a quick supper of meatloaf, green beans, and mashed potatoes. Good thing he'd prepared for the weather, for just as he finished his lemon meringue pie, the heavens opened again. The rain's steady drumming on the broad brim of his waterproof hat matched the rhythm of his thoughts as he strode to city hall.

The Staminon River had flooded only five times since the 1930s. On each occasion, proposals to beef up the city's flood control system came to city council. But the council always refused to act.

Smells of stale smoke, musty carpet, and disinfectant greeted him when he stepped into the second-floor conference room. It was like visiting an earlier age—ivory walls, dark walnut woodwork, green faux-leather chairs, and a Formica-topped table. He suspected Tim Benson wanted the meeting here instead of in the council's chamber to reinforce the fact that state law gave him all decision-making power, thus removing council from its customary role of policymaking.

When the council members and their guests were seated at the table, Benson rose from his captain's chair, called the meeting to order, and introduced the guests. Among those were Paul Johnson of Renewal House, Norm Taylor of the chamber, Eugene Atkinson of Westfield National Bank, and Dan Galbraith of Manufacturer's

Bank. Jeremy LeFevre and Betsy Rawlings from the photo club would report on new findings regarding industrial pollution.

"Our purpose tonight is threefold," the emergency manager intoned. "First, to establish our working relationship as council and manager. Second, to share information on the Westfield Dialogues process recently initiated. Third, to discuss the current state of the city's finances. I am about to prepare a recommendation for generating additional city revenue, so I hope to have your input." Benson then turned to Charles Higgins, the noted local attorney and professor at State University. "Charles, tell us about Westfield Dialogues. What will happen?"

Higgins rose, opened his laptop, and turned on the projector. His tweed jacket and elbow patches bore witness to his academic qualifications. His first remarks addressed the efficacy of dialogue and the reasons why citizen participation had the potential to resolve major issues.

The attorney next described the new Citizen Planning Council that would comprise fifty community leaders from all walks of life as the governing board for the dialogue process. This group would also be responsible for developing two plans. The first would be a short-range plan for five years, the second a long-range plan for upcoming decades. Then Dr. Higgins sat down.

Harvey found it amusing that half the council nodded approval, and the other half shook their heads in obvious disgust.

Several individuals raised questions of procedure and representation on the planning council and in the dialogue sessions. Benson stepped in to answer each one. Clearly, Tim was primed and knew the process well.

"Who will approve the finished plans?" Stan Matthews prompted.

"First the CPC must agree on the plan with a two-thirds vote," Benson answered. "Then it comes to my desk. When I feel it's suitable for Westfield, I will pass it to the city council as a courtesy for your informal input. At that point, I will charge the city council with drafting a referendum by which the citizens can vote to approve the plan. The citizens have the ultimate responsibility."

Harvey's hand was in the air, which Benson acknowledged.

"How do you foresee that the city can shed its financial distress?"

"It'll be very difficult," Benson replied, then handed out a two-sheet summary of the city's finances. He discussed the lack of revenue and the deep cuts in services to residents over twenty years. Meeting financial obligations had become problematic. "Since revenue is our biggest problem, I'm planning a 50 percent tax increase over five years. This will enable the city to repair infrastructure, add lighting in the newly developed areas, improve trash collection, and bring back the buses."

"Mr. Benson, please!" Rhett Bennett exclaimed in an angry tone. "If you raise taxes that much, the citizens won't stand for it. They'll revolt! People come to Westfield to avoid increased taxes."

So, the first volley from the ship of financial austerity.

"Rhett's right," Gene Atkinson, successor to Mike Dwyer, interjected in a somewhat calmer voice. He wore a dark green suit with a bright yellow tie. "And it'll bankrupt many local businesses. If that happens, Westfield's economy will go down the tubes fast."

No surprise that Atkinson had inherited the leadership of the cult of sacrifice. But he hadn't told the whole story. What he left unsaid was that the downtown business district had suffered near total destruction under two decades of austerity. How did that square with the aggressive business development policies advocated by the chamber?

With sudden force, a window-rattling clap of thunder shook the conference room. Rain drummed hard on the roof and cascaded down the windowpanes, drawing exclamations of dismay and concern.

Seeming to ignore the noise, Harvey rose again to speak. "Nowhere do I see on your five-year revenue plan, Tim, that you've budgeted any resources for remediation."

"What remediation!" Benson sputtered. "What are you talking about?"

"It's the cost of cleaning up the filth and toxic waste that industry has dumped on the city for a hundred and fifty years," Harvey explained in a matter-of-fact voice. "It may be a heavy burden, but it has to be done."

Norm Taylor's face was nearly purple. He seemed ready to blow a gasket. But Benson held him off, motioning for Harvey to continue.

"I now turn to Jeremy LeFevre and Betsy Rawlings, who will share with you their very recent research findings. It seems the Bottoms isn't our only sacrifice zone."

"Thanks for letting us share our research," Jeremy said, rising and giving a nod to Betsy, who turned on the projector and brought up the first slide.

Together the two young people demonstrated that for more than twenty years, the amount and number of chemicals used for water treatment declined because of restricted budgets. This resulted in higher levels of toxins in the city's water system, yet the public was never informed.

"Additionally," Betsy noted, "city engineers knew of the problem, but they received requests from several city council members to not report the contamination."

Jeremy reviewed the results of city groundwater tests. Levels of metals, oils, solvents, and acids had tripled in twenty years. Soil samples from developments south of the river also showed substantial amounts of heavy metals. Additionally, several spills of toxins into the river were never reported to the public out of fear of expensive lawsuits.

"Something new has happened," said Jeremy. "Toxic chemicals have migrated from the river into the groundwater both north and south. A contamination plume is now affecting the water table."

"Our next stop was Westfield General Hospital," said Betsy. "There was a 7 percent rise in breast cancer and a 12 percent rise in lymphoma and leukemia in patients living south of the river."

"To complete our report," Jeremy stated, "our citizens should know that the entire city of Westfield has now become a sacrifice zone."

Silence held sway for a moment. The young people had done a remarkable job. Involving them had been the right move.

In that moment of silence, Harvey stood. "As Betsy and Jeremy have demonstrated, it's not enough just to keep the city solvent, Tim. You'll have to fund remediation of all that toxic waste. The last estimate I heard was an estimate of five to ten million a year for twenty years."

An explosion of denials, gasps, and expletives arose from the businessmen.

Harvey held up his right hand for quiet. "We must raise taxes 100 percent over the next ten years. We're considerably behind where we need to be."

The bankers shook their heads in determined resistance. Remediation apparently wasn't in their plans.

"I'd like to add some good news," he continued, giving them a smile of encouragement. "Further help is available from both state and federal governments and foundation sources. But we must create a separate, higher taxing structure for the polluting corporations. This will achieve a more just distribution of economic resources. It will also be a warning that Westfield citizens will no longer tolerate continued sacrifice of its citizens to the cause of industrial waste."

The moment he resumed his seat, six hands went up.

"The duty of elected officials," boomed the mayor, "is to see that costs are so low that taxes don't rise."

"That's not true," Doug Thompson objected. "The duty of elected officials is to serve the public. Not business. Not themselves. For fifty years, business leaders have taught the public to fear taxes in order to quash expectations for city services."

"Not wanting to pay taxes is ducking one's responsibility," Stan Matthews remarked.

"Corporations have no responsibility to the community or anyone else other than their shareholders," roared Gene Atkinson. "That's the gospel according to Milton Friedman, and I stand by it!"

"I give Harvey two thumbs-up!" Alice crowed, both fists in the air, thumbs exposed. "If the CPC adopts that view, it would shift city hall's focus from profits to people. And that's exactly where it belongs!"

"If you support that," Atkinson seethed, "don't come to my institution to borrow money. You'll soon regret your change of focus!"

"The point is," Paul Johnson intervened, "industry regards blacks, browns, and the poor as waste people. We saw that clearly in the attempt to put the waste disposal system in the Bottoms."

"Look!" shouted Dan Galbraith. "If you want a bright future for Westfield, just follow technology. We in business hold the keys to a better future for everyone. We can give people much greater protection than they have now."

"Oh, what insolence!" stormed Alice. "You call using the council majority as a weapon to enforce self-interest good management? Come on! A little pollution wasn't enough? Now you're pushing industrial filth all over the city! And then you want to come in and make more millions by managing the whole shebang? Hah!"

Someone banging on the conference room door interrupted her. Seconds later, the fire marshal and three firemen burst in with the news that the Staminon River had overflowed its banks and the downtown area had to be evacuated.

With great urgency and no little confusion, everyone exited the building.

Wading through the growing flood toward his van, Harvey reflected that human beings seemed to enjoy making trouble for one another. They were good at orchestrating change but deficient in creating improvements that served the common good. How could arguing turn into dialogue, and how long would that process take?

CHAPTER 19

A NEW WAY FORWARD II

A chill west wind forced Harvey to bundle up in his warm woolen coat as he walked to the Sixth Ward committee meeting at Oscar and Natalie Peterson's home the following Saturday. Papers and trash blew around the downtown streets, and the neighborhood tabby minced along, ears laid flat in the wind. Forecasts expected rain by midnight, then turning to snow. But the possibility of having thousands of his fellow Westfieldians join in his struggle to stop pollution warmed him from the inside.

Answering his knock, Oscar Peterson welcomed him, took his coat, and put a mug of hot coffee in his hand. In the living room, fifteen folding chairs, each with a tray table, faced a projection screen to the right of the fireplace with its comfortable warmth.

While Natalie finished loading up the sideboard with delicious-smelling food for the buffet supper, Oscar joined him in the living room, and they sat in a pair of matching wingback chairs upholstered in a bright-colored damask pattern. Presently, Jeremy LeFevre and Betsy Rawlings joined them as presenters of their recent research into the city's pollution.

"I see the dialogue groups started the first of October," Oscar commented. "They also want four people from each ward on the Citizens' Planning Council."

266

"Are you thinking of volunteering?"

"I may," Oscar replied. "But I also know several people I'd recommend."

Just then, the doorbell rang. "Looks like the rest of the folks have arrived," said Oscar as he went to receive them.

When everyone had assembled with their buffet plates in hand, George Spencer opened the meeting and then turned it over to Harvey.

"A year ago, you elected me to improve city services in our ward. As I reported to you last spring, the reason we have inadequate service is that the business interests dominate city policy decisions. For twenty years, the business and finance people on council enacted policies that increased their own personal wealth. This damaged both workers and consumers, and it's the source of today's problems. They've held down taxes despite increasing costs. So there's a shortage of revenue. All the wards are suffering." He took a sip of his water. A look around revealed he had their undivided attention.

"However, I bring you excellent news. Our new city manager, Tim Benson, has instituted a program called Westfield Dialogues. I'm sure you've heard of it by now. I support this process because I think it's a more effective way to change the system. I've asked Jeremy LeFevre to tell you the latest about this effective new program."

He thanked the committee members, then took his seat.

Jeremy summarized the structural nature of Westfield Dialogues and the selection of members of the Citizens' Planning Council, then moved on to the issues to be discussed.

"Our first issue is financial trouble. The city needs more revenue. Second, pollution is spreading. We must stop it and clean it up. Third, we must insulate governance from business so the city can rein in polluters and provide citizens better service. As they work through those issues, the people of Westfield will have direct input into the planning process."

Several heads in the group nodded. They seemed united in concentration.

"What are we voting on in January?" Nancy Caruthers asked.

"The voters will choose from several options derived from the dialogue groups. We'll have a better idea of what those options are by the end of the year."

"Who gives final approval to the plan options before the people vote?" Joe Lingonberry asked.

"That will be done by the emergency city manager," Jeremy stated.

"What does the city need from us?" Natalie asked.

"We need people to take part in the dialogue groups. We hope to have a minimum of fifty groups dialoguing by the end of the year. We also need people to get out and vote in the January 6 referendum."

As Jeremy thanked them and took his seat, Harvey rose to introduce Sybil Higgins, daughter of one of the creators of Westfield Dialogues.

Sybil rose from her chair, walked to the projector, then faced her audience.

"Thank you for allowing me to share our research," she said. Sybil then removed her sweater and bent her arms at the elbows, hands up to her face. "Can you see this rash on my arms? It's caused by TCEs in the ground that my little brothers and sisters play on. TCE, by the way, stands for tetrachloroethylene." She nodded to Jeremy.

Jeremy stood and removed his jacket. "These boils on my face, hands, and arms," he said, "resulted from TCE and beryllium in the water my family drank from our well for many years. We now use city water, but it's not free of hazards either."

As Jeremy resumed his seat, Sybil described the budget limitations that had resulted in higher levels of toxins while residents were never informed. She bent to the table, took a sip of water, then looked up with a cherubic smile. "This is distilled water, in case you're wondering."

A few of the committee members chuckled.

Sybil further spoke about groundwater contamination and local industrial spills, noting substantial amounts of three industrial chemicals had been released—TCE, beryllium, and chromium.

"But that's illegal!" Retha Galloway exclaimed.

"What about the river?" Bill Ferman asked.

"The news isn't good there either," Sybil commented, bringing up the next slide. "Toxic chemicals have migrated from the Staminon River into the groundwater, both north and south."

"What do the doctors and clinics say about health concerns?" Claudia Douglas asked.

"We found a substantial rise in breast cancer, lymphoma, and leukemia cases," Sybil replied. "The doctors also report increases in strokes and miscarriages."

"This sounds pretty scary," Retha Galloway said. "Is there anything we can do?"

"I think we should all get busy!" Susan Mintz exclaimed. "I don't know about the rest of you, but this is news to me. And I'll tell you, I'm scared to death!"

As Sybil, having finished her comment, sat down, Harvey's ears picked up the sound of voices and a truck engine with a bad muffler. A chill crawled down his spine. He'd heard those sounds before at Isaiah Jones's house after the community workday. After a few moments, two thumps and a groan could be heard from the front porch.

"What was that!" George Spencer rose from his chair, went to the living room window, and looked out. A series of pops, thumps, bumps, and minor explosions could be heard on both sides of the house.

"Someone's paintballing the house!" George exclaimed.

Fear sent prickles to Harvey's skin. A few deep breaths couldn't slow the rapid beating of his heart.

"They're ruining our home!" Natalie cried as she peeked out the side window, then ducked as a paintball shattered the glass above her face.

Bill Ferman joined Spencer at the front door. They opened it and scrambled out on the porch.

Heat flushed through Harvey's body as Spencer drew an automatic pistol from his sport coat pocket.

The paintballers ran back to the dark blue pickup truck and disappeared inside.

Spencer fired. The rear window of the pickup exploded in glass fragments. George fired a second time, and someone in the truck screamed. A silhouette from the passenger seat grabbed the wheel and appeared to wrestle the truck farther down the street, then around the corner.

Embarrassment heated Harvey's face with the realization that this was happening because somebody knew he'd be at this meeting.

After a few moments, the roar of the truck's engine drowned out the squeal of tires.

"Must've switched drivers!" Ferman speculated.

Turning to go back inside, Harvey tripped over something on the porch floor, and he banged his head against the open screen door. Two bodies occupied the porch, bound, gagged, and blindfolded.

As he bent over for a closer look, fear gripped him. They looked as if they were dead. "Oh, God! What have they done?" he wailed. He bent to remove an oily rag out of a mouth.

"Hi, Mistah Harvey! Sure glad to see ya!" Hassan Higgins croaked.

"Hassan!" he gasped.

With trembling fingers, he removed the blindfold and gag from Derek Robinson's face. "Derek! Oh, thank God you're both safe!" He hugged them to his chest.

"We're still alive." Derek struggled to sit up. "I don't know how, but we made it! I thought we were goners."

Rising to his knees, Harvey turned around and poked his head in the front door. "Jeremy, Sybil, everybody! It's Hassan and Derek! Help me get 'em loose!"

Six pairs of hands reached for the boys, lifted them from the porch, and carried them inside. In a few moments, the boys had been freed and sat upright. Everyone welcomed them, offered them food, and asked a thousand questions.

After taking a few moments to clear his emotions, Harvey dialed Steve Hastings at the state police. "I've got marvelous news!" he shouted when Hastings picked up. He described how the paintballers had thrown the boys on the porch and defaced the home.

As Steve described the procedure from this point forward, his calm, authoritative voice assured him the lawbreakers would *not* escape.

When he'd finished the call, George Spencer closed the meeting. "That's our meeting for tonight, folks. Good night and thanks for coming!"

For the moment, everyone seemed jubilant, though stunned. For his part, Harvey put on his coat and hat and walked home.

The evening had been an informative one. The committee members of Ward Six had seemed as enthusiastic as he felt about Westfield Dialogues. They were stunned by the revelations about the spread of industrial pollution and had witnessed firsthand the kind of punishment the cult had meted out since his arrival at city hall. He only hoped Alice and all the rest of his team were out there having similarly uplifting experiences.

Derek and Hassan were safe. The ward committee seemed to appreciate the presentation on Westfield Dialogues and the pollution report. Aunt Harriet had been right—perspective was the key. But the battle for hearts and minds in Westfield was just beginning. If only he had the strength and was allowed to live long enough to see his friends succeed!

During the three weeks following his breakdown, Harvey put his new perspective to work. All the air-monitoring devices were mounted and working. Volunteers collected the data daily and fed it into a central database. Using that information, they filed grievances against the worst air polluters. Charles Higgins led the team in writing and submitting those complaints, which claimed that particulate matter in the air had caused physical harm to the people of Westfield.

Another team held weekly demonstrations at city hall on Saturdays from ten in the morning to noon. Thirty people volunteered from the churches and nonprofits to train citizens in the many types and consequences of pollution. Alice and Stan used their contacts to inform the media about the potential for Westfield Dialogues to change the city's governance structure.

Finally, Harvey expanded his support base by using more volunteers on the streets and phones canvassing the neighborhoods. So far, he'd established a dozen teams working both north and south of the river. On this particular day, his job was to debrief four of those teams.

His first conference was at ten in his studio downtown. Alice, Martha Ruggles, and Stan Matthews were reporting on their meetings with ward committees. They had been assigned to encourage ward leaders to participate in the dialogue groups and recruit their neighbors to do the same.

"Those old ladies for our ward had undergone quite a change by the time I got back with them," said Martha. "I mean no disrespect, but most of them are friends of mine, and they're all old like me."

"What caused them to change?" Alice inquired.

"When they heard Clarence's speech, they swore he'd never get their nod for another term. Two women and one man have applied to run for Clarence's seat. They're each hoping to have the committee's backing. The warders also agreed to support Westfield Dialogues, and I signed up three for the groups right after our meeting."

"I wasn't as fortunate with the Ward Five committee," said Alice. "I walked in on a fight between two chamber volunteers. The rest of the committee were teachers, doctors, and professional people. After a few tense moments, I got them settled down. In the end, they voted to support Westfield Dialogues and select their own candidate for council."

"Half the ward committee I talked with couldn't remember why they'd ever supported Rhett Bennett," said Stan Matthews. "Almost all those folks came on the committee after Bennett's election. But all agreed that a top industrial polluter was a poor candidate for election to council. I signed up four people for the groups."

Harvey's second stop was a catered lunch at Renewal House with Paul Johnson and two teams doing neighborhood recruiting for the dialogues. Pizza and soft drinks were the perennial favorite of the younger generation. However, once he smelled the delicious odor of tomato sauce, pepperoni, and bread, he thought he wouldn't mind a slice or two himself.

"We walked into a fight between neighbors," said Hassan of his and Sybil's adventures. "One couple—parents of two younger children—enthusiastically supported dialogue. They wanted to know where they could sign up to participate. The other fellow and his wife were older, dead set against it. Said they had no use for getting together with their neighbors about anything political."

"What did you do?" Harvey asked.

"Well," Sybil interjected, flashing an engaging smile, "I asked them if they felt everything was right with city government, and did they miss any of the services they used to have. The woman said she thought garbage pickup was slow, and they had some damage to their pickup truck when it hit a deep pothole."

"Her husband didn't say a thing and had a scowl on his face," said Hassan.

"He was also on oxygen," Sybil added. "He had a small portable tank strapped to his back. So I asked him was he ill, and he replied, 'Lung cancer.' Then I asked if he had worked in the mines. He said no, he'd worked as a foreman for one of the companies."

"Then I asked him how he felt about the quality of the air in Westfield," said Hassan, "and he said it stank. So I suggested that if he expressed that opinion in the dialogues, maybe he could accomplish some changes."

"That made him think," said Hassan, "but he still had a very mean look on his face, and he didn't want to take part."

"That was our only difficult experience," said Sybil. "We signed up eight people for dialogues out of sixteen homes. I thought we scored pretty well."

"We were nearly the same," said Rachel, obviously eager for the competition. "We talked with twenty-one homeowners and signed up eleven for the dialogues."

"One experience was kind of sweet," said Jeremy. "We talked to a family with five young kids who asked all sorts of questions. They got the message right away and couldn't understand why everybody in the family couldn't participate."

In the early afternoon, at the United Methodist Church phone bank, Betsy Rawlings and Amy Cunningham were working the phones. Their supervisor was Rev. Melissa Gravenly, and they called people to promote Westfield Dialogues and recruit people to sign up.

Though he didn't consider himself a religious person, Harvey nevertheless appreciated the presence of the churches in this campaign. It made a public statement associating issues of governance with a much broader perspective of values than just monetary worth.

"Lots of hang ups!" Amy complained about phoning people. "I still can't get used to that. But I did have five or six delightful conversations. One lady went on about how she looked forward to being in a dialogue group. She would make a good contributor to any conversation."

"I started by saying I was doing a phone survey on health, then asked people three questions," said Betsy. "That seemed to break the ice, and when we got to a place where there was discomfort or where they reported some illness or lack of service, I'd tell them about Westfield Dialogues."

"Did you find instances of pollution causing health problems?" he asked.

"Lots of 'em," Betsy said. "Three of them mentioned relatives who had sickness attributed to bad air or water."

"I seemed to reach lots of older folks," said Amy. "They had lots of conditions to talk about, but only five of them connected their condition to smoky air or bad water. So I said if they got into a dialogue group, maybe they could make a difference."

Later that afternoon, Harvey drove to Bethel AME Church just as Derek Robinson, Tom Monroe, Sam Washington, and Tyler Smith came in from a day of talking with residents door-to-door in the Bottoms. Their pitch was that Westfield Dialogues was the perfect place for any resident who wished to have input on the city's future.

"Six out of twenty signed up for me," said Sam.

"I got twelve out of twenty-four," said Tom.

"Sixteen out of twenty-two," boasted Tyler.

These guys enjoyed competing with and besting one another.

When he arrived back at the studio that evening, he decided to walk over to the Busy Bee for supper. He had his eye on the Monday special, which was smothered pork chops, rice and mixed vegetables, with apple crisp and vanilla ice cream for dessert.

As he finished his meal, Eugene Atkinson, the new president of Westfield National Bank, stopped by his table after saying goodbye to some people who had joined him for supper.

"Can I have a moment of your time, Harvey?" the banker asked with a thin-lipped smile.

Atkinson wore a navy suit with a red tie. His face was old and jowly, and he had the eyes of a cobra and a voice like a used-car salesman.

"Sure, have a seat," Harvey replied, letting caution slip into his voice. "To what do I owe the honor?"

"Harvey, I've been reviewing the bank's assets, and I happened to come across your mortgage," Atkinson said with an obvious tone of reproach. "I don't know if you remember, but there's a clause in that document saying the bank can dissolve the agreement at any time, for any reason. So I've decided we must do that. Now."

A chill snaked down his spine. Could he withstand such a bite?

"Why would you want to do that, Gene?" he queried, trying not to let apprehension color his voice. "I've made my payments on time for fifteen years. I only have five more to go. What's the big rush? You can't get my money fast enough?" He added a brief chuckle to mask his momentary dread.

"Frankly," Atkinson said, his tone flat, the expression on his face as if he were inspecting a dead plant, "you're not the kind of person the bank wants as a customer. You have thirty days to pay the balance of your mortgage, which is—he checked his cell phone—$23,425.75 as of today. If you amend your behavior within thirty days, we might consider renegotiating the loan."

It was an angry parent's judgment, no doubt designed to make him feel like a scolded child. Instead, it made him want to punch the guy's ugly face hard enough to bloody his nose all over his white shirt.

"I have a perfect right as a citizen to advocate for processes and procedures I think will make the city better. Who are you to tell me I can't do that?"

"The guy with the money, that's who," the banker hissed.

Without warning, the temptation to laugh at the man hit him hard. He struggled to keep a straight face. "Mind if I ask your reasoning behind this move?" he asked when he'd recovered his composure.

"Simple," Atkinson said. "We don't need you."

"You're a financier, Atkinson. Why don't you ever make the industries you invest in clean up their act and pay for the damage and death they've dispensed?"

"Sorry I couldn't talk sense into you," said Atkinson, lapsing back into his parental role, rising from his seat. "I'll expect the balance of your loan in the next few days."

As the banker left, Harvey realized he had a way to cover the payoff of his mortgage. He breathed a sigh of relief on the walk back to the studio. He also discovered he'd just been hit with an unfamiliar punishment. When Dwyer was alive, he used physical violence to punish enemies. Atkinson's approach was to take away whatever he thought an enemy held dear. The takeaway was that one shouldn't want anything controlled by untrustworthy people.

At seven thirty Thursday morning, Harvey discovered a problem. He had a full schedule of appointments to sign up people for dialogue groups. But the warning light for the generator in his van shone bright red. The engine was operating on the battery alone. Good way to get stuck if he didn't attend to it. He was already running against time. Now he was also competing against circumstances.

He consumed a quick breakfast of coffee and toast, then started for Herb's Auto Emporium to get there the moment it opened. Maybe he could have the generator installed and still proceed with his appointments. *What a nuisance!* This was no time to fool around with mechanical problems.

He parked at the rear entrance to the service bays, then walked around front to the cashier's desk. As he entered, odors of gas, exhaust fumes, tires, day-old coffee, and hotdogs assailed him. His stomach did a flip-flop.

"Good morning, Mr. Davenport," the young brunette in the cashier's booth said in a pleasant voice, flashing a wide smile full of perfect teeth. He could have sworn she got younger every year.

"I need a new generator, Sue," he said. "Can I get that done right away? I'm in a rush."

"I'll have Dan talk with you. He's got a heavy schedule." She rose and went into the shop to consult with the mechanic.

Her guarded reply caused a knot to form in his stomach. How long would he have to wait? Would he be here all day?

The Emporium featured auto parts, snacks, soft drinks, beer, and liquor. These sections formed a large semicircle around the service desk and cashier's stand. The repair shop and parts department occupied a separate building connected by two short pass-throughs.

"Hi, Harvey." Dan appeared at last on the edge of the shop door, wiping his oily hands on a rag. He wore a black jumpsuit and a handkerchief tied around his head. "What can I do for you?"

"Generator's on the fritz. Can you replace it?" His words were almost overwhelmed by the vvreee! vvreee! sound of air wrenches farther back in the shop.

"Hang on, I'll check," Dan replied. "You've got a ninety-eight. Is that right? Twenty-five hundred is the model?"

Harvey didn't know but nodded and gave him a thumbs-up.

In a moment, Dan returned. "You're in luck. I've got the part. It'll take an hour. Want to wait or take the shuttle?"

"I'll wait," he replied. A smile of relief fluttered across his face. "Thanks, Dan. I appreciate it."

Harriet's admonition returned to bolster his attitude. *Perspective. Stay focused. Keep an eye on the larger picture.* Then a thought came to him—why not use the occasion to recruit Herb and his customers for Westfield Dialogues?

Smiling to himself, he poured half a cup of overheated coffee, then sat in one of Herb's antique metal lawn chairs in the waiting section. The coffee tasted bitter with an echo of petroleum.

Seated two chairs over, Michael, the local vagrant, sat reading the previous day's soiled newspaper, likely retrieved from the trash. An older man with a shock of wild graying hair and grubby overalls, Michael inhabited the same blue metal chair every morning, five days a week.

After a while, Herb Tenebry, owner of the place, strode into the waiting room, a smile on his face, his hand outstretched. "Hello there, Mr. Davenport." Tall, a smidge overweight, and tough as nails, Herb reminded him of a bouncer.

They shook hands.

"What's our favorite city council member pedaling today?" Herb sat in the chair next to Harvey's.

A painful tightness in his throat made it hard to swallow. He'd known Herb for fifteen years, and the fellow was naturally contentious. A quick-tempered racist and a political conservative too. He'd argue with anyone about anything. Yet he had little education.

"I'm talking about Westfield Dialogues today," Harvey replied. "Have you heard of it?"

"Sure! Nothin' like that gets past me," Herb countered. "What about it?"

"It's an opportunity for you, Herb," he explained, choosing his words with care. "Get in there and talk with others, share your point of view about city government."

"Well, hell, they can come in here and do that! Don't have to go to city hall to run off at the mouth!" Herb emitted a scornful laugh, leaned forward, and put his hands on his knees.

"We hope dialogue will generate novel ways for the city to meet residents' needs."

"Like what?" Herb turned to face him.

"How to keep special interests from dominating the city, bring back services, rid ourselves of industrial waste."

"You sure know how to raise a fella's dander, don't you?" Herb chuckled. "I'm real angry when it comes to crackin' down on polluters, don'tcha see?"

"Why is that? Do you pollute?"

"Bury it in the ground out back. Just like my granddaddy did fifty years ago. It's fast and cheap. What does anybody care? It's my property. I'll do what the hell I want."

The remark set his teeth on edge. The place seemed warmer, and his breath came in brief bursts. He hadn't known Herb was a polluter, and he didn't want to offend the man. No sense ruining a friendship. Still, he had to keep his cool and stick to his guns.

"Maybe so, but what's on your property may damage the people surrounding you."

"Look here! I'm a small shop owner. I don't have money for expensive disposal equipment like the big guys use. You want to help the people of this city? Then help guys like me who live on the edge!"

"Well, Herb," Michael interjected, looking up from his newspaper, "how many people are gettin' sick because the stuff you're burying out back is seeping into their water? D'jever think of that? D'jever think you might be gettin' cancer because you drink the stuff?"

"Shut up, Michael! Who asked you?" Herb shot back. "You want ole Herb to crawl off and die o' cancer because he buried his grease and oil in the ground?"

"What could be better?" Michael returned, head buried deep in the newspaper.

The growing enmity between the two made Harvey's heart beat a little faster. "Get in there, join a group, let 'em know how you feel," he said, reaching into his folder and giving Herb an application sheet. "Here's how you get started."

The loud clatter of an air compressor in the shop interrupted them. Then, just as the noisy machine shut off, a large man with curly blond hair came into the service desk to pick up his car. Gunther

Betelhausen was the top commercial land developer in the state. He sat in the waiting room while the cashier completed his paperwork.

Meanwhile, Harvey tried to resurrect the conversation with Herb. "Part of the dialogue will be about paying for remediation of the toxins in the ground and water."

"Bullshit!" Herb exploded. "You know as well as I do it's all just a big communist plot to destroy our society."

"There are no more communists." Gunther scowled at Herb. "But listen to this. I just had the soil at my place tested last week. Water too. Know what they turned up?" He bent down and rolled up his left pant leg. "You see this?" he boomed. A red rash covered his leg. "You know how I got this? Plantin' my garden this spring, that's how! The soil all over my place has carbon coal in it. You know what that is? They call it lampblack."

"Call a doctor," Herb countered. "Looks like diaper rash to me. Try a little baby powder!" He cackled.

"That's what you think, old fart!" chided Gunther, glaring at Herb. "I'll tell you something else. We use wells on my estate, and the water there has PCBs and TCE. You know what this is?" He pointed to the rash. "It's cancer! Westfield needs remediation. Now!"

He sympathized with Gunther's concern. *Shades of half a century ago. The doctors said the same thing to my mother, and still no one has stopped the polluters!*

"And who d'you think's gonna pay to have your property remediated?" Herb growled with a contemptuous tone, followed by a snort and a shake of his head. "I'm not gonna pay for it. That's for damned sure!"

Just the sort of attitude that let the polluters go unquestioned.

"Don't be so sure," Gunther retorted. "The industries that put waste in the ground should pay to clean it up. But I wouldn't oppose a nice tax increase either. We've gotta do something now or it'll be too late!"

"Oh, no ya don't!" Herb objected. "I'm not gonna pay out of my business *and* outta my pocket too! No sirree!" He shook his head. "Next thing ya know, they'll be takin' me to jail and confiscatin' my property. And that'll be the end of good ole Herb and his Emporium. You hear?"

The mounting tension brought another adrenaline rush. This wasn't just friends fooling around. These two were fast becoming enemies. He searched for some way to throw water on the smoldering fire. If Gunther built up enough steam, he might pull a gun, and it wouldn't be the first time.

"Harvey!" Dan the mechanic shouted from the shop door. "Your machine's runnin' perfect. We'll have you on your way in no time."

On his way to the cashier, Dan took him aside. "Listen, man," he said in a confidential tone. "No charge on this. There was nothin' wrong with your generator."

"What?" Harvey croaked. "No charge? What do you mean?"

Dan motioned for Harvey to join him in the shop. "The only thing wrong with your generator is that someone pulled the hot wire from its connection. All I did was reconnect it, and it's working fine. We gave the generator a thorough test, and it runs like a top. As I said, no charge."

"Vandalism?"

"Could be," Dan said, shrugging his shoulders. "Wouldn't happen with ordinary road vibration. If you have more trouble, we'll fix it. But you've got another fifty thousand miles on that generator."

"So, whoever did it left me just enough battery for Mina to bring the van home and for me to drive it here," he mumbled, half to himself.

"Why? Did you leave it out overnight?" Dan asked.

"In the Downtown Grocery's parking lot. I had an emergency."

"That could be it," said Dan.

As he slid behind the wheel of his van and turned the key, he smiled to himself. The van purred like a racer, and the generator light remained off. Who would vandalize his vehicle in a grocery store parking lot?

The answer soon became apparent. As he parked, the damage to his home was obvious. Vandals had destroyed his garden plots, pulled out his rose bushes, sawed off his shrubs. The first-floor windows were smashed. In a panic, he exited the van and ran to the back door. It was locked. So was the front door.

He let himself in. Broken pumpkins littered the living room and dining room floors. The Delft vase Aunt Harriet had given him lay in pieces on the floor, flowers scattered over the carpet. Pumpkins had also shattered the kitchen and bathroom windows.

There was one rock in the dining room, tied with stout string to a cardboard square with the words "Quit the Dialogue or Die!"

His blood ran cold. In one swift motion, he locked the house and headed for the barn. Turning in at the driveway, he brought the van to a halt. His landscaping lay in ruins. The marauders had cut down trees, shrubs, and flowers. They had bulldozed one entire embankment out to the front driveway. Another pumpkin had smashed the largest studio window. He ran up the staircase and let himself in. Another rock. "Quit Meddling or Die!"

He strode to his office and dialed Steve Hastings. When he described the damage to his van and home, Hastings agreed it was time to act.

"I'll have two men stationed at both locations around the clock until further notice. Can you handle boarding up both places? And where can I reach you?"

"I'll call the board-up service now, and you can call this number twenty-four seven."

Perspective had now slipped away as surely as time was fleeing from his grasp.

CHAPTER 20

A NEW WAY FORWARD III

At ten o'clock on a cold, gray October Saturday, Alice Morrison hurried to persuade fifteen hundred teachers to participate in Westfield Dialogues. Her sunny yellow dress mirrored the bright ray of hope shining in her heart. Indeed, the contagion and excitement of promoting this experiment in public choice had awakened within her a new vision for the future of education.

The Confederated Teachers' Union Hall was an old brownstone building, blackened with age. Union members had built this monument in the sixties when greater confidence and more money supported visionary changes to the school systems of the nation. By contrast, the union gathered little money now. Education had dropped to the lowest rungs of the national agenda as the world had turned market-centric, embraced austerity, and become more polarized. The one constant remaining for many of these teachers was loyalty to their students.

When she arrived, strangers marched on the sidewalk surrounding the union hall. She caught the sleeve of Amy Terrapin, the union's vice president, walking ahead of her. "What's with the demonstration?" she asked.

"Chamber of commerce. They're against the dialogue," Amy replied.

Alice shrugged, wondering whatever possessed them to try to tell teachers not to dialogue. Such a tactic seemed self-defeating.

As Alice entered the auditorium, the noise overwhelmed her. A thousand conversations competed with a teen garage band hammering out their latest hit. The spectators clapped in time to the music. Then, as she walked down the aisle and onto the stage, the crowd stood and gave her enthusiastic applause. Hank West, president, along with other union officers, were already in their chairs. All were good friends and colleagues with whom she'd served more than thirty years. Hank gave her a particularly kind introduction.

She began her speech by asking her colleagues to spread the word about Westfield Dialogues and participate in the dialogue groups. "This is how we make a difference," she told them. Then she announced the latest discoveries regarding the city's increased pollution and discussed issues of city services, remediation of toxic waste, and higher taxes.

The audience groaned with resistance to taxes.

"Well, sure!" she declared, flinging her right arm out to its fullest extent. "You got off easy for twenty years! It's long past time to pay the piper!" She nodded her head and smiled. "And a raise in taxes means a raise in your pay too. Don't forget that."

Heads nodded. Many smiled and commented.

"Above all," she cautioned, "we *must* get out the vote on January 6 for the new city plan. By that time, we'll know what elements are included, and we'll be able to choose which ones we want."

Applause erupted from the more excited attendees, but she held up one hand. She wasn't through making her point. She bent toward the people, elbows resting on the podium, assuming a more confidential tone. "Tell me, friends. Do you go home at night feeling like slaves, teaching in chains and unable to affect the system?"

Scattered applause and shouts of "Yes!" and "Amen!" echoed throughout the room.

"Does the ghost of Sisyphus haunt you as he rolls his immense, unwieldy ball of administrative detail uphill every day?"

Many applauded, and a few laughed outright.

"With a new plan," she told them, leaning back, extending an arm and hand out toward her audience, "maybe now we'll have a voice in city hall and the pay we deserve for teaching with excellence." She raised her voice a notch. "Don't let the opposition shake you up! Keep your cool. Get out the vote!"

The applause started again.

This time, she rode the wave. "Maybe now we'll have the budget, the materials, the help, and the time we need." She raised her voice up another notch and shook her finger at them for each word. "Maybe now we can *inspire*, and *mentor*, and *train*, and *teach* our students how to carry our society forward!"

More breakthrough applause. But she again held off the crowd as she stood straight.

"Now is *our time*, my fellow teachers!" She threw her hands in the air. "Woohoo!" she yelled.

The crowd emulated her—"Woohoo!"

"Time for Education with a capital E to have its day in the sun! Let's get out there and make the most of it!" She stepped back from the podium and bowed deeply.

The room erupted into unrestrained applause and cheering that lasted several minutes. People were out of their seats, on their feet, in the aisles. Catcalls could be heard throughout the room. People began to stomp their feet and chant. "It's our time!" they shouted. "It's our time!"

Her heart thrummed in her ears to the rhythm of the crowd's affirmation. With a brilliant smile of assurance and a sheen of tears streaming down her face, she turned and embraced each of the union officers.

From the rear of the auditorium, the sound of shattering glass broke the bubble of enthusiasm. One window after another down the sides of the building imploded. Large brown stones rolled or skidded along the side aisles. A shock wave rolled over the teachers as energy and excitement turned to shrieks of horror.

Just as Alice and the union heads finished their embrace, five shapes in black jumpsuits and masks bolted through the stage door. A strong dose of adrenaline shot through her body. Her muscles tensed for the impact as three of the intruders came for her while the other two went for Hank, obviously unaware that Mr. West not only taught history but coached wrestling and boxing at the high school.

One of her attackers grabbed her left arm, but Alice, at six feet and a hundred and fifty pounds, walloped the intruder in the face with a roundhouse right. Blood spurted onto her yellow dress as her assailant fell backward, mask askew revealing a woman's face distorted with pain, accompanied by long auburn hair.

A second thug seized her right arm. She pivoted on her right foot, then kicked him in the groin with the sharp toe of her red left shoe. He went reeling, hands in his groin, knees locked together, to a corner of the stage where he collapsed in a heap.

Number three caught her by the hair pulling her backward so hard her knees buckled. She had just a quick second to snatch the mask off before she fell hard on the wooden stage. It was a guy with a gray beard. Using the momentum of her fall, she rolled to the right, springing up on her feet, smashing her fists into the intruder's face again and again. Then as the bloody-nosed woman bounded forward with arms outstretched to push her backward, biology teacher Jane Gutierrez tackled the woman from behind, then sat on her knees, slapping the thug's face from side to side.

Then they hurried to where Hank sat on the remaining thug, pounding him in the face with almost maniacal force, his upper lip curled in a snarl. She gave the thug a hard, swift kick to the side of the head, heard bone crack, and saw the fellow go limp. The fight was over. Three of the thugs were disabled, and two had fled.

While Hank calmed the teachers and coaxed them back to their seats, Alice met with the state police, led by Steve Hastings, as they interrogated the attackers.

The woman was Marian Burke, a branch manager for Westfield National Bank. The bearded man, Guy Reid, was plant manager at Superior Plastics. Sam Fuller mumbled that he was a cement truck driver for Materials Management.

"One of the parade marshals drafted us for capturing the speakers," said Reid. "We were supposed to let the teachers see their leaders taken hostage."

"We were assigned to leave a bad taste in people's mouths after the event," Burke told the officers.

"Did you know Mike Dwyer?" Officer Doug Steele asked.

"I used to work for him," Burke replied, looking at the floor. "Best manager I ever had." She wiped her nose, then lifted her head. "There was a model to follow. He said if we kept taxes low, the economy would thrive, and he was *right!*" she keened with a thin, insistent moan, tears streaming from her eyes.

Bingo! Shaking her head, Alice rose and walked away. She had to cleanse herself from the presence of these horrible, violent toadies.

Absorbed in thought, she walked to the podium where Hank and the remaining teachers had been planning to publicize the day's incident. The highlight was a panel of four teachers on Channel 7 the following night. Marvin Feldkamp, widely known for his impartiality, would moderate.

What a lovely toothpick in the throats of Frederick Dwyer and Norm Taylor! Well-deserved retribution for their nasty tricks. If the industrial and financial community continued these attacks, the public would soon hold them in contempt, and that augured well for the January vote.

Two weeks shy of her seventy-fifth birthday, on the first Saturday in December, Martha Ruggles sat in her favorite leather wingback chair in the spacious living room of the Westfield Senior Citizens Center. She had volunteered to inform the seniors about the Westfield Dialogues process and enlist their participation. From her wardrobe, she'd chosen an elegant floor-length dress in a batik orange and brown sunflower pattern. It hid her aging figure well, and the side pockets were deep enough to carry the pistol she kept "just in case."

Tonight was part of a series of Sunday-evening events held throughout the fall and winter for the enjoyment and education of the center's residents. She, therefore, expected a large crowd despite the wet, chilly weather.

The staff had pushed the faux Victorian furniture back against the walls and substituted a hundred folding chairs in rows of ten. At the front, they'd placed a movable dance floor to serve as a small stage. She'd created a few short skits with several high school students to give her fellow seniors a simple message that Westfield Dialogues could improve their lives. At the front of the stage, to one side, stood a podium, behind which the staff had placed her favorite chair, where she now sat.

When the ancient grandfather clock chimed seven, she rose and stepped to the podium, calling the group to order.

"As most of you know, Westfield has been a divided community since its inception. Middle-class and wealthy whites to the south of the river, blacks, immigrants, and poor whites here in the Bottoms. We've also had an immense amount of toxic waste poured in on us over the last century and a half.

"Tonight I bring you good news! There's an opportunity brewing to change both the segregation and the pollution. It's called Westfield Dialogues, and it will give us a chance to say how we want to make the city better. The best part?" She gave them a wide, toothy grin. "You're all included."

Suddenly, her blood ran cold as she spied Clarence Williams entering the salon and taking a seat at the back.

"This dialogue," she continued, keeping her face as neutral as possible, "is a great opportunity for us to have a voice, bring services back, and restructure our city government so it's more equitable and fair for our people."

"Amen!" said several women in the audience, nodding their heads.

"For the first time in history, friends, we can vote on a new plan for the city."

"Amen!" rang out again, along with some applause.

"Another measure we can vote for is remediation. That means cleaning up all the pollution that's been dumped into our neighborhood."

"Amen!"

"Our third opportunity is to vote to bring city services back, so we can use the buses and don't have to wait so long for the firefighters to get here."

"Amen! Preach it, sister!"

"And finally, my friends, we've got to make sure that our representative on city council isn't tied to the corporate interests. You all know who I mean."

"Amen!" a woman confirmed.

"Hallelujah!" shouted a man.

"Did any of you see him last Sunday night?"

About a third of the audience raised their hands.

"Wasn't that the saddest, most disreputable thing you've ever seen? He sold us right down the river!"

"Amen!" came the lead.

"Tell it like it is!" others responded.

She watched Clarence. Unpredictable as he was, she wanted to be prepared for whatever he might do. Her hand patted the pocket of her dress, just for reassurance.

"Whoa!" came his bellicose shout from the back. "Just a damned minute!" Clarence Williams stepped out to the side of the crowd and several rows toward Martha. "You've stopped preachin' and gone to meddlin'! I ain't sold nobody down the river, as you so nastily put it!" His manner was rough, imperious.

Her blood pressure rose with a tightening in her chest. His manner here, with his own people, was completely different from the docility he affected when in the presence of powerful whites.

"Well, if it isn't the ole two-faced jackal himself, in the flesh!" she announced with an ironic tone. "What about that pledge you made at Renewal House to support your own people? And then you turn tail and tell the whole world on television that we don't need dialogue and don't need remediation?"

"Now wait a minute! I never said nothin' like that," Clarence shouted. "You aren't bein' fair. I'm not running away. I'm right here in the midst of the fight!" He paused as if to collect his thoughts. "We don't need no dialogue, we don't need more services, we don't need no remediation here in the Bottoms, and we sure as hell don't need to pay more taxes!"

"Baloney! You're a pathetic specimen of humanity, Clarence. And deep down you know it too!" she growled. She looked at her audience. "Y'all know how his momma and daddy died—from being poisoned by industrial waste. Probably the same chemicals killin' him right now!"

"Don't forget his sister, Tanny," shouted a woman in the third row. "She died o' cancer, age thirty-three. Oh my, she was a beautiful child!"

"You'll pay for this, Martha Ruggles!" he shouted, shaking his right fist.

"Nonsense, Clarence!" she countered. "You're part of the problem, part of what's holdin' us down. Slaves on the modern plantation."

"Why you on city council when you ain't got a lick of sense in how to run a city?" someone in the back called out. "All you eva' see is your own skin."

"Oh, he only on city council 'cause he represents the money guys," said a woman close to where Clarence stood.

"You people be careful what you say," Clarence cautioned. "Not a word of truth in any of it. Jus' remember. The walls have ears, and one day you'll pay for what you just said."

"Okay, that's enough time wasted on your sorry ass, Clarence," Martha said with a sharp tone of finality in her voice. She drew the pistol from the pocket of her long, flowing dress, pointing it at him with two hands. "Get outta here, Clarence! You're not welcome!"

Clarence backed away from her, hands out in front to fend her off. "Take it easy with that thing, Martha. You could hurt someone."

When he had left, the audience buzzed with fear but also excitement.

Martha replaced her pistol in the pocket of her dress, then turned to her audience. "Friends, we can overcome Clarence Williams and a whole lot more by getting into those dialogue groups and telling our story. I've invited a few of our high school young people to portray my message to you this evening. I hope you like the little skit we've worked out." She named the players, then said, "Please give them a big welcome."

The audience responded with enthusiastic applause.

She walked from the podium to the center of the stage carrying a yellow cardboard sign. Facing the crowd, she raised the sign. "Act One—Dialogue" was printed on it in black letters. Then she walked back to her chair and sat down.

Sybil walked onstage in jeans and a gray sweatshirt, swinging a tennis racquet. "I'd like to play tennis. I love to execute my powerful serve." She swung the racquet as for an overhand serve.

Bart entered behind her in a Westfield High baseball uniform, swinging a baseball bat. "I wanna play baseball. I love to swing my bat. Bats are the coolest!" He swung the bat hard as if hitting a home run.

Jeremy followed, dribbling a basketball, wearing white sport shorts and a T-shirt. "Basketball is my sport, man!" He faked a jump shot.

Sybil gathered the two around her. "Did you ever notice none of us can play our game alone?"

"Yeah," said Bart. "I need a pitcher and an outfielder."

"I want someone to feed me the ball," said Jeremy, "and to block me as I shoot for the backboard."

"And I need an opponent to play a good game of tennis," said Sybil.

"Why don't we team up?" Jeremy offered. "We could play tennis for a while. Then we could play baseball. Then we could shoot some hoops."

"You know what?" said Sybil. "We're doin' a great job of *dialoguing*, aren't we?"

"Is that what it's called?" Bart asked. "I thought it was just cooperation."

"Of course it is, silly!" said Sybil. "But we had to do the dialogue to get here, *didn't we?*" Then she gave him a fist to the shoulder and a big smile before they all scampered offstage.

Before the audience could applaud, Martha was on her way back to the stage area with another card, which she held up. "Act Two—Time to Vote" was printed on the blue card.

This time, Derek led off in slacks and a sport shirt, carrying something under his right arm. Close behind were Hassan in jeans, Rachel in a red-flowered shift, and Jeremy in Bermuda shorts.

"Let's go down to the polling place and vote," Derek proposed.

"Where's that?" asked Rachel.

"What's going on over there?" Hassan wanted to know.

"What are we voting for?" Jeremy asked.

"I'll show you when we get there," said Derek.

On the other side of the stage, Derek unfolded a portable voting booth. The others gathered around.

"Here's a sample ballot," said Derek, holding up an imaginary ballot. "There are four issues. We have to mark our choices on the paper. More services? Separate business from government? Remediation of toxic waste? Raise taxes to pay for it all?" He handed out four imaginary pieces of paper and pencils.

Each turned away from the others, pretending to think carefully. Then they marked their ballots and placed them in the slot of the voting booth.

"Is that all there is to it?" Hassan asked.

"That's it. Really simple, isn't it?" said Derek.

"Yeah," said Rachel. "I never thought it would be so easy!"

Then they exited the stage.

As soon as they disappeared, Martha held up a green card that had "Act Three—Remediation" printed on it. Then she moved back to her chair and sat down.

Bart entered in gray slacks and a red shirt. He dropped a stage-prop smoke bomb, which ejected a low cloud of smoke over the stage area.

He coughed and wheezed as the smoke engulfed him. "Yuck!" he exclaimed, waving his arms in the air. "A fellow could die of this stuff!"

"Yeah," Sybil said, walking onstage. She bent to finger something black on the floor. "Look at all this black stuff. Looks like carbon. I got a rash from this stuff. Maybe I'll be poisoned and die too!"

Derek entered, limping with a cane. "My doctor says I have thyroid cancer. I've got only two years to live."

"You can join Bart and me in heaven," said Sybil. "It'll be a lot cleaner there. I hear they have special white cleaning angels to tidy things up."

Chuckles rippled through the audience.

Hassan appeared in gray sweats, drinking from a glass of water. "Yuck! This stuff tastes terrible," he exclaimed, wrinkling up his face. "What if it's poison?"

"How we gonna get rid of this bad water, this black soil, this ole poison smoke?" Sybil asked.

"We can vote for remediation!" said Derek. "That'll wipe all the old nasty stuff away!"

"What's r-r-r-r-e-med-ton mean?" Hassan stuttered, tripping over the word.

"Means to get the bad stuff out of our neighborhood," said Sybil.

"Yeah, that's what I wanna do—get it outta here!" said Hassan.

Martha rose from her chair. "Let's give 'em a hand!" she called out. She laughed, eyes sparkling, trembling with excitement.

The seniors applauded with raucous enthusiasm as the players returned to the stage for their bows.

When the cheering and clapping had subsided, Martha nodded to Rev. Benjamin Booker, who dismissed the assembly with prayer.

As the seniors left the room laughing at the funny parts of the skits, Leone Hawn said to her, "Best Sunday-evening program this year!"

Martha smiled in acknowledgment. It was the one comment that made it all worthwhile. Now if they'd all get out and vote, she'd be very happy.

CHAPTER 21

CONCLUSION

Two days after the vote, Harvey and three hundred volunteers met at the Bethel AME Church Community Center to celebrate the vote and plan the next phase of their work.

When the votes were counted, the city manager announced that the people of Westfield had voted for Financial Plan 2. This prioritized a disengagement of business from government, increased taxes on residents and businesses proportionately so city services could be restored, and approved a special additional tax on companies that released toxic waste of any kind into the city's environment. The funds from that tax would be used for remediation throughout the city, preference to be given to the Bottoms.

Was it a triumph? Just barely. But with humans, everything was a compromise. Nothing was ever simple or easy.

He'd been right to release his grasp on the wounded galleon of self-made victory and let the people carry the day. He'd been overly ambitious to expect total transformation. Still, the people had sent a strong message that twenty years under the yoke of enterprise was enough.

When he arrived, the community center's lounge was packed with noisy, excited volunteers enjoying lunch. At one end stood a majestic stone fireplace with merrily dancing gas flames. At the back of the room, tables groaned with a huge buffet, courtesy of the church ladies.

When everyone had finished eating, Paul Johnson welcomed the attendees, praising them for their hard work.

"You did it, folks!" Johnson crowed. "In less than four months, you mounted a citywide effort to organize and carry out Westfield Dialogues, and you've all done a marvelous job! While we used a somewhat unusual approach, we helped our citizens reinvent our city. You're a shining example of what can be accomplished! So give yourselves a round of applause!"

The attendees applauded and cheered themselves with vigor.

When Johnson resumed his seat, Charles Higgins stood to address the crowd.

"The framers of our national Constitution got it half-right," he said with a smile, raising both hands in the air, palms up. "Involving the people in governance is important because it gives everyone a stake in the policy our representatives enact on our behalf.

"But they didn't go far enough." He paused to clear his throat. "Majority rule is insufficient for our day. We must ensure no one is left out of any policy decision. Dialogue is the wave of the future because it gives everyone a voice, and we learn from everyone's experiences."

Mild applause for the attorney broadened into fervent celebration as Martha Ruggles rose and replaced Higgins at the microphone.

"Thank you, Charles, for showing us how we've taken another marvelous step toward using democracy as a way of governing ourselves." She shuffled her note cards.

"We have also come closer to freeing ourselves from slavery. Back in the day, slavery trapped black men and women in America's economic machinery. But today, the engine of capitalism enslaves whites too. We are *all* shackled by industry's disregard for human health and safety, putting profits before people."

This woman was exactly the right person to deliver the critical message. She'd been through a lifetime of struggle for civil rights and policy that focused on the needs of the people.

"I'm so glad we could all work together here in Westfield because we're bringing all the business world back within appropriate bounds—so it can serve the common good, as was its intended purpose."

As the old trooper took her seat, the volunteers gave her a standing ovation. When the applause died down, Rachel Jefferson stepped to the podium.

"When I was taking samples with the city's engineers, I was amazed at how many chemicals threaten our lives and how much toxic waste is all around us. I think that took all of Westfield by storm, which is one reason we had such a strong turnout in the election four days ago. Seeing the true figures for industrial pollution makes a difference, doesn't it?"

Heads nodded, and several enthusiastic comments could be heard in the room.

"I've learned that industry and economists think that waste in the production process has no cost. But they're dead wrong. They typically throw their waste away. But there is no "away." It always lands somewhere. In our case it lands in the Bottoms. But what we need to do is motivate government officials at all levels to charge industry for the waste they create. We need to be able to see the cost of industrial waste on every company's balance sheet. The physical cost for disposal and de-toxification, *and* the human cost for lives wasted in disease and death.

Loud applause broke out as Rachel took her seat.

Then Derek Robinson rose to speak.

"We've put up with a great deal of opposition during this campaign," he said. "I never realized how much violence city council members were prepared to unleash until Harvey got beaten up at Mama Lulu's. And then, just a few weeks later, Hassan and I were kidnapped. That experience gave me a fresh look at what public service involves. As we plan for the future, we'll need to take this opposition more seriously and be prepared to resist it with more effort. We need to be trained in the techniques of countering violent opposition in ways that bring our opponents to the table for discussion and dialogue. Compromise, not domination must be the name of the game going forward."

These kids were too young to have to experience that kind of violence. One day, perhaps, such early exposure to the worst side of human nature might be unnecessary.

"I'm exceptionally pleased to have been able to work with Harvey Davenport for having taught me so much in the photo club. I'm happy to tell you that I've been accepted by Arnie Anderson Photography up at the state capital for an internship this summer, and I am looking forward to that!"

During the applause for Derek, Hassan Higgins rose from his seat in the front row and went to stand with Derek, giving him a comradely hug.

Harvey stood, nodding to the rest of the photo club members, who stood as they clapped in recognition of Derek's achievement. Then he proceeded to the lectern.

"Well, I'm just so glad you're still alive, Derek!" he exclaimed into the microphone. "We were pretty worried for those two weeks you fellows were taken from us."

Once again, the volunteers let their feelings be known through enthusiastic applause.

"As I'm sure it has been for many of you, the last year has been an eye-opener for me. When I began this journey, I had a fourteen-year-old's understanding of the world and my place in it and what I could expect of it. I say that because when my mother died, I was just fourteen. The person who had loved and guided me was wrenched away. And since my father had died two years before, I was left with no one. I was deeply hurt and angered by that experience. Except, of course, for the fact that Humphrey Marshall came to my rescue." He smiled and gestured with his right hand toward Billie Marshall, who sat in the back of the room.

Billie gave a quick, embarrassed little wave of acknowledgment.

"When the doctor said industrial pollution had caused my mother's cancer, I grabbed hold of that and hugged it like a teddy bear for fifty years. Someone should pay for my loss—I wanted revenge with an urgency I didn't fully comprehend." He coughed, trying to hold back hot tears.

"Unfortunately, by the time I moved back to Westfield, those memories had become fixed. I pursued vengeance on industry simply because I had sworn to do it. It had become an obsession. But the world of 1962 no longer existed, and neither did my fourteen-year-old self.

"I am, therefore, indebted to several of you sitting here this afternoon for helping me lift my goal to a higher plane. Today my goal is to have a world without pollution. One where young mothers don't have to die and leave their children to fend for themselves.

"The best part of my journey was when Charles Higgins told us about dialogue as a way of letting a whole community decide its values and future. That's when I saw the light. I was thrilled that we could, indeed, have a world without pollution. But first we'd have to go through the hard struggle to identify shared values and define our common purpose." He shifted his note cards.

"So now we come to today. The community is on its way to changing a pattern that has existed for a century and a half. Thank you, one and all, for your hard work making these first steps possible. I'm looking forward to what we can do together in the years ahead."

When the crowd finished clapping, Paul Johnson rose and declared a short recess while all the volunteers found their assigned classrooms, where they were to work on the various aspects of planning next steps.

A warm feeling of acceptance enveloped him. Harriet had been right—perspective was the bullwhip of success. He'd done the right thing, and his mind was already busy painting a canvas featuring future achievements for Westfield's people.

The following morning, in the cold, with a bright blue sky and still air, Harvey stepped out onto his back porch, wearing dark wool pants, a blue dress shirt and cardigan, and a wool topcoat. He inhaled a great, cleansing lungful of air, letting it sweep from his mind the detritus of the previous year's effort. Then he descended the porch steps into the cult-fashioned ruin of his backyard. This would be a bittersweet day.

He was on his way to a client meeting in the morning, after which he was due for his first chemotherapy appointment, followed by a radiation treatment. Working with the client would be a treat, but he wasn't so sure about the cancer treatments. However, he first had to stop at the neighborhood postbox to mail a letter.

Reaching into his inside coat pocket, he retrieved a letter he'd received in the previous day's mail.

> Dear Mr. Davenport,
>
> As is our right, according to your mortgage contract for remodeling both your Westfield properties, we are canceling that contract and hereby instruct you to pay the full outstanding amount of your loan. The balance is $23,425.75. If we do not receive payment within five working days, we will initiate court proceedings against you.
>
> Sincerely,
> Eugene Atkinson
> President and Chief Executive Officer
> Westfield National Bank

Good ole Gene! Another dirty trick. Would they never end?

Smiling, he removed from his pocket another envelope. This one was addressed to Atkinson at the Westfield National Bank. It contained a check written on Harvey's own bank in New York for the exact balance of the loan, along with a copy of Gene's letter requesting payment. He marched across the street and down a block to the mailbox on the corner, then deposited the envelope and rubbed his palms together in a washing motion.

"No more interest for Mr. Atkinson," he said with satisfaction.

He'd learned that people with money, occupying positions of authority, had few moral scruples, ignored the common good and were often untrustworthy. To the degree that they caused human hardship, sickness, or death, he would say they were evil. But there were also many whom one could trust. The key lesson he'd learned was how to tell the difference. That bit of learning had made it possible for him to let go of his search for revenge and put the matters of governance and pollution in the hands of the people.

On the walk back to his studio, he considered the results of his first year's work as a city councilman. He had played a role in fashioning positive political change among a people burdened with bargain-basement governance. Never mind that it had to some extent been their own fault. The change had happened one step at a time, herky-jerky, with plenty of reversals. He supposed no one, except perhaps a dictator, could make substantive changes rapidly in any society. And often throughout history, even that had turned out to be illusory.

He longed to develop a geologist's sense of time when considering matters of public policy. That might ease the stress of pursuing the democratic process. Yet he felt fortunate that he'd accomplished at least a beginning for the fight against industry before the cancer had gotten bad enough for the doc to operate. And, through it all, Harriet's wisdom had stayed with him—the secrets of endurance were perspective, focus, and anticipation. This was the formula he'd come to rely on.

As he approached the sidewalk in front of his studio, the loud crack of a high-powered rifle split the air. He thought the sound came from a pavilion in the park overlooked by his building. As his chest exploded, he collapsed on the pavement. Just before his world turned to black, Martha Ruggles's words came to him. *What keeps the people of the Bottoms in line is the ambush we know will come.*

EPILOGUE

Harvey Davenport's life and work was celebrated the following Sunday at Bethel AME Church. Attendees filled the sanctuary as well as both floors of the community center. Ben Booker's eulogy inspired those in attendance to carry on the fight until the city prohibited pollution and its governance policies benefitted all citizens equally.

The state police, under Steve Hastings's leadership, initiated a thorough investigation of Harvey's assassination until they unearthed Robert Kravitz, who had fled to Canada. They also found and arrested truck drivers Coot Dodson and Pete Peterson. All three were tried and found guilty.

Mina LoPino inherited the photography business as planned. She too established a worldwide reputation as an advocate of social change through her photography.

Citizen dialogue and planning groups became a tradition within Westfield, continuing to guide citizens in reshaping their local government to serve the common good. At age ninety-two, in a press conference informing the media of the completion of the remediation project in the Bottoms, Alice Morrison said, "I had a feeling maybe things would gradually turn around in this city. It just took longer than I thought."

AUTHOR'S NOTE

A *sacrifice zone* is an area of land chosen by industrial manufacturers or agribusiness firms to be sacrificed to intense pollution of air, water, and soil with toxic chemicals that are part of the manufacturing or agricultural process.

Sacrifice zones are often situated next to residential areas inhabited by minorities and the poor who unwillingly, and often unwittingly, sacrifice their health and well-being.

Sacrifice zones are created by collusion between government regulatory officials and industrial managers. Euphemistically called "lobbying," this reckless violation of pollution standards set by law takes place behind closed doors, far away from exposure to the media or local residents.

Today, nearly all cities of any size, and rural areas containing agribusiness installations, have sacrifice zones. In these "fenceline" neighborhoods one will find greatly increased instances of many diseases caused by chemical pollutants in the water, the soil, and the air. If you'd like to know more about this growing menace to Americans' health and well-being, you might read the following:

Steve Lerner, *Sacrifice Zones: The Font Lines of Toxic Chemical Exposure in the United States* Cambridge, Massachusetts: MIT Press, 2012), ISBN 978-0-262-01440-3.

Naomi Klein, *This Changes Everything: Capitalism vs. The Climate* (Simon & Schuster, 2014), ISBN-13: 978-1451697391.

Lightning Source UK Ltd.
Milton Keynes UK
UKHW040422171220
375384UK00008B/452/J